Joy Dettman was born in country Victoria and spent her early years in towns on either side of the Murray River. She is an award-winning writer of short stories, the complete collection of which, *Diamonds in the Mud*, was published in 2007, as well as the highly acclaimed novels *Mallawindy*, *Jacaranda Blue*, *Goose Girl*, *Yesterday's Dust*, *The Seventh Day*, *Henry's Daughter*, *One Sunday*, *Pearl in a Cage*, *Moth to the Flame*, *Wind in the Wires*, *Ripples on a Pond* and *The Tying of Threads*. *Thorn on the Rose* is Joy's second novel in her Woody Creek series.

Joy Dettman

THORN ON THE ROSE

PAN
Pan Macmillan Australia

First published 2010 in Macmillan by Pan Macmillan Australia Pty Limited
This Pan edition published in 2011 by Pan Macmillan Australia Pty Limited
1 Market Street, Sydney

Reprinted 2011

National Library of Australia
Cataloguing-in-Publication data:

Dettman, Joy

Thorn on the rose / Joy Dettman.

9780330404020 (pbk.)

A823.3

Typeset in Times by Post Pre-press Group
Printed by IVE

MIX
Paper from
responsible sources
FSC® C018183

Thank you to Shani, Kay and Don —
my fine trio of fearless early readers
who now appear to be tied into a series.

Previously in PEARL IN A CAGE

Characters, in order of importance:

Gertrude Foote, the retired town midwife; her daughter and son-in-law, **Amber and Norman Morrison**; Gertrude's granddaughters, **Sissy** and **Jenny**.

Vern Hooper, Gertrude's long-term lover, sawmill owner and farmer; his daughters, **Lorna** and **Margaret**, and son **Jim**.

Maisy and George Macdonald; their twin sons, **Bernie** and **Macka**; and their many daughters.

Elsie, an Aboriginal girl, raised since the age of twelve by Gertrude. She is wed to **Harry Hall**. They have several children.

Woody Creek shopkeepers: **Charlie White**, grocer; **Mr and Miss Blunt**, drapers; **Mrs Crone**, café owner; **Horrie Bull**, publican; **Mr Foster**, the postmaster.

The railway line is Woody Creek's only link with distant Melbourne. Norman Morrison, the stationmaster, a plain and unlovable man ignored by the community, now finds himself the centre of attention. His obese, overbearing mother, old Cecelia, is dead. Her relatives, who have travelled far to attend the funeral, overrun the country town, and Norman's small house. Amber,

Norman's wife, daughter of Gertrude Foote, the local midwife, is heavily pregnant for the third time in four years.

On New Year's Eve of 1923, Gertrude is awakened at midnight. A dying woman and her newborn infant have been found beside the railway line. There is no doctor in Woody Creek. Gertrude, more farmer than healer, can't save the unidentified mother.

When Amber is delivered of her second stillborn son, a series of incidents sees the living child exchanged for the dead. Amber, desolate at the loss, is not fit to mother. The consequences of this decision will prove disastrous for her, and for the infant they name Jennifer.

We watch Jenny grow as Australia and the world sink into the Great Depression.

'You are a golden songbird, hatched into a nest of grey sparrows,' says her adoptive father. 'You are a classical portrait, framed in gold and hung in a gallery of fools.'

Norman adores Jenny, but she is despised by her mother, Amber, and by her older sister, an impossible child who grows into an impossible woman.

Gertrude — Granny — who loves unconditionally, is the one Jenny runs to when she is raped and impregnated by the hell-raising Macdonald twins.

Amber and the twins' father, George, decide there is but one way out for the eighteen-year-old twins, threatened with twenty years' hard labour, for fifteen-year-old Jenny's good name — and for the unwanted fruit of that rape. A wedding is planned.

At seven o'clock, on the Friday evening prior to the wedding, the Melbourne train leaves Woody Creek with Jenny on board, hidden in the goods van.

Is there a life for her away from Woody Creek?

THE WEDDING DAY

At eleven fifteen on Saturday, 24 May 1939, Vern Hooper's big green Ford made a right-hand turn off the forest road and down a bush track that led to Gertrude Foote's fifteen acres. He didn't agree with that hurriedly arranged wedding, but someone had to transport the bride to church. It would be a marriage in name only, or so they said — which, as far as Vern was concerned, was making a mockery of church vows, as was allowing that girl to wear the white wedding veil. He'd expressed his views to Gertrude, who for once in her life agreed with him. Not that she had any more say in the matter than he. It was what both sets of parents wanted, what Jenny said she wanted, and, when all was said and done, none of Vern's business.

He nosed the car into the fowl yard, parked it between the walnut tree and the wood heap, and was unwinding his overly long frame from behind the steering wheel when Gertrude came from the house, clad in the same working trousers and green cardigan she'd been wearing yesterday.

So she'd decided to make a stand. He was pleased. 'You're not going in with her,' he said.

'She's gone, Vern.'

'I agreed to drive her in, didn't I?'

'Gone, as in caught last night's train.'

'Her fool of a father finally came to his senses?' Vern said.

'He hasn't got any to come to, and the longer I know him, the more I know it. Joey was saying she used to talk to him about stowing away in the goods van. That's probably what she's done.'

'How long have you known?'

'Since last night. She gave Joey a letter before she went for her walk.'

'You could have saved me putting my suit on.'

'I haven't told anyone. They had no right to consider doing it anyway.'

'They'll be up there waiting for her.'

'Then let them wait a bit longer. Brides are expected to be late. The kettle's boiling.'

'Keep it boiling, Trude. I'll be back.'

At eleven twenty-five, when Vern made a U-turn in front of the C of E church, Bernie Macdonald, the groom, waiting at the vestry door, took a decent swig from his flask and looked beyond the green Ford towards Blunt's crossing, still expecting his barefoot twin to come like the cavalry and save him.

Not that the gaining of legal rights to Jenny Morrison wasn't tempting, but not if it was going to drive a wedge between him and his brother. They'd damn near killed each other last night. This morning, Bernie's left eye was closed, though still more red than black. He'd got the worst of it. At midnight, his father, brother-in-law and Constable Denham had driven Macka out to another brother-in-law's farm and offloaded him there, bootless. All night, Bernie had been expecting him back. He hadn't slept. He wouldn't be doing much sleeping tonight either — which was what he'd said to Macka last night, which was what had got Macka riled up in the first place. Neither twin was a happy loser, though this morning, Bernie wasn't too certain that he'd won.

George, his father, trussed up like a turkey for the oven in his out-of-date wedding suit, made a grab for the flask as Bernie lifted it again.

'You'll be on your arse before she says "I do", you stupid little bugger.'

Bernie wasn't little. He and his identical twin were slightly larger, much younger replicas of George — same bullet head, a little more hair, built like apes, faces like Freddo Frog. George was a hard-working teetotaller. Bernie and Macka hadn't done a day's work in their lives and both youths had been drunk for a week.

It was sweating out of Bernie as fast as he poured it in this morning, and seeing his mother and eight sisters running to Vern Hooper's car, surrounding it, caused a new flood to drip down Bernie's face, from beneath his armpits, down the crack in his bum. He stepped back from the door, looking now to his father to save him. It didn't look as if Macka was going to get here.

Maisy Macdonald, mother of the groom, clad this morning in puce chiffon and a matching hat, didn't appear too surprised to learn that the bride had flown, though one of her daughters asked why.

Vern lit a smoke instead of replying. Any girl with half a brain ought to run a mile when she saw one of those raping little bastards coming in the distance. He locked his lips around the smoke, inhaled a good dose and glanced at the clusters of onlookers waiting to see the bride. There was not a lot to do on a Saturday morning in Woody Creek. A wedding always drew a crowd. Two dozen or more women stood in groups, two dozen or more kids ran wild, three dogs barking at them. He blew smoke at his windscreen, sucked more, then nodded towards the church.

'Norman and Amber inside yet?'

'They're coming now,' Jessie, an unmarried Macdonald daughter said.

Vern turned to where she was looking and saw Norman and Amber crossing the road out front of Charlie White's grocery store.

'What did she say, Mr Hooper?' Maisy said.

'Not a lot,' Vern said, blowing smoke and nudging the accelerator, not wanting to deal with the missing bride's parents; not yet.

Maisy's head was inside his car, as was one of her daughter's. 'Have you spoken to her grandmother?'

They wanted answers. Vern had none to give. He slapped the stick into gear and eased off on the clutch, the big car as eager as he to get away from Norman Morrison, who, having sighted the car, was heading towards it.

'I'm going back out there now to find out for myself,' Vern said. 'I'll let you know more when I know more.' They removed their heads. Vern got away before Norman closed the gap.

There were not a lot of details to be had. Gertrude offered him a sheet of writing paper with his mug of tea.

Dear Granny,
I'm going down to Melbourne to Mary Jolly. I've got most of the money Dad gave me. It will be plenty until I get a job, so please don't worry about me.

'You should have told them last night,' Vern said.

'Try finding a black horse on a dark night — in a pea soup fog.'

'You could have sent Harry in.'

'I could have.'

'Mary Jolly?' Vern said. 'That's that penfriend she was writing to, isn't it?'

'She sounds like a decent woman. Jenny will be all right with her.'

Mary has said heaps of times that she and her mother have got a spare bed and I know her mother gets a pension so they might rent me their spare room.

I'm sorry I didn't tell you to your face, but you would have told me not to go, and to take them to court. My head is so tired of all the talking and arguing about everything. I just want it to be over, and it never will be if I stay here.

Please ask Mr Hooper to give the Macdonald to the hospital and tell Elsie I'm sorry she had to look after it for so long.

I'll write as soon as I get to Mary's. Don't worry about me, and don't tell anyone I've gone until tomorrow because they all deserve it.

All my love,
Jenny

'Where does Mary live?' Vern said.

'Surrey Hills. I got her address from one of her old letters.'

'That girl has never set foot outside this town. How is she going to find her way out to Surrey Hills?'

'As far as I'm seeing it, what she's done is the lesser of two evils — and she's got a tongue in her head — but to tell you the truth, I'm trying not to think about how she's going to find her way out there.'

Vern swallowed a mouthful of tea and looked at the clock. 'All dressed up and nowhere to go,' he said. 'We could take the infant down to the hospital today — stay the night . . .'

'Maisy will have some say in that.'

'She didn't seem too surprised when she heard the wedding was off.'

'She went along with it to get her hands on her granddaughter. She'll want to raise the child herself. I'll speak to her as soon as things settle down a bit.'

She'd speak to her sooner than that. They heard a car motor and left their tea to go to the door.

The car still moving, Maisy and George sprang from opposite doors, George flushed red from his billiard-ball dome to the starched white collar choking him. A man with no neck doesn't wear a collar comfortably. Maisy's plump cheeks were almost a match for her ensemble. A slip of a girl when she'd wed George, she'd broadened with each babe she'd borne.

Gertrude greeted them with Jenny's letter. George snatched it, squinted at it, then passed it to Maisy. Her eyes were twenty-odd years younger than his.

'The crazy little bastard took off on his bike —'

'In his wedding suit,' Maisy said.

'Drunk as a skunk,' George said.

'They'll kill themselves on that thing one day,' Maisy said.

No loss, Gertrude thought as she added a dash more boiling water to her teapot, gave it a shake, then turned to her kitchen dresser for two more mugs.

'What have you done with the other one?' Vern said.

'He's fifteen miles out. That's where Bernie will have gone.'

'And he forgot to take Macka's boots,' Maisy said, handing the letter back.

'What's it say?' George asked.

'That she's gone to Melbourne, George.'

'Sit down,' Gertrude said.

George was too agitated to sit. He'd worked this wedding out with Amber. His boys had been charged with the statutory rape of a minor and God alone knew what would have happened to them if not for Amber. Not that he could stand the woman — few could — but she'd saved his boys from the hangman's noose and for that he was grateful.

Maisy sat, and on Vern's chair. He always sat at the western end of the table; Gertrude always sat on his left, on the north side. So Vern stood and George stood.

Both men were landowners, mill owners, both had money to burn, both were town councillors, important positions in Woody Creek. That was all they had in common.

Ludicrous, the sight of those two standing side by side. The short and the tall of it, George five foot five and a half, and thick, Vern six foot six, thickening a little around the waist but long enough to carry it. George had more hair on his eyebrows than his head. Vern's head was covered by an abundance of steel grey wire.

'You're making my kitchen look untidy,' Gertrude said. 'Move those newspapers off that little chair, Vern.'

Vern lifted the pile of papers. There was nowhere to put them down. Nowhere to swing a cat in Gertrude's kitchen — if she'd had one to swing. She didn't like cats. He dumped the papers onto her cane couch, pulled the small chair up to the south side of the table and sat, leaving George the hot seat, his back to the wood stove, where Gertrude was attempting to squeeze two more mugs of tea from her pot.

'She must have said something,' George said.

'She said we all deserved it, George. And we did,' Maisy told him.

'She's going down to that penfriend she's been writing to,' Vern said.

'Was she meeting the train?'

Vern shrugged. He folded the letter, slid it into its envelope. Gertrude took it and placed it on her mantelpiece behind her old mantle clock.

'You should have seen Amber, Mrs Foote. She was as white as a ghost and rigid,' Maisy said. 'And Norman looked as if he wanted the minister to bury him.'

'Was Sissy with them?'

Maisy shook her head and sugared her tea. 'She's said all along that she wasn't going. She told me again yesterday. There was a crowd waiting at the church. The McPhersons were there. John brought his camera, too.'

John McPherson, the local photographer, had gone home. The crowd had dispersed. The street out front of Norman's house looked much as usual for a Saturday morning.

Sissy Morrison left the window, relieved she hadn't been made a fool of, but wanting the details of the aborted wedding.

Her parents weren't talking — to her, or to each other.

Norman sat at the table, in his immaculately clean kitchen, head in his hands. He had raised Jennifer from infancy, as his own, and on his own for six years — his golden songbird, beating her wings against the bars of his common cage. She had escaped; battered, bruised, but free. He envied her flight.

There was no escape for Norman. A waddling wood duck, his wings clipped by his mother, his tail feathers plucked by his first-born, his quack silenced by his wife, the whore, still clad for the wedding that never was.

Had he wanted that girl wed? Perhaps he had, for her good name's sake, for his own and her sister's good name's sake, for his grandchild.

His grandchild? Was it his grandchild? He could not think of it as such.

He glanced at Amber, busy at the stove, sweeping up a scattering of soot with a small shovel and brush.

She had given up her own bridal gown when Jennifer asked for it. He had not expected that. She had taken it willingly from its box, aired it, sponged it, pressed every crease from it, hung it for a week from the curtain rod in the parlour, the long train draped over his couch. She'd spent two days baking for the wedding feast at Maisy's house — eager to see his golden songbird wed to a dirt-scratching mole, her belly swelling each year with Macdonald litters. His wife, the whore, had wanted that wedding. She had been happy these past weeks, had dressed happily this morning. His wife, the whore, was not often happy.

She was cleaning now, in her new wedding suit, a muted checked beige. A beige woman, Amber, afraid to show her true colours. Red anger was in her brow this morning, white rage in her compressed jaw as she swept. She liked a tidy kitchen.

Kept her distance from the western window. Kept her distance from the jubilant eyes of Mr Foster, their postmaster neighbour. He had been at the church, and certainly his eyes had laughed, as had John McPherson's and his schoolmistress wife's — as had a few.

Mr Foster's eyes would be pressed to a knot hole in the paling fence, or peering from his bedroom window, which offered him a fine view of Norman's kitchen window.

'How did she get on the train without you seeing her?' Sissy said.

Norman waved her question away. He didn't know how Jennifer had boarded the train, or if she had boarded the train. He hadn't seen her.

'He knew,' Amber said.

Norman glanced at his wife, the whore. During the early years of his marriage, he'd attempted to understand her. Now he attempted to stay well clear of her. He had his station and a few comforts there. Not this morning. Not yet. First allow the town's laughter to die.

He glanced at his daughter and saw his dead mother. A big girl, Sissy, a Duckworth in build, wide in the hip and buttock, heavy in the thigh and ankle, but longer than the usual Duckworth. She had inherited her maternal grandmother's height and perhaps her maternal grandmother's hair. Her saving grace, that hair, dark and heavy.

'How did he know, Mum?' she asked.

'He sold her the ticket,' Amber said, her face aged by her grimaced words, mouth lines deepening, indentations from outer eye to jaw. A pretty girl at twenty, his wife, the whore. She had not aged well.

'If he sold her a ticket last night, why bother getting dressed up to go to the church this morning?' Sissy argued.

Norman nodded, pleased by his daughter's logic. Her arguments were not always so logical.

His wife, the whore, did not appreciate logic. She vacated the kitchen, Sissy behind her. Norman was free to sit then, free to stare at the window, at a fly buzzing to get into Amber's kitchen.

Fool of a fly, he thought.

UNRESOLVED

Jenny's unnamed infant sucked on, unaware of the part she'd played that Saturday. Born a pale, hairless midget, she'd put on little weight in her six weeks of life but grown no hair. She was as bald as her grandfather, her naturally pale Macdonald complexion was made more obvious by the darker than average breast of her surrogate mother.

Had Elsie Hall been sighted walking down a street in Spain, she wouldn't have received a second glance. She had her father's European features. Every time she ventured into town at the side of her lanky redheaded husband, she received more than her fair share of second glances. In Woody Creek, Elsie was recognised as a light-skinned darkie.

Harry Hall, considered by most to be a reliable and decent enough young bloke, drove one of George Macdonald's mill trucks, had been driving for George since '31. He wasn't a good-looking boy; snub-nosed, watery blue eyes, a blotch of freckles, long boned and not enough fat on them — and a city blow-in to boot, which hadn't stopped a couple of the town girls from giving him the eye. He'd got himself involved with Gertrude's darkie, and like a fool, done the right thing by her — or that's what they said in town. They didn't know much in town.

Harry was going on for twenty-three, and already raising three of his own kids along with Elsie's niece and nephew, plus Joey, Elsie's fourteen-year-old son. And no happier man lived in Woody Creek.

He'd started losing his first family at twelve. Two weeks after his thirteenth birthday, he'd buried his father. Orphaned, he'd caught the train west to spend the worst years of the depression with a dirt-scratching cousin, fighting the bunnies for a blade of grass to chew on. At fifteen he'd caught the train back, to try his chances alone.

An accident landed him in Woody Creek. A second accident had given him a home with Gertrude. He called her Mum, but considered her more angel than a mother. She'd built him and Elsie a little house in her front paddock, built it high enough off the ground to keep it above the floodwaters she knew would come again one day. Only a two-bedroom house, it hadn't been designed to contain a tribe, but it had front and rear verandahs.

On the day of the cancelled wedding, Harry was working on the conversion of his back verandah into two sleep-outs, while keeping his eye on the traffic piling up in Gertrude's yard. The bike of Denham, the local constable, had joined Vern's and Maisy's cars.

'What's he want?' Elsie said.

'The twins or Jenny,' Harry said.

Gertrude's visitors left as they had arrived, Denham first, followed by Maisy and George, then half an hour later by Vern. That's when Gertrude started her search for Amber's wedding gown.

Yesterday when Maisy had delivered the gown, Jenny had hung it from a nail driven into one of the lean-to rafters. Gertrude hadn't thought about it until this morning. Like Jenny, it had gone missing.

It wasn't in the lean-to wardrobe. She looked beneath the bed, opened and closed drawers, searched her own bedroom for it, opened old trunks. She wasted an hour in looking for that gown, then gave up and went over to watch Elsie and Joey hold up a prefabricated wall while Harry hammered.

'Did you find it, Mum?'

'Not yet,' Gertrude said.

'She's took it with her,' Elsie said.

'It's the last thing she'd take.'

'What did Denham want?'

'She's too young to be out there by herself. I'll feel better when I hear that she got to her penfriend.'

For three days Gertrude looked for Amber's wedding gown, or for scraps of it. She caught sight of white against her fence. Only paper, only white feathers.

For a week she waited to hear that Jenny had arrived safely. From Monday to Friday, she, Joey or Harry called into the post office, hoping for a letter that never came, then Gertrude gave up waiting and wrote to Mary Jolly.

The crippled postmaster recognised the name, the address on Gertrude's envelope. He had addressed Jenny's first letters to her penfriend and saved every reply in a box beneath his counter, each one addressed to *Cara Jeanette Paris*, a small deception he had allowed. Mail was sacrosanct. Gertrude's letter went into the mail sack and would be delivered. Mary would not know the Jennifer Morrison Gertrude had surely enquired after.

He sent a telegram to the same address, asking if *Cara* had arrived safely.

If the telegram was delivered, it was ignored.

Previously he had interfered in Jenny's life. He had no wife, no child, no niece or nephew. He did it again. He spoke to Denham, who spoke to Gertrude, and on the fifth day of June, she drove with Vern to Melbourne.

A bitter day of sleeting rain, but they found Surrey Hills, they found the address, found the house in a street of similar houses. Gertrude knocked on the door.

It was opened by a girl of ten or twelve. She didn't know Mary Jolly. Her mother came, an infant on her hip. They'd moved to Surrey Hills back in February, she said. She didn't know who had rented the house before them.

'The lady next door has been there for years. She might know the person you're looking for.'

They went next door where they learned that old Mrs Jolly had died in January, during the heat wave, that Mary had moved in with one of her brothers.

'She's a cripple, you know. She couldn't manage alone, even if her brothers had kept on paying the rent.'

'Has a young girl been here looking for her?' Gertrude asked.

'No, dear, no young girl. I had a couple knock on my door one day, but I told them the same as I'm telling you.'

'Miss Jolly had a job in the city, I believe,' Vern said.

'She did too, and lord only knows how she got herself in there and back every day. The poor girl is terribly crippled, but a real lovely girl anyway. Always a smile for me, and as I said a hundred times to my husband, she didn't have much to smile about.'

'You wouldn't know where she worked?'

'For some lawyer chap, I think. She was one of those typewriters. There was nothing wrong with her hands.'

'No idea of his name?'

'I'm not the sticky nosing type, my dears. I leave my neighbours to themselves as much as I can. The worst thing you can do when you live so close by is to live in your neighbours' pockets — or so I've found.'

There were a lot of lawyers in Melbourne. They couldn't knock on every door. And who was to say that Mary was still working, and who was to say that the brother she'd gone to live with lived in Melbourne?

Gertrude had kept in touch with Ernie Ogden, who had been the law in Woody Creek through the twenties. Six or so years ago he'd put in for a transfer to Mitcham, which according to Vern's city map wasn't a lot further along the road they'd taken to get to Surrey Hills. Ernie would be the chap to speak to.

In mid-June, the newspapers printed a photograph of Jenny, taken on the night she'd come third in a radio talent quest. It was on page five, and not large enough to catch most eyes. Nor was the caption: HAVE YOU SEEN THIS GIRL?

The front page was full of Hitler's escapades. Page two's headlines shouted NATIONAL REGISTER OF MANPOWER. And there

15

could be only one reason why the government was registering its manpower. War. There was a column on the same page mentioning that the Defence Act would be extended to include New Guinea as a territory where conscripts might be sent. Those with sons of fighting age read every word of page two. Vern Hooper's son, Jim, was of fighting age. Ogden had seven sons, all of fighting age.

Norman Morrison had no sons. His wife had carried three. They'd died at birth — or soon after. Poor eyesight had saved Norman from the first war, though it did not prevent him reading the *Sun* newspaper from cover to cover.

He read of a gunman terrorising Melbourne, who had made his escape in a green Ford.

The car pulled into the kerb beside Mr Thompson. The gunman alighted and demanded the canvas bag. No shots were fired. Mr Thompson was able to give police a description of the wanted man. He is approximately six foot in height, of medium build, was wearing grey sports slacks, a tweed jacket and a grey felt hat. He is thought to be in his mid-thirties and was last seen driving west on Whitehorse Road.

Then he turned the page and his eye settled on the photograph of Jenny. He had not reported her missing. Life in his house had been . . . difficult since May. Sissy's social life having revolved around Jim and Margaret Hooper, who had been keeping their distance since the aborted wedding, Sissy housebound was vocal. Norman craved an end to her tantrums. He craved peace.

HAVE YOU SEEN THIS GIRL?
Fifteen-year-old Jennifer Carolyn Morrison, missing from her home since May, is described as five foot five, of slim build, short golden blonde hair and sapphire blue eyes. She was last seen wearing a long black overcoat and green beret. She is believed to be somewhere in Melbourne. Anyone with information on her whereabouts is asked to contact their local police station.

Back in '24 that same newspaper had printed a photograph of Jennifer's dead mother, with a similar short paragraph beneath it.

The circles of life, he thought.

Jennifer had not been meant for this town. He had taken that dead stranger's child into his house and given her his name. He had wanted the best for her, and done the worst by her.

He turned the page.

Charlie White, Woody Creek's grocer, stood behind his counter, reading that same newspaper and knowing it was only a matter of time, a matter of how far Hitler intended pushing his luck and his borders, a matter of how far England and France would allow him to push those borders before they were compelled to stop him.

Roosevelt had been in touch with Hitler and Mussolini, urging them to give assurances of peace. They'd given no assurance. War was coming — and too soon after the last. Just a case of when.

For years Charlie had been telling anyone who'd listen that the Versailles Treaty the Allies had forced on Germany after the last war had left that country nowhere to go but back to war.

'Miserable warmongering old bugger,' they called him.

Maybe he was.

He was a widower and a lonely man once he closed that store. He lived with his daughter and son-in-law, who didn't want him living with them, but as he owned the house they lived in there was little they could do about that. They did a few hours' work at the shop. He paid them well, and paid their bills, and lectured them over the dinner table each night.

'Relations between Japan and the United States have been deteriorating for years. Britain has got bases in Singapore, Malaya and Hong Kong, a bare cat's whisker from Japan.' Charlie knew what was coming.

'For God's sake, Dad. Can't we have one meal in peace?'

'You won't know the meaning of that word soon, girl. You mark my words. The Japs have got a navy second to none, and there's millions of the little yellow buggers crowded onto a few islands. They'll look down at Australia and see land for the taking,' Charlie said.

Australia wasn't ready for war. Compulsory military training had been abolished back in the early twenties. The depression had further depleted the size of the regular army. Bob Menzies had allocated forty-three million to be spent over three years in expanding the defence forces, but by July of 1939, anyone bar a fool knew they didn't have three years.

'I'll give it three months,' Charlie said.

The Melbourne gunman was doing his best to push Hitler and Mussolini from the front page of newspapers. He never struck in the same place twice. He got away from a jewellery shop in the middle of Melbourne with rings worth hundreds of pounds. He held up a bank sixty miles out of Melbourne, held up the owner of a big furniture store in Richmond. He struck at another bank in Frankston.

That one made the front page, with a photograph of a young couple and an artist's sketch of the bank robber.

Mr Victor Howard and his fiancée, Miss Martha Williams, a young couple saving for their wedding and accidental victims of yesterday's bank robbery, were able to give police their first clear description of the bandit who has been eluding Melbourne police for months. He is believed to be between twenty-five and thirty, in excess of six foot and of slim build. The couple entered the bank at ten thirty yesterday, where they handed over their deposit to a redheaded male installed behind the teller's cage. The gunman had entered the bank earlier that morning and locked bank staff in the manager's office.

'He seemed to know what he was doing,' Mr Howard said. The brazen thief wrote the amount of their deposit in their book then stamped and signed it before the couple departed, unaware that they had been the victims of a bare-faced robbery.

'He was a very nice-looking chap and very well mannered,'
Miss Williams told the reporter.

Hitler and his goose-stepping troops took a step too far on the first day of September: they invaded Poland. Two days later, Britain and France declared war.

The news came to Woody Creek on the wireless. Bob Menzies' words sounded like a death knell.

We are at war.

Anyone over the age of thirty could remember the carnage of that last war. Speak to any man, woman or child and they'd tell you of a son, brother, nephew, cousin, uncle lost to that war to end all wars.

Charlie White's son-in-law had lost an arm to it and a brother. Tom Palmer had lost a brother. John McPherson had lost his father, his wife, a fiancé. Lonnie and Nancy Bryant lost two sons. Thousands upon thousands of boys had died in that bloody war — and now their sons would die.

'Where's the government going to raise money to equip an army?' a few of Charlie's customers asked. 'They couldn't raise five bob to put shoes on kids' feet a while back.'

'Governments will always find money for their own causes. You watch it start to flow now,' Charlie White said.

'They're not getting their hands on my son to use as cannon fodder. I'll cripple the little bastard before I let him go.'

'You can't put an old head on young shoulders,' Charlie said. 'They'll go like they did the last time.'

They'd go. Since the aborted wedding, since George had cut off his twin sons' allowance, they'd been working at the mill. The day war was declared they took off to join up, which left George two men short at the mill — or maybe one.

'Useless little bastards. Maybe the army will knock 'em into line.'

On Friday 8 September, Charlie was alone behind his counter when the train came in with the city newspapers. He wanted his newspaper, hated waiting for it until midday when he could close his doors for half an hour.

The mail came in on the train. Always a pile of it for the store, a pile of bills he wasn't eager to open. He paid for his grand-daughter's board and tuition at the Willama convent school — money he considered well spent. Three generations coexisting in one house is rarely an ideal situation. He'd bought a car so his son-in-law could deliver her down there on Mondays, pick her up on Fridays. That's where they were this morning, both his daugh-ter and son-in-law. It didn't take two to drive that car, and the kid didn't get out of school until three thirty. They could have waited until he'd got his newspaper.

He was flipping through yesterday's, looking for something he hadn't read when Foster walked in with his mail. Bills, bills and bills, and one envelope the postmaster stayed to see opened. He said he recognised the handwriting.

THE SALVATION ARMY COUPLE

September was usually Woody Creek's most pleasant month; warmth without heat, gardens blooming, even the weeds looked good in September. Charlie closed his shop door at noon on fine Saturdays, spent enough time in the house to clad himself in his bike-riding shorts, then he took off to someplace.

He had good legs for an old bloke. Jean had said so. She'd bought those shorts in Melbourne two years before she'd died, wanting him to show off his legs. They'd had a good thing going, him and his Jeany.

Gone now, long gone.

On Saturday 9 September, the sun shining, Charlie pushed off along the forest road. It was quiet riding out that way, few cars and trucks to spray him with grit, to force him off the crown into the ruts and gravel. He'd passed the bush sawmill, was four or so miles from town when the sun clouded over. They'd forecast rain for the weekend. Forecasts were more often wrong than right. They could have got this one right.

'You can rain on me all week, you miserable bloody cow. Why go and do it on a man's bloody weekend?' he yelled, and his bike wobbled into heaped gravel. He had to put a foot down to save himself.

Two kids setting rabbit traps heard him, Joey Hall and his blond-headed brother-cousin, Lenny.

'What are you doing hiding there?' Charlie said.

'Listening to you swear,' six-year-old Lenny replied.

'How's your grandma?'

'Good.' At fifteen, Joey was as tall as he'd ever be, five-six or so, and of an age to be conscious of his darker than average skin, his need to shave. He'd known Charlie all his life, but had little to say to him. Lenny said more. He looked white to Charlie, though he wasn't. He was Elsie Hall's sister's kid, and his father must have had blue eyes.

The kids mounted a battered bike and headed towards home. Charlie turned his bike around and followed them in. He didn't like the look of that sky.

He glanced at Gertrude's land as he passed. He was nobody's favourite visitor and he knew it. Jean had been the favourite, and he tolerated at her side. He needed an excuse to knock on doors — and maybe he had an excuse to knock on Gertrude's today.

The sky decided him. It spat in his upturned eye.

'Out of eggs?' she said, inviting him in.

He reached beneath his sleeveless sweater and withdrew an envelope. 'Something you might like to look at,' he said, offering it. 'It came yesterday. Foster reckons he recognised the handwriting.'

It contained the front page of last week's newspaper, with the headline WE ARE AT WAR. Written in the margin were six words.

You told them so, Mr White.

'Foster swears it's young Jenny's writing,' he said.

Gertrude picked up her reading glasses and moved to the doorway, to the better light.

'It does look like her writing,' she agreed. She looked at the envelope. According to the postmark, it had been posted in Melbourne. She studied the written address and the few words on the newspaper. 'Those are her curly Ws. That's her C. Was there nothing else in the envelope?'

'Just what you're holding,' he said.

'Thank God for small mercies. At least I know she's alive. Bless you, Charlie White.' Gertrude held the envelope to her heart, then, realising what she was doing, handed it back. 'Have you got time for a cup of tea?'

All he had was time until he opened his shop on Monday morning.

He was eating his third biscuit when the car drove up. Vern spent his Saturday afternoons with Gertrude, and if he arrived late enough, a few of his Saturday nights.

'She's in Melbourne,' Gertrude greeted him at the door.

Vern glanced at the page of newsprint, shrugged and turned it over, seeking more. There was no more. 'Anyone could have sent it.'

'It's her writing. Mr Foster recognised it,' Gertrude said.

'Whether it is or isn't, it's not worth getting your hopes up.'

'I've been doubting lately that she even got on that train. I've been seeing her lying dead under a log somewhere, face cut to shreds like those other little girls. At least I know she got there — and that she's got money to spend on a newspaper and a stamp.'

The rain cleared on Monday, and by Wednesday arms were being bared to the sun.

Norman sat on his station platform, enjoying both sun and solitude, a mug of tea on the bench beside him, sparrows pecking at biscuit crumbs at his feet. He liked birds, spent a lot of time watching birds.

The telephone disturbed his peace. He sighed, put his paper down, emptied his mug and carried it with him to his ticket office and telephone.

'Woody Creek Station,' he said, expecting the familiar voice from the city.

'Mr Morrison? I'm ringing on behalf of your daughter . . .'

The train due in at ten arrived twenty minutes late on Thursday. Norman was a punctual man; he expected punctuality in others.

He was expecting a broken child to be led by her keepers from the second-class carriage and saw no sign of her. He watched Mrs Flanagan step down, saw one of the Martin youths alight, saw a Salvation Army couple, the man carrying a red case, and behind them a city woman, clad in red. Norman's hangdog eyes continued their search for his broken child. He understood defeat, and if he might not welcome her, he would support her.

The Martins' oldest son was waiting to meet his brother. Mrs Flanagan's son had been pacing the platform for half an hour. Danny, Norman's station assistant, waited with the trolley, and all five pairs of male eyes fixed on the city woman, who was more suitably clad for a Flemington race meeting than a country station.

Norman's eyes were on her when the Salvation Army captain offered the stationmaster his hand.

'Donald Delahunt.'

Norman took the hand. Donald Delahunt and his wife had agreed to return Norman's missing child.

They had returned a woman, her hair hidden beneath a folde-rol of a hat, her frock emphasising her womanly shape. Neckline low cut, belt cinched tight, slim skirt flaring at the knee. The frock flaunted her. He looked down at her red sandals. The heels, four inches of them, lending her height. He looked up to a mouth painted as red as the frock.

Blinded by the glare of her, struck speechless, Norman turned to his train. Jenny turned to his ticket office, walked towards it, leaving her travelling companions to explain how she'd been found.

She hadn't been found. They just thought she had.

A good distance between them, she stood watching Norman. He looked smaller today — or maybe her outfit was making him cringe smaller. She hadn't dressed for him. She'd dressed for Amber. All the way from Melbourne, she'd known that Amber would be waiting at the station, waiting to put on a good show for the Salvation Army people. There was no sign of her. Maybe Salvation Army people weren't important enough to bother putting on her show for.

She looked towards the railway house, scanned the length of the fence. Her mother and Sissy were probably down behind the lavatory, looking between a gap in the palings.

Jenny turned her back on them and on Norman, and walked down to the station's long bench. Same old bench. She had spent hours of her life sitting on it. One of her first memories was of sitting there with Jimmy Hooper, looking at the most beautiful picture book she'd ever seen.

Same old station clock, telling her the time was now ten twenty-eight. That clock was always right. Flyspecked light globe with its dusty shade, ticket cage. Everything the same — of course it would be the same. Time was a weird sort of thing. To her, it seemed as if she'd been away for years, but in real time it had only been four months. In twenty years, that clock would still be telling the right time, the light globe might have been replaced but the shade would be the same.

She sat down and unbuckled her sandals, which looked perfect with the dress but were useless to walk in. She removed her hat and combed her hair with her fingers, lifting higher what little the hairdresser had left her. She didn't like hats — or what hats did to her hair.

Her toes, relieved to renew their acquaintance with the station's platform, wriggled in ecstasy as she stood to look at Norman, who was attempting to get away from the Salvation Army couple. His train already late, he had to attend to it.

I know him too well, Jenny thought. I know everything about him; his nods, when he isn't even listening, the way his hands try to will people to keep their distance, the way his bloodhound eyes rove.

Danny, the station boy, knew him too. Danny saved him. Norman got away.

'How's it going, Jen?' Danny said.

She'd known him since he'd started working for Norman, since he was fourteen and she was eight or nine. She smiled her reply. The bonneted Salvation Army woman caught the tail end of the smile, and returned it.

Dorothy Delahunt. Dorothy and Donald. They sounded like characters in a picture show, the goodies. They should have been wearing white hats.

Her walking shoes were in her case, the case at Donald's feet. He was watching the unloading of goods, watching bundles of newspapers being tossed from goods van to platform, watching as the mailbag was tossed.

Her sandals and hat left on the bench, she slid the strap of her handbag over her shoulder and turned to watch the people on the train. Most faces showed the same expression, the longing to get to where they were going.

A little boy standing at a first-class carriage window, his eyes greedily absorbing the world, his little hand waving. She waved to him, and he turned to tell his mother about the lady who had waved, as Jenny had once turned to Norman to tell him that a lady with a fox around her neck had waved to her.

She loved this station, or her memories of it. Loved Norman too — or once upon a time she'd loved him. Didn't know what she felt now, if she felt anything now.

Train huffing and puffing to get away. Little boy waving again. Norman standing with Donald.

Still waving to the small boy, she walked with the first-class carriage to the western end of the station, until she could go no further.

Glanced back. Dorothy was watching her, or watching the train — or maybe just wondering how she was expected to fill the eight or nine hours until it returned.

Amber would offer them lunch; she'd serve them tea in her best cups and she'd tell them how pleased she was that her daughter had been found, how appreciative she was that their absconding girl had been returned to the loving arms of her family. Dorothy and Donald would get on that train tonight thinking only nice thoughts of their hostess.

People were rarely who you thought they were, or most of them weren't, though most people didn't want to look any deeper than the surface. Certainly the two Salvos didn't. They hadn't asked the hard questions.

Norman picked up the red case. Too late now to worry about walking shoes. The final carriage had cleared the lines.

They were watching her when she hitched her frock's skirt up, baring her knees, when she jumped off the platform and ran across the railway lines.

'Jennifer!' the woman called.

Norman didn't call. He didn't want her back in this town. Maybe if he'd called her name, she might have turned back.

'Jennifer!'

Down through the station yard she ran. The ground hard on city-tender feet, her fine city stockings offering no protection. Over the road, down past the hotel. She was still running when she passed Hooper's corner. Ran straight by Vern's house.

There was only one place to go in this town. There'd only ever been one place for Jenny to go.

THE VENEER OF A WOMAN

'I thought you were a bushfire coming down my track. You're lucky I didn't greet you with a bucket of water,' Gertrude said, but only later, after the kissing, the neck-breaking hug, only after the biscuit tin was opened, the tea poured. 'So, tell me all about it.'

'Your tea tastes of goat udders, Granny.'

'You'll get used to it again.'

She wouldn't, though she didn't say so. She was only here for a day, or maybe two.

'What did your father have to say?'

Jenny shrugged, sipped goat's milk tea, ate another biscuit to kill that taste — and waited for Norman to come. Gertrude expected him to come.

'Did you find your penfriend?'

'No.'

'Where have you been working?'

'Cleaning houses.'

Mick Boyle, the local carrier, drove in at twelve. Norman had sent Jenny's case down with him, plus a cardboard carton of bits and pieces, books, old clothes, her red sandals and fancy black and red hat balanced on top.

She glanced through the carton, smiled at a black-covered book that looked like a Bible. It didn't belong to her. Norman must have thought she needed it. Pitched it back into the carton, pitched the lot back in. She'd left nothing of value in Norman's house, had never owned anything of value to leave there. Sighed, wished she could stop sighing.

They were shaking up the mattress of the lean-to bed, the clean sheets waiting to be spread, when they heard Norman's bike hit the chicken wire fence. Gertrude left her bed-making. Jenny remained to finish it.

He'd sent her case down; he wasn't here to take her home. She crept to the green curtain — always hard to creep in Granny's house. Boards creaked.

'It's good to see her looking so well,' Gertrude said.

That old curtain had only ever offered the illusion of privacy. Norman didn't understand about curtains, or maybe he didn't know Jenny was behind it.

'She is my daughter, Gertrude. I will support her financially while she remains in your care,' he said.

'She needs your support not your money, Norman.'

'I have . . . have a second daughter to consider.' He cleared his throat. 'As you may understand, these past months have not been easy for . . . for Cecelia. There has been a recent reconciliation with the Hooper family. It must not be jeopardised by her sister's . . . her sister's immoderation.'

'Immoderation?' Gertrude said. 'She's fifteen years old, Norman. She ran from two sods who deserved the hangman's noose.'

He cleared his throat. He had things to say. He would get them said. He took a pound note from his wallet and offered it. Gertrude turned her back on his money. He held it a moment longer, then placed it on the table.

'I would, at this time, suggest she make no attempt to see her mother and sister.'

Like a red whirlwind, Jenny exploded from behind the curtain.

'As if you could pay me enough to go within a mile of either of them,' she said. 'As if there was enough money in the entire world to make me go near them.' And her hand reached out to swipe his pound note to the floor.

Paper doesn't fly well. It fluttered to his feet. He stepped back from it, from her, stepped back to the door, out the door.

'I have explained to your grandmother that I will continue to support you while you remain in her care.'

'All I need from you is a train ticket back to Melbourne, and I'll pay for it, too.'

'You are a fifteen-year-old child,' he said. 'You will remain in your grandmother's care.'

She picked up the pound note, ripped it in two and threw the pieces at him.

'Give them half each, Daddy. That's all either one of them ever wanted from you. And you know it, too.'

Daddy. He took a reflex step towards her. But he was a controlled man. He stepped back. Perhaps he stood in the yard an instant too long, staring at one green half-note dancing in the dust. Perhaps he glanced briefly at the hem of that red frock before turning and walking back to his bike, leaving Gertrude to chase the two halves of the pound note, to pursue one half to the weeds growing alongside the wall of her shed.

'He looks like something even a cat wouldn't drag in on a wet morning. What have they been doing to him?' Jenny said.

'He's lost weight,' Gertrude admitted. She'd placed the note on the table, its ragged edges together. 'Pass me the sticking plaster, darlin'.'

'Burn it,' Jenny said.

'You don't burn money,' Gertrude said. 'It's in the middle drawer.'

Jenny found the plaster. Gertrude cut a strip. She joined the note and reached for Jenny's handbag, looped by its strap over the back of a chair.

Jenny whisked the handbag out of reach. 'I don't want his money.'

'Anger doesn't suit you, darlin'.'

'You won't have to see it for long.'

'You're too young to be out there by yourself. He's right about that.'

Jenny stood opening, closing, click-clicking the handbag clasp. It was near new, the clasp had a positive click.

'I'll bet you he'll sell me a ticket. He'll be so pleased to get rid of me, he probably won't even charge me for it.'

'When things don't go to plan for a man like your father, they've got no fallback plan, darlin'. Don't be too hard on him.'

'What about my fallback plan?'

'Look at yourself. You've come home here in your fighting colours, ready to take on the world. I'm proud of you, and so is Vern and half the town.'

Handbag clasp clicking. Click-click. Click-click. It was something to do with her hands. She had cigarettes in that bag but wasn't game to light one, not here. Click-click. Click-click.

'Are they still here?' No need to say their names.

'They told Maisy they were joining the army. She hasn't heard if they went through with it.'

'I hope they did and I hope Hitler is waiting for them with a cannon,' Jenny said. 'I hope he blows them to smithereens and the dogs eat the bits.' Click-click. Click-click. Click-click. She glanced up. 'Did Vern get rid of it?'

'Get rid of what?'

'Don't make me call it what you know I will.'

'She's with Elsie. Maisy named her Margot.'

'Swap the *r* for a *g* and you've got maggot.'

'She was named for some film star.'

'I asked you to get Vern to give it to the hospital.'

'Mothers have to sign papers when they give up their babies.'

'I'll sign them before I go back.'

Gertrude watched the handbag clasp click six, eight times before she reached for it.

'You'll wear it out, darlin'. It's a lovely bag.'

'Where do I get the papers to sign?'

'Maisy is going to take her as soon as she's old enough to wean.'

Jenny slept well that night in her sagging old bed, slept safe. Granny's creaking old house had always radiated safety.

Sitting opposite her at the table at lunchtime, walking three steps away from her when they went for a walk in the moonlight, was safe — like being joined to her, like knowing that nothing bad could ever happen, not while Granny was close by. She wasn't ready yet to give up that safety. She had to go, but not until the end of September.

Vern drove down on Saturday. He asked the hard questions. He asked where she'd bought her handbag.

'There are heaps of secondhand shops down there,' she said, which was true.

'Where were you living?' he asked.

'Where I cleaned.'

'Where?'

'A few places. One beautiful big house built on the side of a hill. It belonged to a man and his wife who went on a tour of Europe.'

'They wouldn't want to be touring over there now,' he said, and she got away, went down to the creek to sit, but Joey and Lenny came down, so she went fishing with them.

She'd almost forgotten the feel of that nibble at the line, that tugging take of a fish on the hook, the pulling weight of the fish, and the surprise of what she had on the line.

'It's a yellow-belly, Jen. It's a beauty.'

She remembered the taste of Elsie's fried fish, of her fried potatoes, Granny's lemon tree.

Loved this place. Loved Granny and Joey and even little Lenny. Hated Woody Creek, and Amber and Sissy. Norman? She didn't want to think about Norman.

She loved playing cards. They played that night in Elsie's kitchen, and when she told Elsie she was going back to Melbourne sometime next week, little Lenny told her she'd better stay home or he'd punch her up. She'd made a comfortable card night foursome uneven, so Lenny, a card sharp born, had been propped on pillows at the table to make up the sixth. He could play canasta like a champion.

Gertrude had put his age at two the day Mini carried him and his baby sister in from Wadi's camp — he may have been an undernourished three. Given a diet of eggs and goat's milk, he'd sprung up, filled out. Smart as a whip, little Lenny Hall, feisty and fair.

Elsie and Harry Hall cared for seven kids, a mixed and growing bunch. Joey had taken Harry's name, for convenience, as had Lenny and his sister Joany. Ronald, Maudy and Teddy were legitimate Halls. The Macdonald, fed at Elsie's breast during the card game, was the seventh.

Jenny didn't look at her. Couldn't. She saw the shape of her, smelled her baby smell. Knew that baby had come out of her. Couldn't stand the memory of her coming out, or the memory of how she'd got in. That baby made her head go cold, made it crawl, made her play the wrong card. She had to go. On Monday.

She didn't. And on Tuesday, Vern Hooper popped in for a cup of tea.

'You found a job right off, your grandma tells me,' he said.

'Yes.'

'Your grandma tells me that you're thinking about going back this week.'

'Yes.'

Vern was pleased to see that girl back home, though he may have been more pleased had she been returned to her family. These past months he'd spent a few Saturday nights in Gertrude's bed. Having a third party in the house would curtail his night-time activities.

He knew the price of a snakeskin handbag, and he'd taken a look inside it while she was fishing on Saturday. She'd told Gertrude she had her own money. Vern knew how much money she had, and he had his doubts that she'd earned it house cleaning.

'How much a week do they pay a fifteen-year-old maid these days?' he asked.

'He thought I was nineteen.'

'Your grandma was saying that you lived for a time in Collingwood. House cleaning there?'

'Laundry,' she said.

'It's a rough area.'

'You had to watch the things you hung on the clothes line or they disappeared.'

'You wouldn't make much money as a washerwoman.'

'I lived at the house.'

She got away from him, went outside to walk Granny's land and to watch silly little newborn goats chasing their mothers for milk through grass as tall as they, to look at Granny's funny little house getting ready to bloom; the climbing rose which had taken over the west and part of the north side of the house was covered in buds. Another week, maybe two, and she'd see those roses open.

THE LEAVING

September's end crept up on her. No one worried much about dates in Gertrude's house, then suddenly it was October.

She was scared of starting again. Ready though. Her case was packed, and lighter than when it had travelled home. Gertrude's black coat, which had kept her warm through that long Melbourne winter, hung again on its hook behind the door.

The red dress would remain in the lean-to wardrobe. It was made of a beautiful heavy material, and was probably the most expensive dress she'd ever own. Granny called it her fighting colours, Norman's eyes had said 'tart's dress'. Perhaps she'd seen what he'd seen when she'd hung it beside the gold crepe she'd worn on the night of the talent quest.

Hanging side by side, those frocks were like the two halves of Jenny Morrison, the before half and the after half. She wasn't sure which one she was, or if she was either, but the red one wasn't going back to Melbourne with her.

Her case, almost as red as that dress, lay open on her bed. She was folding the last few items of underwear into it when Gertrude lifted the curtain.

'You're too young to be out there by yourself, darlin'.'

'I stayed longer than I said I would, Granny.'

Vern swore that case wasn't secondhand, swore that the handbag had been bought new. He had a fair idea of what they may have cost, what the red frock may have cost new. His wife had spent a fortune on her wardrobe. His daughters had expensive tastes. He believed she'd been with someone down there.

'Every day that you were gone, I thought you'd been murdered, that you were lying somewhere out in the bush like Nelly and little Barbie. I don't want to go through that again, darlin'.'

'I have to go, Granny.'

'What's so bad about staying down here with me?'

'Nothing.'

'Then stay.'

'I can't,' Jenny said.

'Have you got a boyfriend waiting for you down there?'

'No.'

'Have you got a job to go back to?'

'I'll get one. Please stop nagging me and just let me go.'

'Tell me why you have to go and I'll stop nagging you.'

'Because if I stay, you'll wish I had been murdered, that's why!'

'You're not that hard to live with.'

'Can't you just trust me? I'll come back. I'll come home for Christmas. I promise.'

'I think you have got someone down there.'

A girl of her years would have been struggling to keep herself, Vern said. A girl of her years wouldn't have been spending money on fancy frocks and handbags — and she had fifteen pounds plus change in that handbag, as well as her talent quest money, still in its envelope.

'Vern was my boyfriend when I was sixteen. You can tell me if you've got a boyfriend.'

'I haven't got a boyfriend!' She turned back to the case.

'If you haven't got a boyfriend, who do you have to meet down there?'

'A doctor. All right?'

It wasn't the reply Gertrude had expected.

'What does a healthy young girl like you need with a doctor?'

'Because it's happened again, that's why.' She closed her case and lifted it to the floor, her back to Gertrude.

'What has happened again?'

'Stop making me spell things out!'

'You're not . . .'

'I've got the name of a doctor in Richmond who can fix it this time.'

'No. No. *No*.'

'You shouldn't have nagged me if you didn't want to know.'

Gertrude was at the stove, one, two, three lumps of wood hammered into the firebox, and the firebox door didn't like its glut of wood. It wouldn't shut. She kicked it shut.

Old boiling hen, simmering for two hours in her big soup pot, rattling the lid to get out. Gertrude yanked open her cutlery drawer, found her two-pronged fork then slammed the drawer shut, tossed the saucepan lid to the hob, stabbed the old boiler and lifted it, dripping, from the pot to a large tin dish. The dish, attempting to get away from her anger, slid, would have slid over the edge of the table, had Jenny not stopped the slide of dish and chicken.

'He's a proper doctor. He does it all the time.'

'Murders babies?'

'It's not a baby. It's not anything.'

'Murder is my name for it — and there's no other name.' Gertrude picked up the knife she'd been using to prepare vegetables. She'd cut two onions into relatively neat pieces. Not so the two carrots she attacked now with the knife. 'Butchery,' she said. 'That's another name for it. Carnage. Bloodbath.'

'It's breaking an egg that might have hatched into a chicken, that's all.'

And Gertrude tossed the knife down. It slid across the table and fell to the floor. 'It's slaughter of the innocent, you fool of a girl. What the hell did you get up to down there?'

'I shouldn't have told you. I should have just gone.'

'Who was he?'

'It doesn't matter.'

'It matters to me!'

'It doesn't matter to anyone. It will be over and done with in less than half an hour. He's a proper doctor. He does it all the time.'

'Your father was a proper doctor. He did it all the time.'

'Dad?'

37

'Amber's father!' Gertrude said and she walked outside.

No use following her. No use trying to explain. Shouldn't have told her. Shouldn't have stayed so long.

Jenny returned to the lean-to where she tested the weight of her case. She'd grown accustomed to carrying it.

No use carrying it anywhere until six. She'd have to wait out the day, get through it, and not say one more word because whatever she said would make it worse.

For fifteen minutes she sat staring at the rough walls, willing time to pass. Then Gertrude was back at the curtain. 'How far along are you?'

'I don't know.'

'You've got a fair idea, my girl.'

'The doctor won't do it after four months and I'm not that far.'

'Do it. Fix it. Get rid of it,' Gertrude said. 'You've got as little respect for life as your grandfather. Where is the boy now?'

'It doesn't matter, I said.'

'Do you know who fathered it?'

'If you think I don't know what you mean by that, then you're wrong. And if you think I don't know what Amber did in Melbourne then you're wrong about that too — and you can stop mixing me up with her because I'm not like her.'

'Well you're doing a damn good job of imitating her, my girl.'

Gertrude let the curtain drop, knowing that she'd lost Jenny as surely as she'd lost Amber. She didn't know why, didn't know what she'd done wrong, but she'd clearly done something very wrong. Maybe it was that she hadn't wed Vern. She'd set no good example to follow.

The chicken stock, boiling too hard on the stove, was spitting fat, hissing steam. She moved the pot to the hob, closed up the flue, and when she turned, Jenny was standing behind her.

And today, in the gloom of that kitchen, the window light showing only one side of her face, Gertrude saw Archie written all over it. He was in the mouth, the hair, in those defiant eyes.

That was her big mistake. She'd married that viper of a man. He'd poisoned everything he'd ever touched, and there was no doubting that his seed was in Jenny.

Gertrude walked away from the sight of him and kept on walking, not seeing her chooks today, her land, the rutted track she walked; seeing only that evil bastard of a man she'd wed, and a tiny baby boy dying in an enamel basin.

Her anger was foreign to Jenny. She'd known Granny's love, her cuddles, her care, but never this side of her. She stood at the open door watching her stride to the boundary gate, until a blowfly flew inside. The chicken at risk on the table, she snatched up a tea towel to cover it.

It was her fault that Granny wasn't in here making her soup, her fault the hacked carrots were turning brown. She picked up the knife and cut the chunks of carrot smaller. She diced the parsnip as Amber diced parsnip, then tossed the lot into the pot. Stood stirring it with a wooden spoon, and that spoon brought back memories of stirring another large pot with a spoon that had turned blue — brought back memories of Amber's old ball gown, and the ball, and everyone looking at her pretty blue ball gown. And . . . and . . .

Two blowflies buzzing, smelling that chicken and wanting to get at it and to lay their maggots . . .

Filthy.

She picked up an old newspaper from the hearth, rolled it and mashed one fly to pulp, chased the second fly into the lean-to. Lost him.

Stood, scratching at her crawling scalp, staring at her case. She had to get through this day. She had to get on the train to Melbourne, get what was inside of her out, then start again. She had to.

And that fly still buzzing somewhere. Whether Gertrude came back or not, she had to leave soon; the chicken would be safer in the pot than out of it.

Quickly, efficiently, she stripped the meat from chicken bones and pitched it a handful at a time into the pot. At five thirty she tasted the soup. It had no taste. She added salt, pepper, a dash of Worcestershire sauce, a spoonful of tomato chutney, desperate to do one thing right before she left. She added a handful of pearl barley — only because the jar was on the table. She added a tea-spoon full of ground ginger — only because she thought it was curry. Then she found the curry so she added a teaspoon full of that.

At five thirty she killed the other blowfly; got him against the Coolgardie safe and squashed him all over the newspaper.

She was opening the fire box to stuff in the outer pages when she saw him on page three, and in a black and white photograph he looked even more like Clark Gable. Stared at him. She knew she should burn that page — knew she should have wanted to burn it. She didn't. She ripped out page three, folded it and took it into the lean-to.

A dusty old shoe box had lived on top of the wardrobe for as long as Jenny had known this room. She took it down, lifted the lid enough to slide the folded paper inside, then picked up her case and handbag and left the house.

Elsie's kids were running around squealing. At any time of day, kids could be heard squealing around and under Elsie's house. Lucky kids. She turned her back on them, and walked towards the boundary gate.

Gertrude was waiting there.

'Get yourself a watchdog, Granny.'

'You're not leaving me like this.'

'I have to!'

'Your father won't sell you a ticket.'

'I'll tell him why I'm leaving and he'll give me a first-class ticket.'

'Why would you go and do a stupid thing like that? Your body is something precious. You don't give it to just any man.'

'If you don't give it, it gets taken — and who cares?' Jenny lifted the case over the fence, climbed between the wires and con-tinued on towards the road.

Gertrude reached it before her. 'If you leave in this frame of mind, you'll end up repeating the same mistake, over and over again.'

Jenny set her case down. 'You can't unlive things once you've lived them. I can't make what happened to me go away. I can't go back to school and sing at concerts. That part's gone Granny, all I can do is change mistakes before they become real — and I'm changing this one.'

'Women die of abortions.'

'Then I won't "jeopardise" Sissy's relationship with the Hoopers, will I? And I won't jeopardise yours with Vern. And I don't care much anyway.'

'Your grandfather took my first baby at five months. I almost bled to death.'

'If he'd got rid of Amber too then I wouldn't be here to upset you,' Jenny said, and she picked up her case.

'You're not leaving me like this . . .'

'I'm not having it, Granny!'

'Then the time to think about that was before you went with the boy.'

'He wasn't a boy — he was a third option,' she said. 'And he was better than the worst.'

'God help me.'

'God helps those who help themselves,' Jenny said, and she walked on.

'Come back and talk it out with me.'

'There's nothing to talk out, Granny. Can't you see . . . can't you understand? My life stopped. It stopped when I was fourteen. They even had to make my fourteen-year-old talent quest photograph dirty. They wrapped it around greasy fish and chips.' And, too close to tears, she ran.

'Don't make me follow you all the way to town. You know I will.'

'Why didn't you tell me there were such doctors when I was fourteen?' she yelled over her shoulder. 'Why didn't you take me down there when I was fourteen?'

'A dear little baby would have been dead!'

Jenny threw the case down as her eyes gave up their battle to stay dry. 'That Macdonald thing took every dream out of my head and I can't get them back! It took me — and I can't get me back, so stop trying to treat me like me.' She walked on then without her case, walked fast, blind. Gertrude had longer legs, longer strides. They walked side by side until a truck moved them from the road to the gravelled edge. Gertrude raised her hand to the driver, Jenny turned her back and wiped her eyes on her petticoat.

'You can't go without your case. Come back and talk, and if you still want to go tomorrow, I'll go with you to your doctor. '

'You're just saying that to make me go back. You'll say different tomorrow.'

'It's a promise — if you come back with me now.'

Jenny's nose was running. She couldn't wipe it on her petticoat, didn't have a handkerchief. Her eyes would be red. She looked towards the town, wanting to go there and get it over and done with. She didn't want Norman to see her with red eyes. Never again would he see her with red eyes.

Gertrude had turned back. Jenny was free to go. She'd made a start. She could come back for her case when it was over.

Or go tomorrow, with Granny? If something went wrong at the doctor's, Granny would know what to do.

She wouldn't go with her. Saying that she would was just a trick to make her go back to the house.

Not if she'd promised. She had promised.

Gertrude picked up the case, brushed it clean of gravel, then continued on. She didn't look back.

Jenny turned around. She followed her home — or as far as the door.

Inside, Gertrude was stirring, tasting the soup. 'It's nice. What did you put in it?'

Jenny sighed, 'I didn't come back to talk about soup.'

'It's still nice.' She left her soup and came to the door. 'I told you once a long time ago that no matter what else changed in your life, I'd be here for you. I'm upset by what's happened — I'm more than upset — but that doesn't change what I said. I love you and I'm here for you. That's unchangeable.'

Tears weren't any use but they wouldn't stop trickling. Jenny stood, her back to the wall, staring at Elsie's house through the blur of tears. The kids had all gone inside to eat. No screaming now. Goats still moving around, white goats.

Behind her, bowls and cutlery rattled, soup was ladled from the pot, bread sawed, tea brewed while Jenny stood staring at the land, at the distant trees.

The fading light was washing the colours away. Elsie's house looked like a carton, too tall, too narrow — a house on stilts, just a splash of colour clinging here and there.

'What are you looking at, darlin'?'

'A mirage,' she said. 'This place isn't real.'

'What about me?'

'I don't know anymore. I thought I was looking out on fairy land when I got to Melbourne.' She shook her head, shook tears, licked at the few trickling to her lips. 'It wasn't real. Nothing is.'

'Life isn't always what we want it to be. We learn to make the best of it.'

'How?'

'By walking ahead, by taking one step at a time and never looking back at the bad times.'

'How can you keep going when everything you are is back there? I don't know who I am, who I'm supposed to be. I can't feel anything that's real. I can't . . . I can't feel *me* inside. It's like I'm lost, and every day I get more lost.'

'Life is a one-lane track, darlin'. It has to be, or there'd be a stampede of folk running back to fix up their old mistakes,' Gertrude said. 'A long time ago, I put up big signposts warning me not to go looking over my shoulder. I looked over it this afternoon. That's what upset me so much. I saw a tiny baby boy lying in a basin and your grandfather standing over it smiling.'

Jenny turned her eyes away from the land, and for an instant looked into Gertrude's face then away to stare again at Elsie's house.

'All I can think about that doesn't hurt, that doesn't make me feel dirty, is over my shoulder. There's nothing in front of me, except black — like there's a giant black pit there and I can't get around it.'

'If we're walking side by side, my darlin' girl, we'll get around it.' Gertrude took the smaller, softer hand in her own, held it between her hands. 'If we're holding on tight to each other's hands, we'll find the way.'

'I've loved you for every season of my life, Granny, but I can't think like you. I can't want the same things you want.'

'You can make a tastier chicken soup. Come in and eat it while it's hot.'

WALL BUILDING

Busy hands make busy minds. Many hands make light work. Idle hands are the devil's tools. Gertrude had a thousand such adages. *Never put off until tomorrow what you can do today* was another of them. She'd woken at dawn with that one playing in her mind.

For ten years she'd put off lining the walls of the lean-to. Today she'd make a start on it. The roll of hessian that would form the lining's backbone was still in her shed somewhere.

It took a while to unearth it. It was dusty, it smelled of mice, but she draped it over the clothes line, gave it a good belting with her broom, then let the sun and the morning breeze do the rest while she fed her chooks, milked her goats, saddled her horse.

Young Robert Fulton opened his shop doors at eight thirty. For twenty-odd years, the sign painted across the verandah had been advertising *Fulton's Feed and Grain*. Robert Senior had closed his doors in the early days of the depression and was dead a year or two later. Robert, his firstborn, a boy of twenty-five or so, had reopened it twelve months back.

From the outside, it looked like the same store. Inside, it was not. Young Robert had diversified, adding hardware, furniture and household appliances, and the last time Gertrude had been in there she'd seen a display of wallpaper samples. That's what she was after this morning, something pretty and not too expensive.

Fulton's carried little wallpaper stock but Robert had a good range of samples and a telephone. If a call was made to Melbourne before four o'clock, he assured her, he could have her order on tomorrow's train. Australia needed more like him,

Gertrude thought — as would the army. The shop, Robert now being the family breadwinner, might keep him out of the war, but God help his younger brothers. Gertrude had delivered nine Fulton offspring, five girls and four boys.

She ordered five rolls of wallpaper, a cream with green stripes and panels of pink roses. Four may have been plenty but a spare roll wouldn't go astray. She ordered three rolls of heavy-duty lining paper, half a pound of tacks with large heads and a wide glue brush. Gertrude carried little cash. She wrote a cheque.

She shouldn't have gone to the post office; Mr Foster always asked after Jenny. She had to lie to him.

'She's well,' she said.

As she walked by Norman's house, she glanced in. No sign of life there. She could be seeing Norman tonight. She'd made a promise and she'd keep it if she had to, though this morning she hoped she wouldn't have to. Jenny had been born with a pair of capable hands. She'd get those hands busy and keep them busy, then see what tonight brought.

Her horse tied in the shade out front of Fulton's, she mounted and started for home.

Vern's car was missing from his yard. He'd be at his mill or out at the farm. Not that she wanted to see him. She'd end up spilling what she knew to the first friendly pair of ears. Time enough for him to know when she'd come to terms with it — or not come to terms with it.

The hessian still smelled a mite mousy. She spread it out in her front yard where she took to it with a tape measure and scissors, and by ten thirty she and Jenny had moved the dressing table and wardrobe out to the kitchen, and moved the bed to the centre of the room so they could work around it.

'You think you're going to sidetrack me, Granny.'

'I think it's time to make this room look less like my shed,' Gertrude replied.

By midday, the hessian, wet down in the old tin tub, was being stretched and tacked over bare timber walls. It would shrink as it dried. Gertrude had done it all before: Thirty years ago she and Amber had given the bedroom walls the same treatment.

They spoke of tacks and hammers that day; there was no talk of Richmond doctors, and at train time, worn out by labour, they spooned up Jenny's chicken soup and ate it with stale bread fried in bacon grease.

'I love your food,' Jenny said.

'You cooked it.'

They boiled up a large pot of glue before they went to bed, and the following morning started in early, pasting newspaper, page after page of it, covering the hessian. Jenny continued the pasting while Gertrude fed her chooks, milked her goats, packed eggs into cardboard cartons for Charlie and Mrs Crone.

At six, Harry came over with more newspaper and a pound of sausages. He stayed a while to paste and he didn't need to stand on a chair to reach the top of the wall.

It took another day to use up the last of the newspaper. It took three days for the many layers to dry out. Then the bad old news disappeared beneath strips of lining paper and the walls of the lean-to turned white.

Harry helped them with the hanging of rosebuds. They finished the papering by lamplight, determined to be done that day with glue.

It was an amazing transformation. Elsie and the kids thought so. Once the furniture was back where it belonged, once the green curtain had been washed, when a scrap of lace had been found to hang on elastic over the flywired window hatch, it looked like a bedroom.

Vern, the realist, saw it for what it was, but he had other things on his mind.

'I see where they're planning to bring back compulsory military training for boys over twenty-one.'

'That's no surprise, is it?' Gertrude said.

'Jim will be twenty-one come April. That's why they did their registration of manpower. They were counting up their cannon fodder.'

'Nothing much seems to be happening; it could all come to nothing,' Gertrude said. 'And a few months in camp won't do Jim any harm.' It might even do him some good, she thought. He'd spent his life with his sisters — who were no role models.

'I worked too hard at getting him, in raising him, to have him caught up in a bloody war.'

Gertrude had heard it all before. 'I'm thinking of getting Harry to hammer a few batons along the rafters. The kitchen ceiling is only batons and paper.'

'Stop wasting your money on it.'

'You're a tactless man, Vern — and you're worrying needlessly about Jim. Even if the worst comes to the worst, they're not going to take a farmer's only son away from the land. Someone will have to feed their armies. Move out to the farm with him.'

'Move out with me and I will. You can spend your days papering Monk's old place and have something to show for it when you're done.'

'You insulting coot of a man! We're proud of what we've achieved.'

'I'm a truthful man, Trude,' he said. 'Where is she?'

'Down at the creek with Joey. They promised me a feed of yabbies for tea.'

'Are you stuck with her for the duration?'

'She's here for as long as she'll stay and I don't know how long that will be.'

'Has she told you yet where they found her?'

'Leave it alone, Vern. And don't you start giving her the third degree as soon as she comes in either.'

'She's been with someone down there. I don't care if she was cleaning houses from daylight to dark seven days a week and telling her boss she was twenty-one, she didn't earn the sort of money she's spent, then save fifteen quid to bring home with her. I've been paying maids for years — Oh, Christ,' he said, hearing a bike land against the chicken wire fence.

Charlie came to the door, and when asked to sit, he sat on Vern's chair.

'I see when I rode past that they've started clearing the block for the new telephone exchange,' he said.

'Which block?' Gertrude asked, and Vern walked outside for a smoke.

'Old man Lewis's, near the Presbyterian church. His son hadn't paid the rates on it in ten years. The council sold it to them.'

Charlie could talk town gossip for hours and had come prepared to do just that. He asked after Jenny, he praised Gertrude's paper hanging when she got him to his feet, and while he was on his feet, praising it, Vern reclaimed his chair. He saw enough of Charlie White at council meetings, heard enough out of him, too.

Woody Creek was changing. The world was changing. Ten years ago, girls of good family had stayed at home until they wed, while the girls of poor families were paid a few bob a week to clean up after them. Before the depression, the Fultons might have paid a maid to do the dirty work. Now three of the Fulton girls held down jobs. Charlie employed one, another one worked at the post office and the third did the typewriting for the council.

'The dark-eyed Macdonald girl has applied for one of the jobs at the exchange,' Charlie reported.

'Dawn,' Gertrude said.

'They say the middle Palmer girl has got work there.'

'Dora?'

Charlie knew everyone in town, Gertrude knew their names. They spoke of the town and the folk of the town while Vern sat, barely getting a word in edgewise. His Saturday nights had been ruined, now Charlie White seemed determined to take his Saturday afternoons.

He hung around until Jenny came in with a bucket half full of yabbies — and Charlie obviously pleased to see her. He wasn't known for his smile, but he smiled at Jenny as he took his wallet from his back pocket and withdrew the page of newspaper.

'I was in a hairdresser's shop when I heard about the war and I looked up and you were in the mirror, saying, *I told you so*, Mr White,' Jenny said — which was more information than she'd given Gertrude.

Charlie stayed ten minutes more, until Gertrude picked up the bucket of yabbies, preparing to execute them in boiling water. He couldn't stand the stink or the squeaks of boiling yabbies.

Vern stayed on to eat his fair share; he stayed on until nine. Gertrude walked him out to the car. Jenny was seated at the table when she returned.

'Does he know?'

'Not yet.'

'Why didn't you marry him when Itchy-foot died? Everyone thought you would.'

She'd been full of questions once. These days, she rarely spoke unless she was spoken to. Maybe Charlie's visit had been good for her.

'The time for us to wed was when we were young, darlin',' Gertrude said. She'd been looking forward to her bed, but she pulled out a chair and sat. 'We were too old to bother with wedding rings by the time your grandfather was declared dead.'

'Why didn't you marry him when you were young?'

'Our grandfather. His sister had wed a cousin and they'd ended up having three idiot babies. Rightly or wrongly he blamed the close blood ties. Vern was the apple of his eye, his only grandson until he was fourteen — until his father took a second wife.'

'Did you ever love Itchy-foot?'

'Queen Victoria was on the throne when I wed Archie. They were different times. He was a doctor, an educated man from a good family. I fed chooks, milked goats, slept at night down the bottom end of this kitchen in a homemade bed. My mum and dad thought I'd made the match of the century when he came courting me.'

'Did they make you marry him?'

'I was encouraged to, maybe expected to, but no one pressured me into doing it.'

'What was Vern doing while Itchy-foot was courting?'

'Never having a good word to say for him — but not prepared to stop me from marrying him. Our grandfather had told him he could have the land or me. Vern wanted that land — and I don't blame him for it.'

'What was he like when he was young — Itchy-foot?'

'What was he like?' Gertrude repeated. 'He had no fear in him. He'd go anywhere, do anything. I saw the world at his side —'she started, then knew she'd spoken those same words before, and she closed her mouth on them. She'd filled Amber's head with pretty tales of travelling in strange lands, of rich maharajas and grand ships of the line. A mistake, and one she wouldn't make a second time.

'His people were very decent, very good to me. I lived with them in Melbourne for six weeks. Then they booked us on a boat to Africa to work with a group of missionaries. I was given no reason why, though in hindsight I'd say it was probably the worst place the family could come up with on the spur of the moment to send Archie.'

'Why?'

'He'd broken an unwritten family law, darlin'.'

'What?'

Only once in her life had Gertrude spoken of what that man had done. She'd told Vern. It wasn't the sort of thing to tell a fifteen-year-old girl, but Jenny wasn't the average fifteen-year-old girl and Archie wasn't dead. She knew it. Vern knew it. Back during the depression, Archie had hung around Woody Creek for two or three years — and she had a fair idea why he'd hung around.

Forewarned was forearmed against vipers.

'He had been interfering with his little sister. He got her in the family way,' Gertrude said. 'She was fourteen at the time.'

'His sister! That's why you left him?'

Gertrude shook her head. 'He told me his sister had tuberculosis, that we were going to Africa so he could study the disease. I was nineteen. I believed him.'

'How did you find out the truth?'

'He told me. I was on the other side of the world, had no way to get home, no money to get home, and back then women didn't leave their husbands — or not women of my class.'

'He looks like such a beautiful boy in that old photograph.'

'If evil wore an evil face, darlin', we'd all know when to dodge.'

'When did you leave him?'

'When your mother started growing inside me. There was some vital connection missing in Archie's head. Maybe it was the drugs that did it. He used his drugs on me the night he took my little

51

boy. I'd gone to bed, gone to sleep, and woke up with him standing over me. "All fixed, Tru," he said, and my baby boy lying in a basin, his unformed little mouth trying to call out to me for help.' She stood, shook her head, shaking that image away. 'And there I go again, looking back. It's never done me one scrap of good.'

She opened the glass covering the face of her old clock, inserted the key and took her time in the winding of it. 'It's past my bedtime,' she said.

'That's like reading a book and finding the last pages missing, Granny. You have to tell me the end.'

'There's never been an end to it, darlin'.'

'Tell me how you got home then.'

'We were in India at the time. He used to do a lot of doctoring on ships. I saw countries I'd only read of in an atlas, lived in countries where no one spoke my language. He could make himself known. He was a clever man, and a good doctor, too, when he worked at curing. We were on a boat when Amber got started. It took us to India. Drugs were easy to come by there, and his allowance was due. His family paid him to stay out of Australia . . . Anyway, the money came through and Archie disappeared, as he was apt to do.

'I'd been on my own for over a week when a boat full of diphtheria came in to port and one of the officers came looking for Archie. I didn't know when he'd be back or if he'd be back. I told the officer I'd nursed diphtheria cases and asked him if I could work my passage home. An hour later I'd packed up that room and paid out my last coins to two porters to carry my trunks down to the boat. It brought me to Melbourne. I travelled with my trunks by dray to the station, and a day later I was walking down that track.

'My mum and dad hadn't seen me in near on eight years. They looked at me as if they were seeing a ghost. When I saw what was left of me in that washstand mirror, I thought I was seeing a ghost. I should have told them the truth, but if I'd told them the half of it, they would have thought I was losing my mind. I told them I had a baby coming, and that Archie had sent me home for my health.

'I can remember that day as clear as I can remember today. I walked this land for hours, walked it end to end, corner to corner, vowing at each corner that I'd never leave again — which maybe answers your first question about why I never wed Vern.'

'You should write it down. It's like a book.'

'A few of the pages would be banned reading, darlin', which is why I don't spend a lot of time in rereading it. I learned a lot from the years I spent with your father —'

'Grandfather.'

'With your grandfather. Some of it has been useful to me. The past is only useful to learn from.'

Jenny sat picking at a fingernail. The hour was late. They should have been in bed. Gertrude started taking the pins from her hair, but Jenny sat on.

'You knew you had to come home, Granny, like I know I have to go back. I'm going tomorrow. You don't have to come with me.'

'I told you I'd go with you, and I will.'

'You don't have to. Just promise you won't make me fight you again.'

'Will you tell me who he was?'

Jenny shook her head.

'You asked me about your grandfather. I told you,' Gertrude said.

'I sprained my ankle and Mary's mother had died and Mary wasn't there. He offered me a job cleaning his house.'

'Was he a married man?'

'No. He was . . . he was kind to me. He mightn't have been a good man, but he wasn't evil. He looked after me.'

'Maybe he was looking after himself, darlin'.'

'That's what they do, isn't it? We're just things to them, just pretty things they want to play their dirty games with.'

'Not all of them.'

'Can I please go without us fighting?'

'What you're considering is putting your life at risk.'

'I haven't got any choice, Granny.'

'No doubt it feels that way to you right now, but out there somewhere tonight, it feels that way for a lot of women who can't carry their own babies. There are hundreds of married women who would sell their souls to change places with you, hundreds who would take your baby and raise it as their own.'

'Is that what you want me to do?'

'To me it's the better choice.'

'Would someone take both of them?'

THE ARGUMENT

Maisy wouldn't agree to her granddaughter being signed over to strangers. She had the time to raise her, the room, and an addiction to babies. Since her birth she had been visiting Margot regularly. Through November, she spent hours with her. After Christmas, Maisy said, after Jessica's wedding, she'd take Margot into town.

In late November, she carried her granddaughter across the paddock to visit with Jenny, convinced that no one could help but fall in love with that chunky, bald-headed infant.

Jenny saw them coming and went out via Gertrude's window hatch. There was a cool spot beneath the tank stand. She'd used it more than once. Her condition was becoming obvious to the experienced eye.

By December, anyone with a good pair of eyes could see she was in the family way. Vern required glasses. He'd have to be told.

Gertrude chose her moment. Jenny was off somewhere reading. She poured two mugs of tea, cut a wedge of apple pie, then sat and said her piece in as few words as possible.

His response was not what she'd expected — or maybe it was. 'That's where she got the money for her snakeskin handbag,' he said.

'Not another word, Vern.'

'I told you when I first set eye on that handbag that she'd been with someone.'

'Eat your pie and forget I mentioned it.'

'Admit that I told you so.'

'Change the subject. I don't want to argue with you.'

'There's no argument to be made. I told you she hadn't bought those things on a maid's wage. Whether she was with one or fifty-one, she earned that handbag on her back.'

Gertrude reached for his plate of pie. 'Go home, Vern.'

'You can't deny the truth in what I'm saying.' His grip on the plate was stronger. She released it, and he filled his mouth. 'Who does she say is responsible?'

'She'll tell me when she's ready to tell me.'

'Or take a stab in the dark when she sees its eye colouring,' he said.

'You force me to take sides in this and you know whose side I'll take.'

'Like you took your snake-eyed daughter's side against me all of your life.'

'If you hadn't put your grandfather's acres before me, I would have married you when I was eighteen years old.'

'Don't you start dragging that up again and throwing it at a man.'

'I'll drag up more than that if you don't drag your mind out of the gutter when you're in my house.'

'House?' he said. 'I live in a house, and I've asked you a hundred times to live in it with me, you independent bugger of a woman.'

Through the years Vern and Gertrude had disagreed on many topics. There was rarely a lot of heat in their disagreements. Hoopers were slow to burn, but get a good fire blazing and the embers took a long time in dying. They knew it. Gertrude allowed him the last word and, content, Vern spooned up his pie, then lit a cigarette.

'Who is going to raise this one?'

'My tank has got about two inches of water left in it. I'll need to fill it tonight.'

'I asked a civil question.'

'I made a civil statement. I could have been uncivil and told you that it was no concern of yours.'

'It concerns me. I spend half my bloody life hanging around

down here after you. Who does it concern more than me? Charlie bloody White?'

'Count to ten, Vern.'

'Don't give me your count to bloody ten. She's been back here for weeks; you've known she was in the family way for weeks and you didn't even have the decency to tell me.'

'And look what happens when I do tell you. Go home.'

'The day the Salvos brought her home, Lorna saw her running by the house, dressed up like a little trollop, advertising her wares —'

'Anyone who dresses like a lamppost in mourning has got no right to sneer at the way others choose to clothe themselves.'

Vern was allowed to insult his daughters. She wasn't. He stood, pitched his cigarette at her hearth, and was out the door.

'She'll be dropping her brats on your doorstep until your dying day,' he said.

'If you stay away you won't need to see them, will you?' She followed him out.

Kids were running around over at Elsie's. Kids' voices carried.

'Your bloody land is looking more like Betty Duffy's every bloody time I come down here.'

'And you're looking more like your pig-headed grandfather every time I see you — and sounding more like him.'

'He was your bloody grandfather too, you pig-headed bugger of a woman.'

There would be no winner. There would be no backing down. The argument continued out to the car, the insults becoming more personal.

'If you'd try using your legs to walk on instead of cramping them in behind a steering wheel, you might be able to reach your bootlaces for a few more years. You're getting a gut on you like your father had.'

'It won't be worrying you, I can assure you of that.'

'I was pitying your pallbearers.'

Maybe Vern got the last word to her chooks. He left in a cloud of dust and chook feathers, leaving one hen squawking on the track.

*

He stayed away all week. He stayed away for two weeks, three.

Charlie rode down a week before Christmas, his bike crate loaded with stale goods for the chooks and a tin of condensed milk for Jenny. He never came empty-handed. He offered a pound of butter, one corner of it mutilated by a rusty nail. Butter was a rare treat; Gertrude didn't waste money on it. She cut off the mutilated corner and Jenny boiled it up with brown sugar and honey, then added it to oatmeal, flour, crushed walnuts, a good teaspoon of cinnamon and a teaspoon of vanilla.

Charlie and Lenny had shelled the walnuts. They sat side by side at the table, waiting for their hot-biscuit payment. If Charlie noticed the young cook's swelling belly, he made no comment. No one had cooked him hot biscuits since Jean, and no one else in town had told him he'd been right about the war either. He'd liked that kid since the day the postmaster had snatched her battered little body from her mad mother, and they'd laid her out on his shop counter, thinking she was dead. It would take more than a beating to kill that girl, and more than a swollen belly to turn him off her, so he ate hot biscuits and drank his tea, with condensed milk. Like Jenny, he couldn't stand the taste of goat's milk tainted tea.

Gertrude had too much to do to sit talking all day. She was at her sewing machine, running up a loose-fitting smock. The machine lived beneath her kitchen window, an eastern window, midway down the side of her kitchen, which offered a better light in the mornings than the afternoon. She was leaning in close to her work, reading glasses perched on her nose, when Vern arrived — and waited at the door for an invitation to enter. In the fifty-odd years he'd been coming down here, he'd never waited to be invited in. Gertrude knew he still had a bee up his nose.

'Sit down,' she said. 'There's tea in the pot, Jenny.'

Charlie was using Vern's favourite chair. Jenny vacated her own to pour Vern's tea. She passed it to him then disappeared into the lean-to.

Vern sat and Gertrude sewed.

The two town councillors sparred like a pair of roosters that afternoon; not well-matched roosters — Charlie, always a small man, had shrunk a little in the wash of life; Vern had expanded.

At four, Charlie gave up Vern's chair, and Jenny came from behind the lean-to curtain to walk him out to his bike. She didn't return. Vern moved to his preferred chair and sat alone until Gertrude brought her sewing to the table.

'A man stays away for a couple of weeks and you start hanging your hat up to Charlie White.'

'He'd be a good catch,' she said. 'He was saying how a few are paying off their bills.'

'What does he think about your granddaughter's addition to the family?'

'He's got manners enough not to comment.'

'You're saying I haven't.'

She spread out the smock, a pale blue floral, and began snipping threads. 'I'm saying he's got manners enough not to comment.'

'What's he doing coming down here all the time?'

'Jean White was one of the few women in this town I called a friend and he's still mourning her, and if he wants to come down here for a cup of tea, he'll be made welcome.'

'You're having a go at me now for not mourning any of my wives.'

Gertrude put her scissors down. 'I'm not into censoring every word I utter, and I meant no such thing, but if the cap fits, feel free to wear it.'

'You've had a bee up your backside since that hot-pants little bugger came back into this house,' Vern shot back. 'You don't want her here any more than I do. She's her parents' responsibility, not yours.'

'Her mother and sister snubbed me the other day in the butcher's. My own daughter, my own granddaughter, the only blood I've got in this world, and they snubbed me, and you come out with something like that. That little girl has got less blood in this town than me —'

'She's doing something about fixing that up —'

'Damn you for your thoughtlessness, for your heartlessness!' She was on her feet. 'A fourteen-year-old schoolgirl doesn't go through what she went through and come out the other end unscathed, and anyone who thinks she does has got less brains than a rabbit and less heart than a worm. Go home to your old maid daughters. You've got more in common with them than me.'

'At least they haven't dropped their illegitimate brats on my doorstep. At least I haven't had to go looking for them in lunatic asylums.'

'And hell would have frozen over while they'd waited for you to go looking for them, too, you hard-hearted sod.'

Gertrude shook the smock and cottons flew. He lit a cigarette and she returned to her sewing machine, offering him her back while she hemmed one sleeve then set the other one up.

'Are you going to sit there all day?'

'I'm going to sit here until it's done,' she said.

'You've got no room in your life for me.'

She swung around to face him. 'I've got room in my life, just none in my bed, and that's what's been getting up your nose since Jenny came home — and if you think I don't know it, my lad, then more fool you.'

Her words were too close to the truth. They bit. 'Take your bed and go to buggery with it,' he said. 'I won't be back.'

'Don't run over my chooks this time. You broke one of their wings the last time you drove off like a maniac.'

He stayed away through Christmas.

On the Saturday after Christmas, Jessie Macdonald married Joss Palmer. The couple didn't want a formal wedding; they wanted a party. A handful of invitations were posted early to a few who lived out of town. A sign was posted for the rest in the newsagent's window.

George Macdonald is getting rid of another one. Everyone welcome to celebrate with him at the town hall. Ladies, please bring a plate.

The party continued until the wee hours. The Willama band, hired until one, continued playing until two, and when the last of the guests went home, the party continued at George's house. His eight daughters didn't get together often. A night of bedlam, that one, the bride as rowdy as her sisters, the groom as drunk as his brothers-in-law.

The bedlam continued the following day, screaming grandchildren adding to it, and no mill for George to go to. The mills closed down between Christmas and New Year. George's house was full until New Year's Eve, then they left, all of them, other than Dawn, one of the middle girls he'd never get rid of.

He was sitting still though, wallowing in silence, when Maisy asked him if he was driving down with her to pick up Margot.

'No,' he said.

'Someone is going to have to hold her while I drive, George.'

'Not today,' he said. Not tomorrow, or the day after either. He kept delaying the matter, in the hope that Maisy would forget about it, like he'd been delaying the purchase of the larger refrigerator she been after for a month or more.

'When then?'

'Haven't you had enough of the little buggers?'

'She's as much our grandchild as any of the others.'

'She's Norman's, too. Let him raise it.'

'They couldn't raise dogs.'

'Then leave her where she is.'

'Do you want your grandchild growing up calling Elsie and Harry Mum and Dad? That's what's going to happen if we don't take her. The other kids already think she's their sister.'

George couldn't see a lot wrong with that.

He'd given Maisy pretty much all that her heart had desired. If he hadn't already given her eight daughters, who between four of them had already produced umpteen granddaughters, he may have given in on their raising of Margot. Had the infant been a male he would have relented. The two little bastards he'd bred to take over his mill were wearing khaki, or they were the last time their parents had heard from them; they'd never taken a liking to pen and ink. They hadn't come home for Jessica's wedding either — were probably in the stockade.

Then Maisy shanghaied him. They'd been out to visit Patricia and instead of driving him home, she turned down the forest road.

Some of George's worst memories were associated with

Gertrude's land. That day his illegitimate granddaughter added another one. Maisy, convinced of Margot's charms, handed her to George. The baby took one look at him, slapped him in the eye and screamed blue murder, screamed herself purple until Elsie put her to the breast to shut her up.

'She's not even weaned,' George said, safe in the car.

'Elsie started to wean her but she got bad diarrhoea . . .'

'You want to take on washing shitty napkins again?'

'She's our son's daughter, George. Someone has to be responsible for her.'

'I was past kid-raising when those little bastards were born. I'm a damn sight further past it now, and that's the last I'm saying on the matter.'

'I told Mrs Foote we'd raise her, and I'm going to.'

'Not in my house, you're not. Buy yourself that fridge you've been magging about and leave that kid where she is.'

Gertrude's apricots always ripened between Christmas and New Year; the plums were at their peak for jam-making a week later than the apricots. Elsie spent several nights in Gertrude's kitchen helping to prepare fruit for jam-making. Jenny sat with her at the table, a knife in hand, halving the fruit, tossing it into the preserving pan and tossing the seed into a bucket.

She wrote the labels for the jam jars and saw the jars sealed with a skin of paraffin wax before the lids went on. Last January she had been here through the jam-making and she'd seen nothing of it.

Jar after jar was stored behind a canvas curtain in the shed, along with a few jars of preserved apricots and plums. The fruit season didn't last long, but while it lasted, they laboured.

Nothing was wasted in Gertrude's house. The chooks ate the rotting fruit, then Joey shovelled out their pens and dug chook dung into the garden beds. He raked up the goat and horse dung and made piles of it down behind the orchard.

Nothing was wasted. Beer bottles, discarded by drinkers and picked up by Lenny on his way home from school, were washed and used for the storing of tomato sauce.

Australia sent her first troops over to the Middle East in January. Maisy came with the news that George had decided that he was too old to raise another child. He raised Harry's wages and offered Joey a job, no doubt to assuage his guilt. They missed Joey when he started going to work in the mornings with Harry.

'There's no reason now why I can't sign her away, Granny.'

'Harry and Elsie,' Gertrude said.

Vern stayed away, but maybe that was to the good. February was as busy as January. Tomato chutney to be made and they'd used up their available jars. That presented no problem to Gertrude and Elsie. Jenny watched them tie circles of string below the narrow necks of beer bottles, watched them soak the string with methylated spirits and hold the necks to a candle flame until that string was burning in a circle, then a fast plunge into a bucket of cold water; the necks snapped off clean and they had their chutney bottles.

A withering onion was planted to grow babies. A shooting potato could yield up a bucketful of its own kind. Water wasn't wasted, hand-washing, dishwashing, bathing water was emptied onto the garden.

Everything must have been the same last summer but Jenny couldn't remember last summer — couldn't remember if her belly had been as big, if her back had ached when she stood too long.

She could remember the Christmas before the Macdonald had been born. She could remember the night she'd been born. But those months between Christmas and April were gone. How could someone forget three months? It scared her. What if she was mad like Amber?

Reading stopped her thinking. Gertrude had a trunkful of Itchy-foot's books and one after the other she read them, the good, the bad and the indifferent.

They made more tomato sauce in late February, and the storage shelves in the shed became crowded, then the late peaches were ready.

Elsie was at the table helping to prepare peaches the night Jenny found a newspaper bookmark in one of Archie Foote's novels.

'It's from 1924, Granny.'

Gertrude came to look over her shoulder at the newspaper photograph of the foreign woman who had died in her kitchen sixteen years ago, and her heart skipped a beat.

'Where did you find that?'

'In his book.'

A terrible photograph; the rough pine box, the eye sockets twin dark smudges, the high-necked frock, hair pulled back hard from her face, ringless hands crossed on her breast.

'When did Itchy-foot die, Granny?'

'The family said he went missing in '24,' Gertrude said.

'He was reading this book, reading this page in 1924. It feels weird, like he's sent a message from the grave.'

Maybe he had, to Gertrude. The night was hot but Gertrude shivered as the ghost of that woman walked over her grave. If there had been any doubt left in her mind as to who had fathered Jenny, that page of newspaper killed it.

Sooner or later, Jenny had to be told, and if it didn't come from Gertrude, it would come from someone else. There were dozens who knew the truth of her birth. Gertrude watched her read and tried to think of a way to begin.

'It's about that J.C. tombstone, Granny. You know, that little grey one. J.C. LEFT THIS LIFE 31.12.1923.' Gertrude knew it. She'd been there when they'd put that poor soul in the ground. 'That's why there's no name on it. They didn't know who she was.'

Gertrude glanced at Elsie. She knew the facts of Jenny's birth. She'd been here the night Nancy and Lonnie Bryant had brought the woman and baby down here.

Jenny didn't see the glance. 'You must remember it. It says here about the midwife,' she said.

'I remember it well, darlin',' Gertrude said. Elsie shook her head and chose another peach.

Maybe she was right. What would be gained by telling that girl the truth right now? And when all was said and done, what was there to tell? That she'd been born to an unwed foreign woman — that Archie was probably her father. Why else would he have ripped that page from the newspaper?

It was the sort of knowledge that might push her over the edge, and just when she'd started clawing her way back.

'Did you put it in the book?' Jenny asked.

'Who knows, darlin',' Gertrude said. 'It was a long time ago.'

WOMAN POWER

On 26 March 1940, Sissy Morrison would become an adult, for all intents and purposes. She could vote, even wed without her father's permission — if someone asked her to wed, which appeared unlikely.

Sissy, a bitch of a girl, had grown into a bitch of a woman, who, nearing twenty-one, was no less bitchy and no more popular than she'd been at five, eight, fifteen. The local boys steered clear of her; their sisters, having learnt in kindergarten to give her a wide berth, gave her a wider berth now. Most crossed the road when they saw Sissy approaching.

Her only friend was Margaret Hooper; nine years Sissy's senior, and as desperate for companionship as she. At sixteen, Sissy had decided to marry Jim Hooper. Her friendship with Margaret gave her limited access to him. He accompanied them to dances, to balls. He drove them to Willama to go shopping. Then he dropped Sissy off before driving home with Margaret.

Everyone was getting engaged and married. Jessie Macdonald, who was Sissy's age, was getting a new house opposite the cemetery — as if anyone would want to live opposite a cemetery.

As if anyone would want to live in a railway house, practically on the train line. As if anyone would want to live with Norman, who Sissy had to crawl to for every pair of stockings. She wanted to live in the Hoopers' house, to be Margaret Hooper, who had an inside toilet and could buy a new ball gown whenever she felt like buying one. In March of 1940, Sissy decided to do something about getting what she wanted.

The idea had come to her at Jessica Macdonald's wedding party. She was going to have a huge twenty-first birthday party at the town hall, hire the band and invite everyone, get heaps of presents and return what she didn't want for refunds.

She told Norman to book the hall, to book the band. He told her she could have a small party at home.

'I'm having it at the town hall, and that's final,' she said.

In her youth, Norman had attempted to guide that girl down the paths of moderation. Many years ago he had retired defeated. He gave in early now and paid for his weakness in hard cash and embarrassment. Since Jenny's misfortune, he had spent his life in cowering shame. Only at the station, clad in his stationmaster's uniform, did he take on the approximate shape of a man.

He booked the hall for the Friday night but didn't hire the band. Maisy owned a portable gramophone and multiple records. He didn't allow Sissy to invite everyone. He told her the country was at war and that all must trim their sails to suit the available canvas. He bought three dozen stamps and told her to write invitations.

She used every stamp, and as each invitation was addressed to husband and wife, to old classmate and partner, the three dozen could mean seventy-two guests to feed and water. She wanted wine for the toasts, like Jessie had wine for the toasts. Norman purchased twelve bottles, convinced he could squeeze six toasts from each. His wife, the whore, had a light hand with pastry. She cooked all week, and on the Friday afternoon, she iced and creamed the cakes, made multiple sandwiches.

A hot and steamy Friday, the butter melted to oil, whipped cream refused to hold its shape, the ice in the bucket of fruit punch melted, but as Norman carried it across to the hall, a clap of thunder caused some spillage — which left room for more ice.

All day the storm circled the town threatening, and as night came down, the sky over Woody Creek turned on a fireworks display for Sissy Morrison's twenty-first. The invited guests came; a party was a party, the guest of honour unimportant. Gifts were offered, weighed, placed unopened on a trestle table beside Maisy's portable gramophone, which was playing a waltz, when

67

at nine lightning lit the town and thunder rocked the town hall. The waltz died. As did the lights.

Norman had been organising Woody Creek functions for years. He lit lamps and candles; a few boys who lived nearby went home to fetch lanterns. It became a better party in the half-dark.

Gertrude had not been invited, which was as well. She was needed at home.

'I don't know any honest labour a woman can do on her back. Giving birth is labour,' she said. 'Stay on your feet for as long as you can, darlin'.'

Jenny's six and a half pound infant came before midnight. A lesser newborn may have gone unheard above the rain now thundering down on Woody Creek, hammering on the low tin roof of the lean-to, but the babe arrived with red hair six inches long and a temper to match it. For fifteen minutes she attempted to outdo the storm, until the storm found its way inside. Old gaps between the roof and chimney had opened up. Water was spilling, hissing to the stove.

'Hang on to her for a second, darlin'. I think we've got a flood in the kitchen,' Gertrude said, and she ran to place her pots and pans to catch the water. Her old chimney was prone to movement. She'd known that storm was coming. She should have asked Harry or Joey to get up on the roof and check it out for her this afternoon.

If not for the late hour and the storm, she would have called Elsie over and had a second pair of hands. If not for the torrent pouring down on her stove, the newborn would not have been placed on the bed. It would be going to Willama in the morning, going to some childless couple.

If not for that mop of red hair, Jenny may never have set eye on that now silent scrap of life. The Macdonald had been born bald, was still bald. She couldn't believe a baby could be born with so much hair. Wondered if it had his green eyes. She wasn't going to touch it to find out, but using the corner of the sheet, she brushed the hair back from its brow.

It looked like the baby orang-utan she'd seen at the zoo, its brow creased in a frown, its hands clawing, attempting to get a grip on its mother's fur. One slightly dazed eye looked at her, but she couldn't see its colour.

If not for one of its clawing hands, Jenny wouldn't have touched it. She didn't mean to, but it wouldn't keep its hands still.

'Granny!'

'Just a minute, darlin'. I'll have to get Harry onto that roof first thing tomorrow.'

'Do hands change?'

'What do you mean change?' Gertrude was on her knees mopping up water from her hearth.

'Just change.'

Gertrude rose from her knees, emptied the contents of a small pot into a bucket and set it back beneath the trickle; she rinsed her hands in the bucket and walked down to the looped-back curtain.

'What's wrong with her hands?'

'It's got my square-topped fingers.'

Gertrude's eyesight wasn't good by lamplight, but the doorway was close enough to see Jenny holding open what could have been a miniaturised replica of her own hand.

'Do they change after they're born?'

'She's the finished article,' Gertrude said. 'He was a redhead?'

'Not red, more like melted pennies, and he didn't have one freckle on his face. She hasn't got any freckles.'

'She hasn't seen a lot of sun yet,' Gertrude pointed out.

'Can you . . .' Jenny tried to ease the red-topped bundle towards Gertrude.

'Give me five minutes,' Gertrude said as she returned to mopping up — and she took her time about it.

Lorna Hooper was at Sissy's party, only to keep an eye on her scatterbrained sister. A tall ungainly woman, Lorna spent the evening at the piano. She'd had ten years of lessons and played as she had been taught to play, note perfect, but without imagination.

Jim was there, taller than his totem pole sister, better looking, though perhaps not as manly. He had one dance with Sissy, two with Peggy Fulton and one each with three of her sisters, while Sissy sat glowering at him, willing him to her side.

Margaret was at her side, plump Margaret who would never be the sharpest tack in the box, nor did she carry a trickle of Hooper blood, though she was unaware of her failings. She loved to laugh and to dance. Norman danced with her. He danced with Sissy. There were rules to dancing, steps to learn, instruction manuals. Norman danced correctly. He didn't dance with his wife; he ate the supper she provided.

The Hoopers had walked across the lines to the town hall. They'd walk home through mud — unless Vern got the car out and drove around to pick them up. He sat on his verandah, watching the rain and considering getting the car out.

He was thinking of Gertrude, too, wondering if they'd invited her to the party and knowing they hadn't — knowing she'd be appreciating the rain, celebrating a full tank. He knew her too well. He missed her too much.

And he didn't want to miss that arguing, bugger of a woman. He told himself ten, twenty times a day that he wasn't missing her. He couldn't tell a lie to save his life. He couldn't even convince himself.

They'd had a good thing going before her hot-pants granddaughter had come home and ruined it. He might have been heading fast for seventy-one, but he was a big man with a man's needs, and the only woman who had ever filled those needs was that independent bugger of a woman. He loved her, and tell himself what he might, he missed her in the mornings, at night, on fine Saturday afternoons and during rain storms. Missed her.

And the rain kept pouring down. He didn't get his car out.

Norman had booked the hall from seven to midnight. Midnight was long gone, but no one could be expected to walk home in that storm. They were still there at one, Norman yawning, desperate to blow out the candles, to sweep the floors, to lock the doors.

One fifteen before the rain eased off. One fifty before he swept the last of the guests out with the cigarette butts, the trodden-in pastries and some of the mud, before he blew out the last of the lamps and candles.

Woody Creek was awash; its fine sandy soil didn't know what to do with water given too fast. Cemetery Road looked like Cemetery Lake and South Street was no better. He squelched home carrying the punch bucket, heavy now with presents, a tin dish heavy with more.

His wife, the whore, and Maisy, had made numerous trips across the road with gifts, plates, glasses. Amber was washing dishes at the sink when he entered. Sissy, clad in her nightgown, sat watching her and complaining about Jim Hooper, about an embroidered tablecloth given to her by the Fulton family.

'What do I need with a tablecloth and serviettes?'

Norman placed the tin dish and bucket on the table then leaned in the doorway watching Sissy riffling through the new assortment of gifts, greedy hands seeking something of value. Another girl may have delighted in placing a sugar basin, a pretty dish, into her hope chest. Sissy had no hope chest and tonight Norman had little hope of her ever needing one.

As he turned to stare at the back of the scrawny whore at the sink, a tidal wave of despair washed up from his muddy shoes to his brow and he swayed while the kitchen swam in nauseating circles. He gripped the doorframe and turned away, forced his feet to carry him across the passage to his junk room where he sat heavily on his bed, the room circling, the memory of gentle hands removing the studs from his collar, circling.

Pretty songbird, shot through the heart by time's arrow. Head in his hands, hot and exhausted tears dripped to muddy shoes he had no strength to remove.

LAURENCE GEORGE MORGAN

If Vern hadn't been sulking, Gertrude would have asked him to drive her and the baby to Willama on Saturday morning. She hadn't seen him since before Christmas. The garage man would drive her down, for a price, but she didn't like disturbing him at the weekend when it wasn't an emergency. It could wait until Monday.

Elsie, who wouldn't hear of giving Margot up to strangers, kept her distance from the new baby — on Gertrude's instruction. She'd told her it was Jenny's decision, that she'd promised not to interfere.

The fates interfered. Rain poured down for most of Monday. They delayed the trip again. Jenny had the resilience of a rubber band; by Wednesday, she'd be up to travelling, which would allow them to get the papers signed while they were down there.

'Will I know who they give her to, Granny?'

'It's all done with great secrecy, darlin'. They can't have the new mother falling in love with her only for you to change your mind and want her back.'

'I can't,' Jenny said.

On Wednesday morning, she put the fear of God into Elsie when she came to the back door, asking to see Margot.

'I don't want to fight with you, lovey, but I'm not letting you take her down to give to strangers,' Elsie said.

'I just want to look at her, Elsie.'

She looked at Margot that morning, and for the first time. She looked at her for a full fifteen seconds, at her hands first.

Margot had the stubby Macdonald hands. She had their pale purplish eyes, was as fat as lard and as pale — and she didn't like strangers.

'Tell me what to do, Granny.'

'I told you that you shouldn't be running around yet. Do you ever take a scrap of notice of anything I tell you to do?'

'I do. I can't . . . I can't think straight.'

'I'm not saying a word.'

'I want you to.'

Gertrude stood watching as Jenny dressed the redhead for travelling, handling the tiny mite as if she'd been doing it for years.

'All I know, darlin', is that a wrong decision, made for whatever reason, can't be undone. Whatever you decide to do today, you have to be very certain you can live with forever.'

'I can't live with any decision I ever make. What if the people they give her to don't look after her? What if they give her to people who don't like her red hair? Some people don't.'

Jenny liked it. She liked brushing it. She liked watching that silly little mouth suck its bottles dry.

Sixteen is not far enough removed from the time of the dressing of dolls. She'd stitched frills to one of Margot's hand-me-down baby gowns, wanting the baby to look well dressed when she gave her away. Now she brushed her hair, tied it back from her brow with a yellow bow.

'She's not a doll to play with, darlin'. She'll be walking in twelve months' time. When you're twenty-one, she'll be at school.'

'You're saying you want me to give her away?'

'I want you to know the consequences of not giving her away. You can't hide her. Her birth will have to be registered. You'll need to tell me her father's name.'

'He's gone.'

'If you write *Father unknown* in some city office now, that's what that little girl will carry through her life.'

'I won't even know *her* name. They'll probably call her Cecelia . . . or Florence.'

'It will be her new parents' right to name her. She'll be given a birth certificate with their names on it.'

'Will mine be on it?'

'No.'

'She shouldn't have been born with my hands!'

Silly little hands, tiny gripping, clawing things, determined to hang onto what little they had.

'Her name is Georgie,' she said. 'He was Laurie.'

'Laurie who?'

'Laurence George Morgan, if you must know,' Jenny said, expecting Gertrude to recognise the name.

She didn't. She didn't send word in to the garage man either. She watched and she waited, then on Friday while she was preparing to go into town, Jenny asked her if she'd be angry if she said she didn't want to give her away.

'I'd be proud of you,' Gertrude said. 'But she'll be your responsibility.'

'I know.'

Sometimes there are no options. Sometimes you have to weigh up the good and the bad and find a balance you can live with.

There'd been no good and bad to balance the night she'd got into the goods van. All along that had been her plan — while they'd talked about weddings, while she'd agreed with everything they'd said, she'd planned her escape. Nothing ever goes exactly to plan.

As a three-year-old she'd known the names of every station between Woody Creek and Melbourne. As a ten-year-old, since she'd watched Sissy opening her first mail order parcel, since she'd smelt the essence of the distant city, she'd known it was a magic place, and that she'd go there one day.

Her first glimpse of Melbourne by night hadn't disappointed. It was a fairy land, a giant's star-studded cloak flung over all of the earth. She'd known before the train had pulled into Spencer Street that she'd find Mary Jolly's house and finally live happily ever after — or Cara Jeanette Paris would live happily ever after. Jenny Morrison wasn't getting off that train.

No one took a scrap of notice of her at Spencer Street. No one told her she couldn't spend the night in the ladies' waiting room. She'd bought a cup of tea and raisin bread toast for breakfast, bought a ticket out to Surrey Hills.Which was when Melbourne had stopped being magic. Mary's station wasn't as she'd imagined it to be, nor were the streets around the station.

She'd addressed a hundred envelopes to Mary; she'd known for years that Mary's street was only two blocks from the station, that she lived at number thirty-three.

Two blocks east? West? North? South?

Jenny couldn't find Mary's street. She should have written to her, should have arranged to meet her in the city — or should have paid a taxi to drive her to the address.

She returned to the station, but the stationmaster only worked at Surrey Hills; he didn't live there. She asked a dozen people. She asked in a ladies' wear shop where the woman told her to speak to the chap at the post office, that he'd have a map of the area.

The post office was on the far side of the road — a busy road that Saturday morning. She'd been crossing over, watching cars, watching people on bikes, watching drays, wondering if any of them knew where they were going, when a car backed out from the kerb. One second she was waiting for a loaded truck to go by, the next she was flat on her backside, on the road.

People came from everywhere.

'Stay down, dear,' they said. 'Someone get a doctor. Someone call the ambulance.'

Faces circling her, bike riders stopping to stare and the crowd stopping the traffic. Car horns bleating.

She didn't stay down; she scrambled to her feet. As soon as she put her foot on the ground, she knew her ankle wasn't going to walk anywhere.

The driver who had knocked her over, a businessman wearing a suit and hat, looked worried. He said he'd drive her to the hospital. She told him she had to go to her friend's house.

A taxi driver might have found Mary's address faster, but the businessman found it. She thanked him. He apologised again for knocking her over then drove away up the long street.

A woman with a baby in her arms opened the door of number thirty-three, and she'd never heard of Mary Jolly.

And the businessman hadn't gone after all. He'd turned his car around and was watching her as she closed the gate.

'Not home?' he said.

'There must be two streets with the same name,' she said.

'We'll try the neighbour.'

It wasn't the wrong street. The neighbour knew Mary Jolly. She knew her mother had died.

'January it was when she passed,' she said. 'It was that terrible heat wave that took her, deary. I think the eldest son took Mary in. There's four brothers. I don't know which one she went to. She couldn't have managed here alone of course, not with her leg the way it is. What's your name, deary, just in case I happen to hear from her?'

'Cara Paris.'

Rain spitting down, settling like dew on her black coat, on his grey hat, and her ankle starting to swell.

'Where to now, Cara Paris?' he said.

'Nowhere,' she said, and dared a glance at his face. He was the image of Clark Gable. She looked away fast.

He took her arm and led her back to his car as the spitting rain became a gusty shower. She got in out of the rain. He offered her a cigarette.

She'd smoked with Dora Palmer; she'd smoked with Joey. She smoked with a redheaded Clark Gable that morning while heavy rain thrashed the car windows and condensation settled like fog on the windscreen.

She could barely see the house where Mary Jolly had once lived. It was like looking at a mirage. And that's all her plan — to stay with Mary — had ever been: a mirage that disappeared as you ran to grasp it.

'Where do your folk live?' he asked.

'They're dead,' she said.

'How old are you, sweetheart?'

'Nineteen,' she lied. Cara Jeanette had always been older than Jenny.

'So, where to now?' He started the car. He wanted to go.

'I'll get a job somewhere.'

'Not with that foot, you won't. The hospital?'

'Is there . . . a cheap boarding house somewhere?'

'I don't know the area,' he said. 'Are you any good at cleaning?'

'I don't care what I do.'

He told her he was staying at a big house that needed a good spit and polish.

'Could I live in?' she asked.

'It's well out of town, sweetheart,' he said. 'Nothing around it for miles.'

'Yes please,' she said.

And maybe there was a God who knew that Mary's mother was dead. Maybe He was watching over her — like Norman thought he was — and he'd sent down a guardian angel, and made him look like Clark Gable, who was her favourite film star.

His house was built on the side of a hill. He led her in through the back door. She thought his wife would be inside, or his mother. No one was there and the house was freezing cold.

'Keep that foot up until I can get something to bandage it with,' he said. 'I've got a bit of business to attend to.'

He left her alone in a house nicer than Vern Hooper's, and she went to sleep on his couch, her feet tucked up beneath Granny's coat. She didn't open her eyes until he returned with fish and chips wrapped in newspaper.

No cup of tea, no stove lit to make tea, but he poured her a glass of something red she thought was raspberry cordial, until she took a sip. It tasted like poison, but he drank it so she drank it. He strapped her ankle later, then showed her to a fancy bedroom, offered her a silky pink nightgown — his sister's, he said.

Her shoe wouldn't fit on over the bandage. He produced a pair of fluffy slippers, also his sister's. She wore them for a week, with her ankle-length overcoat, while she cleaned his house, dusted his beautiful things — and felt like Amber, polishing off every flyspeck.

Then, on the Friday, he paid her *five pounds*!

Irene Palmer had worked as a maid for Vern Hooper; she hadn't made five pounds in a month.

'That's too much,' she said.

'As far as I'm seeing it, sweetheart, you've got three options. You buy a ticket back to where you came from with that money —'

'No.'

'Or I drop you off to the Salvos.'

The Salvation Army people would try to make her go home. She'd shaken her head.

'They're good people. They won't ask you the hard questions.'

He'd said three options. She waited for the third option, and when there was no third option, she asked him if she could keep working for him.

'Any chance of me getting you out of your nun's habit?' he said. He meant her overcoat. Twice before he'd called it her nun's habit.

'I could light the kitchen stove,' she said. 'There's plenty of wood.'

'You're already lighting more fires than you know. You're a beautiful thing. Do you know that?'

She should have known what he was after. She didn't. She should have had the sense to go to the Salvos, but he said the house belonged to his sister, that she'd be coming home soon. And Jenny was scared of Melbourne without Mary. Scared of starting again somewhere else. Scared of everything — except him, her guardian angel. She trusted him.

For three weeks she trusted him and cleaned his house, ate what he brought home.

Then one night he'd come home with two brown paper parcels.

'Open them up, sweetheart,' he said. 'I need to go out and celebrate.'

Parcels from city shops had always been Sissy's to open. She shouldn't have opened his parcels, but she did, and that same city essence had sprung out, swamping her with that same old envy of Sissy's pretty things.

He'd bought her a lime green dress, stockings, and a belt to hold up the stockings. She shouldn't have tried that dress on. She did. She put the stockings on, worked out how to keep them up.

It was like being in a film that night, like acting in a movie with Clark Gable, his hair dyed red for the role, like being Cara Jeanette. All she had to do in that movie was wear a modern dress and sit at a restaurant table smoking his cigarettes while waiters in fancy black suits called her madam and filled her glass with fizzy wine.

And dance with him, dance close with Clark Gable.

He put his arm around her when he walked her out to his car, and it felt so safe, like she'd always felt safe when Granny's arm was around her, so safe she'd leaned against his warmth. He kissed her in the car — not on the cheek, like Granny had kissed her, but it was only a movie kiss.

She'd had a baby forced on her, but knew nothing about life, about the way normal men went about getting what they wanted from girls. He kissed her again when they got back to the house. He lit a fire and opened a bottle of wine. She drank it, and smoked two more cigarettes.

And he was no guardian angel. She didn't even cry when she found out what he wanted. It wasn't worth crying about — just a final understanding that whether two of the mongrels held you down on a tombstone, or one poured fizzy wine for you on a couch, they were all the same in the end.

Nowhere to run, even if her head had been clear enough to run. No use screaming, or fighting him. Closed her eyes and watched him from a great distance.

He didn't hurt her — not as the twins had hurt her. He hurt her in a different way, hurt her trust. But when it was over and done with, he was still kind and asking questions.

'Who have you been with, sweetheart?' he wanted to know.

'No one.'

'You've been with someone.'

That was the night she learned how to balance the good against the bad, or the bad against the worse.

After the house on the hill, he took her to a guesthouse in Frankston where he left her alone for three days. She walked the sandy beaches collecting seashells, poking at jellyfish washed in by the

79

waves. She stood for hours, watching boats bobbing on green water, miles and miles of water. Loved it. Loved those miles of water.

He came back with more parcels. She opened them.

He liked bright colours. She'd unwrapped the red dress in Frankston and the red sandals, had danced with him in Frankston, and afterwards, in bed, she'd thought about seashells, about Sissy coming to Frankston with the Hoopers, and about the guesthouse bathroom and the hot water that poured from shiny taps. The trick was learning how to concentrate on the good bits and not even think about the bad bits.

He had many names. He'd told her his name was Laurie London. He told the Frankston guesthouse he was Laurence Porter, told a country hotel he was Mr Brown, told another hotel his name was Laurie York.

He'd changed his cars as often as his name. He liked driving fast down country roads. They stayed at a small guesthouse at Lakes Entrance for a week and he spent that week teaching Jenny to drive a little maroon car. Like a boy, he laughed at her when she let out the clutch too fast and the car went kangaroo hopping down the road. She learned how to get it moving without the kangaroo hop.

She drove it halfway to a town where they made Melbourne's electricity, and he'd only decided to go there because she'd told him about the valve men she used to believe lived inside wireless cabinets.

'Where are your folk?'

'I told you: they're dead.'

'How did they die?'

'I don't remember.'

She didn't tell him anything that was real. Cara Jeanette wasn't real. Pretty frocks and driving cars weren't real. Nothing was — not even the bed. She learned to be a starfish in his bed — a starfish washed in by a wave, a seagull pecking at it. It would fly away and the ocean would sweep in and wash the dirt off.

He was a car salesman, he said, but he parked that little maroon car near a country station and they caught a train back to the city, where they stayed for a week in a city hotel, in a room fit for the King of England. He took her to the pictures, took her dancing in a huge ballroom, took her to the zoo and bought her a yellow balloon blown up so tight that one little pinch would burst it.

She slept with him in a wide bed. Bathed for an hour in the king's bathroom.

Then Collingwood, and an old boarding house and not much of a room, and not much of a bathroom. She spent two days alone in Collingwood, worrying and waiting for him, playing with the yellow balloon.

It grew smaller during those two days. It became her hourglass in Collingwood. When the air had all seeped away, she'd have to be real again. Something had happened.

The balloon was wrinkled and the size of a duck egg the night he brought home a parcel of fish and chips wrapped in newspaper. They were sitting on the bed eating chips when he snatched a sheet of the paper.

'Bugger that for a joke,' he said, chips flying everywhere. 'That's you.'

Her photograph, taken after the talent quest, had been used to wrap the fish and chips. In her mind, the talent quest part of her life had stayed clean. Greasy now, stained like the rest of her.

'You're fifteen years old,' he said.

She looked at the date on the paper. It was months old. 'It doesn't matter,' she said.

'It matters to me, sweetheart. You told me you were nineteen.'

'You tell lies all the time.'

'You're jail bait.'

Jail bait. A beautiful thing. A play thing he liked to dress up in bright colours. A play thing he'd got into trouble.

He told her that night she had to go home. She told him she could never go home now, and why she couldn't go home.

'There are doctors about,' he said. 'Don't worry about it, sweetheart.'

He came home with the handbag a few nights later, and she'd never seen anything like it in her life — except in Sissy's magazines. He told her it was made from the skins of snakes.

He wasn't like other people. He never worried about money, about eating normal meals at normal times. At times he was a boy of sixteen. At times he was older than Granny.

He'd found a doctor at Richmond. 'We'll get you fixed up,' he said. But they moved again, and he hadn't taken her to Richmond.

Her eyes had started seeing too much, watching him too much. He was looking through a newspaper one day, when he laughed.

'I'm sending in your accounts, Dad,' he told the ceiling. 'The bastards are finally paying up.'

He was strange that day, quiet, he'd sat, watching her for an hour, then he'd said, 'What say we have a clutch of them, sweetheart? George the first, George the second, George the third.'

Then September. She felt sick in the mornings, sick at night, and he went away and left her in a room with a winged mirror like Amber's. She could see all of herself in it, but she no longer saw herself in who she was looking at. Without Granny to cut her hair, it had grown long, grown frizzy. The clothes she wore were not her clothes. He bought what *he* liked.

She killed the balloon that day. Squeezed it until one end of it popped — hardly a pop at all. Then she picked up her handbag and went out to find a hairdresser.

A middle-aged woman standing behind her, snipping off curls, the hairdresser's wireless playing a melody Jenny had never heard, when the announcer cut into the music with a news bulletin, and Bob Menzies said, *We are at war*.

The scissors stopped snipping, and in the mirror, as clear as day, Jenny saw Charlie White shaking his finger at her, saying *I told you so*.

Of course it wasn't Charlie. It was the woman's husband, but she knew Charlie would be standing behind his counter, shaking his finger and saying, *I told you so*.

He was real.

That snakeskin handbag she clutched to her stomach wasn't.

What was behind the handbag was growing more real every day.

Laurie wasn't. Nothing about him was real.

The snipping scissors were, and she forgot to watch them.

They snipped too much. Still no Jenny in the mirror, only a wide-eyed spaceman staring back at her, a Martian who had lost his spaceship, who wanted to go home to his own planet but had no way of getting there.

The following day she ripped the front page from a discarded newspaper, bought an envelope and addressed it to Charlie — just to prove to herself that her planet was still out there.

You told them so, Mr White.

That night, or near dawn, Laurie came home limping. 'Up you get, sweetheart,' he said. 'I've got a taxi waiting.'

The taxi was waiting. Its driver wasn't.

'Where's the driver?' she said.

'You're it tonight. I've buggered my foot.'

If she lived for a million years she'd never forget that dawn. He told her to drive, so she drove, followed suburban streets to roads. One road ended in Geelong, or that's where the taxi ended its journey. It ran out of petrol. He tried to walk away from it. He couldn't.

'Go home, sweetheart,' he said. 'When it's over, it's over.' He pushed her handbag at her. 'Find the station and get yourself back to where you came from.'

'I can't,' she said.

She sat with him until the man from the café on the corner came out to sweep his section of footpath. He sold her a packet of APC powders and a bottle of lemonade. He raised his eyebrows when she ordered two double-header ice-creams.

She did more than raise her eyebrows when she opened her handbag to pay him. She dropped the bag on the shop floor and a roll of banknotes bounced free.

Couldn't remember how or with what she'd paid him, just took the change and ran back to the taxi, handed Laurie an ice-cream, then showed him the contents of her handbag.

'Elves have been at it,' he said. 'Pesky little buggers.'

'Why did you put it in my bag?'

'I won't need it where I'm going, sweetheart.'

'Did you take the taxi driver's money as well as his car?'

'They don't make enough to bother with,' he said, licking in a circle around the ice-cream cone before handing it to her to hold while he poured three APC powders into his palm, then he licked them up, washed them down with ice-cream and lemonade.

She smoked two cigarettes with him, shared that bottle of lemonade, and when the APC powders had done their work, she asked a dog walker where she'd find the station.

They were halfway there, she was walking ahead carrying both cases, when a newsagent on the far side of the road placed his large wire-caged posters out front of his shop.

REDHEADED GUNMAN FLEES WITH JEWELLER'S TAKINGS.

Maybe there is a switch in the mind that can cancel out logic, cancel fear of consequences. Her switch flicked back to the full-alert position on that street in Geelong. She dropped the cases as the double-header ice-cream and lemonade rose up to her throat and spilled to the gutter, then, the cases left lying on the pavement, she ran across the road.

No war, not even Bob Menzies could compete for the front page of the *Sun* that morning. She grabbed a copy, paid over her pennies and walked out to the street to read all about the injured redheaded gunman.

Mr Quinn, a St Kilda jeweller, was on his way to the bank yesterday when a black vehicle pulled into the kerb and the well-dressed gunman stepped out and demanded Mr Quinn hand over the two hundred pounds he was carrying in a canvas bag. When the bag was denied him, the gunman brandished his firearm and wrenched the bag from Mr Quinn's hand. His clean getaway was foiled by quick-thinking carrier Mr Colin Matheson who, having witnessed the incident, drove his horse into the path of the gunman's car. In swerving to avoid a collision, the car mounted the footpath and hit a brick fence. The gunman was last seen escaping over the fence. Mr Matheson told police the gunman was limping.

Mr Quinn and Mr Matheson, though shaken, were able to give police a good description of the bandit who has been eluding police for months. The wanted man is approximately six foot in height, aged between twenty-five and thirty-five, and has dark red hair worn in a brushed back style. He is

clean-shaven, and when last seen was wearing a grey pin-
striped suit and a dark tie. The grey hat found in the vehicle,
size six and seven-eighths, is believed to belong to the thief . . .

The injured gunman was sitting on her case on the far side of the
road, no grey hat on his head this morning. Sun glinting on his
hair, turning it to melted pennies.

She couldn't remember dodging the cars on the way back.
All she remembered was throwing her handbag and Mr Quinn's
money at his injured foot.

'Jewellers make enough money.'

'They wear nice suits too,' he said.

Sun shining on that handbag, making it squirm like poisonous
vipers, but his hand reached for it.

'Where's your gun?'

'Not enough in there. Want to stick up the newsagent,
sweetheart?'

'You're as bad as . . . as Squizzy Taylor.'

'Better looking though.'

'You pointed a gun at a man and stole his money!'

'You're not yelling it loud enough, sweetheart. They can't
hear you over the road yet,' he said, and with the handbag beneath
his arm, he limped on towards the station.

She should have turned around and run the other way, but her
talent quest prize money was in that bag and it had become more
than just a five-pound note. It was the only piece of herself that
hadn't been lost, the only clean piece of the before time, the songbird time, before the world had gone mad. She picked up the cases
and caught up with him. He swapped his case for the handbag.

'Walk away from me, sweetheart,' he said. 'We're out of
options. Get lost now.'

She walked eight or ten yards towards the station, but turned
back when a car blasted its horn. No more good or bad to balance.
No more guardian angel or red devil either, just Laurie, who had
swallowed so many APC powders he was going to get himself
run over. And she knew why. Two policemen were waiting out
front of the station.

A truck braked hard, but he got to the other side of the road. She stood watching him until he limped into a hotel.

They'd see his red hair. They'd know who he was. She looked towards the station. He'd told her to get lost. She crossed the road and followed him into the hotel.

Stood back until he'd signed in, until the key to number eight was in his hand, until he limped towards the stairs, then she booked a single room. *Cara Paris*, she wrote. *Surrey Hills*. The man at the desk handed her the key to number eleven.

She thought Laurie's door would be locked. It wasn't. He was lying face down across his bed, asleep or feigning sleep, when she crept in. She opened her handbag, opened his case, and stuffed Mr Quinn's money into the toes of his dancing shoes, all but three five-pound notes — enough to pay for the Richmond doctor, enough to buy a roll of bandage, a tin of antiseptic salve, a bottle of strong painkillers and a pair of size ten canvas boots.

She bought a dark brown cap to cover his hair, bread, cheese, bananas, cigarettes, two bottles of lemonade and a string bag to carry her shopping in. She'd get lost soon, but he'd looked after her when she'd sprained her ankle and she couldn't leave him to starve in a hotel room.

He was like a little boy, sitting with his eyes scrunched shut when she took his shoe off, soaked the blood-caked sock from his foot. He kept his eyes shut until she'd plastered his foot with salve, bandaged it, until she'd tried to get the oversized canvas boot over the bandage.

'I'm not going anywhere, sweetheart,' he said. 'It's over. Go now or you'll get caught up in it.'

'I will when you put that shoe on. If you don't put it on now, you won't get it on,' she said, and she felt like Granny, giving advice.

'You'd make a good nurse,' he said.

'I could have been.'

'What did they do to you?' he asked.

'What's the Richmond doctor's name?'

'Poor little Georgie,' he said, but he told her the doctor's name and she wrote it on hotel paper.

She didn't leave that day. For three nights she stayed at the Geelong hotel. His foot was no better. He needed to go to a hospital — and he couldn't go to a hospital. She brought food to him, cigarettes, told him he looked like Clark Gable.

'Why, thank you, sweetheart.'

'Did you think that you could keep robbing people forever, Laurie?'

'I hoped so,' he said.

'You could have shot someone, then you would have been hanged for murder.'

'It leaks when I load it,' he said, and he told her his father had bought him a fine water pistol for his thirteenth birthday, told her he'd loaded it once too often. The rubber butt had perished.

She asked him about his sister, who had lived in the house on the side of the hill. He told her the house belonged to a man who had worn nice suits and taken his wife on a grand tour of Europe.

'I read about them in the social pages, sweetheart, and thought what a damned pity to leave a nice house like that sitting empty for six months.'

Maybe he was like Itchy-foot. Maybe he had no conscience. Maybe she was like Itchy-foot, too. She knew who Laurie was, but she didn't hate him. Like a snatch of disconnected time, those three days in Geelong, like Mr No one and Miss Nobody smoking cigarettes in some halfway place between yesterday and tomorrow, where consequences and conscience didn't apply. She got to know him in that room. Maybe he got to know her.

When she opened his door on the fourth morning, he was sitting on his bed, dressed for travelling, his canvas boots and too large cap looking silly. He told her he'd take the train back to Melbourne, then try to get up to Sydney.

'Don't budge from here for a day or two,' he said, then he picked up his case and limped away — hadn't even said goodbye.

She watched from the hotel balcony, watched him disappear into the station, and she felt more for the redheaded gunman than she had for the well-dressed businessman.

She was standing, willing a train to leave for Melbourne, when two police cars drove up and stopped in front of the station. Six policemen got out.

She left the balcony and ran downstairs where she joined a group of onlookers beneath the hotel verandah.

They saw the gunman limp to a police car, his hands locked behind his back, his too-large cap falling forward over his eyes and no hand to push it back.

He didn't look for her. He didn't turn towards the hotel. She looked at him but hers was just one of many staring faces.

A Salvation Army couple stared, their rattling tins silent. Had Laurie put a penny in their tin? He'd always had a coin for the Salvos. Were they the ones who'd recognised him? Or was it the man at the hotel? Or the stationmaster?

One police car drove away, three policemen and Laurie in it. Jenny hoped they'd drive him to the hospital. The second car remained. There was no sign of the other police.

Were they looking for the gunman's companion, looking for a girl wearing a long black coat who had bought a bandage and antiseptic salve, who had bought that brown cap? She shouldn't have bought that. How many dark brown caps, size seven and a quarter, had been sold in Geelong that week?

Scared then, blind panicking scared then.

And the hotel maid had seen her going into his room once. She'd end up in jail. She'd end up having a baby in jail. He'd end up hanged for the rape of a minor. She was fifteen. She was jail bait.

One policeman crossing the road to get her.

The Salvation Army couple walking on, tin rattling.

'There's always the Salvos,' Laurie used to say. 'They don't ask the hard questions.'

If he knew what she'd done that morning, he would have laughed like a boy. She caught up to the tin rattlers and told them her name, her real name, told them she'd run away from home in May and was too scared to go back.

Laurie was right; they didn't ask the hard questions.

A few days later they returned her to the loving arms of her parents.

*

She'd learnt Laurie's real name from the newspapers, learnt that Laurence George Morgan had been arrested at the Geelong station following information given to police by an observant stationmaster. A later newspaper told her that twenty-six-year-old Laurence Morgan was the son of a Sydney tailor who, in '31, had lost his business and maybe his mind. He'd shot his wife and daughter and wounded his eighteen-year-old son before shooting himself.

For a few days journalists attempted to turn Laurence George Morgan into the new Ned Kelly. WATER PISTOL BANDIT, they dubbed him.

Water pistol bandit sentenced to three years' hard labour.

MOTHERHOOD

Breastfeeding was nature's own form of family planning, Gertrude said. It was Elsie's only form of family planning. She'd weaned Ronny and Maudy at six and eight months. Teddy had arrived before Ronny's third birthday. She'd nursed Teddy for eleven months, then Margot had taken his place at the breast. At ten months, Margot hadn't had a tooth in her head. A month later they'd erupted, front, back and sides. She had a bad habit of clenching her jaw, which had necessitated her weaning.

Elsie was pregnant again. They had no room for more, but it would be welcomed, and all thanks to Margot, Elsie's insides had had a rest from carrying.

On a morning in late May, Margot still miserable with her teething, a pile of washing waiting to be started, Elsie heaved Margot's dead weight up to her hip, picked up a bucket of napkins and tripped over Teddy as he came running up the back steps.

Teddy made a reflex grab for the stair rail. He saved himself, but with no free hand Elsie went down, down five steps, Margot cradled against her. She may have saved the baby growing within, but not herself. Elsie's bones were always too fine. Her right arm snapped.

Harry and Joey were at work. Lenny was at school. Gertrude couldn't leave Elsie alone. Jenny had to run into town to fetch the garage chap to take Elsie to hospital.

'George Macdonald will know where to find Harry,' Gertrude said. 'Go to his office. It's on the left side as you walk into the mill yard.'

It was the first time Jenny had set foot in town since arriving home — and she couldn't force herself to walk into that mill. She walked fast past it, walked fast to the garage in North Street, midway between Blunt's corner and the Catholic church. The mechanic drove a modern car, Woody Creek's unofficial taxi cum ambulance. She passed on Gertrude's message then continued over Blunt's crossing to Maisy's door.

'Well, look who's knocking on my front door. And when have you ever needed to knock?' Maisy greeted her. 'Come in, love. Jessica's just making a cup of tea.'

Maisy knew about Georgie, so Jessica knew. Jenny didn't want to see her. She'd shared a bedroom with her, back when the world had been an almost sane place. Jessica was married to Joss Palmer, brother to Dora, who had been Jenny's best friend. She'd know about Georgie. Everybody would know. Granny had warned her that she couldn't hide her. She couldn't, but she could hide herself.

'Elsie broke her arm. Could you find Harry, please,' she said, and she left, got out of town fast via the short cut through Flanagan's land which would bring her out behind Gertrude's orchard, preferring this morning to run headlong into Flanagan's bull than someone from town.

The garage man was waiting when she got back to Elsie's and minutes later he drove away, Gertrude and Elsie in the back seat, Margot screaming for the only mother she knew. She wouldn't have anything to do with Jenny. Then Georgie, who never cried, realised she could, and they screamed a duet. Bedlam.

'Thank God,' she said when Harry came home. 'Thank God.' Margot recognised him as her father, and for fifteen blissful minutes there was silence.

Gertrude was away for four hours. The Macdonald screamed for three of those hours. Gertrude yelled her news. Elsie would be in hospital for a couple of days. She'd broken her arm in two places and they'd have to give her chloroform to set it. They didn't hold out a lot of hope that she'd keep the baby.

Jenny tried to silence the Macdonald with a cup of milk. Margot showed how much she didn't want that cup of milk. Jenny cleaned up the spillage. They tried to silence her with one of Georgie's bottles. She pitched it at them, pitched a biscuit at them. They tried to settle her in a warm bath. She tried to drown herself. They put her into her cot, and Gertrude stood rocking it while Harry took his lot out for a walk and Jenny took off across the paddock with Georgie.

That kid was a monster. It weighed half a ton and never shut up. It screamed until Elsie came home — still pregnant and with her right arm in plaster, from above the elbow to the tips of her fingers. She silenced the screamer but couldn't handle her with one arm.

That was the day Gertrude moved the Macdonald across the paddock, the day Gertrude's house lost its sanctuary status.

Maisy came the next day. She'd raised ten Macdonalds. She pandered to her granddaughter until she got her sucking goat's milk from a teat. She stayed from ten in the morning until four in the afternoon, and there was peace. Then she went home.

Jenny bribed that kid silent with bottles — and it started coming out green from the other end.

'I'm signing her away Granny.'

'She's teething,' Gertrude said. She cleaned up the green backside; they took her off goat's milk and gave her boiled water to suck on. She knew the difference. She belted Georgie with the bottle, left her with a lump on her brow the size of a pullet's egg.

What happened to June that year? Italy declared war on Britain and France in June; Nazi troops occupied Paris in June, just walked in and took it.

'Why?'

'I dare say it's better than seeing a beautiful city bombed.'

'Have you been there?'

'Your father liked Paris.'

'I'm not Amber.'

'Your grandfather. You knew who I meant.'

He hadn't liked London — and going by what they wrote in the newspapers, there'd be none of it left soon to like or dislike. Through July, Hitler's planes tried to bomb London into submission. Through August the battle of Britain, for Britain, raged, while the battle of green napkins was fought in that two and a half room hut.

Gertrude and Elsie blamed Margot's teeth for her napkins and her tantrums. One of Georgie's lower teeth came through in August and no one had noticed she was close to teething until Jenny felt it scrape against the feeding spoon. No time to notice anything. Margot stole time.

Australian boys were being sent overseas to fight. The Macdonald twins were overseas, so Maisy said. Soldiers were being killed, planes were being shot down, cities were being bombed, and it was no more real to Jenny than that last morning in Geelong. She wiped backsides, washed napkins, boiled them, hung them on a sagging clothes line, then watched the sky for rain, watched the clothes prop fall down every time a good drying wind blew up, and when she fell into bed at night she was too damn tired to worry about anyone, anything.

Dreamed of war. Dreamed she was carrying that kid into town to give her to Maisy but Maisy's house had been bombed — and why couldn't it have been Norman's house? Woke thinking of Amber, knowing she was in town, laughing about the mess Jenny had made of her life.

Then September again, and it couldn't be a year since she'd come home. Elsie's arm was freed of its plaster in September. For a day or two there was hope of an end to purgatory. But Elsie was six months pregnant, and Margot wasn't her responsibility, so Gertrude said.

She wasn't Jenny's either. She'd asked Gertrude to give her away. Elsie had decided to keep her.

'I don't even like her, Granny. Elsie likes her.'

'She's your flesh and blood, darlin'.'

'There's nothing of me in her.'

'You were as bald at her age.'

'I wasn't as fat.'

Almost eighteen months, more than old enough to walk but too weighty ever to do it. Her legs were white rolls of fat to her knees, bent pins from knee to ankle.

'I'll be hauling her around until I die of old age,' Jenny said.

'She'll walk when she's good and ready.'

Charlie White took to riding his bike again in September. He came with his stale and damaged offerings for the chooks and his town news. He sat at the table, drinking tea, dunking biscuits, feeding pieces to the kids, poking Margot's Buddha belly until she smiled. She didn't do it often — and when she did, she showed her father's teeth.

'I hear your sister is sporting an engagement ring,' Charlie said. 'When did that happen?'

'What?' Jenny said.

'Who?' Gertrude said.

'The unwed Macdonald girl was telling Hilda that she's wearing Vern Hooper's boy's ring.'

'I thought he was in the army camp,' Gertrude said.

'He is — or was,' Charlie said.

'Engaged to Sissy?' Jenny couldn't believe it.

'Don't quote me,' Charlie said. 'I only heard it third or fourth hand.' He spoke then of another new house going up, out towards the slaughteryards, and they forgot about Sissy, who had probably bought the ring for herself at Coles.

She hadn't. On the Thursday morning, Elsie came across the paddock with a copy of the *Willama Gazette*, open at page six, at a photograph of the happy couple: Sissy, her broad chin and brow separated by a self-satisfied Cheshire grin, and Jim, startled into exposing every one of his mouthful of china cup teeth.

'Vern will be pleased,' Gertrude said.

'Why?' Jenny shovelled a mush of vegetables into baby mouths.

'The war.' Gertrude read aloud the report on the happy couple while Elsie stood watching Jenny's feeding style. The two kids seated on the floor, Jenny squatting between them, spoon in one hand, bowl in the other, shovelling mush, scooping up what oozed out of one mouth and feeding it into the other.

'He was worried sick about Jim being caught up in it,' Gertrude said.

'Does it say when they're getting married?' Elsie asked.

'Not here. It will be soon if Vern's got anything to do with it. The army won't call up a married man.'

'He'd be safer dodging Hitler than dodging her for the rest of his life,' Jenny snorted.

'She's built for it. Hoopers have a bad habit of killing their mothers,' Gertrude offered.

'Harry says he's been courting her for years. He says Jim was taking her around before we got married,' Elsie said.

'She's been courting his indoor lavatory since she was sixteen.' Jenny shovelled faster, Margot getting two mouthfuls to Georgie's one.

'Let her swallow it,' Gertrude scolded. 'You'll get her stomach playing up again.'

'All the Hoopers have ever been to Sissy is a car to ride in and a lavatory chain she can pull on.' Jenny scraped the bowl, feeding the last scrape to Margot, who didn't know much, but knew enough to know that once the spoon was in her own hand, there was nothing left in the bowl. She threw the spoon at her feeder and crawled over to Elsie. Next best to food, she liked Elsie, who stooped to lift her to her feet.

Margot smiled for Elsie, crowed when she praised her, screamed when she went home. Gertrude picked her up to soothe her screaming.

No one had been expecting miracles when they'd moved Margot across the paddock. Jenny now referred to her as the Buddha, but she handled her, which was a minor miracle. Gertrude still had hope of Margot's bald head producing a crop of Jenny's golden curls, though not much hope. A slight fuzz was visible in strong sunlight and it appeared to be Macdonald white.

Georgie had the curls. Georgie had Jenny's hands. Georgie wore the pretty yellow dress, the matching yellow pants over her napkin. Margot wore a napkin and Maudy's hand-me-down brown.

'She's always known how to get what she wanted,' Jenny said.

'She's only a baby. All she's ever known is Elsie and a tribe of kids tripping over her. Her little life has been disrupted.'

'I meant Sissy,' Jenny said. 'Though probably her, too. Some people are born knowing exactly how to get what they want while everyone else learns to accept what they get.'

'There's always been too much of Norman's mother in Sissy. She was a wilful woman.'

'I wish I'd taken after her.'

'Don't ever wish that on yourself.'

'I didn't wish this on myself, but I got it.'

'You could say that about a lot of people.'

'You mean yourself.'

'I mean half the people in this town — speaking of which . . .' Gertrude walked to the door to look out, to listen. Car motors always announced their approach before they were sighted. 'I hope they don't want me in town.'

Her midwifery days were all but over. A few still came for her opinion on whether a pain might be appendicitis or just a belly-ache. She'd had her seventy-first birthday. She didn't look like a woman of seventy-one, didn't move like a woman of seventy-one, didn't dress in a grandmother's garb.

'It's Vern,' she said, placing Margot down and turning to her washstand mirror to tidy her hair before walking out to the yard to meet him.

Margot crawled after her. Jenny hauled her back. Margot clenched her jaw and screamed.

Both kids went down for a nap after lunch. Jenny poured milk into two bottles while listening for the car motor, hoping it wouldn't die, hoping someone in town had a pain in the belly, that Gertrude would get into the car.

The motor died.

'We just now saw the announcement,' she heard Gertrude say.

The car door slammed.

Maybe the kids would nap on her bed. Jenny didn't want to see Vern, didn't want him to see those kids.

She heard the wire gate open. He was coming in.

'She's been after him for years,' he said.

Jenny hauled Margot down to the lean-to and dumped her on the bed. She went back for Georgie and the bottles — grabbed Margot before she nosedived off the bed, gave them a bottle each and tucked them in. They eyed her, but sucked in unison.

He was in the kitchen; a chair complained as he sat on it. She knew the sounds of this house, knew by Gertrude's rattling that she was making him a cup of tea. Knew he'd be in that kitchen for hours.

'I'm going to do up Monk's old place for them,' he said.

'Does it need much work?'

'The back section needs re-roofing. It leaks like a sieve. We'll put in a kitchen. I can't see her running through the rain to cook him a meal.'

Sissy cooking anything other than toffee was a joke. And the kids thought that being in Jenny's bed was a joke. Georgie dropped her bottle overboard. Margot was on her feet, rattling the bedhead bars.

Jenny lifted them to the floor and sat with them, her feet propped against the dressing table, her legs forming a barricade across the doorway, behind the green curtain.

'The front rooms don't need much,' Vern said. 'We'll need to do the bathroom.'

Bet you'll be putting in an indoor lavatory, Jenny thought.

Vern spoke of Monk's garden, of the weeds riddling it, while the kids found shoes to play with and Jenny sat listening, visualising Sissy living in a mansion.

She'd heard of Monk's house all of her life, heard of the grand parties they'd had out there. She knew that Itchy-foot had been related to the Monks, knew that Gertrude had met him out there, had married him out there.

Margot pitched a shoe at the barricade. She attempted to bulldoze through it. She clenched her jaw and squealed, and when that didn't get her what she wanted, she got to her feet and for an instant Jenny thought she was going to walk. She flopped to her backside.

'I've been looking around for a car for them,' Vern said. 'There's not a lot around, or not a lot worth owning.'

Sissy driving a car? I can, Jenny thought. Hard to believe it now. Hard to believe any of Melbourne happened. Hard to believe I once came third in a radio talent quest.

Bastards.

And that kid standing there, determined to storm the barricade — and looking more like those twin bastards every day.

Bastards, bastards, bastards, bastards.

One day she'd say that word aloud to them. She couldn't force her throat to say it yet, but chanting it in her head could sometimes dull memory of that night.

Bastards, bastards, bastards, bastards, bastards.

And their kid took a step! She did, alone and unassisted. One step and she flopped down, but she'd done it. And about time.

If Elsie had been here to see it, she would have praised her. If Granny had seen that step, she would have picked her up, swung her around and told her she was a clever girl.

Goose bumps crawled up Jenny's spine, wave after wave of goose bumps. They washed up to her scalp, made her hair stand on end. She scratched her scalp and looked Buddha in the eye, looked at the washed-out rag of a frock she wore. Looked at Georgie, so cute and pretty in yellow.

And saw herself too clearly. Saw what she was doing to those kids.

It was herself and Sissy all over again. She was trying to reverse what Amber had done to her by repeating it with those kids . . . like she was getting her own back . . . on Amber and those . . .

Bastards, bastards, bastards, bastards.

Not that kid's fault. She hadn't been there. She'd had no more say in being born than Georgie. She'd had no more say in who she looked like than Georgie.

There was too much going on in her head to listen to Vern and Gertrude's conversation — until they mentioned Amber. Her name could still cause Jenny to flinch.

'She's offered to help Margaret with the meal,' Vern said, and Jenny stilled her mind to listen.

'How is she?'

'She looks older than you but seems normal enough. She was at the house with the girl yesterday, going through Margaret's recipe books. You'll come?'

'Of course I'll come. She's my granddaughter.'

Vern was giving the couple a party on Saturday night, or giving himself a party so he could invite Gertrude. He was pleased to be back in that kitchen. Gertrude was pleased he was back. Jenny could hear it in their voices.

He'd be back every Saturday now. She couldn't hide in here, hide those kids, every Saturday.

And Margot was on her feet again, and this time Jenny held out her hands to her. Margot took two wobbling steps, squealed and landed in Jenny's arms.

'She just took two steps, Granny,' she said, lifting the curtain and carrying Margot out to stand on her bent pins and show off her new trick.

Kids never perform on command. Georgie followed them out and made a beeline for Vern's shoes. Margot got down to her knees and followed her.

'When's the wedding?' Jenny asked.

'December,' Vern said, giving her a slit-eyed look he might have offered a disease-carrying cockroach.

It crushed her, and like the cockroach she was, she crawled back into her hole, or back into the lean-to. The kids would get rid of him.

THE PLANTING OF SEEDS

Fashions come and go in cycles; during the past fifty years Gertrude's hairstyle had been in mode as often as it had been out. The loose plaits, held in place by crossed ivory pins, once put up in the morning stayed up all day. She dyed her roots every month or two; the silver stripe in her parting disappeared on Friday night. Her black suit hung on the clothes line airing all day Saturday. It only came out of her wardrobe for weddings and funerals.

She had two nice blouses, a pretty blue silk and a black and white stripe, both purchased by Vern many years ago. A blouse never went out of fashion. She dusted off a pair of black shoes with heels, also bought by Vern, in Melbourne, found a pair of stockings. They'd been repaired but no one would be looking at her legs.

'Will you buy something new for the wedding?'

'I'll wear my blue blouse — if I'm invited.'

'You look about fifty when you're dressed up.'

'Flattery will get you everywhere,' Gertrude said.

'You're happier since he came back.'

'I've never liked being on his bad side, darlin'. He's the only one of my blood that I'm close to.'

'What about me?'

'You're a piece of my heart,' Gertrude said.

'What's Amber?'

'Another piece of my heart — which I do my best to live without.'

*

Gertrude's heart was flopping around like a frog in a mud puddle when she entered Vern's house that night. She looked for Amber, hoping Sissy's engagement might lead to a reconciliation.

Norman was there, looking like an abused terrier wearing the stretched skin of a bloodhound. It hung on him, folded around him. He informed Gertrude that Amber would not be attending the function. Apparently she had been laid low by one of her headaches.

Maisy was there with Dawn and Jessie. George sent his excuses. Joss, Jessie's husband, was there. Robert Fulton and his bride and two of Robert's sisters were there. It wasn't a large gathering. Nelly Dobson managed the serving. Vern filled the wine glasses — and too often his own.

He wasn't a drinker, and with a few glasses of wine under his belt, he could be a fool. He told Gertrude at midnight he was too drunk to drive her home, that she'd have to spend the night in his bed. She told him the walk home would do her good.

He drove her home, and at the garden gate he kissed her like a lover and told her she was marrying him before they had another argument.

'And wouldn't we look like a prize pair of doddering old fools, walking down the aisle in our dotage.'

'You're never going to do it, are you?'

'You know he's not dead, Vern. Do you want me had up for bigamy?'

'There's nothing to stop you putting a ring on your finger and moving out to Monk's place with me. We'll do the house up for ourselves.'

'Jim might have something to say about that. He sounds fired up about that house.'

'Your granddaughter's not. She's no farmer's wife.'

Nor any man's wife, Gertrude thought, but she held her tongue.

Vern had never required a lot of encouragement. He dropped by on Tuesday morning for a quick cup of tea; he was back again on Saturday and Jenny was back to dodging him.

There was only so much time she could spend at Elsie's house, which Margot still considered to be her rightful place. She was treated like a deity by Elsie's kids; there wasn't an ounce of fat on any one of them. That pale Buddha waddling on tiny feet was looked on much as Jesus's disciples may have looked on His walk on water. Jenny left her there to be praised and took Georgie down to the creek to teach her to swim — and she paid in full measure when Vern finally left and she hauled Margot home.

'Mumma. Mumma.'

The following Saturday when they heard that car coming, Jenny left, a kid under each arm. She borrowed Elsie's worn-out pram and took the two kids for a walk down one of the forest tracks — and ran into Bobby Vevers and Johnny Lewis, out setting rabbit traps.

Dragged that pram around and headed fast back the way she'd come, the youths following like two eager dogs panting behind one of Duffy's bitches.

'We're not going to hurt you, Jen.'

They wouldn't get a chance. Pushed that pram faster, ran with it once she was back on the road, mouthing 'bastard' with each revolution of worn wheels and vowing she'd never set foot off Gertrude's land again.

She put the kids down for a nap one wet Saturday and hid in the shed with a book Norman had sent down in the carton of bits and pieces — a book which, until the kids had upended the carton that morning, Jenny had believed to be a Bible.

It had a black cover like a Bible, but it wasn't. She had in her hands D.H. Lawrence's banned book, and what Norman had been doing with it, and why he'd sent it down with her old junk, she didn't know, but fifty pages into it she didn't care why he'd sent it. It was about a woman married to a crippled man, a rich man, and the woman spent half her life getting her clothes off with the gamekeeper.

She didn't hear them until they were in the shed.

'You could smell it on him at the council meeting,' Vern said.

'I noticed him putting it away at the party.' Gertrude was poking around where the chooks' wheat was stored, feet away from where Jenny sat in the partitioned rear corner, Gertrude's bathroom, her store room for preserves, and no door between them, only a wheat bag curtain. Jenny stopped turning pages, stopped breathing — almost.

'What sort of a wage would he be getting?' Vern mused.

'Not much above the basic,' Gertrude said. 'The railways never did pay more than they had to.'

'I don't know how he pays that girl's dress bills. Did his mother leave him much?'

'I doubt it. Amber used to say that she'd never put a penny into the pot.'

'She's around there with Margaret now, talking about ordering her wedding gown from some Sydney bridal wear place.'

'She needs her backside kicked — and the way she was talking to her father at the party, I felt like doing the kicking.'

'A couple of kids will settle her down,' Vern said.

Eavesdroppers rarely hear what they hope to hear. Jenny didn't want to know that Sissy was still treating Norman like a dog with a chequebook. But why should she pity him? He hadn't come near her since the day she'd come home, and that visit had only been to tell her to stay away from Amber and Sissy. And he'd sent down a book that was so . . . so hot it almost steamed.

'All he ever had was his pride in that bugger of a girl's voice,' he said. 'Where is she?'

'Over at Elsie's or down at the creek with the boys.'

'You'll need to watch her around Joey.'

'Don't talk such blatant rot! Those kids have been friends since they were toddlers.'

'A girl who looks like her won't live long as a nun. You fool yourself into thinking that she will, and you'll be in for a fall.'

The afternoon sun glaring through a rough-cut opening in the shed wall, burned Jenny's face; the book she held open burned her hands, and knowing that Vern believed she was like the woman in that book scorched her soul. And as if Lady Chatterley could do it all the time without having babies. It was fiction, that's all, fiction written by a man who had Vern's dirty mind — and Bobby Vevers's and Johnny Lewis's dirty minds, and those twin bastards, and probably every man.

'That boy looks five years older than he is, and if you think he's not out there looking for it . . .'

'Don't judge him by yourself,' Gertrude said, her voice growing distant.

'And don't you get your back up every time I open my flamin' mouth.'

'Then stop attacking that girl every time you open your mouth.'

Too far away for Jenny to hear more. The car left fifteen minutes later.

Vern went home to where no one attacked him, where he was free to say what he liked — other than to his future daughter-in-law, who he found fiddling with the knobs of his wireless.

He hated people fiddling with his wireless, changing it from the station of his choice, but he kept his distance, walked by his sitting room and on down to the kitchen where he sought comfort in cake. That independent bugger of a woman could make him feel like a callow youth caught with his fly undone. And what had he said today to get her back up? He could have said a lot worse than he had.

He'd helped himself to a fair sized chunk of fruitcake before Margaret heard him rattling the tin.

'Would you like a cup of tea to go with it, Father?'

'It would go down well enough,' he said.

He had no intention of taking tea with his future daughter-in-law, who he'd expected to be gone, and if Margaret would stop encouraging her, then she might have been gone. He made a point of dragging a chair to the table, Margaret's work table. She served him there, allowing him to make his point.

A tray loaded, she carried it into the sitting room. Lorna smelled it and came from the library, a book in hand. She didn't tolerate fools gladly, and tolerated Cecelia Morrison less gladly than most, though she had not interfered with the engagement. With the war still escalating, the safest place for her brother was wed and living out at the farm.

Margaret sat with Sissy, delighted they were soon to be sisters.

She was nine years Sissy's senior, though at times seemingly the younger of the two, and excited as a child. She was to be Sissy's bridesmaid. She'd never been a bridesmaid.

They'd chosen the wedding frock. She'd taken Sissy's measurements and together they'd filled in the order form, ticked the *Cheque enclosed* box.

Lorna placed her book down and took her teacup and cake. She bit, swallowed tea, watching the two heads together, still praising the gown modelled by a slim-hipped slip of a girl. Lorna, never a womanly woman, who shuddered at the thought of wedding gowns and bridal beds, left them to their oohing and aahing, and joined Vern in the kitchen.

'What time will Jim be back?' he said.

'Not before six.'

Jim was playing cricket. As Gertrude had once suggested, a few months of military training hadn't done him any harm. He'd trained with the second Fulton boy, a top cricketer who had encouraged Jim to join the team. Jim wasn't much good with the bat or ball, but he had good reflexes and the height to take catches.

'Why isn't she up there watching him play?'

Well may you ask, Lorna's eyebrows said, as she helped herself to more cake.

Vern wasn't pleased with Jim's choice of bride, though he had no one but himself to blame for it. He'd planted the seed.

During his nine or ten months away from Gertrude, needing something to keep his mind off her, he'd decided to do what he could about keeping Jim out of the war. He'd pointed him towards the Fulton girls. There were four of marrying age, and a nicer bunch of girls you'd never meet.

As Gertrude liked to say, you can lead a horse to water but you can't make him drink.

The army had a herd mentality; Jim, born a sheep, had taken a fancy to military khaki. He'd come home on leave from the camp talking about joining up. It was a disease of youth. During the last war, there'd been a stampede of young chaps joining up to see the world. They all believed they were immortal.

'There's more to winning a war than putting on a khaki uniform,' Vern had said. 'A country needs her farmers at home growing food. That's where you'll do the most good.'

A man's heart had to be in the land. Always a bookish bugger of a boy, Jim might have been something had Vern forced him back to that city school — might have made him into an architect.

He'd dragged Vern across the paddock one morning to look over Monk's house, to point out its leaking roof, the bathroom floor rotted through in one corner. It had been a grand old house once.

'It needs people living in it,' Vern had said. 'Not worth putting the money into doing it up if no one is living there.'

He'd never told him to marry, or not in so many words. 'I'll do it up for you as a wedding present.' That's all he'd said.

He'd never come near to suggesting he ought to marry Sissy Morrison — though in hindsight, maybe he was responsible for that, too.

For years Jim had been squiring her and Margaret to every ball, to every dance, which would need to be stopped if Jim was ever to have a chance of taking up with a nice girl. So back when the ball season started, he'd tried to toss a spanner into the works.

'Stop carting that girl around with you and your sister and let her find someone who'll marry her. She's not getting any younger,' he'd said.

'I'm not stopping her,' Jim said.

'Of course you're stopping her! You walk into the hall with her. You walk out with her. Everywhere you go she's beside you. Half the folk in town think that you're courting her.' That's all he'd said.

Then came the mushrooms.

Jim arrived in from the farm telling of a crop of mushrooms growing in the corner of Monk's grand old dining room.

'The least we have to do is to fix the roof, Pops. It's a magnificent old place. If we don't fix it now, we'll be pulling it down in a year or two.'

Arthur Hogan, master builder, wed to one of the middle Macdonald girls, had taken a run out to the farm with them to give an estimation for roof repairs. Jim, as he was apt to, had gone off on a tangent.

He knew every inch of that house. He'd led Hogan from room to room, led him into the old bathroom where they'd stood for half an hour praising the falling tiles. Too much like his mother, that boy — with her same ability to spend money.

'Fix the roof,' Vern had said to Hogan. 'You can do the rest when he weds — and at the rate he's going, I'll probably have twenty years to save up for it.' That's all he'd said.

Toss a seed into fallow ground and, given the right conditions, it will sprout. He'd planted that seed in Jim's book-addled brain and the bloody thing had grown twisted.

With a bit of help from Margaret.

She'd been scratching around in Joanna's jewellery box one wet afternoon, trying on rings. Every time she saw Arthur Hogan she started dripping and trying on rings.

She'd tried on a nice diamond, with a couple of smaller diamonds on the shoulders, and Vern had got talking about how he'd bought it for Joanne when he took her down to the races the year Artilleryman won the Melbourne Cup.

'A late engagement ring,' he'd said.

You could have knocked him down with a feather when a week later that same ring turned up on Sissy Morrison's finger.

'I'm over twenty-one, Pops.' That's all Jim would say when Vern had tried to argue about it. 'I know what I'm doing.'

That military camp had done more than give that boy a yearning for bloody khaki.

Vern had been trying ever since to look on the bright side. He doubted there was any love between the engaged couple, but in his experience love and marriage didn't necessarily go hand in hand. Marriage was for the producing of legitimate offspring, which he'd done three times, without love. He'd loved Gertrude for fifty years and that bugger of a woman wouldn't wed him.

And when all was said and done, he had achieved what he'd wanted: to keep his boy safe from war. And whatever else he might think of Sissy Morrison, she was one of the few girls in this town built to bear Hoopers — even if his grandkids did take after her. And when all was said and done, the engagement had been responsible for him getting back with Gertrude — even though he now had to censor every bloody thought in his head before he let it out of his mouth, thanks to that hot-pants little bugger.

SPLIT PINS

On the first Saturday in November, two cars left the Hoopers' backyard and drove in convoy out Three Pines Road. Vern was behind the wheel of his new maroon Chrysler; he turned right at the fork. His two-year-old green Ford, with Jim behind the wheel, continued over the bridge. Jim was taking Sissy out to introduce her to the farm manager and his wife, who would be her nearest neighbours come December, and to show her over Monk's house before Arthur Hogan and his crew started on the renovations.

The farmhouse Vern had been born and raised in was as old as Monk's, a third of its size, but in better repair. Sissy, wearing her best manners and a near pleasant demeanour, was ushered into a parlour much like Norman's. There the manager's wife poured tea and offered cake. Sissy was no longer a child; she'd learned when not to behave as a child. She smiled when a smile was expected, preened when her ring was admired, smiled until Jim led her out the back door then expected her to walk over rough ground, through drying grass, across wide paddocks, to climb between fence wires while flies swarmed like bees around their queen.

'You could have driven me around there in the car,' she said.

'Petrol,' Jim said. The V8 Ford drank the stuff and the monthly ration was next to useless to those accustomed to driving to Willama every week or so. Jim conserved his petrol when he could. 'It's only a hop, step and a jump, Sis.'

Jump being the operative word. The garden Vern had envied as a boy was overrun by sheep, the gravel path leading to the back door was scattered with sheep dung. Sissy, her mouth shut, her eyes slitted against the flies, stepped over, around, in sheep poop. There was more of it on the rear verandah where a few sheep had been taking advantage of the shade.

If he expected her to live on a stinking sheep-poop, fly-riddled farm he could think again. She wanted to live in the Hoopers' house in town, with Margaret. Since she'd turned sixteen, she'd coveted the Hoopers' house and everything Margaret had. And she would live there too — though she'd keep her mouth shut until December.

Jim opened the rear door and the smell of mould and mice hit her. She took her handkerchief from beneath her bra strap and held it to her nose, making her point without saying a word.

He led her into a large room overlooking the creek. 'We're going to put a wall up in here. This end will be the kitchen and the other half a dining room.'

'It stinks.'

'It's nothing to what it was. We had a crop of mushrooms growing in the corner,' he said with pride. He loved this house with a passion he didn't feel for his fiancée. Love grew, so the books said. If it was going to grow anywhere it would grow in this house. Anything was possible out here.

As excited as a kid, Jim led her though empty halls while in the yard sheep bleated and shook off more dung. Sissy wanted to go home, wanted to put her head under a pillow and scream.

'Down here, Sis. You've got to see this.'

She hated him calling her Sis. Just hated it. Her name was Cecelia and no one ever used it — except her mother and father, and she hated them, too.

'I'm not your sister. I'm your fiancée,' she said, shoes clomping on bare boards, following his voice to a room as big as a church where she found him running his hand over a carved monstrosity of a fireplace, mirrored inserts going up to within feet of the ceiling — a fifteen-foot ceiling, and dark. And they didn't even have the electricity on.

'How could anyone live out here without electricity?' How could anyone live out here without ten maids? 'The whole place smells mouldy.'

'The rain has been getting in. They'll fix that. We'll get the electricity connected. No one has lived here since around '32.'

'The Monks had maids?'

'That's why the bank sold him up,' Jim said, leading the way to his bathroom, which might have been the height of luxury a hundred years ago. Today, two legs of the bath had gone through the floor and the pipes feeding it swung free.

'Look at those old tiles, Sis. I told Hogan I want to reuse them if we can get enough off intact.' She was backing away from his tiles. 'Watch where you walk,' he warned. 'The floor is rotten.'

'It's rubbish,' she said, stepping onto the solid ground of the passage. 'It deserves burning down not fixing.'

He wanted to show her the cellar, to tell her its history. She wanted to go home.

'Why do we have to live out here anyway, when that house in town belongs to you?' She shouldn't have said that. She probably wasn't supposed to know. Margaret had told her in confidence. Maybe he'd think her grandmother had told her.

'It's Pop's for his lifetime, and I don't want it anyway. Since I first saw this place as a kid, I've wanted to live in it. You won't recognise it when it's done up, when we get the garden going again.'

'What's wrong with living in your house?'

They live in it, Jim thought. He'd had a dose of living away from them. It had given him a craving for his own space.

That was one of his reasons for marrying: to have his own space, his own house. He wasn't too certain he'd recognise love if he tripped over it, but being with Sissy was like being with Margaret. He'd been tagging around behind her and Margaret since he was sixteen — which was the second reason why he'd decided to marry her.

Until Vern had suggested that his squiring her around had kept other blokes away, he'd never considered it. But it was probably true. Sissy had been slimmer, better looking, less demanding at sixteen than she was at twenty-one. If she'd been going to find a husband, it would have been at sixteen or seventeen.

The third, and most convincing reason why he'd put his mother's ring on her finger, was her size. Jim's great-grandfather

111

had gone through four wives and produced three kids. His grand-father had gone through two and produced two sons. Vern had gone through three. Lorna's mother died in childbirth; they'd cut Jim's mother open to get him out, and he'd never known her to be well. She'd died when he was six years old. He had no intention of letting his kids kill anyone. Sissy Morrison had the build to birth a dozen Hoopers.

She got on his nerves at times, but out here he wouldn't have to live in her pocket. The house had eight bedrooms. It had an acre of neglected garden and seven hundred and fifty acres of sheep and wheat surrounding it — and today every acre of it clinging tenaciously to its green. Sissy was seeing that land at its best. Give it another month and the green would be gone.

'It's beautiful out here at this time of year,' he said.

'Hmph.' Sissy waved away a fly and looked down at the poop-splattered verandah boards.

A perfect grass-perfumed spring day, the barest feathering of cloud, one of those days you know you've lived before, you know you'll live again, a day for long bike rides — an ice-cream day . . .

The two babies in Elsie's pram, Jenny pushed it towards town wishing she had the guts to push those kids into town and buy an ice-cream. She didn't. She didn't even have the guts to push them down bush tracks. Too many headed out to the bush on fine days.

She stood a while where the forest road ended, wishing she could push on over the bridge and out Three Pines Road. Norman used to take her riding out there. He'd always found something interesting to look at.

And speak of the devil — or think of him — just as she was about to leave the shelter of the trees, she sighted her father rounding McPhersons' bend, heading towards the bridge.

She backed the pram into the trees and watched him stop, lean his bike against the bridge railing. It brought back a rush of memories. He used to strap her into a little wooden seat he'd fixed to the back of that bike, and always lift her down at the bridge to look at the birds. He could name every one: the spoonbill, the blue heron, the musk duck and crane, the dab chick, kingfisher.

She wished . . . wished Amber had never come home. Wished there was a tablet available from Charlie's shop that would wash memories out of the brain. Wished she could stop feeling sorry for him.

She watched him until he mounted his bike and rode on, until the kids started trying to climb out of the pram. They wanted more walking and less trees. And why not? She swivelled the pram around and pushed on towards the bridge.

No sign of Norman on the road. He'd probably ridden down one of the bush tracks. No sign of anyone.

Jackass laughing at her, a few waterbirds playing, a white heron looking for a fish. She could have stood all day at the railing watching birds but she had to get over the bridge before he came back or someone else came.

Almost across, one of the pram's front wheels jammed in a gap between the bridge boards. She should have lifted it out, not tried to drag it. The pram moved forward but the wheel didn't.

'Hell. Hell and damn it!' She kicked it, and the wheel dug in deeper. She cursed it, kicked from a different angle. The wheel jumped free, and rolled merrily towards the railing, Jenny behind it, desperate to catch it before it dived overboard.

The kids, now sitting at an angle, watched with interest as she lifted them level and pushed the wheel back onto the axle. With no split pin to hold it on, it wobbled for a yard or two, then *clunk!* She stood searching the bridge for that pin, knowing it had probably fallen through a gap and was in a fish's gullet — or maybe back on Granny's road where she'd swivelled that pram around.

Dust in the distance, a car coming, she tried tilting the pram, running it on two wheels, and almost lost Georgie overboard. The car was close enough now to recognise. It was Vern's green Ford, and Jim would be driving it. And he was the last person on earth she wanted to see her pushing two kids in a pram. Or maybe not the very last person on earth. The very last person on earth was sitting in the passenger seat.

Helpless, she stood with the wheel in her hand, expecting the car to run over her, to flatten her and her kids like frogs on the road. She almost hoped that car would flatten them and be done with it, but it stopped a few yards short. Jim got out while Sissy leaned on the car horn.

'Are you thinking of moving sometime soon, Jen?' Jim said.

'Not in the near future,' she said. She hadn't seen him in two years. He was thicker around the shoulders, thicker in the neck and face, more like Vern, though also nothing like him, not around the nose, the eyes, maybe the jaw. He'd grown into his goblin ears.

She stepped back as he lifted the pram to study the wheel's mechanics, its contents tilting to the side but clinging on.

'It would have had a split pin in it,' he said.

'I don't need a diagnosis, just a cure,' she replied, and he showed a flash of his teacup teeth. He hadn't grown into those teeth.

'I'll have something in the car,' he said.

'Just help me lift it off the bridge and I'll use one of their napkin pins.'

'It might get you home,' he said. The axle dropped back to aged boards, the kids flopped back to their original tilt, chortling, enjoying the game.

'Twins,' he said. From his great height maybe they looked like twins.

'Sounds logical to me,' she said. She'd clad them today in identical pink frocks and sun bonnets, which hid some of Georgie's hair and all of Margot's, which made Georgie look like a little old-fashioned lady and made Margot look like George Macdonald wearing a sun bonnet. They looked nothing like twins, though she preferred him to think they were.

Car horn beeping, McPherson's old dog adding the base notes, kookaburra laughing.

'I'll put the pram in the boot and drive you home,' he said, and he walked back to empty his rear seat of papers and sweaters, to place them at Sissy's feet.

'You're not putting them in this car,' she said.

'Her wheel came off.'

'You're not putting them in this car, I said.'

'She can't push it back out there on three wheels. Be reasonable, Sis.'

Sissy had never been reasonable, and those kids were coming towards her, one under each of Jenny's arms. 'You put them in this car, and I get out, Jim.'

'Wait over at McPherson's. It will only take me a couple of minutes.'

'As if I'm standing around waiting there while you play good Samaritan to the town slut.'

If Jenny had had a free hand to grip, Sissy's well-dressed hair may have lost some of its curl. She had no free hand — but Sissy hadn't had the last word since Jenny was eleven years old.

Jim was holding the car door open. Jenny placed both kids on the seat and got in to hold them there.

'Try not to breathe, kids,' she said. 'Your Aunty Sissy has got terrible BO.'

A CHANGE OF PLANS

Jim drove down on Monday morning with a selection of split pins. The pram was back at Elsie's, its four wheels intact, but Gertrude thanked him for his thoughtfulness. Jenny remained inside.

On Thursday night, while Gertrude was writing her list to take into town, she brought up the subject of prams. 'I'll ask around while I'm in there and see if someone wants to sell one,' she said.

'Why not advertise in the *Willama Gazette*? *Pram wanted by town slut*.'

'I told you not to use that expression.'

'Tell Sissy that. Tell Vern, too. Tell Bobby Vevers. Tell everyone.' There was a freedom in being herself, in saying what she was thinking.

'That's enough.'

'Then it's enough of you talking about prams, too.'

'Your father is still sending me money for you.'

'Give it back to him to pay for the wedding.'

Gertrude had considered it. She'd burned his first few cheques, thinking he wouldn't find out. He had, and he'd started doubling the figure. She deposited his remittances into her account now. Ten shillings a week wasn't a lot, but Jenny had been home for over a year and those ten shillings mounted up.

She raised the subject of prams again when Elsie's new son was born and the old brown pram back in full-time service.

There is little more heart-stirring than the lusty wail of a newborn child, though Gertrude hoped it might be the last of them.

Her land was overrun by accidental grandchildren, and not a dribble of her blood running in any one of them — yet she felt more for the smallest of them than she felt for Sissy.

At night, when she sat alone in the moonlight, she wondered how she might feel about Sissy's children. They'd be hers and Vern's grandchildren. Maybe that could be excuse enough to wed him — or to put his ring on her finger. She'd be sure of getting her hands on her blood grandchildren — maybe the only way she could be sure. In time she might even form a relationship with Sissy. Becoming a mother matured most girls.

She didn't consider the possibility that Sissy wasn't pregnant. Why else the rushed wedding?

Not so rushed, as it turned out. The postal department delivered the box from the Sydney bridal wear store ten days before the proposed wedding date. It was a beautiful gown, but never trust a friend to take an honest waist measurement. Depending on the nature of that friend, they might add two inches, or deduct two. The frock didn't come within four inches of doing up at Sissy's waist. Amber repackaged it carefully. Norman posted it back, and that night, while Sissy howled on her bed, Norman prayed for a refund.

'Dress or not, it will still go ahead won't it?' Gertrude asked.

'In February. She's having a frock made by Margaret's dressmaker. The woman says she's run off her feet until January,' Vern said.

'The sooner it's done the better, Vern.'

'That's what I said. But I don't think that boy has worked out what a woman is for yet — I've got my doubts that he ever will,' Vern said, and Gertrude thought no more about wedding rings.

Christmas came. They ate homegrown chicken at Gertrude's house, homegrown vegetables, soggy plum pudding, two threepences poked into every slice and more threepences required each year. They ate the festive meal in Gertrude's kitchen, which was larger than Elsie's, though the Halls' chairs and kitchen table made the trip across the paddock. Always controlled bedlam,

Christmas Day at Granny's house. Worse when Gertrude tested her present from Harry and Elsie, a small whistling kettle. It boiled fast and screamed its success.

They were washing dishes, stepping over and around kids and building blocks, when Maisy arrived with a knitted gollywog for Margot and scented soap and rose water for Jenny, Gertrude and Elsie.

Her own house was full, she said. She'd popped out for a breather. 'Patricia and the kids and Rachael are staying in with us until New Year. They want to see *Gone with the Wind*.'

'Up here?' Jenny said. 'Up here already?' Hiring new movies cost the council too much money, so Norman used to say. They never hired any of the good shows until they were worn out.

'They're showing it in Willama this week. The council made some deal with the theatre.'

'Are you going?'

'I'll be looking after the kids, love.'

'Would you come in with me, Granny?'

'I haven't seen one of those ratbag things since the projector chap almost burned the old town hall down.'

'How?'

'Before we had electricity,' Maisy said. 'A travelling chap used to come up here on the train with his light thing.'

'Limelight,' Gertrude said. 'Dangerous stuff. It burned a few theatres down. I remember once when Archie was —' She closed her mouth.

'What?' Jenny said.

'It was some sort of a cylinder they filled up with lime, then burned it by blowing oxygen or some sort of gas mixture onto it. It gave off a good light.'

'I meant what about Itchy-foot?' Jenny said. She liked hearing stories about Itchy-foot. Knew she looked like him — probably was like him — which was probably why Amber hated her.

'He was fond of the limelight,' Gertrude said.

'Come with me, for my birthday. Please.'

'Joey will go with you.'

Joey had grown a moustache. He looked like a Spanish pirate, but knew he wasn't — as did most in town. He worked in the bush, was happier in the bush.

'You can sit with my girls,' Maisy said.

As if they'd want to sit with her. The subject was dropped though not forgotten by Jenny. She'd read about that movie. Clark Gable was in it.

Then, on the Saturday it was showing, Vern came down talking about it. Jim had been staying out at the farm, but he was coming in to see it. Margaret and Lorna were going.

Everyone in Woody Creek would be at the town hall tonight and Jenny didn't have the guts to go.

She spent the afternoon with Elsie, watching Vern's car, listening for its motor. It didn't move from the yard. She fed the kids at Elsie's, gave them a bath, clad them in borrowed napkins, borrowed nightshirts. She ate at Elsie's table, but by seven both kids were whingeing for their bed. She and Joey carried them home.

Vern eyed them as they walked in. He asked Joey how he was enjoying being a working man. Joey said he liked the money, then he left. Jenny got the kids down, gave them bottles and disappeared into the lean-to. No lamp to read by. Nothing to do but sit all night while he sat.

And she wasn't going to sit in there all night listening to him. She wasn't going back to Elsie's either. She was going to see that movie.

It was almost dark when she got to the station, where she waited until the crowd filed into the town hall. She waited five minutes more then ran across the road.

Mrs Olsen sold the tickets. Jenny couldn't see if she sneered or not, but she took the money and Jenny slipped into the hall.

The newsreel was playing. She stood, her back to the wall, watching a crippled plane come in on a wing and a prayer, watching soldiers, thousands of them, marching across the screen, and thousands more being offloaded from boats. She saw Winston Churchill get into a car somewhere in London, bombed London, men digging through rubble. She'd heard Churchill's voice on Elsie's wireless and it had given her goose bumps. *We will fight them on the beaches. We will never surrender.*

Was it better to surrender your city to the enemy than to see it bombed into oblivion? Maybe. Paris had surrendered. It would still be standing when the war ended. But what would it feel like to walk the streets of your own city saying '*Heil* Hitler'? Did the French walk around with their heads bowed in shame?

The newsreel was her first sight of war, of its destruction. She had read bits and pieces in the newspapers, just facts and figures, the number of casualties. Tonight she knew the newspaper's casualties were boys, those same boys marching across the screen.

There were a few empty seats scattered around, if she was prepared to squeeze past people's knees to get to them. She considered the long wooden bench seats at the front of the hall where the kids sat, where she'd sat in another lifetime. Everyone would see her, stare at her. Better to stand near the door, be first out at interval.

Then the movie began, the screen lit up with colour and the music swept her away from the town hall to Tara.

She didn't want an interval, didn't want to move, but she had to. She got out the door before the lights came on and ran across to the park where she sat in the shadows of the bandstand as the crowd poured out onto the street, and a stream of the younger moviegoers ran across the railway line to the café. Mrs Crone always stayed open late on picture nights.

Hiding in the park was a mistake. It was a popular place. She watched one couple kiss, wondered what it might be like to be kissed like Rhett had kissed Scarlett, Atlanta burning behind them. Laurie had looked a bit like Clark Gable; he'd kissed her, but not like that, not a waited-for sort of kiss. It was more a warning that she'd be having a bath sort of kiss.

She was sitting, head down, remembering her walk across this park on the night of the ball, thinking about the twins and mouthing 'bastards' when another one crept up on her.

'I thought I recognised that hair,' he said.

Jenny sprang to her feet, sprang away from him. Bobby Vevers, but alone tonight. And she wasn't. Maisy's house was on the far side of the park fence. There were two hundred people at the hall. She'd been scared of him when she'd come on him and Johnny Lewis setting traps. She wasn't going to be scared of him tonight.

The kissing couple must have heard him. They broke apart and walked back towards the road.

'Dora Palmer and Reggie Murphy,' he said. 'They've been going together for six months.'

He'd been over to the café. He offered her a toffee. She hadn't had a toffee in ages. She took it, peeled off the paper. She shouldn't have. He thought his lolly had brought him the right to put his hand on her.

'Don't you touch me!' She dodged around him out of the bandstand and walked to Maisy's fence.

'When did you get to be so fussy, Jen?'

Bastard.

She ran along the fence to the footpath, and around to Maisy's open gate. He didn't follow. He walked back to join the thinning crowd out front of the hall.

She shouldn't have come into town. She'd go home as soon as the crowd cleared.

But she didn't want to go home — she wanted to see the rest of the movie.

The town hall lights dimmed, and Jenny ran — and almost collided with Dora and Reggie Murphy, who had been standing in the shadows of a clump of bushes. There was enough light for her to recognise Dora, who must have recognised her, though she pretended she didn't. They'd been best friends. For the longest time, they'd been best friends.

The music was playing when she entered the hall and took her place against the back wall.

She could see the Hoopers, sitting side by side four rows from the back, Lorna in the aisle seat beside Margaret, Sissy beside her, tall Jim the other bookend.

Then the last light went out and the movie started and Jenny forgot about the Hoopers, forgot about Dora Palmer. That movie got better and better.

And right when Scarlett had just shot a thief who deserved shooting, Bobby bastard Vevers came in to stand beside her.

She moved along the wall. He moved with her.

She had to go.

She'd probably be the only person in the world who had ever walked out of *Gone with the Wind*. And she was not walking out. Hitler could drop a ton of bombs on Woody Creek tonight and he wouldn't blast her out of this hall — and slinking, greasy Bobby Vevers wouldn't drive her out of it either.

'Get the hell away from me,' she hissed.

A hiss is loud in a crowded hall. Eyes turned to identify the hisser, and who cared? Who cared who saw her? She walked fast down the aisle to the front row, down to the kids' hard seats.

'I don't know how she dares to show her face in town,' Sissy whispered loudly.

'If I had a face like yours, I wouldn't,' Jenny tossed over her shoulder.

Sniggers, a murmur of tut-tuts, a giggle or two, but Jenny squeezed in between two kids and returned her attention to the best movie ever made.

POKER FOR PENNIES

The kids pushed out through the side exit, Jenny behind them. Dozens of adults were streaming out through the front door. She cut across the grass to Cemetery Road, then across the road to the post office, walked fast past Norman's house and down through the railway yards.

And that mongrel was leaning against the fence waiting for her.

'Are you scared of me, or something, Jen? I won't hurt you.'

'Stop following me!'

'I was here first. You're following me.'

She wheeled around and ran back to Norman's side gate. It squealed open, squealed as it closed. She waited behind it, watching him through the hand-hole where the gate latched. The Vevers' house was behind the park; she hoped he'd go home. He didn't. He walked over to the currajong tree, leaned against it and lit a cigarette.

She'd have to go the other way, up past Charlie's and over his crossing. She ran down the eastern side of Norman's house, past his junk room window, knowing she was closer to him than she'd been in a year, and knowing too that if she knocked on his door and told him Bobby Vevers was hanging around out there ready to rape her, he'd probably think she'd asked for it. She wasn't asking Norman for anything, not tonight, not for as long as she lived. Anyway, he probably wasn't in the junk room; he was probably in Amber's bed, doing what he'd read about in *Lady Chatterley's Lover*.

And she couldn't get out the front gate. Jim and Sissy were out there. She stood and watched him kiss her — or her kiss him — and it turned her stomach, turned her footsteps back the way they'd come.

She hated her life. Hated it. Hated Sissy for having everything. Hated Vern Hooper for spending half his life in Gertrude's kitchen. Hated Dora. Hated everyone.

Her eye to the latch hole, she searched for Bobby Vevers. He'd disappeared from the currajong tree. He'd probably gone on ahead, would be waiting for her down near Macdonald's mill. She looked towards Maisy's house. Maisy would drive her home.

She'd be making supper for her daughters.

Mr Foster?

No lights showing in his house.

I'm signing those kids away tomorrow, she thought. I'm getting out of this town. I have to. She still had one of Mr Quinn's five-pound notes and her talent quest money. I'll go to Melbourne. I'm old enough to train as a nurse. The army needs nurses. I'm signing those kids away tomorrow.

A family group had taken the short cut through the railway yard. She opened that squealing gate, closed it as gently as she could, and tailed the family over the lines and down past the hotel. They went left and, her protection gone, she ran. Past the Hoopers' house, past King's corner where the street lighting stopped and the dark was darker because there had been light.

She wasn't afraid of the dark, just scared stiff of Bobby Vevers coming out of the dark. She glanced over her shoulder, glanced down side lanes.

There were dark buildings at Macdonald's mill. Too many buildings. Anyone could be hiding in there. Knew he'd come slinking out from behind the piled logs, the stacked timber. Knew he was down there somewhere.

She should have known what would happen. Stupid. Stupid. Stupid. Stupid.

And Dora Palmer . . . Dora Palmer now working on the telephone exchange, and smooching with Reggie Murphy in the bushes.

I hate my life. Bastards. Bastards, bastards, bastards, bastards, bastards. How many times can you mentally repeat a word before your tongue feels the need to spit it out? She was near the McPhersons' gate when she glanced back and saw him coming.

'Bastard,' she hissed and ran to their gate, knowing she dared go no further, knowing that if he caught up to her in the bush she could scream 'Bastard' and no one would hear her.

Heart racing, she watched the road, or the walker, aware that she'd have to knock on the McPhersons' door. Miss Rose, the infant schoolmistress, had married John McPherson. They'd let her in, even if they did think she was the town slut — except there were no lights showing in their house. They would have been at the town hall; they wouldn't have missed that movie.

But whoever was coming down the middle of the road was walking too tall to be Bobby Vevers. She squinted at the shape, at the walk — and recognised those long swinging strides.

With a moan of relief, she walked back to the road. 'You just scared the living daylights out of me, you drongo.'

'Sorry,' he said.

No chance to say more. John McPherson's old brown kelpie didn't approve of people messing around near his master's gate. He came under the gate snarling, and Jim Hooper, never fond of dogs, took off towards the forest road.

'He'll be laying in wait for you on your way back,' Jenny said, following him to the trees.

'He bit one of the Dobson kids a while back.'

The dog, having hunted them, lost interest.

'If he bit anyone, his teeth would fall out,' Jenny assured him. 'He's as old as me. What are you doing down here in the middle of the night?'

'You used to be scared of walking through the bush.'

'I used to be scared of a lot of things.'

'It's good sense sometimes to have a bit of fear, Jen.'

'Then you haven't got much sense, have you?'

'What do you mean?'

'I spent fourteen years living with your fiancée. If I were you, I'd be scared stiff of spending the next fifty with her,' she said and walked on, expecting him to turn back.

He didn't.

Shoes scuffing through the dust, they'd walked a hundred yards in silence before he spoke. 'I've been thinking about joining up.'

'Getting shot would be faster and a lot less painful.'

'You've got a mouth on you these days, Jen.'

'I haven't got much else, have I? I can't even go to a movie without some mongrel trying to pick me up.'

'I . . . you don't . . . I'm not.' He stopped walking. She continued on for a yard or two.

'I didn't mean you, you drongo.'

'Vevers?' he said. 'We saw him.'

'That's why you're down here! You're playing Sir Galahad.'

He didn't deny it. 'What did you think of it, anyway?' he said.

'Brilliant.'

'The book is better,' he said.

'You've read it?'

'I bought it. Borrow it, if you like.'

'Really?'

'Margaret says she's going to read it but she'll take six months.'

They spoke of the book, of the movie, until they reached the boundary gate. She was on the other side of it before she asked him when he was getting married.

'We'll wait until the house is done up now. They've started on it.'

'Granny says it's a mansion.'

'It's been let go. A house needs people living in it.'

'You'll fix that — if the dog doesn't eat you on the way home.' She backed away from him. 'Thanks, Sir Galahad,' she said, then ran down the track.

And that was that. She'd seen *Gone with the Wind* and now she was home, and she was still going to sign those kids away tomorrow and go to Melbourne and train to be a nurse.

Georgie changed her mind on Sunday afternoon. She'd been pulling herself up to her feet for weeks. On Sunday she took off running, and she wasn't even ten months old.

Jenny was bathing the kids on Tuesday evening when Vern's green Ford drove into the yard, Jim behind the wheel. He had a big old cane pram roped onto the drop-down trunk lid.

'It's been hanging around the shed rotting for years, Mrs Foote,' he said. 'I thought Jen might get some use out of it. It needs a good scrub but it's got a decent set of wheels on it.'

'It's a fine pram,' Gertrude said.

Jenny waited until he'd left before she came out to look at the pram. Inside it was the book. She pounced on it and started reading while Gertrude worried about finding space for the overly large cane relic Jim Hooper had once ridden in.

They got rid of the cobwebs the following morning, scrubbed the dusty cane white. They moved a few things around in Gertrude's bedroom, stacked boxes on trunks, newspapers on boxes, and the pram came inside to live.

On Sunday night, the kids asleep, Jenny sat close to the lamp finishing the last pages of *Gone with the Wind*. Gertrude was preparing to go over to Elsie's to bathe and wash her hair when they heard a car coming.

'Who wants me at this time of night?' Gertrude grumbled, watching the car lights bouncing into her yard.

'Sorry to disturb you so late, Mrs Foote. I was . . . was wondering if Jen had finished the book yet.'

'Last pages,' Jenny yelled.

Gertrude invited him in, then she went out with her towel and her nightclothes.

Her finger marking her place, Jenny looked up at him. 'I've got three pages to go. You'd better sit down if you want to wait for it.'

Minutes later, she closed the book. 'It's brilliant, but they should have cut out those last words — the *After all, tomorrow is another day* bit. Everything has been said. That's excess. It sort of . . . sort of steals the power of it a bit.'

They'd been friends since she was four years old. She'd been older than her years, he'd been younger. They'd sat for hours on the station platform, on verandahs, discussing the world as seen through the eyes of kids, discussing books, discussing wireless valves. He'd never seemed older, had never been one of Bobby Vevers's pack — never been part of any pack.

He took the book but didn't rise to leave. She fetched two mugs of water from the Coolgardie. He emptied the mug, then he started talking.

Like a bottle of home-brewed ginger beer when the cork is popped, he spilled words. He told her about his military training, about the mushrooms growing in the corner of the old dining room, of rotted floorboards, of the bathroom.

'You should have seen it before they gutted it, Jen. I'm keeping the tiles. And there's this big old fireplace in one of the rooms that would look at home in a castle; you could burn four-foot logs in it. Hogan isn't touching that room. I'll do it my own way when I'm ready.'

'Why did you let them gut your bathroom?'

'No floor,' he said. 'Half the tiles were off. I spent most of today cleaning them. You wouldn't believe them. They're all the same but side by side they're all different. They must have been hand painted.'

'I bet you're putting in an indoor lav.'

'Why do you say that?'

'Fourteen years' hard labour,' she said.

Mozzies buzzing, the kids breathing in harmony, night birds calling. Big hands playing with the book, hands identical to Vern's. He had Vern's jaw, maybe his mouth. Hard to tell with those teeth.

'We're putting in a septic system. Not in my bathroom though.'

'Told you so.'

He reached for a packet of cigarettes, lit one. She found him a saucer for an ashtray, watched him draw on the cigarette and wished he'd offered her one.

'I've been thinking a bit about what you said.'

'I say a lot of things.'

'The fifty years . . .'

She laughed, and she shouldn't have laughed. She never

128

laughed. Had nothing to laugh about. But she laughed until she started coughing.

'It's not that funny,' he said.

'It is. What made you do it?'

'Do what?'

'Decide to marry her, you drongo?'

'I'm not saying anything against her, Jen.'

'You are so. You said you were thinking about fifty years of her.' And she laughed again.

'I didn't mean it like that. She's all right. We get on all right.'

'People get on all right with the McPhersons' dog as long as they walk on the far side of the road.'

'He doesn't like me.'

'He knows he can bluff you.'

So strange to sit in this kitchen, to see Jim sitting in this kitchen. So strange to be treated like she was Jenny. Strange, too, to laugh at this table. Almost bliss. It was like he'd given her leave to be normal, to talk about normal things.

Then Gertrude returned, in her dressing gown, hair wrapped in a towel, and it was over.

Jim picked up his book and said goodnight.

But it wasn't over. He came down with *How Green is My Valley* and *The Grapes of Wrath* the following Sunday night. Harry was there, checking the level of Gertrude's water tank. He had the water carrier coming in the next day to fill his tanks so he might as well fill hers, he said. Jenny and Joey had been playing poker for matches. The books ended the game, but one way or another, Jim sat down, and all five ended up playing poker for matches while Gertrude questioned Jim about Monk's house, and Jim questioned her about the wallpaper hanging in Monk's house when she'd known it in its heyday.

They spoke of the wedding, now planned for May, and about Norman. They drank tea and Jenny stole a drag of Joey's cigarette and she gambled wildly, never glancing at the clock until it struck midnight.

'I'm so sorry, Mrs Foote,' Jim said, rising too fast, knocking his chair over in his haste to be gone. 'I'm so sorry to keep you all up so late.'

'We enjoyed the game,' Gertrude said.

And when he was gone and the door closed, while the matches were being settled back into their boxes, Gertrude looked at Jenny.

'What's going on with that boy? I doubt he's been inside this house more than half a dozen times in his life.'

'He's going to be your grandson-in-law. He's getting to know you.'

The following Sunday he drove down armed with a bagful of pennies and a new deck of playing cards. Jenny called out to Harry and Joey and the game was on again, Jim's pennies shared into five equal piles.

It became a game of high finance, IOUs written by those who borrowed pennies to stay in the game. It became a loud game. They disturbed the kids. And when the old clock told them they should all be in bed, the pennies were scooped into a jam jar with the IOUs, and the jar placed beside the bottle of medicinal brandy on top of the dresser, Jim's cards placed in the dresser drawer.

'See you next Sunday,' he said.

There was no harm in it, and it was good for all three of those boys. They were of an age. Gertrude knew she ought to mention Jim's visits to Vern. She almost told him when he drove down on the Tuesday following their third poker night — until he referred to Joey as 'young Darkie'. That's what they called him in town, Darkie Hall. She kept her mouth shut. He wouldn't want to know how well those three boys got along.

130

THE LAST ROSE OF SUMMER

Vic Robertson ruined their game on the second Sunday in February. He arrived while Jenny was washing up the dinner dishes. His wife was getting ready to pop her eleventh, he said.

'An inconvenient time for her to choose,' Vic said. 'I hate to take you out at night, Mrs Foote.'

Gertrude smiled. 'Babies don't have a lot of regard for clocks.'

Ten minutes later, they rode into the gloom, Vic on his bike, carrying the basket, Gertrude on horseback, clip-clopping at his side.

Kids are creatures of habit. Jenny's two sat on the table while she washed hands, faces and feet, while she clad them in matching nightgowns. They shared a big old iron cot down the bottom end of the kitchen. It was barely wide enough for two. She tried topping and tailing them, but the kids considered it a game, long aware that their heads belonged on the same pillow.

She tucked them in and told them about Jack and Jill who'd walked up the hill, about Wee Willie Winkie who ran through the town. She sang about the black sheep, just to test her vocal cords, then sang about four and twenty blackbirds baked in a pie. Two sets of eyes watched her, neither one complaining about their private concert, so she tried the Twenty-third Psalm. She loved that one, always had — maybe because Norman had loved listening to her sing it, which should have been enough to put her off it, but it wasn't. And he wasn't here to hear her anyway. No one could hear her, except the kids. She only knew the old songs, but they came, one following the other until the purple eyes and the green gave up their struggle to remain open.

131

The lamp cast its meagre light in a circle over the table, barely extending to the open door and not quite reaching the cot. She didn't realise he was there until she turned and saw his lanky frame holding back the hessian curtain.

'I didn't hear you knock.'

'You would have stopped,' he said, offering a bunch of roses.

She didn't take his bouquet. He placed it on the table with the soapy water and the towel she'd used on the kids. She tossed the water on Granny's rosebush, hung the towel then picked up his bunch of roses and smelled them.

'Thanks,' she said.

'They're the last of them for this year. Margaret picked them today.'

Not for you to bring down here, Jenny thought.

'I was waiting for you to sing *The Last Rose of Summer*. Remember that one? You sang it at the school concert.'

She shrugged, embarrassed that he'd crept up on her.

'Do you remember it?' he persisted.

She shook her head. 'Granny has gone up to the Robertsons' —'

'I know,' he said. 'I saw her riding past your father's place when I dropped your sister off.'

He looked awkward. Jenny felt awkward. 'You're too early,' she said.

'I am,' he admitted. 'We were out at the farm. They've finished the roof, got a new floor down in the bathroom. Your mother came out with us. Her father used to tell her about the house, she said.'

'How nice for you.' She turned her back on him and found a tall earthenware vase which she filled from the bucket of water always waiting ready beneath the washstand. He watched her settle the stems, watched her smell each rose as she placed it.

'You used to walk past our corner smelling the roses.'

'I used to wait for them to bloom. I'd never seen anything as beautiful as your father's roses.'

'Take a look in a mirror sometime, Jen,' he said.

That snapped her chin up. She looked him in the eye, knowing in her bones, in her stomach, that he hadn't been coming down here to question Gertrude about Monk's house, or to play penny poker with Harry and Joey.

And knowing something else too, knowing that it was within her power to drop a bomb on Sissy, on Vern and Amber, and on Norman too, who sent his cheques in the mail so he didn't have to come anywhere near his slut daughter.

She picked up the vase and carried it away from him and from the light, not wanting her face to show what she was thinking. The vase set on top of the Coolgardie, safe from the kids, she stood a moment, looking down at the two small heads, the red and the white.

Babies can change the course of history, she thought. If Jesus had died at birth there'd be no religion. If Hitler's mother had had an abortion, Australia wouldn't be at war. If Margot hadn't been forced on me, I wouldn't have had Georgie. If Mrs Robertson had gone into labour yesterday, or tomorrow, or next week, or during daylight hours, I wouldn't be alone with him.

Making the transition from child to woman with a belly swollen by a rapist's leavings doesn't do a lot for the victim's psychological development. Nor does making the harder transition from local songbird to town slut because of what they'd done — and while Maisy's maladjusted pair of bastards, who had found their forte, killing Germans, were making their own transition from rapists to war heroes.

There was no balance to be made there, not in Jenny's mind. There was no fairness to be found there — and life's lack of fairness to her hadn't instilled in her feelings of fairness towards all mankind, or any feelings for Sissy and Amber.

So drop that bomb, she thought. Blow their wedding plans to hell.

Her mind had covered a lot of territory, but Jim hadn't moved. Perhaps no time had passed.

She shrugged and walked by him to the stove, glanced up at the clock, wanting verification that no time had passed. Harry or Joey could be over soon. She hoped they'd be over soon.

'I didn't say what I said to upset you,' he said. 'It's true, Jen. If you could have seen yourself standing there singing to those kids — you looked like one of those pictures of angels they used to give out at church when we were kids.'

'Tell your father that and watch him laugh,' she said.

She moved the whistling kettle over the hotplate. It started screaming. She moved it back to the hob. She loathed that kettle, even if it did boil fast — wondered if anyone else in the world loathed whistling kettles — if anyone else in the world loathed their sisters enough to do what she was considering.

How much of Amber's blood might be running through her veins, how much of Itchy-foot's lack of conscience had transferred itself to her? Whose frantic heartbeat had she inherited? Maybe Norman's father's. He'd dropped dead from a heart attack. Her heart was racing so fast its beats were tripping over each other. She wanted Harry and Joey to come.

I'm scared of Jim Hooper, she thought. Not scared of him throwing himself on me, but a different kind of scared. I've known him all my life. He taught me how to keep pushing the ice-cream down into the cone so I'd have ice-cream to the last bite. He read his books to me, showed me a book of fairies most boys would have been too embarrassed to look at. He walked home from school with me, tracked ants through the dust with me, worked out on paper how many yards might equal one ant mile.

I deserted him for Nelly and Gloria, for Dora Palmer — or did he desert me for Sissy?

He grew too tall, that's all. I didn't grow tall enough. Sissy was tall enough, and once she claimed him as a friend, she made damn certain there was no room for me.

Sissy had gone with the Hoopers to Sydney, to see the Harbour Bridge opened. She'd gone with them to Frankston, gone with Jim and Margaret to balls in Willama, gone shopping with them. Of course he'd marry her . . .

Unless I save him from a fate worse than death.

Jenny stood, her back to the window, the table between them. Just stood there knowing full well that he knew what she was thinking, and knowing too that her face was flushed by her thinking.

Then that huge hand reached across the table, palm up. She had nothing to give. So easy though to . . . to reach out her own hand.

And thank God she heard the goat fence gate slam. And thank God for Harry and Joey. She walked to the dresser and opened the drawer to get the cards out.

BULL ANTS AND SILENCE

In March Jim spent most of his month's petrol ration on a trip to Willama, thirty-nine miles there, thirty-nine back and a lot of running around while he was there. Sissy, Amber and Margaret needed to look in every shop for wedding gown fabric. Lorna went her own way.

She met them for lunch, ate steak and onions while the others nibbled and discussed styles, discussed the dressmaker, agreed that pink was Margaret's colour, that it always looked well with her platinum blonde hair and pink complexion. Jim drove them home at four. Sissy invited the Hoopers in for a cup of tea. Lorna declined the offer. Jim said he had to get out to the farm.

'You've got a manager,' Sissy said. 'What do you pay him for?'

Lorna humphed, Jim put the car into gear and the Hoopers left.

Sissy mimicked her as she walked inside. She'd bought a Boston Bun at the Willama bakery for afternoon tea. In the kitchen she removed it from its bag and sought a sharp knife.

'I told you not to buy that,' Amber said.

'I thought they'd stay for afternoon tea.'

'Your measurements have been taken. You can't put on weight this time.'

'I didn't the last time, and stop telling me what to do!'

A constant catfight in Norman's house, but an unfair matching of felines — the Bengal tiger versus the feral cat. The tiger snarled, showed its claws and teeth, but the old cat was smarter and more devious, the tiger too lethargic to do much more than snarl.

And into that catfight came the aging bloodhound, his skin sagging, his coat mangy.

Bun on the table, on its brown paper bag, a large triangle cut from it, the last of that triangle disappearing down his daughter's gullet, a blob of creamy icing filling the too small space between top lip and hooked nose. Norman's father had had the good sense to die young. Norman envied him.

'A successful trip?' he asked.

'We got the material, if that's what you mean,' Sissy said.

'Miss Blunt will do the stitching of it?'

'As if,' Sissy retorted.

'The woman makes a serviceable gown.'

'I told you I'm getting it done by Margaret's dressmaker.'

'A stationmaster does not have access to deep pockets.' He had received a refund from the Sydney bridal wear company, though not for the postage.

'It's my wedding day. You ought to be pleased that at least one of us is getting married before we have kids.'

Norman nodded and glanced again at the bun. He spent little time at the house. He ate there; it was not yet time to eat. He slept in the junk room; the day was not near done. He had an icebox at the station and two-thirds of a bottle of gin. He returned to his station and gin bottle.

Jim dropped his sisters off at home, then set off again. He needed petrol and the only place he'd get petrol was out at the farm. Farmers received more than their fair share of fuel. Vern's manager was of the old school, and not yet reliant on tractors and generators.

Since new that green Ford had spent a lot of its life parked in Gertrude's yard. It made the turn into the forest road and Jim parked it beside the walnut tree.

'I was wondering if you and Jen might like to take a quick drive out to the farm with me, Mrs Foote. The old place is starting to look good.'

The kids were missing. Jenny was missing. His eyes searched for her.

'It's taking a while,' Gertrude said.

'There's a lot to do. Hogan and his chaps are camping out there this week.'

'Your father was saying this petrol business is holding them up.'

'That's the problem with employing out-of-town chaps. They're doing a beautiful job of it though. They brought up some wallpaper samples I wouldn't mind your opinion on. Pop's got no memory for detail.'

Then Jenny came, the redhead under her arm. That was the instant alarm bells should have rung in Gertrude's ears. Jim's smile turned his face into Vern's.

'I've got to get petrol. I was just trying to talk your gran into taking a drive out to see what we've done.'

'Your dad will want to show me over it,' Gertrude said.

'He won't show me over it,' Jenny said.

'I'll have her back in under an hour,' Jim promised.

Georgie was passed to Gertrude's hands, and maybe there was a gentle tinkling of alarm bells as Jenny ran to the car.

Vern Hooper's land was eight miles west of Woody Creek. He'd inherited over two hundred acres from his grandfather and during the early days of the depression had added Max Monk's seven hundred and fifty to his holding, which gave him a good-sized chunk of land with the creek marking his northern boundary.

Sounds of industry echoed from within the house, the saw, the hammer; outside, a chap stood high on a ladder, splashing paint about. Jim drove by him, by a small truck advertising *Hogan & Son, Master Builders*. He drove around a stack of timber and parked half in, half out of a shed much like Gertrude's shed while he pumped petrol from a forty-four-gallon drum, Jenny stood looking at the house Sissy would call home.

'Over here, Jen.'

She turned to his voice and saw him standing in the middle of a claypan, stamping his feet. 'Doing a rain dance?' she said.

An ant dance. He'd disturbed a nest of bull ants, giants of their race, heads on them as big as peas, nippers capable of leaving their mark.

It's difficult to keep your eye on angry ants defending their territory. One attacked from the rear and got a grip on Jenny's shoe. She shook her foot, and the old shoe flew. With one foot bare, she hopped back to the car, Jim laughing and fishing for her shoe with a length of wire.

He hooked it and flung it towards her, a few ants clinging on for the ride. He laughed as he flicked them off, while she sat on the running board, brushing grit from her foot, embarrassed by her worn shoe. He wasn't. He slid it onto her foot.

'My God, it fits!' he said, his eyes still laughing.

'And I was prepared to cut off my big toe!' she said. Shouldn't have. He was no Prince Charming and she was no Cinderella. 'I thought you brought me out here to show me your house, not bull ants.'

He showed her his house, led her in through the open front door, into an entrance hall as wide as Gertrude's kitchen and longer.

'My God,' she breathed.

He led her to his bathroom, where a workman was sticking old tiles to new walls with mud. 'My God!' There was nothing else to say. She lived in a hut, slept in a lean-to; she could touch its corrugated-iron ceiling if she reached as she jumped. The ceilings in this house were a mile high, the rooms were huge, the bathroom was as big as Granny's bedroom.

'My God.' She followed him into a kitchen with a shiny sink and the skeletons of many cupboards — and Arthur Hogan, who stopping sawing to stare at her. She'd seen him often at Maisy's house.

She nodded and walked through the kitchen to a room of shelves, while Jim spoke to him about a stove which should be arriving on the train sometime that week.

He found her standing beside an open trapdoor, looking down into a pit.

'That's the best part,' he said, stepping into the pit. 'There's a handrail,' voice without body said. 'Watch your footing. The steps are steep.'

The steps were not quite a ladder, yet not quite a flight of stairs. Carefully she followed him into the hole.

'Your dungeon?' she said.

'Storeroom, so Pops says.' He struck a match and while it burned she made her way down to the floor, hand gripping a rail worn smooth by the grasping hands of the Monks' many maids.

Then the match went out and they were in pitch darkness.

'Strike another one.'

'Let your eyes get used to it, Jen.'

'What's down here?'

'Nothing now. According to Pops, in the old days a bullocky used to bring in a load of supplies once a year. Everything was stored down here.'

'It smells like an ancient burial tomb.'

'I've found a couple of mouse skeletons,' he said.

'I can't see anything. Haven't you got a candle or something?'

'I know my way about.' He struck a match and the little light gave her an idea of the cellar's size, or no idea. She saw a wall of shelves behind him, but no other walls. It was huge. It was like finding an underground world.

'Listen,' he said when the second match died. 'Wait until they stop hammering.' She waited, counting the blows of the hammer. Then silence, dead silence. 'Where else can you hear that, Jen?'

'It's like the world is holding its breath.'

A male voice overhead wasn't holding his. He yelled and something fell on wood above her head.

'Granny would love this place for storing her preserves. What are you going to use it for?'

'I sleep down here when I camp out. I dragged an old bed down. It's never colder than it is now, never hotter.'

She'd ventured well away from the steps, and when she turned back to where she'd thought they'd be they weren't there. He was. She touched him with an outstretched hand, but stepped back fast.

'Strike a match.'

'Sing *The Last Rose of Summer.*'

'Strike a match and stop being stupid. I'm lost.'

'Me too,' he said, and his hands found her shoulders and he kissed her, a soft, achingly sweet kiss; not a Rhett Butler and

140

Scarlett waited-for kiss, but Atlanta was burning anyway, or his underground world was burning.

Jenny pulled away from him, bumped against the shelves she hadn't been able to find, followed them with her hand to the steps and clambered too fast up to the light. She followed the sound of hammering to the kitchen, nodded again to Arthur Hogan, then got out of that house through a rear door, knowing that he was no better than Bobby bloody Vevers.

She didn't say a word on the way home, and all he said was 'Sorry'. She didn't even thank him when she got out of the car at the boundary gate, just climbed between the fence wires and ran down the track away from him.

BLOOD PRESSURE AND WEDDINGS

That kiss ended the Sunday night poker games. Vern still drove down on Saturdays. Jenny still left when she saw him coming. The days grew shorter, the mornings grew colder, the leaves turned to gold in the orchard and by April they were flying and Gertrude's rake was busy. Autumn leaves made good garden mulch.

Sissy's wedding gown travelled home from Willama on April Fool's Day. Maybe it was an omen. Amber pinned a sheet around it and over it to protect it from dust and interested eyes. With nowhere else to hang it, she used the curtain rod in the parlour.

Norman had been allowed to glimpse briefly what he'd paid for dearly. Certainly it was a pretty thing, all satin and lace. Was it worth the exorbitant price of its making? Perhaps.

Six weeks. Six short weeks and he'd walk her down the aisle and be done with fatherhood. Some managed it with success. He had failed, as he had failed at marriage. As he had failed at much.

The wedding party was to be at the Hooper house. Two women would be hired to assist Margaret and Amber with the catering. Maisy, who owned a set of wedding cake tins, had baked the wedding cake, three square tiers of varying size which would balance on columns and be decorated with sugar flowers by Margaret Hooper. Norman had heard much about the sugar flowers. Margaret Hooper apparently had a clever hand with icing sugar.

The wine had been ordered. A keg of ale would be delivered on the day. Norman had compiled his list of Duckworths and ex-Duckworths. Lorna had offered her services in the writing of the invitations. Norman supplied the stamps, the ivory envelopes and matching writing paper.

Sissy demanded he purchase a new grey suit. He'd ordered it from a city catalogue, at sale price, had ordered his usual size. It arrived, and hung on him like a shapeless sack. The company exchanged it for a size smaller, though not at the sale price. Add to that the sending of the thing backwards and forwards by mail and the suit had been no bargain.

It was written down in his account book. Every penny spent had been itemised, tallied. He'd added the cost of new spectacles ordered from the optical man who set up shop in the town hall two or three times a year. Certainly he'd needed them.

Norman's organisational skills were renowned but there is only so much that can be organised, as there is only so much that can be said about a wedding. His weeks had been filled with the saying, his every meal crammed with it. He longed for May. He wanted it done with.

Six more weeks.

Three and a half dozen sealed and stamped envelopes stood in a row on the Hoopers' hallstand. Half a dozen unused ivory envelopes waited on the writing desk. Jim hadn't completed his guest list. He hadn't been there to complete it. He'd driven his intended and her gown home from Willama, dropped his sisters off, told them he was going out to the farm to get petrol and he hadn't returned.

He'd been spending his days working on the garden, sleeping at night in the cellar, eating with the manager and his wife or with Hogan's men and sitting for long hours in the moonlight, looking over the land.

On Thursday Hogan and his crew packed up the last of their tools and left. On Friday morning the manager's wife came across the paddock to tell him his father had been on the telephone again, that he wanted Jim to call him.

Jim was working in the garden. He didn't make the call.

He worked until nightfall, ate with the manager and his wife. They were drinking tea when the telephone rang. It startled Jim.

There was something about the demanding tone that told him it was his father. He took the call.

'Bring in a drum of petrol when you come. I'll need it tomorrow,' Vern said.

'Righto, Pops.'

Maybe he needed petrol. Maybe he didn't. Jim filled a four-gallon drum and loaded it into the car; he thought about getting into the car.

Then he walked away from it. He couldn't stand the thought of going home.

Or couldn't stand the thought of marrying Sissy Morrison in six weeks' time.

He'd have to tell her it was all off. He'd have to take off, join up.

He wanted to live in this old house.

But not if Sissy was in it.

Would he want to live in it once he told her the wedding was off? Would he want to live at all once he'd told her the wedding was off?

So . . . join up?

He'd enjoyed his time in camp. There wasn't much that he was good at but he'd always been a fair shot with a rifle and, having become accustomed early to taking orders, he'd got on well.

Camp wasn't war.

He had to do it though.

The train went through at seven. He'd tell his family at dinner, tell Sissy before the train came in — just before — and buy his ticket before he spoke to her.

He couldn't. Norman sold the tickets.

He'd drive the car down to Balwyn, leave it at his uncle's place.

He had to. The alternative was fathering a batch of kids with Sissy — on Sissy.

That thought got him to his feet. He'd tell her tomorrow night.

He should have done it sooner. Shouldn't have let Norman pay for that dress. And he'd let Sissy order a pair of white satin shoes, let Margaret dream of being a bridesmaid in pink.

He had to go through with it.

And wasn't Sissy the type of girl a bloke needed to marry? She'd never had another boyfriend and wasn't likely to. He got along all right with her — most of the time. She'd been built to bear Hoopers.

He sat down again, striving to see his father's grandchildren, to see Sissy singing nightgown-clad babies to sleep.

Instead he saw her standing over a cot reciting 'Daffodils'. Saw a batch of little Sissies chanting back at her. And he was up and pacing his house. His house, since he'd been eleven or twelve.

His, but never Sissy Morrison's.

He peered at his watch. The windows had no blinds yet. Moonlight poured in, but offered insufficient light to read his watch face. He'd taken the call from his father between six thirty and seven. It must have been nine now. He had to take that petrol in.

He ran his hand over the newly papered walls, touched smooth paintwork, loving that house, wanting to live in it, wanting to work all day in the garden until he'd got it back the way it used to be.

Lighting one cigarette from the last, Jim stood looking at his garden. He couldn't see the weeds in the moonlight. He could see the paths he'd cleared, see the creek reflecting the moon.

And he had to go home.

The doors locked, he slipped the key into his pocket and started around the house to his car — but diverted, wondering what ants did on moonlit nights, if they slept or had teams to work the nightshift. Stamped his feet on clay then stood immobile looking down. Couldn't see if they were crawling over his shoes, up the legs of his trousers. Stamped his feet again, imagined showing his father's phantom grandson that bull ants' nest.

Saw Sissy's sons stamping on his ants . . .

Wedding dress or not, he couldn't marry her.

The invitations had probably been posted. Had he been staying away from town, wanting them posted, wanting the decision taken out of his hands?

Maybe he had.

He looked up at the moon, bigger tonight, roaming free up there, laughing at him because it was free and he wasn't. He had to get himself free. Somehow. Had to get himself home, too. He walked to the car.

There were few lights burning in town, no lights showing at his house as he eased the car into the backyard and parked it behind Vern's new car. It might have been later than he'd thought. He crept in through the back door, crept up the passage to see if the invitations had been posted. Saw them standing white against the dark wood of the hallstand. Fingered them to make certain they were still there.

The ball had been tossed back into his court. He went to bed to bounce it.

It bounced around in his head for hours. And the moon had followed him home to peer between his drapes. He liked a dark room, liked his root cellar bedroom. He closed his eyes against the moon, but couldn't close down his mind.

Tired, tired of thinking, tired of attempting to find a way out of the mess he'd made and knowing there was only one way out. He tossed until five, when weary from lack of sleep, he rose and crept out to the eastern verandah where he sat smoking until the back door opened. Lorna. She was at it each morning at six, rain, hail, sleet or shine, taking her thirty-minute constitutional. Around and around the verandahs she went, diverging from her straight line on each circumnavigation to avoid his sprawling legs, conversing as she passed, commenting on his early rising, and on the next turn asking after his health. He replied in monosyllables. He'd never had a lot to say to Lorna.

At seven he heard Margaret rattling pots. She enjoyed her kitchen. During the early days of the depression, Vern had paid two full-time domestics. Irene Palmer had wed, Mrs Fitz, the housekeeper, had retired to her daughter's home in Melbourne. Nelly Dobson now handled the heavy work but Margaret had taken over the kitchen.

Water splashing in the bathroom, sluicing down the pipes. Vern was up, washing his face, wetting down his hair. Back door opening, slamming. Vern taking his only exercise, the long walk

146

down the back to the old lavatory, still there, though well hidden behind trellis and passionfruit vines. Vern didn't eat where he peed and he didn't pee where he ate — and he'd resented paying for Sissy's septic system.

'Sissy's septic system,' Jim mouthed as he rose to his feet. It would make a good tongue twister. He yawned. He'd eat, then get some sleep; stay out of their way today and tonight, and before the train came in, he'd tell them. Then he'd catch the train. The decision made, he went inside for breakfast.

'Morning, Pops, Lorna,' he said. Vern sat at the head of the table, Lorna on his left. Jim took his place at the foot of the table.

Margaret served them.

'Morning, Margaret.'

'Good morning, dear.'

Poor Margaret. She wanted to be a bridesmaid in pink.

She served Vern two sausages, bacon and two fried eggs with toast. Served Lorna toast, and a small dish of marmalade. Jim ate cereal, followed it with two hard-boiled eggs.

'What time did you get in last night?' Vern said.

'Late. I got the paths clear, cut a lot of shrubbery.'

'Did you bring my petrol in?'

'It's in the car.'

'Is Hogan done?'

'They packed up on Thursday night. They did a good job of cleaning up.'

'I've paid him enough to do a good job. Did he leave his final bill with you?'

'He said he'd post it.'

A bad choice of word. He shouldn't have mentioned the post.

'We need to get the invitations in the mail on Monday,' Lorna said.

Jim tapped his boiled eggs with the handle of his knife, peeled them, cut them in half, seasoned them, added a shake of curry to each half, then with his fork he mashed the eggs onto slices of buttered toast while Lorna spoke of the ridiculous length of time a letter took to reach its destination, spoke of a Duckworth now residing in Tasmania.

'With a bit of luck they won't come,' Vern said.

'I'll need your list today,' Lorna said, and Jim bit into his own version of eggs on toast. Having been trained early not to speak with his mouth full, he could make no reply. 'Have you completed it?'

'No.'

Margaret's watery blue eyes blinking at him, Vern's red-rimmed eyes squinting at him. He needed glasses but wouldn't admit to his need.

Lorna fixed him with a gimlet eye. 'Get them done today,' she ordered. 'Six weeks is the bare minimum of notice one can give.'

A lump of toast caught in his throat. Jim swallowed. He picked up his teacup, emptied it. Considered filling his mouth again to delay the inevitable.

But it *was* inevitable.

'I'm calling it off,' he said.

Margaret's cup stilled halfway to her lips, as did Lorna's wrist, bent in preparation to swipe marmalade, as did Vern's loaded fork. Jim had risen from his chair and was almost to the door.

'Sit down and finish your breakfast,' Vern said.

'I'm finished, Pops.'

'You don't come out with something like that and walk away from me, boy!'

'I'm not marrying her, Pops. There's nothing else to say.'

'Sit down, I said.'

Jim continued to the door. 'Sitting down won't change anything. It's off. I'll tell her tonight.'

'You never had any intention of marrying her. You used that girl to get me to spend a bloody fortune on doing up that house!'

'I'll pay for it out of Mum's money.' He was at the door. 'I'll write to the solicitor and get him to release some of it early.'

Lorna had spread her marmalade. She bit. Margaret, the never-to-be bridesmaid in pink, wept.

'You'll get back to this table and sit down when I tell you to sit down.'

'I'm well over twenty-one, Pops — and you may as well know I'm joining up, too.'

That got Vern to his feet, got him spitting brimfire and sausage.

Something silenced him mid-roar. He made a grab for the table and, mouth still open, crashed to the floor, taking the table-cloth with him.

Lorna, never one to show her feelings, gasped, inhaled a crumb of toast and was paralysed by a paroxysm of coughing. Margaret screamed, and ran bawling out to the street. Jim came back.

Horrie Bull and Mick Boyle helped load Vern into the back seat of the Ford. He was unconscious but breathing. Lorna rode to the hospital at his side, and for once Margaret travelled in the front passenger seat. They made the trip in record time.

The young doctor diagnosed a stroke. 'At his age, it's unlikely he'll regain consciousness,' he said.

They left Vern in a narrow bed, in a ward filled with old and dying men. His daughters kissed his brow. Jim shook his lifeless hand.

'Your gross stupidity caused this,' Lorna accused.

Jim knew he'd caused it.

They spent the morning in Willama and, before leaving for home, returned to the hospital. There was no change in Vern's condition.

The news of Vern Hooper's collapse swept through Woody Creek like a firestorm with a hot north wind behind it sweeps through a gum forest. The news hit Norman's station at one. He carried it home with him at six where it caused a secondary storm.

'I'm not delaying the wedding again,' Sissy said.

'It's six weeks away. There'll be no need to delay it,' Amber said.

'Some hang on in a vegetative state for months,' Norman said. He'd been hanging on in a near vegetative state for most of his married life. He was not yet sixty and looked seventy-five.

'I'm not delaying the wedding, and that's final,' Sissy said. She'd spent six years in the planning of it, and nothing, no one, was going to interfere with her wedding day.

By eight, Sissy was looking on the bright side. It could alter everything if Vern Hooper died. Jim wouldn't leave two unmarried sisters living alone in town. She wouldn't have to live on a fly-riddled farm. She'd throw huge parties out there though, and invite everyone — and make them green with envy.

There was no bright side to look on at the Hooper house. Vern's offspring went to their beds late and rose early. Lorna called the hospital at seven to hear that Vern was very low. By nine they were on the road to spend their morning at his deathbed.

'I'm sorry, Pops,' Jim said.

'You've been courting Cecelia for years, dear. You've got the wedding jitters, that's all,' Margaret said. 'Everyone gets the wedding jitters.'

'I'm sorry, Pops,' Jim repeated.

THE WORM TURNS

'I'm sorry,' Jim said, ten, twenty times a day. Guilt and Margaret had near convinced him that he was indeed suffering from wedding jitters. Guilt and Margaret may have been enough to get him to the altar, had Sissy not called by on the third afternoon to enquire after Vern's health, had Margaret not invited her in.

He sat beside his fiancée, Margaret's eyes never leaving him, Lorna ready to override him should he attempt to open his mouth. During the two hours Sissy remained, he managed half a dozen words, most of them beginning with S.

'Sorry,' he said when he spilled tea on the table. 'Sorry, Sis,' he said when Lorna spoke of delaying the wedding.

He was sorry he'd caused his father's stroke, more sorry when he escaped the women at four and called the hospital. His father was sinking, the nurse said. Jim didn't want his father to die.

All his fault. And maybe he *had* given Sissy that ring so his father would agree to renovate the old house. He no longer knew why he'd given it to her.

He took his seat again, drank the tea Margaret had poured in his absence, and sat looking at the three women surrounding him.

Knew how a worm must feel when surrounded by squawking crows. Hemmed in by them. No chance of escape. They had him corralled, Lorna on his right, Sissy on his left, Margaret opposite, her cream sponge between them. He watched Sissy bite, the cream squirt, adhere to Sissy's top lip. There was something wrong with her bite, or in the way she bit. Too much chin maybe, too much power in her jaw. Always cream on her top lip. Always

151

crumbs on her skirt. No breasts to catch the crumbs — no breasts, but thighs like tree stumps. He imagined what they'd look like naked. Flinched, bumped Lorna's elbow.

'Sorry.'

Sorry too for wondering if a breastless woman could feed babies. Sorry for staring at Sissy's breasts and wondering why she didn't have any. It was all very well being built to bear babies, but they had to eat, didn't they?

He glanced at the cake crumbs fallen to Margaret's breasts. She could have fed Vern's grandkids, could have fed a litter of them. His eyes dared a glance at Lorna's tight bodice. If there were breasts behind it, they'd issue acid.

'Sorry.'

He thought of Jenny's breasts, recalled the feel of them against him when he'd kissed her. Saw his son at her breast, a curly-headed, blue-eyed, smiling cherub; heard an angel singing him to sleep.

And like the worm he was, he squirmed, spilled tea. It leaked between his legs and through to the tapestry couch.

'Sorry.'

It still might have been all right — if Sissy had left while he was in his room changing his trousers, if she'd gone while Margaret washed spilt tea from the upholstery, if he'd seen the back of her walking home alone, he might have felt pity enough, guilt enough, but she hung around for another half-hour and he couldn't look her in the face, so the worm turned, returned to his room to sit on his bed and wait for her to leave.

He walked out to the gate with her, got her to the far side of it, closed it. She hung back for a kiss; he would sooner plant one on Lorna's mouth.

He couldn't shake the memory of that other mouth. Felt the heat of it in his face now. He shouldn't have done it. Things might have worked out if he hadn't done it. He hadn't been near her since.

And he wanted to go there now. Wanted to empty his head out to someone who wouldn't accuse him — and it was the last place in the world he could go.

And his car was out of petrol.

His father's car wasn't.

Gertrude heard him coming. Fear that he'd brought bad news was etched into her face.

'He's low, Mrs Foote. That's all they'll tell me. I was wondering if you'd . . . if you'd like to take a drive down there with me.'

'When?'

'I wouldn't go putting it off too long.'

Jim stood back as she held his father's limp hand, kissed his brow, brushed that wiry hair back. He heard her tell his father that he was the only man she'd ever loved, and that he didn't need to say a word because she knew he loved her.

'If you have to go, my old darlin', then you're allowed to, though you're too damn young to be doing it,' she said. 'You've raised a fine thoughtful boy in Jim, one you can be proud of.'

Half dead or not, Jim knew his father wouldn't agree with that. He left the ward and walked outside to light a cigarette.

She was still gripping that hand when he returned, and he wished he could sit where she was sitting and grip that hand, pat his father's face and tell him he loved him — or beg his forgiveness.

From the doorway he saw her take Vern's face between her hands and kiss that dry gasping mouth — or take his last breath away.

That's what she'd done. Jim counted the seconds, knowing it was over, knowing he couldn't join up, wanting to scream, *I'll marry her Pops, just breathe!*

Then they heard Vern's great sucking inhalation, and the mumble of exhalation.

'I'm here, darlin'. I'm right here beside you. Jim is here with me. We're here.'

'I'm here, Pops,' Jim said.

And an eyelid fluttered.

'Pops?'

'Vern!'

The eye closed, but Vern's breathing seemed more regular. They stood by that bed, side by side, Gertrude crying, Jim not knowing what to do. He placed a hand on her shoulder, patted her, watching Vern's eyes, wondering if he'd imagined that flutter.

And he hadn't. The eyelid fluttered again and Vern muttered something that might have been 'Trude'.

'We're here, darlin'. We're right here beside you.'

Jim wasn't. He was down the corridor looking for a nurse.

An hour later, they left Vern awake and in the care of his nurses and one of the doctors. Jim drove in silence, knowing that tonight he'd witnessed the power of love, and knowing that he wanted some of the same for himself.

It was nearly four in the morning when he got home and, too wound up to sleep, he woke Lorna to tell her the news. They left Margaret sleeping and created havoc in her kitchen in the making of tea and toast.

The following afternoon they visited briefly with their father; that brief visit was enough to know the stroke hadn't affected his mind. He'd suffered some paralysis of the right side, the doctor explained. Vern's right eyelid drooped, his right hand was weak, he spoke from one side of his mouth, his speech was garbled, he didn't look like Vern Hooper, didn't sound like him, though he still thought he was in control.

He told Jim to stop wasting petrol, repeating his command a few times before it was understood.

'Righto, Pops,' Jim said.

He remembered the wedding — or chose not to remember it had been called off the morning he'd had his stroke. He didn't want them to go putting anything off because of him. He'd be up and about in a week or two.

'Righto, Pops.'

Margaret wept at his garbled words. They shooed her out to the corridor. Lorna and Jim stood on either side of Vern's bed,

154

deciphering what he said, guessing at much, and knowing by the look in that one open eye when they guessed right.

'Trude,' he said. He didn't want them wasting petrol but when next they did, he wanted them to bring Gertrude with them.

'She was with you when you woke up, Pops.'

Vern's eye told him he knew that. 'Tired,' he said, or tired of them leaning over him.

They took the hint. Margaret dripped tears when she kissed him. Lorna stooped a little. Perhaps she sniffed his wiry hair. Jim shook his good hand, squeezed it, wished he had the guts to kiss him. He didn't.

He unloaded his sisters out front of the house and drove on down to Gertrude's. She made him a cup of tea while he relayed every word spoken by Vern. He watched the toddlers being fed a mush of egg and breadcrumbs, and he drank more tea, ate bread and cheese, his eyes never once meeting Jenny's.

He watched her wash the kids' faces and hands, watched her bundle them into matching flannelette nightgowns, and still his eyes avoided her face — until the kids were down for the night.

'I don't suppose you'd like to take a quick run out to the house, Jen, just to see what they've done . . . now that it's done.'

'You know I would,' she said.

The sun had put itself to bed behind tall trees when he unlocked his fine front door and turned on a light switch. Not too much light. The old house was not yet accustomed to the glare of electricity. He walked her through the renovated hall to his kitchen, where she stood in awe before his modern wood stove. He took her to his bathroom. It was of an older world, a beautiful world — and it made Jenny's tin tub in the corner of a spider-riddled shed look like a ridiculous joke. She was visualising Sissy bathing in the shiny white bath when Jim told her the wedding was off.

'I'm going to Melbourne tomorrow to join up, Jen.'

'You said an hour ago that your father is half crippled.'

'Crippled or not, he's too strong for me.' And he turned off the light and walked away from her.

'It will kill him, Jim.'

'It won't,' he said. She followed him to the kitchen, and when that light died, she followed to the cellar trapdoor where she watched his length disappear into a black hole. 'If I don't go while he's stuck in hospital bed, he'll come home and I'll end up married.'

'If you're going to talk, come up here and talk. I can't hear you.'

'Come down. I want to hear what your singing sounds like down here before I go.'

'You're not joining up, you drongo — and it would sound the same as you sound. Swallowed by dirt.'

'It only sounds swallowed because you're up there.'

'We have to go, Jim. It's late.'

'One song, then I'll take you home. "The Last Rose of Summer",' he said.

'You don't have to join the army just because you don't want to get married. Granny said that an only son with a sick father and a farm to run wouldn't even be taken by the army.'

'Life won't be worth living here.'

'What did she say when you told her?'

'I haven't told her.'

'You won't, either.'

'I have to. And while he's in hospital. You don't know him, Jen.'

'I know him. And I can hardly hear you.'

'Come down then. And you only think you know him. He's lying on his back in that bed, wearing an old man's ragged nightshirt. He can't sit up, his face looks lopsided, one side of his mouth doesn't move properly when he talks and he dribbles like a kid. But he tells me to stop wasting petrol. Righto, Pops, I say. He tells me to get my sisters home. Righto, Pops, I say. He tells me not to put the wedding off. Righto, Pops, I say.'

'So, stop saying righto!'

'I tried to and he had a stroke.'

She climbed down, feeling the wall for a light switch. Her hand couldn't find one. She could hear his car keys jingling — until they stopped jingling.

Pure silence then, the hearing of your own breathing silence, hearing the whisper of his arm moving against the fabric of his shirt, the sigh of his intake of air.

'I can't stop thinking about your father paying out a fortune for her dress. I can't face him. Or her. I'm thinking about writing to her, posting it.'

'That's the coward's way,' Jenny said.

'That's me.'

'Then it's not much use joining the army, is it? Where's the light switch?'

'I didn't want lights in here.'

She stood at the bottom of the steps, looking up at a square of grey light, the only light. And it was fading. She clung to the railing and watched the darkness swallow the second to top step.

'In a minute I'm going to see the instant when day turns into night,' she said. 'When I was a kid I used to wonder if anyone ever saw it.' He made no reply and she stood, trying not to blink as the top step was sucked into that darkening square of grey.

'Come down to Granny's and talk about it. We have to go, Jim.'

'You haven't sung yet.'

'We told Granny we wouldn't be long.'

'That sounds so good.'

'What sounds so good?'

'We,' he said. 'You and me. Jen and Jim.'

She shouldn't be down here in the dark with him. She climbed two steps back to the light.

'Run away to Queensland with me, Jen.'

Like Georgie's howl in the dark, his voice moved something deep inside her. All Georgie needed when she howled at night was Jenny's voice, the touch of her hand. All he wanted was to hear her sing. She could give him that much.

She sang 'The Last Rose of Summer'. Sang it through, from beginning to end, and her voice sounded strange, sounded as if it was coming from someone else. She wasn't aware he'd moved until the song ended.

'Remember when we found the picture of the banana palm, when we were going to live on bananas and sugar cane?'

'You remember too much,' she said. She didn't like the sound of her voice. Had to get out of here. She was halfway up the steps when he took her arm.

'Don't you dare touch me, Jim.'

'We were going to sit in the middle of a cane field and eat our way out. Remember? We were going to pick our own bunch of bananas.'

She pulled her arm free, but his other arm was at her waist.

'I can't help myself, Jen,' he said. 'I love you.'

It was a Scarlett and Rhett kiss. She'd been aching for it. It was a blood-whooshing, drowning-in-honey kiss and she didn't want him to stop, didn't want him to ever stop. He did, but he didn't release her, he held her hard against him.

'I knew I loved you when I brought you down here the last time. I knew it years ago,' he said.

Kissing was easier than words. She stood, drowning in feelings she didn't understand. Should have pushed him away and continued on up the steps, but there was nowhere else she wanted to be, no place in the world better than standing on those cellar steps, his huge hand cupping her head so he could find her mouth, cupping it as gently as he'd once cupped a butterfly.

'I knew it the night of the talent quest,' he said. 'I'd never seen anything as beautiful in my life as you standing on that stage with the lights shining on your hair. When you had to sit beside me on the way home, I couldn't breathe for imagining you grown up, and one day doing this.'

People can talk too much. She hadn't been allowed to grow up, or not into anyone decent enough for him. She pulled away, knowing she was going to bawl and she started up the steps too fast. Her bones, only pulsating honey, were not obedient to her brain's commands and the steps were steep; her worn shoe sole slipped and she hammered her knee into the edge of the top step. The shock of pain too soon after the loss of his arms was reason enough to cry, and if it wasn't, then not being allowed to grow up into someone who might have been fit to live in his arms, to live in these rooms with him was more than a good enough reason.

158

And he was holding her again, his giant gentle hand wiping her tears, his mouth finding her bawling mouth.

She clung to him, because she wanted to, and her mouth clung to his mouth, and he took the pain out of her, on the steps, and they ate from each other's mouths, drank, breathed each other. And why shouldn't she feel something beautiful for once in her life? And why pretend she was decent when she wasn't? And why shouldn't she let his beautiful hands wash her clean?

She could have stopped him when he carried her down those steps to his camping-out bed, but it was far too late by then. He was God reaching down from heaven and offering back her every lost dream.

And when it happened, it wasn't a taking of her. It was a joining, a joining of butterflies. Like two perfect butterflies, mating in the sky, flying, flying higher and higher and higher . . .

MISS HAVISHAM

April moving on, King George blushing red on the right-hand corners of three and a half dozen fine-quality ivory envelopes — a battalion of King George heads, standing at attention, awaiting their posting.

Margaret glanced at them each time she walked by the hallstand, occasionally straightened them. Sissy counted them when she called in to enquire after Vern's health and Jim's whereabouts, to ask when next they'd be driving down to Willama. She had to pick up her white satin shoes.

Vern's health was delicate, though improving, Margaret said. Jim was . . . occupied. With his father incapacitated, there was, of course, much for him to do. He had not been himself at all since Father's stroke, she said.

To Lorna, the collection of Sissy's satin shoes was not a priority. The steaming opening of forty-two envelopes, the altering of forty-two dates, may well be.

'Send him around to see me when he comes home,' Sissy said. When. If.

'He has to keep his eye on every teaspoon full of petrol he uses, dear,' Margaret said.

By the end of the third week in April, Vern felt sufficiently improved to demand his own night attire and slippers. That was the day Jim came home from the farm. He didn't turn off the motor, didn't drive in. He beeped the horn.

Lorna didn't appreciate the beep, but with alacrity she claimed the front passenger seat. Margaret sat in the rear, with Vern's case, both sisters sitting in silence as Jim drove towards North Street. A right-hand turn would signal that all was well, that his fiancée would be travelling with them to collect her wedding shoes. A left-hand turn would suggest that all was still not well.

He did neither. He parked the car in front of the hotel.

For years Lorna had crossed the road to avoid walking beneath the hotel verandah.

'Have you taken leave of your senses, boy?' she said.

'Probably,' Jim said. He left them sitting and loped across to the station to give Norman an envelope, which the stationmaster placed in his breast pocket.

The envelope remained in Norman's pocket until six that evening, until he was seated at the kitchen table, his evening meal set before him. Lettuce, beetroot, slim slices of corned beef, a concoction of apple, onion and raw cabbage . . . Amber was keeping an eye on her daughter's waistline. She, as much as he, wanted that wedding.

He'd buttered bread, two slices, before Sissy mentioned the Hoopers, mentioned that when she'd called in this afternoon, Nelly Dobson told her they'd taken some clothing down to their father.

Norman glanced at her, and reached into his breast pocket.

'From Jim,' he said, passing the envelope across the table. 'It appears that his father is continuing to improve.'

'They knew I had to pick up my shoes.'

'Family only at the hospital, no doubt.'

'I'm as good as family,' Sissy said.

She used her butter-smeared knife on the envelope, to protect manicured fingernails. She removed a sheet of paper. There was not a lot written on it.

Dear Sis,
There is no easy way to do this so I'm taking the coward's way out. You've probably noticed things haven't been right for a time. I'm sorry I let it go so far.

161

I'm going to Melbourne to join up. It seems to be the right thing to do at the moment. Maybe it's the cowardly thing to do, too.

Please pass on my apologies to your father. I know he spent a fortune on the dress and the other preparations. Keep the ring if you want it. If not, Pop might like to have it back. He bought it for my mother out of his Melbourne Cup winnings.

There's nothing else I can say except I am truly sorry.
All the best for the future,
Jim

Reading comprehension had never been Sissy's forte. She scanned those few words a second time, then looked at her ring. With all the money the Hoopers had, he'd given her a secondhand ring?

She had the Duckworth eyes, small muddy-green puddles, deep set. They turned to Amber, to Norman. Amber reached for the letter. She read it while Norman masticated on raw cabbage. Sissy, looking from one to the other, saw Jim's note fly, land on Norman's plate.

Beetroot juice seeping through — purple blood staining an ineffective bandage. Norman watched the seepage as he swallowed raw cabbage. He put his cutlery down, exchanged his everyday glasses for reading glasses, removed the letter from his meal and read around and through the beetroot haemorrhage.

And it could not be so! His chair legs shrieking on polished linoleum. 'He is . . . joining up?'

'He doesn't have to put the wedding off for that!' Sissy howled.

He was not 'putting it off', as in delaying it. Norman offered the haemorrhage, and when it was not taken, he returned it to his meal, not wishing its stain to be transferred to the embroidered tablecloth.

'When did he give it to you?' his wife, the whore, said.

It was a hot day in hell before she addressed a word to him. In the doorway, he turned to her, his ragged jowls lifting. For a moment he had a chin. Then it disappeared, settling back into familiar folds, and Norman continued into the passage, out to the verandah. He had been remiss in not delivering the note sooner. Jim had come by the station at ten past two.

Wire door groaning open, Sissy screaming. Norman hurried

down the verandah, through his squealing gate and back to the sanctity, the sanctuary of his station, back to his only self-worth, where he poured a little more self-worth into a glass, a bare inch of gin. The glass was wide. He added an inch of water. Gulped down a mouthful, did his best to stifle the resulting burp. Raw cabbage never settled well in his stomach.

The train was due at seven. It arrived at seven ten and was on its way by seven thirty-two, when he poured another inch of gin, another inch of water into his glass. The station lights turned off, he sat on in the dark, sipping, smoking, listening.

Voices carried by night. His daughter's had always carried more than most.

The contents of his bottle was somewhat depleted before the last light went off at the house. He returned the bottle to his ice-box and walked the short distance home to his junk room.

Amber informed Maisy that the wedding had been delayed. Maisy told her daughters. They told the town. Few were interested, less were surprised, not with Vern stuck in hospital, and from all accounts half crippled.

Jim was not missed; the cricket season was over and he didn't play football. He'd spent little time in town since Hogan had started work on Monk's house. Few noticed he wasn't about — apart from Nelly Dobson, Vern's house cleaner. Jim's bed was never slept in, which in itself wasn't unusual, but with the two cars at home, it was. She told her brother and sister-in-law that Jim had taken off somewhere, but the Dobsons were known for their tight lips. They kept the news to themselves.

'Is that wedding on or off?' a customer asked Charlie White.

'She's still wearing his ring,' Charlie reported.

'Someone told me he'd joined up,' Hilda, Charlie's daughter, said.

Few secrets remain secret in small country towns. Neighbours look over fences, wave to cars as they go by. Elaine Fulton worked behind the counter at the post office. She knew who received bills, knew if they were paid or not.

She was sorting mail into pigeonholes when she noticed two matching letters, one addressed to Mr Vern Hooper, the other addressed to Miss Jennifer Morrison. Same envelopes, same army postmark, same handwriting.

There were ten Fultons and a daughter-in-law sharing the house next door to Charlie's, and by nightfall every last one of them knew about those letters — as did Hilda.

'What's he doing writing to Jenny Morrison, Dad?'

Another letter arrived for Miss Jennifer Morrison, and no one had ever written to her — or not since Elaine had been working at the post office.

'Has anything come for Sissy?'

'Only from that big shoe shop in Willama.'

Jim's divergences down the forest road had to a large degree gone unnoticed. Jenny's first visit to Monk's house hadn't; Arthur Hogan had seen her. Arthur Hogan, wed to one of Maisy's middle daughters, heard via Jessie, who had heard via Peggy Fulton, that Jim was writing to Jenny Morrison.

'He brought her out to Monk's house one night to show her over it,' Arthur said.

Within days everyone in Woody Creek knew that Jim had taken Jenny out to Monk's house near nightfall.

Lorna and Margaret could have set the rumour-mongers straight on the day Jim said his goodbyes in Willama.

He'd parked the car out front of the hospital, its nose pointing towards home, and he'd handed Lorna the keys.

'Stick to the left-hand side of the road and don't try to pass anything unless you can see a mile ahead,' he'd said. 'I'm joining up.' Then he'd given a sealed envelope to Margaret. 'Give that to Pops when he's well enough to handle it.'

And he'd gone. Left Margaret bawling. Left Lorna feeling the weight, feeling the power of the car keys on her palm. Left two magpies warbling in a palm tree. Left his father waiting an hour longer for his night attire.

Hospital visiting hours were from two to four. Lorna

delivered the case with three minutes to spare. She parried a question or two, lied about Jim being out at the farm, lied about having ridden down with the garage mechanic, then got out of the place.

Some years ago, the Hooper sisters had been given licences to drive. Neither was capable of doing it outside the farm gates. Between them they'd got the car started, then with Margaret squealing, Lorna elbowing her silent and a truck's fast application of brakes, they'd got that car out of town. The bridge presented a problem, or its narrow section did. They left a little green paint on one railing, but once on the open road, Lorna's confidence had grown. Her attempt to drive in through Vern's narrow gateway led to more scraping of the paintwork, but she'd braked, and that's where the car remained — for two weeks.

They'd hustled Nelly Dobson from the kitchen, closed the door on her, and with the help of the kettle's steaming spout opened Jim's letter. Its contents sent Lorna to bed with palpitations. Margaret, too distraught to lie still, took three aspros with a glass of sherry. She'd slept, her head on her folded arms, at the kitchen table, with the letter.

It remained unsealed for ten days, was read daily for ten days, was no longer pristine when sealed once more into its envelope — on the morning Vern was released from hospital.

He'd been gone for a month. His arrival home was viewed by many from behind lace curtains, from behind shrubbery, by shoppers who chose that moment to walk up for bread.

'It took him five minutes to drag himself out of the car,' they reported on street corners, over side fences. 'They got a crutch in beneath his arm, and he hobbled to the verandah like a man of ninety.'

'He doesn't look like Vern Hooper. He used to take those verandah steps two at a time. He damn near fell in trying to get up to the verandah.'

'Did you see his useless pair of daughters, standing around letting him struggle?'

A bad, bad day that one. Lorna was exhausted. The car had refused to start until Margaret fetched the garage man who had told them the petrol tank was dry. The big Ford, parked for ten days, nose in, backside out on the street, had tempted a petrol thief. The garage man sold them petrol enough to get to Willama and back. He'd got the car started and pointed in the right direction.

The drive to the hospital may have shattered a lesser woman than Lorna; the drive home, Vern at her side, near crushed her. He was not a good passenger.

But they'd got him home, and on her second attempt Lorna had got the car into the yard and parked it so she might circle the lawn if it became necessary to take the thing out again.

Then he'd wanted to use the toilet. They'd seen him to the indoor toilet and left a defeated man to urinate into porcelain.

'Are you all right in there, Father?'

He wasn't all right. He had one good hand and six bloody buttons to undo. He needed his son.

''ere the 'luddy ell i' 'e?'

Difficult enough to understand his speech when face to face, and near impossible with the closed door between them. It took some repetition.

'We will discuss it later,' Lorna said.

'Are you managing, Father?'

He managed. Managed to see that the porcelain he was peeing into wasn't white, and nor was his bath. There was nothing wrong with Vern's sight, not since an optician chap had come to the hospital and fitted him with a pair of glasses. There was nothing wrong with his sense of smell, either, and his bathroom smelled like a lavatory.

He emerged, his fly hanging open. He clumped on his crutch down the passage where dust mice skittered, and he asked in his inimitable way, what the bloody hell Nelly bloody Dobson had been doing with her bloody time, and where the bloody hell was their brother, and what the bloody hell were they keeping from him?

'Nelly has not been available, Father,' Margaret said.

Much had changed during Vern's month in hospital. Without him and Jim to add some balance, Nelly had got above herself.

She'd asked what Jim's car was doing half in and half out of the yard, and she hadn't believed Margaret when she'd said he was staying in Willama to be close to his father.

'If he's in Willama, what's his car doing here?' Nelly had asked — at which time, Lorna had attempted to teach her her place.

'I'm only asking out of concern,' Nelly had said.

'Your concern is the house, Miss Dobson.'

That's when Nelly told her to shove her job up her skinny old maid arse.

In May 1941, domestic servants were as scarce as hen's teeth, and anyone lucky enough to have one paid her well to stay and treated her with respect. A girl could find employment in shops, in offices, at the telephone exchange and on the land.

Margaret quite enjoyed her kitchen, but not the laundry, a rough building out back. Lorna preferred to wash her smalls in the bathroom; she could spend an hour there in washing one pair of lisle stockings while attempting to keep her talon fingernails dry. Neither sister could iron a garment, and washing a kitchen floor, cleaning a bathtub, touching a toilet — other than to sit on — and now they had been given the care of a bad-tempered invalid father.

Vern's spluttering speech unnerved them, his colour when he spluttered terrified Margaret, the spittle leaking from the corner of his sagging mouth, his swiping response when she attempted to wipe it away. She dithered around him. Lorna kept her distance.

Never, in the many years they'd known Gertrude, had they been pleased to see her or her atrocious attire at their door. At five that afternoon, when she slid from her horse, both girls were waiting to welcome her. They stood back while she kissed their father's wet mouth, uncaring of his spittle; they vacated the room when she sat at his side and buttoned his fly; they hid in the kitchen when he asked after Jim.

Gertrude told him he'd joined up.

A devious pair, Vern's daughters. They brought in Jim's sealed letter and hurried back to the kitchen to await the results.

Gertrude opened the envelope and flattened the page. Vern, his complexion livid, did his own reading. Then threw the letter in her face.

She picked up the page and moved closer to the light, squinted at the handwriting — too small for her to make out more than a few words without her glasses.

'You come in here, crawling all over a man, making a bloody fool of a man —'

'Let me read what he says,' she said, helped herself to his glasses.

Dear Pops,

I'll be in Melbourne when you open this. I'm joining up. I'm sorry I let you spend so much money on doing up the old place, but it was worth doing. I've seen the solicitor and asked him to release some of my money to pay for it, told him that I'd be living in it. He said there shouldn't be a problem.

It will do the house no good standing empty. If I were you, I'd speak to Paul Jenner and see if he's interested in share cropping Monk's section. He's a good farmer and he's struggling to keep his head above water on his land. His wife is the type who would look after the house.

There's nothing I can say in a letter that's going to make you feel any better about what I've done, other than to say that seeing Mrs Foote with you the night she brought you back from the dead convinced me that I want a lot more out of life than Sissy Morrison.

This war is going to change everything. I hope it changes a few of your attitudes. I know I shouldn't be writing the following, but you've got to know sometime and while I'm away it could be the best time for it to start sinking in.

You used to say once that Jenny was worth two of her sister. She's probably worth a thousand. I know that you and Margaret were fond of her when she was a kid and if things had worked out the way they should have for her, you would have been as pleased as punch if we'd ever got together. I've got to know her again these past months, and whatever happened to her hasn't changed who she is.

*That's about all I'll say right now, other than I hope you
keep on improving and they let you come home soon. I'll see
you when I get some leave.*
All the best,
Jim

'You knew what was going on,' he said.

'I knew he was joining up?'

'You knew he was on with that hot-pants little slut.' His speech
wasn't clear. His consonants were lost or garbled, but one word
out of two was enough to decipher the gist of his sentence.

'They were good friends as kids. I saw nothing between them.'

'Liar.' An ugly word, made more so tonight by that twisted
mouth, by the froth of saliva dripping white to his chin.

She stepped back, stung by the word. 'Calm yourself, or you'll
have another stroke. There was nothing wrong going on between
them, Vern.' Or maybe there had been since his stroke. They'd
spent a lot of time together, though she'd been too worried about
Vern to go looking for wrong in it. 'All he says in his letter is that
he's got to know her again.'

'Liar.' He could get his tongue around that word and he was
sticking with it.

'You know me better than to call me that.'

'You knew what was going on. You encouraged it.'

'Wipe your chin. You're dribbling,' she said, placing both letter and his glasses down.

Jim had eaten a few meals with them. He'd spoken openly
about calling the wedding off. He'd mentioned going to Queensland. Jenny had gone out to the farm with him a few times, but
Gertrude had seen nothing inappropriate.

'You're reading more into his words than he's saying, Vern.
You've raised a fine decent boy in Jim —'

'Liar.'

'You know in your heart that I'm the last person in the world
who'd lie to you,' she said, and she left him to his daughters and
his dust mice.

*

169

The wedding gown, meant to turn every head in Woody Creek, hung forlorn from the parlour's curtain rod, its covering sheet removed, the satin and lace of it exposed, the long filmy veil a trap for flies. It should have been packed away, out of sight, out of mind, so Maisy said. Sissy wouldn't hear of it.

Amber was no longer entering into arguments over that frock. She spent her days evading her daughter. Spent them in her bedroom, the door locked, staring at walls, at the draped windows, at the green suit, her mother of the bride suit. She'd been counting down the days more eagerly than Norman, Sissy's wedding like a spring morning after the long winter of that hangdog, bloodhound cur.

She'd walked Monk's renovated house with Sissy and Margaret, had walked the rooms, aware that at a given day, at a certain time, she would be going home to live in that house.

She'd known about it all her life. At thirteen her father had promised to take her away to such a palace.

She'd waited for him. Looked for him for months. Looked for him for years. And as if she hadn't recognised him when he'd come back.

He'd liked them young, the bastard. They all liked them young.

Amber was too old for him by then, too old for any of them, worn down by the hangdog cur she'd wed. No spring left for her now. Dark winter looming, forever the long dark winter. Cold. Bleak. Empty. Nothing.

She couldn't stand the sight of that hangdog cur, the sound of him — or his Duckworth daughter. Couldn't stand the noise of her, the size of her, the demands of her. In the womb she'd been beautiful. In the womb she'd been Ruby Rose. For a day, a week, her Ruby Rose had suckled at the breast. They'd killed her with old Cecelia's name. Murdered her with it. There was no name on the tombstone for her beautiful Ruby Rose, but she'd died as surely as Leonora April, as surely as Clarence, and the other two.

His bitch of a mother, Cecelia, had named them; had named the tiny blue Clarence. He'd had sense enough not to breathe. He'd named the other ones. Simon — his name cut late into the tombstone. Simon Andrew. He wasn't in that hole. He was rotting on top of old Cecelia. She'd named Leonora. They'd put her in that hole — and the last one. What had he named him? Peter? Paul? Reginald?

Amber laughed, but quietly, as she walked the cage of her room, walked the L from door to bed to window, turned and walked back — six, eight, ten times. Her legs needed to walk. It was years since she'd walked further than the butcher's shop. Years since she'd been out to the cemetery. How many years? Barbara Dobson's funeral. She hadn't gone near her baby's tomb-stone that day. Other things on her mind that day. Tonight she wanted to go there to see what he'd named that last one. She lifted the curtain and peered out. Too much light yet. She'd wait until dark. She liked the dark.

They didn't hear her leave the house. She walked too fast, needing to get far away — from them, from his house. She was out of condition. Out of breath. Once she'd been strong. Once she'd been strong enough to do what had to be done. And she'd done it, too. She'd almost got him.

That lying old bastard, standing down at the creek, staring at that girl —

She walked faster. Cut across the road and through the park, catching her breath at Park Road, then continued on to the sports oval. There was no one about. Everyone went home at nightfall and left the world to her. She could take her time now as she walked across the oval to Cemetery Road.

The small gate was always open. She let herself in and, with no need for haste, wandered the dark paths, spat at old Cecelia's stone, spat in the eye of a winged angel, leaned her weight against the wing. Didn't have enough weight behind her to snap granite. Walked on, down the wrong gravel path. Turned back and took another path.

She found her dead babies and sat with them, in the dirt, her back against their stone. Sat and remembered while the lights of the town slowly went out and the slim moon rose up high to light that place of the dead. Cold earth beneath her, cold stone at her back, cold stones in her hand, one for each of them. More stones than names. She'd fix that.

One stone had a sharp enough edge. She used it to gouge at the stone, gouged and kept gouging until she'd cut her firstborn's name on the tombstone.

RUBY ROSE 26.3.1919

No one saw it, not the next day, not the next week.

Norman rarely went to the cemetery. He was a lost man, mourning the lost wedding no less than his wife — mourning the money spent on it, and his father of the bride speech, written months ago, edited several times, now never to be orated. He mourned the cost of three crates of wine, stacked one on top of the other in the corner of his junk room, though by May he was doing his best to get rid of it, the red and white, the sweet and dry. There was enough left to see him beyond the cancelled wedding date.

He ignored his wife, the whore, who was not herself, and his daughter, the toffee-crunching banshee, who was so much more than herself. He ignored and dodged them, slept at the house, helped himself to bottles of wine from the house, but otherwise kept to his station.

By mid-May he was cooking his meals at the station on a twin burner primus stove. He'd purchased an electric toaster, a china jug that boiled water in minutes — the inventiveness of mankind never failing to amaze him. He purchased a small wireless so he might listen in peace to the news broadcasts, was considering a small electric heater. The nights were cool.

On the Friday evening prior to the cancelled wedding day, he sipped red wine while his dinner, a cheese sandwich, fried and poker players gathered at the Macdonalds' house, directly opposite his station.

He had attended those gatherings for a time, had been a part of that card-slapping raucous male company — for a time. He sipped red wine and sighed for the loss of laughter and fine brandy, for the cheese sandwich suppers eaten in his kitchen with his golden child — now tarnished gold.

He ate his sandwich when he deemed it ready; he poured more wine into his mug. It was not a pleasant wine, and though his eyes watered for good brandy, he took his punishment like a man.

'How long since I have held a card, hazarded a silver coin on the turn of a card?' he asked the night, then answered his own question, 'Since the golden child lost her glitter. How long since I have shared laughter? Since the golden child lost her glitter.'

Only a madman talks to himself. He attempted a laugh. Only a madman laughs alone. He emptied his mug and poured more.

Was there laughter before the golden child's coming? Very little. His mother had been in residence. A few rare moments of laughter, a few stolen moments of pleasure.

He sighed, looked towards his house, drank.

He had not expected his wife, the whore, to remain in that house once Cecelia was wed. That girl could cut bread, spread jam, make toffee. Her mother would have gone with her, to cook, to clean. Knowing this, he had paid willingly, each cheque signed a down payment on freedom, a down payment on two wide beds, a kitchen stove to offer warmth, and perhaps a hand of poker on Friday nights.

Laughter rose from across the road and he poured more wine.

By nine forty-five, his bottle empty, the last light at his house turned off, his narrow bed called to him. He rose unsteadily, placed his empty bottle beneath the platform with others of its ilk, and made his careful way along the path he had worn between the station and his side gate.

His bed was not as he had left it. Pillows flung, mattress on the floor, blankets and sheets strewn — and not for the first time. He heaved the ticking mattress back to a hump on the bed, collected the sheets and the blankets, knowing that the chore of bed-making was beyond him tonight. His eye settled on the crates of wine. More red than white remained. Tonight he had attempted to create a balance and been left with the metallic taste of that last bottle on his tongue. He reached for a bottle of white.

A corkscrew was on the windowsill, hidden by the curtain. He'd become quite the expert at cork removal. He got this one out intact, tasted the wine from the bottle. Sweet and fruity. Picked up his pillow from the tumble of bedding, dragged a blanket free, turned off his light before opening the door, then felt his way along the passage wall to the parlour. The couch made a serviceable bed.

Bottle in hand, he attempted to undo a shoelace. Difficult to do with one hand, in the dark, and why bother. There would be another train in the morning. Always another train. Always a reason to get out of bed.

He sipped from the bottle, toasted the bridal gown, mouthed his wedding speech, all three pages of it, sipped and mentally edited that final page.

At some stage of the night he must have placed that bottle on the floor and laid his head down. At some stage of the night his thoughts of the lost wedding turned to dreams, a confusion of wine-soaked dreams. At some stage of the early morning, his dreams took him back to his own wedding, to his own wedding night — more satisfying in dream than in reality. He smiled as he drew the satin sheet over his pretty bride's naked form, the dream so real he could feel the slip of satin between his fingers.

His eyes sprang open.

The glaring white light of morning is a hard light when the sun is aiming its beams directly in through a glass window to dance on a white satin wedding gown.

He flung it from him, and with barely focused eyes followed its flight as he attempted to rise, only to be felled by opposing teams of drummers fighting for supremacy inside his skull. He clutched his head, rolled his feet on the floor, onto white satin. The consequent untangling of his shoe upset his forgotten wine bottle, which spilled its contents —

Too fast he reached to retrieve the bottle and his head bounced from his shoulder to the ceiling. Sat, swaying, headless until it landed, until he had eyes to see, to place the bottle onto the small table. Thankfully, he had selected a white wine.

He sat a moment, staring at the mound of white on the floor, willing it to rise up and hang itself. It did not, and when he again attempted to rise, his head exploded. He got his feet beneath him, and with one hand lending support on the arm of the couch, he stood. Listened. Not a sound.

With great care he stooped, gathered in that glaring white, shook it, and felt the fine rain of wine on his face. Perhaps better eyes than his may have seen from whence the wine-rain had issued. He saw no stain and chose not to don his spectacles — not that he knew where they were.

The hanger remained hooked over the curtain rod. Drummers battling, he raised his chin to study it. Only to study. To hang the dress would require him to mount the couch. Norman was a man who knew his limitations, so he stood, feet planted, while the hundred drummers in his head were felled by one master drummer belting out a solo rhythm on the base of his skull. His mother had dropped dead of a possible stroke. He hoped his would be fast and complete. When it was not immediate, he rolled the gown into a ball and carried it with him to his junk room where he hid it in the carton of hand-me-downs he saved for . . . for a rainy day.

His spectacles were on the small table beside his bed. He settled them onto his nose and surveyed the chaos of his bed. He would keep his door locked in future. Slowly then, each step a considered thing, he returned to his station to boil water, to drink black tea and swallow aspirin.

The train went through at ten, by which time his head was again perched, if precariously, on his shoulders, though his stomach was threatening to leave home. A methodical man, Norman, he saw the train on its way before running to the tin shed station lavatory, where his night of dissipation exploded into the pan.

At ten twenty-five the banshee came wailing across the railway yard for her gown. Norman ushered her home. The key to his room was in his pocket. He unlocked his door, gave up the crushed gown, and while the banshee screamed at him, cursed him, he reassembled his bedding, made up a neat enough bed, locked his door and placed the key in his pocket once more.

His stomach craving a dose of liver salts, he braved the kitchen. No sign of the whore, not in two days. He hoped she had gone. His potion mixed at the sink, he drank it while his daughter stood bawling into her wedding gown.

'Miss Havisham!' he said. 'The name of that book . . . It momentarily escapes my mind.'

Cecelia had not progressed beyond the fourth grade reader. The volume of her bellow increased.

And his wife, the whore, had not gone. She came into the kitchen, colourless, her straw hair uncombed, her dead eyes accusing him as she took charge of the crumpled gown.

'It is past time that the thing was put away, Mrs Morrison,' he said.

'If you were half a man you'd sue that mongrel for breach of promise!' the whore snarled.

'If I were half a man, I would not be here to sue him, Mrs Morrison.'

'Ugly, useless —'

'And yet you remain to torment me,' he said, and returned to his station.

A BAD HABIT OF KILLING

A confusing year, 1941. Australia was at war, but untouched by war, apart from a couple of German raiders laying down a couple of mines. Fashions changed as they are apt to, given any opportunity. Women took a liking to olive green, navy blue, dark brown and khaki.

A lot of boys came home on leave in khaki. One of the Dobson boys wore air force blue. Bobby Vevers was in the navy. Army trucks travelled through town from time to time on their way to someplace else. More planes flew over and kids learned to recognise their various shapes.

There were three fast weddings, and a farmer's daughter who should have had a fast wedding before her fiancée was killed in an army accident, though no one called her a slut when her babe was born out of wedlock.

Petrol was rationed, but there weren't enough cars in Woody Creek for that to be a major concern. A few horses due for retirement were back in harness. There was more money about. Folk paid their rent on time, and a few paid Charlie what they'd owed him for years.

Yes, there was a war. Yes, in distant Europe young men were dying, cities were being bombed, but the mill saws kept on screaming, the price of wool went up, crops still grew, chooks still laid eggs.

In August, Bob Menzies retired from the country's top job and Arthur Fadden took it on until October, when John Curtin was voted in. He'd been anti-conscription during the last war, and vocal about it. There were those who didn't believe Curtin was the right man to lead a country through wartime, and others who knew they'd finally picked the right man for the job.

Vern didn't care who was leading the country. For the first time in half a century, he hadn't cast his vote. He was a dead man walking, though not often seen walking. Petrol rationing no longer concerned him. Two cars stood idle in his backyard, grass growing beneath them, weeds grabbing at their axles.

He'd always worn a lopsided smile. He no longer smiled but his mouth was permanently lopsided, the lower corner inclined to drool. One eyelid drooped in sympathy with his mouth. He'd taken to wearing glasses to disguise his drooping eyelid — and the buggers allowed him to see more than he wanted to see.

He could thank his lucky stars the damage hadn't been worse, the young doctor said. Vern told him to go to hell, but the doctor kept coming back.

'Get outside. Get some sun on your skin,' the doctor said.

Vern asked him if he'd ever been brained with a walking stick.

He could get around with his walking stick, but refused to be seen hobbling around with the bloody thing. He rarely left the house. He never left his yard. Spent his days sitting, listening to the wireless, measured his days with meals: breakfast, morning tea, afternoon tea, dinner, then supper. What else was a man expected to do?

There were moments when he wished he hadn't called Gertrude a liar, more moments when he wished he'd called her worse.

And he had trouble at the mill. Lorna's fault. No man would stand for a woman telling him what to do. Tom Palmer, Vern's foreman, had taken it for longer than most. In September, George Macdonald poached him along with two of Vern's best men. Finding a good man to replace Tom wasn't easy. Finding manpower enough to run the country was becoming a major problem by the latter months of '41.

The young doctor drove up in September. He told Vern he was well enough to drive, that the only way to get over being a cripple was to stop thinking of himself as a cripple. He told him about one old chap at the hospital whose only means of communication was poking his tongue out for yes and keeping it in for no.

'Do him a favour and put him down,' Vern said.

'Keep putting on weight, Mr Hooper, and I won't need to put you down. You'll do it yourself. I'll see you in October. In Willama.'

And how the bloody hell was a man supposed to drive with one hand as weak as a kitten's paw, with one leg that refused to do what he told it to do? He'd end up killing himself or some other bugger.

Lorna offered to drive him. He'd sworn the day she'd driven him home from the hospital that he'd never repeat that experience.

There were a few modern thinkers around in 1941. They spoke of the country needing to rely on her women to fill the gaps left behind by the fighting men. There were others who knew that a woman trained to do a man's job in wartime wouldn't return happily to her aprons once the war was over.

Vern had never been a modern thinker; his stroke hadn't altered his outlook. Fair enough, a man couldn't live well without a woman, but her place was in his bed or in his kitchen, not behind the steering wheel of his bloody car. If not for Jim, those girls would never have been allowed anywhere near a steering wheel.

For a week before he was to see his doctor, he considered his options. He had no control over Lorna. He'd made the mistake of educating that girl. Margaret he'd attempted to educate without success. He could control her. The night before his appointment, he told her she'd be driving him down to his appointment. Margaret never argued.

Lorna argued. She argued until her sister slid in behind the steering wheel, then she stopped arguing, took off her hat and strode back to the house.

Within a hundred yards, Vern knew why. That dithering fool of a girl made the left-hand turn into North Street too fast, as the bank manager's dog took his diagonal meander across the road. She braked, missed the dog, but a kid on a bike hit the rear bumper bar and flew over the car. Margaret ran for home howling and Vern sat like a bloody crippled old fool in the passenger seat, exposed before the town — and a crowd gathering to stare at him — and the dog that caused the accident laughing at him.

179

The kid wasn't laughing. He was gravel-rashed from ear to ankle.

'Is your bike all right, lad?' Vern asked.

'What?'

Vern wasn't repeating his words. He took a quid from his wallet and offered it. The kid understood money. He pocketed it and Vern heaved himself across to the driver's seat and in behind the wheel.

He got the car home, where he told Lorna to put her bloody hat on. She drove like a maniac with a death wish, and God help man or dog who tried to get in her way, but she got him to his doctor, who had the gall to ask why his blood pressure had gone sky high.

He was sitting on the verandah on Friday when Gertrude rode by. She didn't see him, or maybe she did and ignored him. He resented the way she sat astride that horse.

He watched George Macdonald walk by twice each day, on his way to and from his mill. Bull-necked, bull-shouldered, short-legged, compact; his blood didn't need to travel far from heart to head to feet. Vern resented George's circulatory system, and his bandy gorilla legs, and his *I'm off to someplace* stride.

And Charlie White, still riding that bike like a madman, the bike looking bigger every year — or Charlie looking smaller. Vern resented Charlie's scrawny muscle-bound legs pumping those pedals, and resented more than his circulatory system; he knew where that white-headed old bugger was spending his Saturday afternoons.

Self-pity can erode the soul. Vern was eroding. He'd had it all. He'd had it all and now he had nothing. He hobbled around like a man of ninety, braces over his shoulders to stop his trousers from falling down, one daughter attempting to kill him with kindness, the other an overbearing, self-serving bugger of a woman just willing him dead. He hoped one of them would be successful before Christmas. He didn't want to see another Christmas.

He was on his western verandah on the third day of December when a kid came wobbling up to the corner on a bike too large for him; he wobbled into Vern's fence and both kid and bike disappeared from view. The rosebushes, neglected last winter, were attempting to turn into trees. Roses have thorns. Vern thought about getting up to see if the kid was all right but the effort was too great.

He heard knocking at his front door, wondered if the kid's mother had come to complain about his overgrown roses blocking the footpath. A few had. Lorna handled it. He heard her telling whoever it was to remove himself forthwith before she fetched a bucket of dishwater.

Heard Margaret, too. 'Father is not well, dear.' He'd never appreciated Margaret. He relied on her now.

'The garage man isn't home,' the kid said.

'Speak to the constable, dear,' she said.

Lenny Hall walked back to the bike, his fingernail digging at a rose thorn embedded in his forearm. Granny hadn't mentioned getting the constable; he rode a motorbike anyway, and Granny had said to get someone with a car.

Maisy would know what to do. He mounted his bike and wobbled up North Road and over the lines. Maisy's car wasn't there. He was heading for Charlie's shop when he saw Maisy turn out of Cemetery Road and pull up out front of Charlie's. He caught her as she was walking through the door.

'Granny said someone has to get Jenny to the hospital and the garage man's not there,' Lenny said.

Hilda, Charlie's daughter, busy serving Peggy Fulton, stopped serving to walk down to the end of the counter. Peggy got there first. They heard little more, other than something about Hoopers killing their mothers — which was enough to start a rumour.

'That kid is one of Harry Hall's, isn't he?' Peggy said.

'She's done it again,' Hilda said. 'That's why Jim left.'

They watched Maisy back out to the road, watched her drive away, watched the kid work at mounting the too-large bike, then with nothing more to see they returned to their respective sides of the counter.

'It could be something to do with Amber. They took her down to the hospital three days ago,' Hilda said.

'The kid said Jenny. Jim left in April, didn't he?' Fingers at work, busy fingers, counting off the months.

'It's only eight months.'

'Who knows how long it was going on before he left?'

Poor Sissy Morrison, abandoned at the altar, now abandoned by her mother; she couldn't stick her nose outside the door without someone staring at her, whispering about her, about Amber. Half the town had seen Amber taken away in the hospital ambulance.

Sissy remembered the last time her mother had been taken away. She'd stayed away for six years, the worst six years of Sissy's life. She hadn't known what had gone on that time. This time she'd seen it happening. Everyone had.

Sissy had seen her birthdate on the tombstone. Many in town had — after Amber had taken Norman's axe up to the cemetery and attacked his mother's tombstone, beheaded one angel, shattered the wing of another. Sissy hadn't known what it meant, except that her mother had gone mad. Norman paid a man to fix the angel's head back on. He'd done nothing about Amber's head.

Constable Denham had, when she lit a fire against the back wall of Gertrude's house. It hadn't burnt anyone, had barely scorched the wall, but he'd got the ambulance up to take her to Willama — and it was too embarrassing.

Poor Sissy. She'd consoled herself with toffee until she ran out of butter, then sugar. Toffee brought her out in pimples. Toffee, in combination with the time of the month, turned her face into an open weeping wound.

Poor, plain, lonely Sissy. Margaret Hooper, her only friend, hadn't been near her since Jim joined the army. No one came near her, except Norman, who didn't care. She'd tried to make him care. She'd pitched a cup of tea in his face. He'd wiped his face with a tea towel, mopped up the spill with the same tea towel, and left it on the table with everything else.

She couldn't stand living in his mess, couldn't stand him puddling around in his mess. Couldn't stand the long, lonely days when he was at the station, the longer lonely nights when he was home. She considered walking down to Blunt's crossing and lying on the railway line when the morning train came through. Charlie's crossing was closer but Blunt's was busier. She wanted everyone in town to see her being cut to shreds, to care that she'd been cut to shreds. If she'd had a dress that would do up, she might have killed herself during the week of her menstruation.

In the late afternoon of that third day of December, Maisy dropped Gertrude off, drove her car home, then walked over to the station to let Norman know where she'd been and why she'd been there. He was more interested in the whereabouts of a consignment of cigarettes and tobacco, lost between Melbourne and Woody Creek. Maisy left him to his phone calls and went across to his house to check on Sissy.

'Are you there, Sissy?' she called at the back door.

'Where else would I be?'

Maisy let herself in. Sissy, nightgown clad, was in her room, pursuing a fly that wouldn't let her sleep in peace. Maisy didn't enter the room and wondered why a fly would. The overwhelming smell of sweating humanity should have knocked it dead.

'You need to have a bath and get dressed, Sissy,' she said.

The fly had settled on the wall. Sissy swiped at it, but the fly flew.

Maisy had noticed Sissy's pimples, her weight, her nastier than usual demeanour, but with some it's difficult to see the difference between honest despondency and common run-of-the-mill bitchiness.

'What are you doing in your nightgown at this time of the day?'

'Go home if you don't like it.' Sissy had the fly trapped behind the lace curtain. She mashed it between glass and curtain and left it there.

'Open your window. Your room needs airing.'

'Stop telling me what to do.' Sissy went back to bed to bury herself beneath a mound of blankets.

'I saw your mother today.'

'As if I care.'

183

'They've got her on pills again but they don't seem to be doing her any good.'

'I don't care, I said.'

'Then it's time you started caring, at least about yourself. Your room stinks of sweat and so do you. Have a bath and get yourself cleaned up.'

'I've got nothing to wear, have I?' Sissy wailed.

A bad week, for Sissy and for Norman; the weather was bad, the trains were late, the six o'clock news was all bad.

'You need to get Sissy away somewhere, Norman.' The suggestion sounded fine in theory. Norman lowered the volume of his wireless and turned one ear to his neighbour. 'Have you got someone she could go to for a while?' Maisy asked.

Norman had many relatives, though he could not in all conscience inflict that girl on any one of them.

The news broadcaster was speaking of two newborn infants found dead in their cribs. Maisy reached to turn the volume higher.

'They lost two babies down at the hospital,' she said, but the announcer had progressed to a horrendous accident on the Molliston Road, two dead and a third fighting for her life. Maisy lowered the volume. She was at the station tonight to fight for Sissy's life.

'I've seen a lot of her moods, Norman, but nothing like this. She's never got over her wedding being called off, and she knew her mother wanted to name her Ruby Rose. It's affected her mind, Norman.'

'The weather has been conducive to ill humours,' he said. 'I believe they are forecasting a cool change tomorrow evening.'

Maisy gave up and went home.

The promised cool change reached Melbourne, but failed to make it across the Dividing Range. Then, on the eighth day of December, Japan declared war on Britain and America, and to prove they meant business attacked Pearl Harbor in Honolulu, which was home to a large US naval base. America and Britain declared war on Japan and Australia followed suit.

At nine that same evening, Norman's station telephone rang while he sat late over his wireless listening to John Curtin's speech to the nation.

It was the hospital. His wife, the whore, was being transferred to a city asylum come morning. Norman hoped they'd keep her.

'Understandably,' he said to the doctor on the line. 'Certainly. Good evening.'

That was the day the distant war became not so distant, and on 11 December, in order to increase the number of men under arms in Australia, the call-up was extended to include all single men aged eighteen to forty-five and all married men aged eighteen to thirty-five.

Norman lost track of the days in the lead-up to Christmas. There were more trains during harvest time, goods trains spilling wheat. They went through at odd hours and he sat late, waiting for them, his wireless tuned in to the world news.

Adolf Hitler assumed control of his armed forces. The first American troops arrived in Australia. Danny, his station boy, took to wearing khaki.

If not for the Christmas cards he collected daily from the post office, Norman would not have been aware that the festive season was nigh. With no time, no desire to open them, he tossed them unopened onto the hall stand, the wireless, the mantelpiece.

Had a train passed through on Christmas Day, he may have forgotten the church's celebration of Jesus's birth. There was no train on Christmas Day. He dressed himself in his new grey suit, sat in his usual pew. One or two asked after his wife, his daughter . . . his daughter in her bed when he'd left the house, still there when he returned.

Perhaps some effort on his part was required. He found an envelope, wrote a brief note echoing the sentiments expressed by the parson, and wrote a cheque for five pounds which he slipped into the envelope.

Sissy's bedroom door was closed. He knocked, slid the envelope under the door, then went to the kitchen and set about lighting the kitchen stove. Bread in the tin supplied no doubt, by Maisy, tomato supplied by his mother-in-law. No butter.

He set a fat-caked frying pan on the stove, filled the kettle, and when the grease melted in the pan he added tomato sandwiches, then again knocked on Sissy's door.

'Will you join me for a light lunch, Cecelia?'

A wood stove is long in heating. She emerged, with his envelope, before he lifted Christmas lunch from the pan.

'What did you fry them in?'

'The pan.' He glanced at her. Her hair, suffering the loss of her mother's care, hung long and greasy, witch-like. She'd clad herself in a brown print, familiar, but not in his house. 'Maisy's frock?' he said.

'The only taste she's got is in her mouth,' Sissy replied, her own mouth full.

The sandwiches oozed sausage grease, but they ate them, and he attempted to make conversation.

'The Japanese have taken control of Hong Kong,' he said.

'Who cares?'

She made and fried two more sandwiches later. They soaked up the last of the frying pan's grease.

In the late afternoon, Norman was standing at his bookcase, flipping through his small collection of novels searching for Miss Havisham, when he came upon a Bible which should not have been amid his novels; a Bible which, as far as he could recall, should not have been in his house. Surely . . . certainly he had packed it . . . into a carton on that September day when the . . .

He recalled clearly the Salvation Army couple eating lunch in his kitchen while he'd gathered together . . .

A crimson stain crept up from Norman's collar to settle in his ears, in his insignificant nose.

Then he found Miss Havisham, in *Great Expectations*. He spent the afternoon of Christmas Day visiting again with her and Pip — and was better able in his fifties to relate to that woman than he had been in his thirties. Charles Dickens had surely known such an abandoned bride.

It was during the space of days between Christmas and New Year that he noticed the changed atmosphere in his house. He

186

now lit the stove each morning before leaving for the station; a soot-covered stove, pan waiting ready on the hob. He returned one evening and found the pan washed, the hearth swept.

Maisy's hand, he presumed.

The pervasive odour of Amber's cleaning had long given way to the stench of sweating humanity — which had also faded.

The kitchen floor was swept; the table cleared.

Maisy again . . . though surely Maisy would not have opened his Christmas cards. Two late arrivals, tossed onto the hall table, had been opened. He glanced at them, glanced at the dust-free rectangles where they'd lain. Dust had left its stamp on the wireless, where he'd deposited another bunch of cards. They too had been opened.

He picked up a small card, three wise men following the star. *Best wishes to you and your family, Bessy.* He glanced at another, a large card, the head of Jesus, his halo sparkling with glitter — though not well stuck on. He took that one with him to the kitchen to prop on the northern windowsill while he unwrapped sausages.

Sissy came in. 'We need bread,' she said.

'I will see to it,' he replied, displaying his card — sent by Uncle Charles, the parson, who had always had a penchant for Jesus cards, though the glitter was . . . was perhaps more alcoholic Cousin Reginald.

'Aunt Olive has been widowed? Was I informed?'

Sissy required bread, required butter — though perhaps her face looked better for the lack of butter.

'Perhaps I was,' he said. 'In early December, I believe, around the time the Japanese were bombing Pearl Harbor.'

'The baker shuts at half past five.'

'He does indeed.' Norman glanced at the seven-day clock on the mantelpiece. It was not ticking. He took out his fob watch, his father's watch. 'Perhaps you . . .'

'I'm not going outside. I'm staying in here until I die,' she said.

He bought two loaves of bread, bought potatoes. The meal that evening resurrected memories of nights long ago, the golden child with her grandmother, a younger Cecelia sitting across the table, he working hard at conversation.

He tried tonight. 'Your Aunt Olive . . . do you recall her husband's name? For the life of me I can't. Olive and Horace perhaps. Uncle Horrie. Olive and Wilbur? No, Wilbur was Aunt Millicent's, I believe. A belated note of condolence to Olive might be in order, even at this late date.'

They ate lumpy mashed potatoes, overdone sausages, fried tomatoes.

Sissy rose to wash the dishes. To disguise his surprise he collected pen, ink, paper then sat at a cleared table to pen two pages. He apologised for his inability to attend *his dear uncle's* funeral, mentioning that his wife was again undergoing treatment in the city, mentioning that his daughter's fiancée had gone off to fight. He wrote of his appointment with a butchering dentist and of his lingering pain, wrote of the war — wrote too of his second daughter's eighteenth birthday, though he did not mention that, like Jesus's halo, she had lost her glitter.

Aunt Olive, one of the younger Duckworths, replied by return mail. She had not settled well into her widowed state, she wrote; her children, spread far and wide, were not frequent visitors. She wrote of her fear of Japanese invasion, of a bomb shelter she was having constructed in her backyard, then suggested a visit from Norman and his daughters would be most welcome at this time, and perhaps beneficial for all.

God will provide, Norman thought, eyeing the somewhat grease-stained Jesus, who was nonetheless still watching over him from the windowsill.

'Your aunt has suggested a brief holiday at Portsea . . . '

'When?'

The arrangements were made swiftly. On the eighth day of February Sissy boarded the train, a new frock on her back, two in her case and two ten-pound notes in her handbag.

Jesus — or the Duckworth clan — will provide . . .

Uncle Charles, who hadn't seen Sissy in twenty years, had no difficulty recognising her at Spencer Street Station. He saw her out to Portsea where she was welcomed with kisses and a cream sponge. Aunt Olive was known for her kitchen skills. Sissy ate well. She dare not turn on a light at night unless every blind in the house was drawn. If the Japs came to Australia, they'd come via sea, Aunt Olive warned.

A Duckworth among other Duckworths manages well enough. In all bar name, Sissy was a Duckworth. She enjoyed the drama of the approaching Japs, enjoyed the visiting relatives, the visits to relatives, and the more extensive wardrobe found for her by Aunt Olive. The Duckworth family had always passed their outgrown garments around — as they passed around difficult relatives.

The Japs didn't arrive in Portsea, but on 15 February, in a surprise attack, they took Singapore, the Gibraltar of the Far East, considered by most to be an invincible fortress, a bastion of the British Empire, and well prepared to fight off any invasion — had it come by sea.

They came down the Malay Peninsula and caught Singapore napping. More than fifteen thousand Australian troops were taken prisoner there, a Duckworth grandson among them.

'This is the gravest hour in our history,' John Curtin said. A string of islands led from Singapore down to Australia.

Then, on 19 February 1942, they came. They bombed Darwin.

The hideous efficiency of the Japanese war machine appeared to be unstoppable. They bombed Broome, a little town up the top of Western Australia. They sunk the HMAS *Yarra* off the island of Java, and a few days later thirty-five thousand Australian, American and Filipino troops surrendered.

'If something isn't done soon, we'll all be speaking Japanese,' Charlie said.

In March of '42, General Macarthur, an American, arrived to do something. He took command of the South West Pacific region in April, and set up his headquarters in Melbourne. In May, the battle of the Coral Sea halted the Japanese navy's advance.

In May, Norman again retreated to his station. Amber came home.

DOUBLE-JOINTED THUMBS

War or no war, ration coupons or no ration coupons, babies were born, couples were wed, the elderly went to their makers and the mill saws screamed on.

The noise of Macdonald's saws infiltrated the Hooper house, and on difficult days gave Margaret a headache — as did her sister. She missed her brother, missed the dances, the balls, missed Sissy Morrison. Margaret's finest hours were those she spent shopping. She took her time at the grocer's, the butcher's, she browsed at Fulton's, but Blunt's drapery, a cluttered little shop, was the highlight of her day. She could become lost in dark corners, could handle the wools, the embroidery silks, sift through the buttons.

On an afternoon in late April, she was on her way to Blunt's to buy another skein of wool for her father's cardigan when she sighted a pram, an old cane pram with tall wheels. As a child she had pushed her brother up and down the street in such a pram. It had been stored in the shed for years. She'd seen it there. Had she seen it there recently? Perhaps not.

She approached the pram, studied the springs, the wheels. Her father had donated it to the needy. Of course. He had donated much during the bad years of the depression. She could never resist a peep at the newborn. She stooped to steal that peep, and as she did, a hornet, one of those orange and black striped brutes, flew by her ear and under the pram's hood.

She had been stung by one such brute in her childhood. Reflex action saw her lift the hood to release the insect — and the fool of a thing followed it to the foot of the pram. Reflex action saw her snatch the babe from harm's way, step away and into the shop, and that dear wee mite chuckled and grasped at her nose.

'We must find out who you belong to,' she told him.

And his mother turned from the counter and seized him from Margaret's arms.

'A hornet,' Margaret explained. 'One of those nasty black and orange things. It's in the pram, dear.'

Miss Blunt came out with a rolled-up newspaper. She hunted down the hornet and the babe was placed back into the pram.

'Is that Jim's, dear?' Margaret said.

Jenny turned to her. 'He's mine.'

Margaret blushed, a deep cherry red. 'The pram. I . . . I recognise the pram, dear.'

'Oh,' Jenny said, and turned that pram for home.

'Beauty carries its own curse,' Margaret said, her eyes following the swing of black-clad hips.

'It's such a terrible, terrible pity,' Miss Blunt said.

Margaret had of course heard the gossip — this town was a hotbed of gossip — it was up to the individual as to how much she chose to believe.

This morning Margaret believed. She forgot about the skein of wool and followed the pram back to North Street. It continued over the road and on down Blunt's Road, which intersected with Hooper Street at the school end of town. Margaret followed it until it crossed over Hooper Street, then with no good reason to follow further, she stood on the corner watching until girl and pram turned left into King Street and were lost to her view.

But not if she moved quickly. She scuttled for home.

Now in her thirties, she had all but accepted her spinsterhood, her childless destiny; today she knew she was an aunt. Why else had Jim given that girl his pram? And look at the girl's reaction to her queries about the pram. In the letter Jim had written to his father the day he'd join the army, he'd as much as said . . . Of course she was an aunt, and by the look of that infant, had been an aunt for some time.

She stood with the rosebushes, neglected, overgrown, but offering good cover to those who did not wish to be seen spying.

She stood unmoving until the pram was out of sight, convinced that God had sent that hornet so she might have reason to hold her nephew. Her own sweet nephew. And when would she ever hold him again? Never — unless she took matters into her own hands.

She had done her fair share of weeping this past year. She'd wept when the Japs bombed Darwin, when ships were torpedoed and lives were lost, when her father roared. She wept when she remembered the balls she had attended with Sissy, when she thought of her gentle brother, a gun now in his hand. A weeping sort of girl, Margaret. She wept that afternoon while preparing the evening meal, wept when saucepan lids slipped through her fingers and rattled to the floor. Her father and Lorna did not venture out to the kitchen to ask why she was weeping. When one of the better dinner plates skidded from the table, no one came to help her sweep up shattered china. She wept over the broken shards. No one noticed.

They noticed she'd forgotten to put salt in the potatoes, that the peas were a little underdone, but they cleared their plates.

Margaret had no appetite. She chased green peas with her fork while Vern spoke of an offer he'd had for Monk's section of the farm. The money spent on restoring that house was a burr in his underwear. Lorna spoke of the new bank manager's dogs, a burr in her own — they barked at her each time she walked by.

Two of a kind, Vern and Lorna. They sat at opposite ends of the table, discussing the town, the war, the fools in town and out of town, while Margaret dreamed fine dreams of raising Jim's son in Monk's house, her fork chasing, catching peas, placing them individually into her mouth. And yes, they were a little underdone.

The family dormouse, Margaret. She nibbled; she ran from danger; she scuttled into corners, scratched among old papers.

Vern had a box of old papers, his own, his father's and his grandfather's marriage lines, birth certificates, land deeds. She knew that Lorna Langdon, Vern's first wife, had been seven years Vern's senior, that for near ten years their marriage had not been fruitful. She knew from the death certificate that Lorna's birth had killed her mother. It was all documented. Vern had been a widower for two years before he'd wed Rita Jones, Margaret's mother, a girl of eighteen, who had produced Margaret less than seven months after the wedding.

The knowledge that she had been conceived out of wedlock had at first shocked then excited Margaret. At one stage, when courting Arthur Hogan, she had been sorely tempted to . . . to give in to his urging. Had she, she may now have been raising her own little Arthur. Maisy's daughter had not been so moral; her firstborn arrived six months after the wedding, a white-headed, purple-eyed female. And she'd produced another since.

Margaret had three green peas corralled between neatly cut carrot and overdone chop. She invariably placed the worst cuts of meat on her own plate, the burned chops, the broken eggs. A tear escaped, blurring the burned chop, magnifying the peas. Stabbed one, carried it to her mouth, and thought of her mother, who had also served herself the worst cuts.

She'd known her for only nine years, happy years on the farm. Then her mother had died and Vern had sent both girls away to a boarding school. Barely six months later he'd wed Joanne Nicholas.

Never, never would Margaret forget the day she'd first set foot in Joanne's fine house, nor would she forget the first time her new brother had been placed in her arms. Today, she'd held his son.

To bear a child, to love and be loved by that child, was every woman's right, but in order to have that right a woman must first give herself to a man. After Arthur had been stolen away, there had not been another. The cruelty of life; a woman's content or discontent dictated by the whims of man. Life was unfair.

A tear dripped and Margaret blinked, glanced at Lorna, already tapping her talon nails on the cloth, waiting for dessert.

She ate like a horse — a horse with worms. Never an ounce of fat did she put on her bones. Margaret ate like a bird and each year her waist expanded. Wrongly born a female, Lorna never mourned for her children unborn. Tonight Margaret mourned — and she envied that Morrison girl. Three babies. Three, and what was she, seventeen, eighteen?

The tear fell to her burned chop.

No one saw it, or noticed when she rose and carried her untouched meal to the kitchen, where a steamed pudding rattled too merrily in the steamer. No one came to comfort her when the steam burned her wrist. She must control her emotions. She must focus her mind on her tasks. Her tasks — and why hers alone? She had become Vern's kitchen maid, as her mother had been his kitchen maid.

The kitchen maid served their dessert, steamed chocolate pudding and custard. She sat with them, listened to them, until both mouths were full. Hers was not, and she opened it.

'Were you aware, Father, that Jim gave his old pram to the Morrison girl?' Vern turned to her. 'I recognised it today.'

'They should be taken away from the little slut,' Lorna said.

Margaret's mouth opened, closed. She blinked, her head denying the words she was about to say, but God had a plan for her and tonight he would not allow her silence.

'The boy is Jim's, Father, and such a sweet mite.'

Vern froze. Lorna singed her sister with a glance. But a dormouse becomes good at dodging, and must take chances in order to snatch the cheese.

'I held him today, at Blunt's.'

Vern, who didn't rise easily, rose, his good hand on the table, his bad hand raised for silence.

Margaret did not fall silent. She reached for her father's hand. 'I believe he has the thumbs, Father. His hands are so like yours.'

Vern shook her off. He got out, out to his chair on the western verandah — and he forgot to take his walking stick.

'Are you attempting to give him another stroke?' Lorna said.

Margaret spooned up her chocolate pudding. 'I held him, Lorna. I held him, and he knew I was his aunt. You are an aunt. Jim has a son.'

Lorna left the table. Margaret sat on alone with the dirty plates. They'd remain on this table until she cleared them, washed them, dried, then put them away. She had help in the house on one morning a week. She did the rest, washed the linen in an electric laundering machine, sucked dust from the carpets with a vacuum cleaner. She managed.

And she'd manage that babe, too. That girl had three and would no doubt have more. No court in the land would deny a grandfather's claim. However, she must first convince the grandfather.

She gave him an hour, by the clock, then made tea and cut a piece of her specialty, her ginger fluff sponge. Lorna was at the writing desk. She took care of the accounts for mill and farm. Margaret took her a tray, needing her to stay where she was. She took a second tray out to the verandah where Vern sat watching the road. He thanked her. She stepped back but didn't leave, again waiting until his mouth was full.

'If you saw him, it would be as obvious to you as it was to me, Father. He is Jim all over.'

'Enough,' he said.

'He gave her his old pram.'

'Are you deaf, girl?' Vern roared.

A dormouse has excellent hearing. She scuttled back to her kitchen to nibble on cake. Her features, and at times her demeanour, were that of a mouse — a mouse overindulged. She was a younger sister who had never learnt to fight back, the middle child, lost between the first dominant daughter and the only son. She'd spent her life invisible, had grown accustomed to scuttling for cover when the old lion roared. She feared his roar. She did not fear her sister.

Lorna came with her plate for a second slice of sponge. Like her father, she was moderately appreciative of her sister's kitchen skills.

'We could raise him out at Monk's, Lorna. And if it was to become known that Jim has a son, he may be released from the army.'

Lorna scorched her with that raised eyebrow and returned with her cake to her bookkeeping.

Margaret was not an avid reader; mathematics had plagued her in the schoolroom. She knew nothing about the keeping of books, but a mouse, in its own quiet way, in its own element, is smart enough.

Each week she wrote long newsy letters to her brother. On occasions Lorna penned him a line or two. The only time Vern picked up a pen was to sign cheques, written by Lorna. Jim wrote every week or so, his letters addressed to his father. He'd made no mention of an illegitimate son — though of course he would not mention it to his father.

To her perhaps. She'd write to him tonight. She'd tell him she'd recognised his old pram . . .

Or perhaps not tonight.

Out to the verandah again. 'Such a pleasant evening,' she said.

'Have you got any more of that cake?' Vern asked.

She brought him a plate then sat with him to enjoy the pleasant evening. Dark now, the nights were drawing in, winter on its way again, but far away tonight.

'Perhaps there is rain on the breeze,' she said.

'Could be. It's warm enough.'

Crickets chirping, autumn leaves stirring like the pages of a dry old book. She waited until the moment felt right.

'We cannot allow it, Father.'

'Don't you open your mouth.'

'We cannot allow your grandson to be raised by a . . . in that black's camp.'

'Goddamn you,' he roared and cake crumbs flew. She wiped one from her eye, reached over to wipe his mouth with a serviette. He swiped at her wiping hand. She backed away but would not back down.

'If you saw him, you would recognise him. With a dependent child, Jim may be able to get out of the army.'

'Get out of my sight with your manipulating, you blathering bitch of a girl. Get!' He got up from that chair faster than he'd risen from it in months and limped down to look at his neglected roses. They were done with blooming for this year, and the way his blood pressure felt tonight, he doubted he'd see their next blooming.

'Bloody fool of a boy. Bloody book-reading simpleton. A man got himself surrounded by a bunch of feeble-minded bloody half-witted —'

A week passed and not a word did Margaret speak of the child. Midway through the second week, Vern came on her leafing through a photograph album. Few can resist an album. He glanced over her shoulder at a shot of the infant Jim, lying on a blanket. His hand moved to halt her progress at the page displaying a two-year-old Jim, his hair still long and girlish, hiding his ears. Vern remembered it well. He'd argued with Joanne over that photograph, had told her to stop turning his boy into a girl, that he already had two of them, and when he couldn't convince her, he'd carried his boy to the barber and had him clipped to the ears and he'd paid for it when he returned a goblin to his mother.

Pages turned. Lorna's mother, a plain woman, horse-faced, narrow-hipped. No photograph of Margaret's mother, nor of Margaret until she was nine years old. Her mother dead, she had emerged from the wilderness, a worried, saucer-eyed girl, seated on a cane chair, holding baby Jim.

Margaret's hand prevented him turning the page. 'That's the one I was looking for,' she said. 'I knew it was in here somewhere.'

'He was four months old,' Vern said.

'Jim's boy would be around the same age. It could be him, Father.'

'Are you trying to break a man's heart?'

'What chance has he got if we leave him to grow up out there?'

'It's young Darkie Hall's. She's spent half her life hanging around him.'

'I kissed his little hand. It's a replica of your own and Jim's. He grasped my nose with it. He's your grandson, my nephew, and I want to raise him, Father — out at Monk's.'

Vern turned the pages back to a photograph of himself, holding his long-haired two-year-old. Just a young man then, strong in the leg, strong in the mind, he'd thought he'd live forever.

'Put the bloody thing away,' he said. 'Put it away and leave it away.'

She put the album away.

But a mouse is a rodent and rodents have a bad habit of gnawing. Margaret gnawed during the following weeks. She altered her angle and gnawed, then on a Saturday evening, having claimed a headache, she sent Lorna off to the movies alone.

At eight o'clock, in the kitchen, the cake tin between them, she
moved in for the kill.

'I spoke to Mrs Foote at the grocer's yesterday. Jimmy was
born a month early and he weighed nine pound eight ounces at
birth. She says he has . . . has the thumbs.'

A mouse can undermine a wall if given time.

CLOSED DOORS AND BIRTHDAYS

Vern woke feeling old on his birthday, woke up wanting to be young and sitting again in Gertrude's kitchen, his life ahead, not behind him.

Lorna presented him with a large atlas, which he'd paid too much for and didn't want. Margaret offered a cardigan, which he also didn't want. Old men wore cardigans, though maybe not of that shade of blue.

'You'll be crocheting me a knee rug next.'

'You can button it like a sweater or leave it open, dear,' Margaret said.

He tried it on. It was warm. It buttoned across his belly. It felt comfortable. He left it on.

At ten, when the girls emerged from their rooms dressed for church, Vern was waiting in the hall, car keys in hand.

'You can't wear that thing to church,' Lorna said.

'I'm going down to have a look at that boy,' he said. 'Don't wait lunch for me.'

'I'll come with you,' Margaret said, church forgotten.

They came in force to Gertrude's kitchen that Sunday morning. They filled it: Lorna, tall and ungainly; Vern, all height, belly and electric blue cardigan; Margaret, her ample chest heaving, her eyes watering. It may have gone better had Vern driven down alone.

The infant, kicking long legs in his father's pram, crowed at his visitors. Lorna picked up a foot, studied then dropped it. Vern went straight for the hands, in particular the tiny thumbs. Gertrude stood back, knowing what he'd find.

And he found those double-jointed thumbs. And a hammer fist slammed into his gut. He hadn't expected to see them again, hadn't expected that grasping little hand to grab onto his finger. Vern couldn't get a breath; his vision blurred. That wild little slut had made him a grandfather. There was no doubting it.

He looked at Lorna, busy taking inventory of a kitchen she had not previously entered. He watched Margaret cooing at her nephew. He looked at Gertrude. She had her back turned to him.

It was his birthday and she hadn't remembered. She hadn't told him to sit down either, hadn't offered him a cup of tea. If she'd given an inch, he might have given two. If she'd said happy birthday, he may not have said what he did.

'I'll take him off your hands. We'll see that he's raised decent.'

Jenny, who had been holding the two small girls behind the green curtain, released them. Georgie catapulted out to the kitchen where she dived into the thick of the Hoopers. She moved them away from the pram. Jenny wasn't far behind her. She scooped Jimmy into her arms and was out the door, Georgie at her side.

The Hoopers followed them out to the yard. 'You bring that boy back here,' Vern demanded.

With eight or ten yards between them, Jenny turned. 'I'll raise him decent and without any interference from you.'

'You couldn't raise dogs,' Lorna said.

'You could teach them how to snarl,' Jenny said, continuing on towards the goat paddock gate.

'Get that boy back here,' Vern roared. Jenny was on the far side of the gate. 'You bring that boy back here now or I'll have you in court next week, you hot-pants little bitch. I'll have the lot of them taken away from you.'

'You take me to court and I'll tell everyone how Lenny knocked on your door to get help for me when your grandson was stuck inside me, and how your witch of a daughter threatened him with a bucket of dishwater.'

Vern had seen that kid fall into his rosebushes. He hadn't known why he'd been there. Had he recognised him, had he known Gertrude had sent him —

200

'You're a contagious disease infecting every youth in this town,' Lorna snarled.

'Every man in Australia has been immunised against you,' Jenny said.

'Stop it,' Gertrude said. 'That little boy is no trophy to be fought over. Get over to Elsie's, Jenny, and you take your girls home, Vern. I won't have my land turned into a battlefield, not by you or anyone else.' She went inside and closed her door.

Margaret, the instigator, stood in the yard, watching her nephew disappear into that nest of blacks. Lorna walked to the car, already preparing her case for court. She'd studied law at university, for a time.

Vern was staring at the house, at the closed door. Gertrude hadn't shot that bolt, but he was outside and she was in, and he wanted to howl.

He'd pulled the tail off a lizard on his fourth birthday, just to show Trude how smart he was, and she'd run inside and slammed the door. Today he was that boy again, standing outside her door, the lizard wriggling in one hand the tail in the other.

Without her, all he had to show for his years on this earth was a fool of a son who'd tossed away a fortune for thirty bob a week and a bloody uniform. All he had without that fool of a boy were two middle-aged old maid daughters who liked their comfort too much to leave home. That's all he had.

And an illegitimate grandson with the thumbs.

'Let the courts handle it, Father,' Lorna called to him.

That's what he'd do. He'd show that Goldilocks little bitch that she couldn't get the better of him. And he'd show that independent, lying, door-closing, birthday-forgetting bugger of a woman while he was at it.

Lorna drove the car home. Vern was in no state to drive. Margaret made him a cup of tea. He drank it at Joanne's writing desk while writing that fool of a boy out of his will.

To my brainless, book-reading bloody idiot son, I leave buggar all.

How did you spell 'bugger'? He said it often enough, though had never attempted to spell it. The word didn't look right on paper. He'd had little formal schooling — not that schooling would have taught him how to spell *buggar* . . . *bugger*. His handwriting had never been up to much. It was worse now.

Lorna did the writing these days. He forced his weak right hand to sign his name. It didn't appreciate the sustained effort of writing his will. And who would he leave his all to if not to Jim? The girls? War or not, they'd blow the lot on a world tour.

To Betty Duffy's dogs, I leave my —

He placed the pen down and read his words while emptying his teacup. Signed and witnessed, it would stand up in court — which made it a dangerous document to leave hanging around. He shredded it then sat a while, massaging his right hand. It had half the strength it used to have and did more than its fair share of aching, as did his ankle.

Again he took up his pen, dipped it, then sat staring at a blank page while the ink dried on the nib. Like his grandson's infant mind, that page was waiting to be written on — and that hot-pants little bitch wouldn't be writing a word on it.

He'd left too much of Jim's early training to Joanne. She'd filled his mind with fairytales, bought him picture books of fairies perched on mushrooms. His boy was no fairy though. At least he'd proved that much. There'd been times these past years when Vern hadn't been too certain. But to go and do that to a man, then not to tell him that he'd done it, to let him find out that he had a five-month-old grandson — and on his birthday. Those thumbs would have been a prized gift in different circumstances. It was a good-looking infant too, bright eyed, smiling, shaking hands with his finger. He had the Hooper chin. He looked to have the Hoopers' long bones.

I did the wrong thing in taking those girls down there, he thought. I should have kept my mouth shut, sent them to church and gone down there alone.

He sighed, picked up his cup and drained it. Saw the ring it had left on Joanne's writing desk. She would have had his hide for that.

'Bloody women,' he said, keeping a hold on his cup. 'Independent, door-shutting, birthday-forgetting, lying bugger of a bloody woman I've loved since the cradle.' He rose and walked out the front door.

His doctor told him at every appointment to exercise. Vern wasn't a man to take advice, but unable to sit still, he walked that Sunday, walked down the eastern side of his verandah, around to the back door, in, through the passage, and back out to the front verandah. Around and around he went, his mind doing faster circles than his feet.

The house had been built with verandahs on all four sides. Lorna had been wearing their boards down for years with her early morning marching. Vern's leg-throwing limp was no march, but he continued doing it, taking the short cut down the central passage just in case he fell over. That useless sitting pair wouldn't come out looking for him. He started doing figure eights, turning left at the front door, or turning right, then back around to the rear.

Margaret, seated on the couch knitting, flinched each time the wire door slammed. She was using the leftover electric blue wool, knitting a tiny cardigan to match Vern's, and his slamming of doors wasn't the worst of his ire. He had an admirable vocabulary, learned from his mill men, perfected on sheep in the farmyard. He was exercising it, uncaring that it was Sunday, uncaring of his daughter's finer feelings.

Lorna's expression suggested she may have been mentally mimicking her father's expletives. She slapped the newspaper with the rear of her hand.

'Coupons,' she said. 'They are to issue more rationing coupons. Tea is to be one ounce per week for those over the age of eight.'

Margaret made the tea. She poured the tea. What did Lorna know of the brewing of tea?

'A child of eight does not require tea,' Lorna said.

Vern's expletives suggested he wasn't interested in coupons. He silenced Lorna. He caused Margaret to drop a stitch, caused the girls to look at each other.

In appearance and personality, there had never been sisters less alike than the Hooper girls, seated on opposite sides of the sitting room. Lorna measured a six foot one in her lisle-stockinged feet, Margaret was five three in her nylons.

If Lorna had once developed breasts, they'd been tightly bound for so long her rib bones had reabsorbed them. She had the shape of a lamppost and a face which may have inspired primitive man to carve his first totem pole. Her black hair, prematurely greying, was pulled back to a small knob at the nape of her long neck, accentuating the Hoopers' taxi-door ears. Her hawk nose was her mother's but larger, her eyes were Vern's, small and heavy lidded. She had her mother's narrow hips, her father's height, her father's wiry hair, worn in her mother's style.

A short cut, a permanent wave, available in Willama for only ten shillings and sixpence, would have disguised her ears and softened her features. Another woman, with her unfortunate shape, may have dressed to disguise it. Lorna wore straight grey or brown skirts, wore them ankle length. It's possible the showing of a little leg could have lessened the impact of her great height, though as she was the only one familiar with those legs, perhaps she knew best.

Margaret had magnificent breasts, held high by an expensive undergarment. Her posterior was well cushioned, excellent for sitting, but creating nightmares for her dressmaker, who made allowances for those twin humps of buttock, though whatever allowances she made, Margaret's skirts always hung a little longer in front. Her hair, wildly curling, platinum blonde, was her best feature. For years she'd worn it short. Until Jim had left home, he'd driven her down to her Willama hairdresser every month or two. If allowed any length at all, her hair frizzed out of control. Two months ago it was out of control. Today it was feral.

She ran her fingers through it, entangling them, and considered Maisy Macdonald, known to be handy with a pair of scissors — also known to visit Gertrude's shack. Where there was a will, there was a way. She would find a way to her nephew.

The wire door slammed and Vern came once more up the passage. Margaret's overly large eyes circling — twin fish swimming in circular bowls — waited for the front wire door to slam.

204

It didn't. She blinked once, twice, three times in rapid succession. Her eyelids, by necessity, bulged when she blinked.

'The last letter that came from your brother. Have you got it somewhere?' he said.

Margaret had it. She sprang up from the couch and scuttled to her room.

Jim's letters were in her top drawer. She found his most recent and scuttled back to give it to her father.

BLUNT KNIVES

'A harebrained rabbit doesn't mate with an elephant and live to tell the tale, you fool of a girl,' Granny had said. 'If you've got any regard for your life, you'll get yourself down to the doctor you were so fond of talking about a few months ago.'

The Richmond address, written on a scrap of paper, was long gone. Jenny hadn't planned on needing it.

'You did it to nark your sister,' Granny had said. 'And the only one it will nark is you. Jim was cut out of his mother six weeks early and he still weighed nine pounds.'

Angry Gertrude. Months of her anger. She couldn't believe it. 'You did it right under my nose,' she'd said. 'And I was fool enough to trust you, to think you'd learnt your lesson.'

Jenny had climbed up to the shed roof and jumped off, hoping to dislodge what had lodged inside her. She'd sprained the same ankle she'd sprained in Melbourne, though worse this time. For ten days she'd been a sitting duck for Gertrude's anger.

The others growing inside her had been like cans of maggots. This one had been like the fluttering of a butterfly — for a time. By November it had turned into an elephant wearing football boots.

That's when Gertrude had started talking about hospitals and doctors cutting. Then, on the third day of December, Jenny had woken before dawn knowing the baby had started vacating his crowded premises. She hadn't said a word though. Had been determined to stay away from the hospital. Amber was down there.

She'd gone for a walk at six, hoping to force it out. The other two had come fast. Not this one. Its head had jammed in her pelvis — so Gertrude said at ten, when she sent Lenny into town to get the garage man.

By the time Maisy arrived, Jenny, aware she'd been written down to die with Vern Hooper's grandson stuck inside, stopped arguing about the hospital, didn't care if the doctor sliced her in half with a crosscut saw just as long as he took that pain away.

They knocked her out with chloroform and dragged Jimmy out with forceps, dragged him out alive, but barely. She wasn't allowed to see him. The sisters and the matron knew she wasn't married. They told her it would be easier to give him up if she didn't see him.

Late on the fifth night, she got out of bed and went looking for the baby nursery.

She knew Amber was there, though Maisy had assured her that the maternity wards were well away from where they'd put Amber. But they didn't put unmarried mothers in the maternity wards.

If the hospital had supplied sharp knives, Jenny might have died in the corridor on the day the Japs bombed Pearl Harbor. Two night sisters pulled Amber off, then they took Jenny to the nursery and let her hold Jimmy.

His head was elongated, his face was scratched and bruised, he was the ugliest, most misshapen scrap of Hooper humanity ever born. He looked more Martian than Hooper, but she fell in love with him anyway, almost drowned him in tears, wouldn't give him back for an hour.

Babies' heads find their true shape fast, scratches heal, bruises fade. He was beautiful now. He had the Hooper chin and Jenny's ears, the Hooper hands and Jenny's eyes, though not so blue. He had Jim's mouth — before he'd been fitted with his false teeth. He didn't have the Hooper hairline or Jenny's, Gertrude said. He had Georgie's nature — and he was worth every week of Gertrude's anger, every hour of pain, every day of embarrassment at the hospital, even worth being almost stabbed to death with a blunt knife. He was worth everything.

She'd registered him at the hospital as James Hooper Morrison, but from the night she'd first held him, he'd been little Jimmy.

Gertrude, still convinced he'd been born of Jenny's desire to break up Sissy's wedding, didn't hold it against him. She'd been born a Hooper. Here now was a grandchild of her own blood.

'He's got the Hoopers' double-jointed thumbs,' she said the first time she checked him over.

'Lucky he hasn't got their ears or they never would have pulled him out,' Jenny said.

'You've got no shame, my girl.'

No shame, no conscience, no husband, not much of a life, but a son she couldn't get enough of.

And Gertrude was besotted by him. Her grandfather had those thumbs, she said. Her own father had them, Vern had them. She'd wanted to tell Vern about his grandson when Jimmy was two weeks old. Jenny put her foot down about that. Lenny had told her in detail how he'd knocked on Vern Hooper's door the morning Jimmy was born.

'You can't keep secrets in this town,' Gertrude said. 'He'll find out he's Jim's boy.'

'He won't get close enough to find out, Granny.'

Famous last words. Kids had to have injections and Granny refused to allow Elsie to take him into town.

'You had him,' she said to Jenny. 'You take him in.'

Those damn injections . . . and calling into Blunt's afterwards. That's what had ruined everything.

COMMUNICATIONS

Dear Jim,
You bloody fool of a boy. I don't know what the hell you were
thinking of, but I've just now seen the proof of what you got up
to with that wild little Morrison bugger. There is no denying
that he's a Hooper. I need a letter stating that you're claiming
that boy and that you want him raised by your family . . .

Dear Jen,
I know you don't want to hear from me but I just opened a let-
ter from Pops and I need to know if he's lost his marbles or if
what he told me is the reason you didn't answer my letters. He
said that you've got a son by me and he wants a letter from me
saying that I want my family to raise him . . .

Dear Jen,
I just received five pages from Margaret. She said she's seen
the baby and that you named him for me. They can't all be
going mad so it must be me. I feel as if I am.
    I don't blame you for not wanting to have anything to do
with me. I did the wrong thing by you and I know that you
think I'm no better than the rest, but you've got to know what
being with you meant to me. It's the place where my mind goes
when it's got no place to go. I told you I loved you and I do,
and nothing will ever change that. Please write to me and let
me know what's going on down there.
All my love,
Jim

Dear Jen,

I received an out-of-focus snapshot from Margaret today and I've never seen anything more beautiful in my life. You should have told me. You must have known I'd stand by you.

Thank God, I know now why you wouldn't write to me. I must have said that fifty times since I opened Margaret's letter. I nearly drove myself mad in trying to work out why you didn't write back. All I could think of was that you'd met someone else.

I know how your head works. I've always known. For your own sake you have to stop thinking that way. Pops has got a beehive up his backside about Jimmy and when he gets like this, he doesn't care how much he's stung as long as he is stinging the one responsible.

I can't see much of Jimmy in the shot. Margaret points that camera and if she sees something in the frame she calls it good enough. I want to see him, Jen. I don't know how much John McPherson charges, but I'm enclosing five pounds in the hope that you'll get him to take a good shot and send it to me . . .

Dear Jim,
Please find enclosed your five-pound note and stop writing to me.
Jenny

My dearest Jen,
I love you and I cherish your fourteen words. Please find enclosed five pounds. I still want a photo.

We've got a son together and even if we only do it for his sake, you have to marry me. I've put in for compassionate leave, though how I'll get down there and back I don't know.

Margaret told me what has been going on between you and Pops. He likes to get his own way and Lorna is as bad as him. He's spent years telling me I'm too much like my mother, and Lorna has spent the same amount of time telling me not to be like my father. The best thing I ever did was join up and get away from them, and find out that I'm a bit like Mum and Pops.

I'm like him in knowing what I want, and I want to marry you . . . and Jimmy. I'm as determined as him, too. The day he had his stroke he accused me of getting engaged to Sissy so he'd put money into doing up Monk's place. Maybe I did . . .

Dear Jim,
Please find the five-pound note, which is a pittance compared to what your father just offered me. He came down here this afternoon with his solicitor wanting to buy Jimmy for five hundred pounds. People come down here to buy eggs and goat's milk, don't they? Why not buy a baby? Anyway, to get to why I'm writing. I told him I was going to marry you as soon as you can get home, so just in case he says anything to you, you'll know I only said it to nark him . . . like Granny thinks I only had Jimmy to nark Sissy.
Jenny
PS One hundred and six words.

'I ought to marry him, Granny.'

'You ought to get those napkins on the line, too.'

Wilma Roberts had married Ron Davies in June. Barbara Duffy broke from the family tradition to wed a Willama boy. Dora Palmer was engaged to be married. Love happened faster during wartime.

Attitudes changed, too. Mrs Bull, the publican's wife, in her mid-fifties, caught the train to Melbourne in June, a pillow stuffed down her dress, so Maisy said. In July she came home with a new baby. She told Maisy he was a change of life baby, that she hadn't known he was on the way. Maisy swore the baby was Gloria's or Victoria's, but no one really cared if it was or not. Horrie Bull, never seen on the wrong side of his hotel bar, was out every Sunday pushing a pram.

'I could have trained to be a nurse.'

'I could have been the Queen of England if I'd been born in a palace. I was born here, and this is where I am. And we're going to have to do something about putting on another room.'

'You could live with me out at Monk's if I married Jim.'

'My goats wouldn't get on with his sheep. Now stop your pipedreaming. There's a good wind out there today for drying.'

They were reliant on the elements at Granny's house; on the rain to fill the tank, on the wind to dry the napkins, on the frost to sweeten the oranges.

Dear Jim,
You'll wed that hot-pants little slut over my dead body . . .

Dear Pops,
They'd give me compassionate leave if there was a death in the family. They might even fly me down there. We could do the wedding before the funeral . . .

Dear Jen,
Please find enclosed a well-travelled fiver. I've got it on paper now and two witnesses to prove you said you'd marry me. Lorna writes a fiery letter.

It looks as if we might be going south. There's talk around that they're moving us. If it's true, I should get some leave . . .

Dear Jim,
Enclosed, one photograph, now leave me alone.
Jenny

Dear Jen,
He's beautiful. I know I should write handsome, but he's beautiful. He looks like you. You told me you loved me on that last night, and until my dying day I won't understand why you kept him from me. You must have known I'd be home like a shot if you'd told me he was on the way. I was in Victoria for months after I left home. I would have gone AWOL . . .

Dear Jim,
Stop writing to me. I've got three kids. Would you like a photo of all three? I've got a good one.
Jenny

Dear Jen,
If you'd stop wasting blank paper and stamps, and write to me,
I might know what you were thinking — or are they rationing
ink down there now . . .

Dear Jim,
Herewith, the last of Granny's watered down ink, just so you'll
know exactly what I'm thinking.

I received a letter two days ago from your father's solicitor, telling me a court date would be fixed for some hearing before a judge which will prove me an unfit mother. Granny says she's got ten accidental grandchildren. I'm an accidental mother so of course I'm unfit. Then, this morning, two strangers turned up at Elsie's door wanting to see her kids' living conditions, and when they'd finished with her they came over here and stuck their noses into Granny's house.

What's going on between me and your father has got nothing to do with Elsie. She's a quarter black and she's scared stiff. Two of her kids belong to her sister and even Granny says that the authorities are going to try to take them away from her.

I'm more scared than Elsie, and I hate your father for what he's doing. He knows that we've got warm beds, and that we eat better food than half the people in town, but all he cares about is getting Jimmy any way he can.

You also asked me why I didn't tell you I was having Jimmy. Hating your father and sisters is why, and having two other kids is why.

If I could go back and undo every single thing that has happened to me since the talent quest, I'd go back and undo the lot. I'd be at a Melbourne school now, learning to be something, or I would be training to be an army nurse like Gloria Bull. One day, if you hadn't married Sissy, we might have even got together, got married and lived happily ever after. But I can't undo one single thing that happened to me, and if you want to know the truth, I wouldn't even want to undo Jimmy and Georgie.

Right now, right at this moment, it would be so easy for me to say, yes, I'll marry you, even if it was just to get out of this mess, except I know that when the war is over, you'll come home and start seeing me as your family see me, as dirt beneath your feet. I've already lived for most of my life with people who hated the sight of me. Even at the hospital, a few days after Jimmy was born, my mother tried to stab me with a blunt knife, and if you think for ten seconds that I'm going to spend the rest of my life living with people who hate the sight of me, then you're wrong.

If you want to do one single thing for me and Jimmy, then get your father and Lorna off my back or I'm going to lose him, and Georgie and just for good measure they'll probably take Lenny and Joany away from Elsie, too.
Jenny

Dear Jen,
I sent a telegram to the solicitor demanding he ignore Pops' instructions. I've written to him, too, and told him that we're engaged, and getting married as soon as I get back down south. He was Mum's solicitor before he was Pops', and he's holding a lot of her money in trust for me. He'll do what I ask.

You, dirt beneath my feet? Moon dust maybe, sprinkled down from a moon far too high above my head for me to ever reach. Think back for a minute, Jen. While you were winning talent quests, having your photograph in newspapers, I was the town drongo, tagging around behind Margaret and Sissy and pleased to have someone to tag around behind. I wouldn't wish on anyone what happened to you, but it put the moon within my reach.

I've been giving a bit of thought to how I might have felt about that photograph of your other kids, and all I can say with any honesty is that they are half you, they're Jimmy's half-sisters, and they'd probably grow on me — and even if they didn't, I promise I'd always do the right thing by them. There's one sure way to put a stop to Pops' plans, so stop putting up your barbed-wire fences, and say you'll marry me.

214

You told me that you'd loved me since you were four years old and since I taught you the right way to eat an ice-cream. Just try for a second to imagine what that must have been like for me, Jimmy Hooper, town drongo, hearing that, and being able to write that on paper today. It makes me a bigger and better man . . .

Rainy days through August, tank overflowing into the yard and turning it to mud, then Joey turned eighteen. The army didn't mind his winter suntan. They took him. He was missed. And the rain kept pouring down.

Wet napkins draped all over the shed, the kitchen.

'I'm marrying him, Granny.'

'Your mother said those words to me and regretted them twelve months later.'

'Did she ever love him?'

'I doubt it.'

'Why does she hate me?'

'She's got her father's head and something very wrong going on inside it.'

'She loved Sissy.'

'Sissy was her . . .' Gertrude started, then shook her head and completed packing a row of eggs into a small carton. 'She was her firstborn. She wanted to be a mother.' She spread sheets of newspaper over the eggs and began a second layer. 'Had those two little boys lived, things might have been very different. She got over the loss of Clarence, but never the second boy. Then the little girl, Leonora April, was born. We thought she'd live. She was born strong.'

'What happened to her?'

'Who knows, darlin'. We got her down to the hospital but the doctors didn't know what was going on. A city doctor said it could have been caused by some blood incompatibility between Amber and your father.'

'Two babies died when I was at the hospital. The sisters said they'd stopped breathing in the night.'

'It happens.'

'If it was Norman's and her blood at fault, why did I live?'

'You were made of stronger stuff.'

'She must have had one a year. How much space was there between Clarence and Simon?'

'I can't recall,' Gertrude lied.

'Between Simon and me then?'

Gertrude shook her head and spread more newspaper. Charlie White's son-in-law would be knocking on her door this morning, wanting those eggs.

'Does she hate me because I look like Itchy-foot?'

'I doubt anyone knows how her mind works. I gave up trying to work it out years ago,' Gertrude said.

She hadn't laid eyes on Amber since she'd come home from the Melbourne hospital. She hadn't expected her to come home, but according to Maisy she was well. Sissy had been home for a month or two. Gertrude hadn't seen her either.

Alfred Timms arrived for the eggs and only one arm to carry them. Gertrude carried the carton out to his car, and as he drove away she saw a second visitor at the boundary gate, a bike rider.

'Telegram for Miss Jennifer Morrison,' he said.

'Burn it,' Jenny said. 'It will be Vern's court date.'

Gertrude opened it.

WILL BE IN SYDNEY SEPT 19 to 26 STOP HAVE TO SEE JIMMY STOP WILL NEED TO BOOK RETURN MELB SYDNEY IMMEDIATE STOP LETTER FOLLOWING LOVE JIM

'What is that boy thinking of? Expecting you to go traipsing half-way across the country with a nine-month-old baby,' Gertrude said.

'It's only five hundred miles from Melbourne.'

'If he wants to see Jimmy he can come home and see him — and see his father.'

*

216

Three days later, Jim's letter arrived, a ten pound note inside it.

Dear Jen,

It's official. We're going over to have a go at the Japs and we'll get a week's leave before we go. I know I'm expecting a lot of you, but you always said you wanted to see Sydney. You'd have to get the train to Melbourne, stay somewhere for the night then get the Sydney train. If you can't, I'll try to get home — which will mean spending most of my leave travelling and the rest of it arguing with Pops. I want to spend it with you and Jimmy . . .

'Jimmy deserves to have a father,' Jenny said.

'You might have thought of that sooner rather than later, my girl.'

'You don't wish we didn't have him.'

Gertrude had no reply for that. He was her beautiful boy. Everything he did pleased her. A new tooth was a miracle. When he pulled himself up on the cane couch to stand on sturdy legs, the world stopped to applaud. His gabbled 'Nan-na' delighted her.

A second letter arrived, hot on the heels of the last.

Dear Jen,

Nobby just heard that his sister has got him and his wife a room at a boarding house for the week we'll be in Sydney. He said to tell you that you and Jimmy can stay with his wife and we'll bunk down where we can . . .

'I'd be staying with his mate's wife, Granny.'

'He's not taking you up there to share a room with his mate's wife, and his mate isn't taking his wife up there to share with you. Use your God-given brains, Jennifer. Those boys have been living for months in camps with a lot of sweaty men. They probably haven't seen a white woman since they've been up there. You're not a fool so stop talking like one.'

'Would you at least talk to Norman and see if I can get a return ticket?'

'No, I won't. Now that's enough about it.'

It wasn't. Jim wanted to see Jimmy and she wanted it too. She wanted to get away from Vern, wanted to see Sydney — and wanted to see Jim. She knew she shouldn't, but you can't help what you want.

Maisy asked Norman to book the ticket. She paid for it, offered to take Margot into town for a week.

'I know you're against it, Mrs Foote,' Maisy said. 'But she's eighteen years old. She needs to see something other than kids. I had two kids when I was her age and by God, if someone had offered me a week's holiday, you wouldn't have seen my heels for dust.'

'If she comes home pregnant, Maisy, I'll drop her on your doorstep and walk away,' Gertrude said.

ILL-EQUIPPED

Two days of travelling with a crawling baby on a crowded train. Two days of changing napkins on railway benches, train seats, lavatory floors, of hauling her case, Jimmy and a string bag full of wet napkins, and when she got there, Jim wasn't waiting.

Anyone can be late — ten minutes, even half an hour late. She'd been searching the crowd now for over an hour. He'd changed his mind, or his father had changed it for him. He'd probably sent another telegram after she'd left.

There were uniforms everywhere; khaki, navy, white. Everyone was in uniform; station people, Salvos, Red Cross. Even the women who weren't wearing uniforms looked as if they were. And there she stood in her best blue and green floral frock and black cardigan, looking like a bunch of week-old wilting flowers but not smelling as sweet. She mightn't be able to find Jim in this crowd but he'd find her. Every napkin she'd packed for Jimmy was now stuffed into her string bag, and smelling worse by the hour. And he was wet again and not a thing she could do about it except soak it up with her hip.

Jim had said in his last telegram to wait at the station, that he'd find her, but anything could have happened. The Japs could have landed up the top of Australia for all she knew about the last two days.

An elderly woman and her husband, waiting an hour for their daughter-in-law, shared their bench seat with her, bought her a cup of tea and a slice of station cake, but then their daughter-in-law found them and now she waited alone, with their newspaper,

219

their half a bottle of flat lemonade and a fractious and sopping wet Jimmy. He needed a dry napkin and his nap.

She poured lemonade into his bottle, placed her handbag and cardigan down for a pillow and lay him down on the bench. He didn't argue about the lemonade or the bed.

The newspaper, the Melbourne *Sun*, was three days old, though its news wasn't old to Jenny. She hadn't seen a paper since she'd boarded the train in Woody Creek. Battle at desert oasis, German campaign stalled at Leningrad — all too distant to be real, though maybe not so distant in this place. The evidence of war was everywhere, and not only the uniforms. There were war posters, urging women to join the Land Army. *Keep the farms going while the men are fighting.* There was a poster of a nurse playing Florence Nightingale.

His bottle empty, Jimmy rolled onto his stomach to sleep and she sat turning pages, seeking news of war at the top of Australia where Jim had been stationed. She read of well-equipped US forces fighting in the Solomons, which were somewhere up near New Guinea. They said there had been heavy fighting up there. How far was Sydney from New Guinea? A while back, Jap submarines had come into Sydney Harbour and been sunk. If they'd done it once, they could do it again — and blow up the bridge before she'd walked across it.

She stood again, scanning the crowd for Jim's head. He hadn't come. Sat back down. She was stuck up here with a baby and a return ticket for next Saturday. She'd been crazy to do it. And why had she done it?

The arguments she'd been putting forward for weeks no longer seemed valid. She shouldn't have come. She should have known that every plan she ever made turned out bad, should have known that the only place in the whole world where she was safe was in a two and a half room hut with Granny . . . except it wasn't so safe now, not with Vern Hooper hounding her. That's why she'd come. And Jim, who kept saying he'd marry her, and why shouldn't she marry him?

Some people were born to have everything. Others were born to have nothing — which didn't stop those others from wanting everything. Which was why there were wars, she thought, which was why cities were bombed, boats were sunk, boys were shot, all because of someone wanting more than he had and someone else determined to stop him from getting it.

How long am I supposed to wait here? she wondered. Will I be able to get a seat home? Her ticket was paid for. Surely they'd change it.

Where? This place was too big, too crowded.

She turned a page, read an advertisement for a corset that would make a fat woman slim, read of headache powders — and wanted ten — read of *Clement's Nerve and Brain Tonic*, guaranteed by Mrs Rosenfield, who had bought a bottle of the tonic and after only a week felt so much better. *I cured my husband after an accident and gave it to my little boy who had the measles.*

Wish I had a bottle, Jenny thought. Wish I'd listened to Granny.

She had Jim's last telegram in her handbag, now Jimmy's pillow. She couldn't get at it without disturbing him. And she'd already checked it. She was at the right station.

Stood again, praying he was there. He was tall enough to be seen above the crowd. No sign of him. He hadn't come. She'd have to spend two more days on trains and without napkins. Or buy some from somewhere before she left. Where? Where was anything in this place?

I should have brought the pram. I could have brought it up in the goods van.

The immensity of the station scared her, the strange faces scared her. She wanted Jim's familiar face to come walking through that crowd.

Closed her eyes and breathed, breathed in strangers, breathed in Sydney. The smell of trains, the smell of cigarette smoke, the smell of Jimmy's wet napkin. She breathed, knowing that she had to stay calm. There was always the Salvos. That's what Laurie used to say. She had to stay calm, wait, and remember there was always the Salvos.

Laurie could have been up here somewhere or still in jail. They might have let him out to join the army. She smiled at the thought of him shooting Japs with his water pistol — his leaking water pistol.

September '39 when she'd gone home. Three years ago. The papers had said he'd been sentenced to three years. She'd followed that story. They'd used the same photograph of him each time. She saw the photograph face now when she thought about him, not the flesh and blood face.

She flipped newspaper pages, flipped pages until she came to what was on at the theatres. War or not, they were still showing films, people were still dancing.

She'd packed the red dress Laurie had bought for her; it was the only thing she owned that looked expensive, looked city — it was the only thing she owned she could wear with her red sandals. She hadn't had them on her feet since that day at the station.

Never would she forget the expression on Norman's face that day. She hadn't dressed for him. She'd dressed for Amber, sure she'd be there waiting.

Red didn't seem to be in fashion in Sydney. Dark brown was in fashion, navy, black — and huge shoulder pads. Women, now doing the work of men, were trying to look like men.

She frowned at one slim woman wearing a dark brown frock, with shoulder pads that made her look like a champion wood cutter. She looked at the woman's shoes and knew that red sandals were out of fashion.

Her gaze fixed on passing shoes, she saw Jim's oversized army boots before she saw him.

'You're hiding from me,' he said.

'Thank God,' she said, springing to her feet, spilling her newspaper. 'I thought you'd changed your mind.'

'We got held up at Newcastle.'

Like strangers, hardly daring to look each other in the eye, they looked at the one thing they had in common, on his stomach, wet bum up, and sound asleep.

'God almighty,' Jim said.

'He thinks he is.'

'God almighty.' Standing, hands not daring to touch, looking at her, then back to the tiny boy, his cheek on the snakeskin handbag. 'He's fair like you.'

'Granny says he'll go dark like you.'

'God almighty.'

They had to take a train to the boarding house, Jim said. They'd better move.

She lifted Jimmy carefully, hoping he'd continue his nap on her shoulder. He flopped against her, legs dangling.

'He's too heavy for you. Let me carry him.' Jim touched a chubby leg, marked by the wooden bench slats.

'He's sopping wet. You carry the case.'

'Nobby's sister got us a room with them.'

'Good,' she said. And it wasn't, but she was desperate for space of her own, for a door she could close.

He took charge of her case. She slid the strap of her handbag over her shoulder, heaved Jimmy higher, slung the string bag's handles over her wrist, and followed in Jim's wake. He was big enough to clear a passage.

He looked healthy too, looked suntanned, looked like a soldier. She felt like a crumpled country bumpkin.

He found the right train, someone gave her a seat and Jimmy woke up to look around.

'G'day, nipper,' Jim said. Jimmy buried his face against Jenny's shoulder. 'He's shy.'

'He's not. He'll wake up properly in a minute and drive you mad.'

It took longer than a minute. He was still clinging to her like a koala when she followed Jim from the train. They'd have a bit of a walk, Jim said. He had a map, hand drawn on the back of an envelope. He knew where he was going, or thought he did. She swapped Jimmy from her shoulder to her hip and followed, swapped him to the other hip, walking unfamiliar terrain until her arms threatened to disconnect from their sockets and she had to set Jimmy down.

'Are we even going the right way?'

He showed her his map, pointed to where he thought they were. 'It looks like there's this block, then we turn left,' he said. 'Let me carry him?'

'He's wetter now than he was before.' The weight of Jimmy's napkin was pulling his romper pants down. She heaved them up, heaved him up, and they walked again, turning left then heading up a hill, whether to the north, south, east or west, Jenny didn't know. She'd lost her bearings at the main station — and if Jim thought he was going to find a boarding house in this street, he was wrong.

'There's nothing up here that looks remotely like a boarding house,' she said, swapping Jimmy to her dry hip. The homes on either side of the road were classy; they had green lawns, fancy fences. And she was going no further. She set Jimmy down again.

Jim continued past two more posh houses while she stood holding Jimmy's hands and allowing him to walk. He'd take off alone soon. Georgie had walked early.

'Got it,' Jim called.

He'd brought her to the wrong street but he was her only life-line so she hauled her load up to where he was waiting, at a fence wearing a name. *Amberley*.

'That's not a boarding house.' She sat Jimmy on the fancy brick fence, knowing now that she'd have to carry him all the way back to the station. 'That's some la-di-da dame's house, Jim.'

'Nobby's sister said it was until the depression. Here,' he said. 'Put this on.' And he offered her a ring, wrapped in tissue paper.

'I'm not marrying you and this isn't a boarding house.'

'Its name is written on the envelope.'

She looked at his map, saw *Amberley* printed there, underlined. She sighed, looked at him, at the ring, which anyone could see was a mile too big.

'Is that the one you bought for Sissy?'

'I bought it in Newcastle. The landlady thinks we're married.'

She turned to look at the house, a double-storey red brick place with a tiled roof, a leadlight window that any one of Woody Creek's churches would have sold their soul to own. She'd lived in boarding houses with Laurie. None had given a damn if she was married to him or not — and none had looked remotely like this place. She took the ring. It might have fitted her thumb.

'It won't stay on.'

'The chap said that any jeweller will take a bit out of it.'

'It won't stay on until he takes a bit out of it.'

'Hold it on,' he said, and he picked up the case and walked to the porch where he rattled a fancy brass knocker while Jenny stood well back, knowing he'd brought her to the wrong *Amberley*, even more convinced when an overweight middle-aged woman with a plum in her mouth opened the door.

'I've booked a room,' he said. 'Jim Hooper.'

'The lodgers' entrance is down the drive,' the woman said. And she closed the door.

'Get me out of here.'

'We won't get another room.'

'I stink and so does Jimmy. We can't go in there, Jim.'

'She'll know you've been travelling.'

She followed him, hauling her load by that pretty window, then down a gravel drive by more common windows. Midway down, they found another entrance and a painted sign — *Lodgers' Entrance*. The same dame stood waiting at the open door.

'Jim and Jenny Hooper,' Jim said. 'And Jimmy.'

'Mrs Norris,' the la-di-da dame said. 'I hope you had a comfortable trip.' Her words were as rehearsed as her stretched smile of greeting.

Jenny followed Jim inside, saw a *Gone with the Wind* staircase and smelled her bag of wet napkins. Jim signed the la-di-da dame's book in what looked like a kitchen cum dining room; tables, chairs, refrigerator, gas stove and electric hotplate, polished linoleum on the floor.

The woman was pointing to more signs when an army man came to the open door and Jim swung around, clicked his heels and slapped his head like a puppet who'd had his string jerked.

'My wife had given up on you,' the army man said.

'We got held up in Newcastle,' Jim said.

'Enjoy your stay,' the army man said and he went on his way, Jenny staring after him, wondering if he was Nobby.

'The situation with accommodation being what it is at the moment, we keep two of the smaller rooms available for short-term use by the services. We were not made aware there was to be a child until last evening,' the dame said. 'It is not our policy to let rooms to family groups.'

Jenny clung to her wedding ring and to Jimmy, who wanted to get down and find Granny and the girls. He didn't want to look at Granny's replacement, and Jenny didn't blame him. That landlady had about as much warmth in her as a wet blanket hung out to dry on a frosty night.

He crowed when the dame opened a refrigerator and he saw the milk bottles. The landlady flinched, but continued.

'I take no responsibility for items left in the refrigerator,' she said. There was a bottle of milk on the top shelf named *Glenys*, one labelled *Mrs Collins*, *Robertson* printed in a heavy hand. There were names and signs everywhere; an instruction sheet stuck to the refrigerator door, another one over the gas stove, one over a sliding hatch in the wall.

'The kitchen is to be left as you found it.' The la-di-da dame opened cupboard doors, displaying saucepans, frying pans, an assortment of crockery — the rattle of a cutlery drawer suggesting to Jimmy that he might get down and play with Granny's spoons. Jenny held him prisoner.

'All food is to be consumed in the kitchen,' the woman said, then she led them from the kitchen and up those incredible stairs to more signs. Bathroom, indoor lav — labelled *WC*.

Left turn away from the WC, past a closed door to one that was open, number five, where the landlady completed her tour, where Jenny sighted a double bed. She remained in the passage with the landlady. Jim carried her case in, stood it beside his army bag, beside that double bed. Jimmy was fighting to get down now.

'My brother's room,' the la-di-da dame said. 'He resides in New Zealand with his wife and son. The cot is small but quite stable.'

Cot on the far side of the double bed. Nice wardrobe, dressing table with a big mirror, large rug over polished boards, side curtains, brown roller blind and the prettiest light shade, hanging so low Jim's head was going to hit it.

'As I said, Mrs Hooper, the house is not equipped for children, and I will ask you, in deference to the other guests, to keep his noise to a minimum . . . also that you leave no . . . no laundry soaking in the troughs.'

She'd smelt Jimmy, or that string bag of wet napkins. Jenny nodded, cringed.

'You'll find an ironing board in the laundry. An iron is available. You will see a sign in the kitchen. I hope you enjoy your week with us.' And with another brief stretch of her lips, she was gone, her soft-soled shoes whispering down the passage. For a heavy woman, she moved fast.

Jenny watched her disappear down the stairs. Released a breath held too long. Released Jimmy, closed the door, placed the string bag on her case then stood staring at the double bed, at the rug, at the curtains. She'd seen herself in a hotel room with twin beds and Nobby's wife in one of them. She hadn't foreseen this room, hadn't foreseen that double bed. Granny had been right again.

'A nice room,' Jim said.

Jimmy didn't like it, or he'd picked up on Jenny's apprehension. He'd wanted to get down, and now that he was down he wanted to get up, and she didn't have energy left in her to lift him.

'Where's the bickies?' she sighed.

Jimmy knew where they were and took off for her case but stopped to stare up at Jim, who perhaps looked like a tree.

'G'day, nipper.' Jim kneeled, got his face down to child level, and finally got his hands on his son.

'He's soaked to the skin, Jen.'

'You're telling the person who has been carrying him for the past half-hour. And I'm out of napkins.'

Green and white striped towels folded on the dressing table, a matching face cloth, a hand towel. She measured the hand towel and judged it near enough, folded it into a napkin shape. Nowhere to change him other than on the rug. She got him down, got his pants and napkin off. He took off with a bare bum and Jim grabbed him, held him down while she pinned the striped towel in place, got a clean pair of rompers on him to cover the green and white stripes.

Nowhere to put anything. A week of this. She shouldn't have come. The dripping napkin on her case, and she had to get into that case again. She stuffed the napkin in with its smelly companions, hung the bag from the door knob, lifted the case to the bed, opened it and retrieved the biscuit tin. Only eight left. She'd baked a tin full before she'd left. Handed one of the eight to Jimmy then removed a brown paper bag. She'd emptied two tins of condensed milk into screw-topped jars before leaving home. One was empty. She'd brought a bottle of coffee essence, an enamel mug, a dozen clothes pegs, Weet-Bix, a large bar of Velvet soap.

'She said no food in the rooms, Jen.'

'It's in my case,' Jenny said, and she handed him the wedding ring.

'You'll have to leave it on.'

'I have to find somewhere to wash his napkins.' She placed the ring on the dressing table, picked up the bar of soap, her pegs, her string bag. 'Feed him biscuits if he yells, or bring him down to me if you don't want to break the rules.'

Tired, near drunk with tiredness and people. She wanted space, an empty place.

The washhouse in the back yard was empty, and it looked more welcoming than that house. She emptied her string bag into a concrete trough, smelled the bag and tossed it in with the napkins. She found a washboard and a plug, found two taps and turned on both, not stopping to wonder why there were two — until hot water came gushing out of the one on the left.

'Oh my God,' she whispered, watching the steam rise. 'God almighty.' If the floor hadn't been formed of bricks, she may have fallen to her knees to offer up a prayer of gratitude to the gods of hot water.

It was as nothing washing two dozen napkins in steaming hot water — two dozen minus three. Jimmy had soiled three on the way up, and after her first attempt to wash one in the train basin she'd dropped it down the train's lavatory hole. It went straight through to the lines. Thereafter she'd dumped the ones he'd soiled.

There was no sun in the sky, or too many clouds to see it. No doubt it would rain, probably rain all week, but she pegged out her washing with the landlady's pegs, praying the rain would hold off for an hour or two. She thought of the Collingwood boarding house and the clothes line no one had dared turn their backs on. Laurie had lost two shirts. It would be safe to turn your back on washing here. The la-di-da landlady would have a sign up somewhere saying *No snow dropping allowed*.

She found an outdoor lavatory behind the washhouse, complete with a chubby roll of white toilet paper hanging on a rope. She'd landed in paradise. At home they cut up newspaper for the lav. She helped herself to a good handful of toilet paper before she went back to the room.

'They've got hot water in the taps,' she said, opening the door to number five.

They weren't there. Her case was on the bed, still open, Jim's bag was on the floor beneath the window. He'd taken him! And her weary heart fell down to her stomach and dropped dead.

She'd been fooled. Vern and his solicitor had set this up, set up Jim's story about *Amberley*, about Jim getting leave, the wedding ring. Everything. And even that la-di-da dame was in on it. All along it had been their plan to get her up here then kidnap Jimmy. She should have known it as soon as she'd seen this house — as if it was a boarding house.

Norman was probably in on it, too. That's why he hadn't argued about booking the ticket.

She ran down the passage, ignoring the landlady's sign. *Noise to be kept to a minimum. Nightshift residents in occupancy*. Ran down to the far end, where a resident in a floral dressing gown was vacating the *WC*. Backed away. Knocked on the bathroom door, opened it. They weren't in there.

Downstairs to a locked door and another sign. *Private Residence*. A back step, a turn, and down another passage towards the rear of the house. *Lodgers' Sitting Room*. And more rooms with numbers, another bathroom. And no Jim or Jimmy in it.

They'd taken him, and of all the people in the world, Jim was the one she'd trusted, trusted enough to come up here to spend a week with him.

Fool.

Out the side entrance and up the drive, looking left up the street, right down it, listening for Jimmy's wail. Running like a hare to the corner, knowing it was no use howling but howling anyway. Standing on the corner, howling, not knowing which way to run, and knowing that running was no use. She'd been fooled. Vern Hooper and his solicitor, Jim and his beautiful letters, had got her up here where she didn't know anyone, didn't even know where she was, and they'd got Jimmy, and that la-di-da Mrs Norris and her captain husband were sitting behind their fancy window patting themselves on the back for a job well done.

She was running back to murder them with one of their own kitchen knives when she saw a tall man pushing a baby stroller downhill towards the boarding house from the opposite direction. She wiped her eyes so she might see. He was wearing khaki and an army hat. She wiped her eyes again, wiped her nose with the back of her hand, and saw blue — the blue of Jimmy's rompers. Her heart jumping back to where it belonged, she ran.

'You had no right,' she howled, snatching her baby. 'You had no right to take him without asking me.'

'You were washing,' he said. 'There's a street of shops just down around the corner.'

'You had no right!'

'I want the right, Jen. That's why I'm here. Put him in the buggy. He's too heavy for you to be hauling around.'

He'd bought a brand-new stroller and a dozen napkins. He'd bought bread, milk, bananas. She clung to Jimmy, who was pointing to the bananas. 'You should have asked me before you took him. I thought you'd kidnapped him.'

'I was bringing him down to you and we saw a taxi dropping off an old chap so I grabbed it. I thought we'd be back before you were done.'

Jimmy babbled and pointed to the stroller.

'He knows who I am,' Jim said.

'He's saying banana, and he's mine. And your father is never getting near him.'

'Put him back in the buggy, Jen. You can push it.'

BEING MRS HOOPER

It was probably the longest day of her life. She'd travelled across two states with a nine and half month old baby, and all the way up she'd been imagining something she hadn't found — like when she'd run off to Melbourne and nothing had turned out as it was supposed to. Too tired to stand up, too wound up to sit, even if there'd been somewhere to sit, and Jimmy as fresh as a daisy and wanting to play. He'd slept well on the way up, he'd napped at the station, and he had a new playmate. Twice she left them playing together in the room while she walked down to the clothes line.

If she could get her bearings, she might feel better. She couldn't; she didn't know if she was facing north or south and as the day wore on she was allowing it to take on too much importance.

And Jim's eyes followed her every move — or he was standing beside her, behind her, leaning over her, even when she changed Jimmy's dirty bum.

They drank coffee in the kitchen, made with her coffee essence and Jimmy's condensed milk. She'd eaten a banana, wrapped in a slice of Sydney bread. He asked about Sissy. She told him she had better things to do than talk about Sissy.

'Sorry,' he said.

'Will you stop saying you're sorry!'

All they had in common was Jimmy, and by four thirty when again she walked alone to the clothes line, she didn't know why they had him in common. But the napkins were dry.

An old chap was looking for space on the clothes line to hang his shirt. She watched him use four pegs on it. Maybe that's how it was done in Sydney. Her napkins were pegged corner to corner, Woody Creek style, where every peg was precious.

'Good afternoon,' he said as she began removing pegs, bundling napkins.

'Good afternoon,' she said, watching him use two pegs to hang one handkerchief. His hanging method reminded her of Norman's hanging style of long, long ago, and before she could stop herself, she asked him what direction the house was facing — as she may have once asked Norman.

He'd hung one sock, hung it heel and toe, then he turned to give her a geography lesson, and offer his damp hand. 'Fitzpatrick,' he said.

Jenny found her own hand amid the bundle of white napkins and took his. 'I'm Jenny . . . Mrs Hooper,' she said.

'The attractive half of the "*young couple with child*" we were warned about.'

'I hope he doesn't disturb you.'

'We could all use the disturbance,' he said, and he hung his second sock, heel and toe.

Jenny Hooper. Mrs Jennifer Hooper. It sounded . . . it sounded cleaner than Jenny Morrison, and she felt better for her geography lesson. Number five was on the western side of a house that faced north. Mountains that way, city that way, Woody Creek south-west. Maybe her shoulders relaxed a little. She felt better knowing that she had a ton of dry napkins too, and that tomorrow morning she'd have hot water to wash the next lot.

And she'd have a bath tonight, wash her hair. It would be all right. She'd see Sydney tomorrow and walk across the bridge that gave Sissy blisters as big as pennies; she'd kiss its floorboards. It would be all right.

And tonight she'd sleep with him in a double bed?

She opened the door to number five and dumped the napkins onto that double bed, feeling like Jesus must have felt on the mountain when he was being tempted by the devil. The house was a palace; she'd been offered hot water, a brand-new baby buggy, an extra dozen napkins and a week in Sydney, and all she had to do in exchange was sleep with him.

She folded the napkins and put them in one of the drawers. She hung her few frocks, shook out a dark navy print that Dawn, Maisy's middle daughter, had bought to wear to her grandmother's funeral years ago and never worn since. Maisy had given it to Jenny with a pair of slightly worn sandals and a black cardigan she'd knitted for herself, knitted too small. It was a mile too big on Jenny, but warm. The navy print would be too short, but it had a hem she could let down — just like before — just hand-me-downs.

Not that red dress, which looked less respectable when hung beside the navy print. She'd packed the faded lime green, also bought in Melbourne. It wasn't a bad style but it would forever more raise memories of the night Laurie changed from guardian angel to devil.

'You're a beautiful thing,' he'd said.

That's all she'd been to him, a pretty toy to play with. She hadn't known anything back then. Hadn't been anything. She'd lost herself in Melbourne. She might have been lost up here too but she hadn't lost herself. And she wasn't lost, anyway. She could point out the window to Woody Creek.

She glanced at Jim. He was sitting on the floor, Jimmy crawling all over him, crowing at him, probably making too much noise, but happy. It would have been hell if he'd taken a violent dislike to his father.

His father? That's what he was. It was on his birth certificate. They looked like father and son when they smiled. They had exactly the same chin, the same mouth, exactly the same hands. It was so weird seeing their hands side by side, Jim's so huge, Jimmy's so tiny. Weird, too, seeing Jim interacting so naturally with his son. She hadn't known what to expect, if he'd even touch Jimmy. She'd half expected him to stand back, hands behind his back, looking embarrassed. He wasn't a bit embarrassed. He was trying to make him say Daddy.

A deep, deep sigh arose from the soles of her shoes. It would be all right. She'd worked out a way of sleeping with Sissy, between the top sheet and blanket. It had been prickly with a woollen blanket against her skin but less prickly than Sissy. That's what she'd do. She was in Sydney and it would be all right.

There was a hum of noise through the house now; the ongoing hum of a wireless, the movement of other lodgers in the passage.

'I'll give him a bath,' she said. 'He's usually asleep before seven.'

'I thought we'd eat somewhere.'

'You go if you like.'

The bathroom was vacant, and like everything else in this place it was clean. She put the plug in, set hot and cold water running, said another prayer to the gods of hot water, then went back to the room to get Jimmy and a towel, soap, clean clothing for him and for herself.

Jim didn't go out to eat. He followed them to the bathroom and stood watching Jimmy's perfect little body stripped, watching him bathed, his hair lathered white, rinsed clean and made sweet again. She dressed him in his nightshirt and handed him to Jim.

'Give him a banana,' she said. 'I'm going to use his bathwater.' She locked the door and turned on the hot water tap to fill the bath higher.

Hot water is restorative. Being clean after days of being dirty is euphoric. Jenny sat in that bath until she heard knocking, heard the door tested. There were two bathrooms, one upstairs, one down, but for how many people?

She'd had her hair cut short for the trip. She dried it with a towel then dressed in the navy print, shorter than most of her frocks, but long enough — and was pleased to be wearing it when she got back to number five where she found a chunky little army bloke and a dark-headed woman sitting on the double bed. Jim introduced them as Nobby and his wife, Rosemary. Rosemary had Jimmy on her lap.

He crowed for Jenny and she swung him into her arms, kissed him for preferring her, then sat on the bed with their visitors, who had been given a downstairs room at the rear of the house, with twin beds they'd moved together, Rosemary said. She'd travelled up from a place near Albury, half as far as Jenny.

They pooled their resources, their sliced ham, bread, bananas, Jenny's coffee essence and condensed milk — once Jimmy was down for the night, and he hadn't gone down easily, or silently.

It was almost eight when she joined the trio around one of the kitchen tables.

'I'm dying to have a baby,' Rosemary said. 'We decided when we got married that we wouldn't have one until after the war.'

And how did she plan to manage that with their twin beds moved together?

Paddy, Artie and Bull were out at Bondi with Paddy's aunty, Nobby said. Paddy's girl was coming in tomorrow. They were still hoping to get a room somewhere.

Easy conversation, Nobby's arm slung possessively along the back of Rosemary's chair, her eyes rarely leaving him. Jim and Jenny sat apart, the table's corner between them, her eyes evading his, Jim's eyes trying hard to look elsewhere but too often failing.

Then Nobby and Rosemary said their goodnights, Jenny and Jim were alone and the conversation dried up.

'If I'd known we'd have a kitchen, I would have brought eggs. Jimmy loves eggs,' she said.

'They would have made a nice mess of your case if they'd broken.'

'I suppose you can buy them up here.'

He stood, ready to go back to the room. She didn't want to go back to a dark room.

'Jimmy might have woken up,' he said.

'He won't move until daylight, and we'll hear him if he does.'

She found a dishcloth, wiped the table, wiped the sink, read the sign about how to get her hands on the iron, read the instructions on how to light the gas oven while Jim leaned against the doorframe, waiting for her to be done with her cleaning.

'I came up here so you could see Jimmy — so he could see you.'

'And to marry me,' he said.

She turned her back, found a broom behind the door and swept the floor, found a dustpan — and realised she was doing an Amber, maybe understood something of her mother's cleaning mania. It was a response to being trapped in a situation she couldn't handle — trapped with no way out.

But she wasn't Amber. And she had a return ticket. And she was stronger than Amber because Granny said she was. She put the broom back where she'd found it, put the dustpan back with crumbs still in it, and led the way upstairs.

They couldn't turn the light on and disturb Jimmy, so they left the door wide open. The passage light lit the room. Jim sat on the bed. Jenny sat on the dressing table.

An elderly woman with a frizzy perm peered in. 'Good evening,' she said.

'Good evening,' they chorused.

'I'm Mrs Collins from next door.'

'Jenny and Jim,' Jim said.

The woman went back next door, and Jim closed their door.

It was pitch dark then, shades of the cellar. He kept his distance, but he was braver in the dark.

'In a way I'm glad I didn't know you were having Jimmy. Having me probably killed my mother.'

'I wouldn't doubt it,' she said.

'You said you were in hospital. Did they have to operate on you?'

'They dragged him out with forceps, if you must know. Now change the subject.'

'I'd make sure it didn't happen again, Jen.'

'Don't worry. It won't.'

Silence then. Footsteps in the passage, music from below, water sluicing through pipes.

'They issued us with . . . there's places down here where a lot of the single blokes will be going.'

'You're single. Go.'

'I'm not going anywhere. I'm just letting you know I've got . . . protection.'

'I've already let you know that you won't need protection.'

'Righto,' he said.

A longer silence, but unlike the cellar, not a true silence. Jimmy breathing, Jim's shoe scuffing the floor, someone rattling pots beneath them.

'They don't want everyone turning up at the boats with a disease . . .'

'I'm not dumb, Jim! Will you shut up about it?'

'I know you're not dumb. You're beautiful, and I love you, and every nerve in my body is aching to hold you.'

'I didn't come up here for that.'

'I know that, too. All I'm saying is that if the rubbers stop diseases getting in then they stop . . . anything getting out.'

'Jesus! What's happened to you?'

'You did,' he said.

'I bet you didn't talk to Sissy about protection and blokes catching diseases.'

'I did more listening than talking.'

Someone walked by. The door opposite opened, closed. Jenny slid from the dressing table and went to the window, struggling to open it. He opened it and stood beside her, head and shoulders out. There was barely room for two to stand. Arms brushed.

Why could standing near him make her feel so breakable? She wasn't breakable. Granny said so. Granny said she had the resilience of Indian rubber; knock her down and she'd spring back up. Balloons were made of rubber. The air eventually seeped out through invisible holes. Standing so close to him was letting her air out.

Then his arm was around her, just resting lightly at her waist.

'I told you it's not happening, Jim —'

'You told me you loved me since you were four years old, too.'

'You were going away!'

'I'm going away again. Just let me hold you.'

She stood unmoving and never wanted to move again. And there had to be something wrong with her; she wanted him to do more than just hold her. She was tired, falling down tired, and all she could think about was whether he would kiss her. And then he did, and she stood there like a bird, head out of its nest, mouth open, begging to be fed, her entire aching body sighing out with the peace of being fed what her body needed to survive.

There was no harm in kissing, half in, half out of that window, but he drew her in and she stood crushed against him, feeling the ache of her seeping into the ache of him and feeling both of those aching souls wanting so much more than kissing. Like that second night in the cellar when she'd sworn there'd be no second night, like every time they'd driven out to the farm, day or night.

She either loved him or there was something unnatural about her. She had babies at the drop of a hat and knew it. It couldn't happen again. She'd promised Granny it wouldn't happen again — and she wanted it to happen, wanted his hands all over her. Loved him, his mouth, his china cup teeth. She wished there was an injection she could have that would immunise her forever against having babies. Wondered how Rosemary could say with such certainty that she wasn't having a baby until after the war. Didn't want to pull away. Had to.

'It's not happening. If Jimmy hadn't come early, they would have had to slice me open to get him out. I'm never, not ever, having another one.'

'I'll use two rubbers.'

Back in his arms again and that bed behind her. She knew about the rubber sheaths a man could use. Granny had told her everything when she'd learnt Jimmy was on the way. She'd told her about times of the month, about things a woman could use to protect herself.

'If you're determined to give your body to every man who looks at you twice, then you'd be well advised to protect yourself,' she'd said.

Angry Granny, angry again when Maisy told her that Norman had booked the return ticket, angry at Maisy and Norman.

'You come home to me pregnant again, my girl, and I wash my hands of you. And that's a promise.' Granny always kept her promises.

This time Jenny got away from him, got out the door, down the passage and downstairs to the lodgers' sitting room, where an old dame who could have been Lorna Hooper's shrunken maiden aunt sat sorting papers beside a wireless.

'Good evening,' Jenny said, and the dame raised a finger. She was listening to the nine o'clock news.

'*Giving the Japanese their due, their advance across the Owen Stanley Range was a remarkable feat, carried out against geography and some of the toughest fighting troops in the world. The chief Allied problem is to combat the Japanese jungle tactics. Port Moresby is the key to defence of our . . .*'

Jim came to sit beside her on a two-seater couch; she never learned why Port Moresby was the key to defence. She heard the announcer say that Sydney could expect a fine day tomorrow, then the news ended and the old dame started questioning Jim.

He'd seen what the Japs had done to Darwin. He knew how many had died there. The dame spoke of the government's censoring of news, the sterilisation of it before it was presented to those at home.

They sat until the wireless told them it was ten o'clock, until the dame took up her papers, gestured towards a sign over the wireless. *In respect to other residents, radio will be turned off at ten thirty.* 'Robertson,' she said, and she left.

Vera Lynn was singing 'We'll Meet Again' and Jenny loved it. She moved to the dame's vacated chair and not a word was spoken until the song ended.

'Go to bed, Jim,' she said.

'Righto,' he said, but made no move to go. Not until the wireless told them it was ten thirty, not until Jenny turned it off, did he rise to go. She stayed where she was.

'You can't stay down here all night.'

'There are no signs telling me I can't,' she said.

'I won't touch you.'

'You won't get a chance.'

He left and she moved back to the couch, convinced for a time that she could sleep on it, until every light other than the sitting room light went out, until the house stilled and the chill started creeping into her bones.

She felt her way back to the stairs, felt her way up, past the permed-hair lady's door, feeling for the doorknob of number five.

He didn't move, didn't speak when she entered the room on tiptoe. She thought he was sleeping. She took off her shoes and frock, and that was all she took off, she felt her way to the bed and slid in between the top sheet and the blanket.

He wasn't asleep. 'You're not in properly,' he said.

'It's properly enough for me.'

'Get under the sheet. It's like I'm in a straitjacket.'

'That's where I want you,' she said.

'I won't touch you. I promise. We'll get married tomorrow.'

'That won't make any difference.'

'It will to Pops.'

'I can't get married. I'm eighteen,' she said, but she slid between the sheets, crisp sheets, crisp soft pillow, no gravitational pull towards the centre of the mattress.

'Put your age up.'

'It wouldn't be legal.'

She turned to face the door, he turned towards the window, and back to back they faced their first night in Sydney.

JEN AND JIM, 1942

Jim told her over breakfast that the married chaps in his unit had the paymaster send money home to their wives. Jenny asked him if he was trying to buy Jimmy like his father had tried to buy him.

'I don't need to buy him. Anyone can see he's mine.'

'Then why can't you be content with that?'

'I want both of you.'

They left the boarding house with the workers and by nine were in the centre of the city, Jim in quest of a jeweller who would resize the wedding ring that refused to stay on Jenny's finger. Near ten, a little man in a side street said he could have it done by four. Jim left it with him. And how they were going to fill the next six hours, Jenny didn't know. She was barely speaking to him.

Eating filled time. They ate a second breakfast at a café. He ordered a glass of milk for Jimmy, who had never drunk anything other than goat's and condensed milk, but he seemed to like it well enough. They looked in shop windows, licked ice-cream in a park while Jimmy plastered his face with ice-cream. They ate lunch too early, and poured a glass of milk into Jimmy's bottle, hoping he'd settle down for a nap in his stroller. He'd had enough of Sydney and the crowds. He emptied the bottle but didn't nap.

They were walking the streets with three hours still to kill when Jimmy let fly with the contents of his bottle, and probably his ice-cream, and when Jenny attempted to lift him from the mess he aimed his breakfast at her. She caught the lot, all over her one respectable dress.

A passer-by pointed them in the direction of public toilets. Jenny had bought a sweater for Jimmy and half a dozen napkins. Jim took one napkin and the stroller into the gents' lavatory while Jenny took Jimmy into the ladies' and gave him a bath in a hand basin. No soap, cold water, but she got him clean enough, dry enough, clad him in sweater and napkin then washed what she could from her frock.

'I stink,' she greeted Jim and the clean stroller. 'We have to go back.'

'We have to pick up the ring at four.' He was keeping his eye on the jeweller's lane, concerned that once lost from sight, it would be lost forever. 'I'll buy you a dress,' he said.

'I need soap. I can't stand the smell of myself until four.'

'I'll get some soap. Wait here.'

He disappeared into the crowd and she waited, watching the cars and the hordes moving about their business like bull ants on a claypan, listening to Sydney's disapproving growl, while Jimmy chortled, happy now that he'd got rid of that cow's milk. She wondered what Jim would buy her; probably a baggy brown frock, big enough to fit Sissy. At least it wouldn't stink.

He returned with a brown paper parcel, and it reminded her of Laurie's parcels. He gave her a bar of green perfumed soap and a bottle of lavender water. There are few worse stinks than a baby's regurgitated breakfast. He'd smelt her.

She opened the parcel in the ladies'. He hadn't bought brown. She tossed the string, the paper and shook the frock free. It was a beautiful deep green linen, and she loved it, loved the style, the colour — until she saw the price tag, which almost floored her. She rewrapped that frock fast and took it back to him.

'That's too expensive, you drongo. Take it back.'

'I know what it cost, Jen.'

'Then stop trying to buy me.'

'It looked like you.'

'I look like ten bob a week, what my father pays Granny to feed and clothe me and my kids. That dress cost three months worth of ten-bob notes. Take it back.'

'You stink,' he said. 'Get changed.'

'I know I stink. I'm eighteen years old and I've got three kids —'

'And one of them is mine. Do you like it?'

'Who cares what I like? Stop being so damn nice to me all the time.'

'If you'd stop being so spiky with me, I might be able to stop being so nice. I bought it for you because I wanted to see you wearing it, so stop arguing and wear it.'

'Stop trying to turn me into someone I'm not.'

'Then stop trying to think yourself into being something you're not.'

She stood with her head down, juggling the parcel, while half of Sydney walked by, uncaring that she was dripping tears on the brown paper. No one stared up here. No one sneered. They were all too busy going about their own business to worry about a tall bloke in an army hat and a weeping girl in a sicked-on navy print — and a baby determined to get out of his stroller. She shook the tears from her lashes, sat Jimmy down and opened her handbag. She'd saved her talent quest money for something special. That dress was special. She flicked away more tears with her index finger and removed the envelope, removed the still-crisp five-pound note and pushed it at him.

He didn't want her money but took the envelope he'd seen presented to her on stage at the Willama Theatre. 'That's what I mean,' he said. 'Who else but you would carry a five-pound note around for five years?'

'Take it.'

'All I want is what that announcer chap said the night you won it, Jen: the golden girl with the golden voice . . . and I want to see Henry Fonda's new movie. It's on at a theatre around the corner. Get washed up while we grab some tickets.'

He left her standing. She watched him disappear with Jimmy around the corner before she walked back to the public toilet and stripped to her petticoat. Washed with the perfumed soap, sprinkled lavender water on her bra, splashed it all over her petticoat. She washed Jimmy's sicked-on things with perfumed soap, wrapped them wet into wet napkins, with the soap, then wrapped the lot in brown paper and tied it with string. Lavender water bottle in her handbag, handbag over her shoulder — it was still a classy handbag, good enough for that dress. Wished she could see more of that dress than she could in a mouldy eighteen by twelve inch mirror.

She loved the colour, which was too dark to be a grass green and too blue to be emerald green. And the shoulder pads, not big ones, enough though to make it sit as it was supposed to sit. She loved the weight of it, the way the skirt fell, not quite straight, but not yet flared, maybe cut on the bias. Granny would know. A quality fabric, she'd say. The belt was as stiff as a board, its buckle covered with the green linen, the small buttons on the bodice covered too. She loved him thinking that it looked like her.

Did men look through different eyes, see the same person differently? Did a man's taste in women's clothing reflect the way he saw the woman or just what he liked? Vern had bought a classy classic suit for Gertrude and the prettiest blouses. Laurie had bought low-cut, tight-fitting red for Jenny, a gruesome lime green that stood out in a crowd, a snakeskin handbag — expensive handbag.

She slipped it over her shoulder and felt like Princess Elizabeth, as long as she didn't look down. Her walking shoes didn't look like Princess Elizabeth's.

There was no sign of Jim and Jimmy. She stood alone on that city street in the heart of Sydney, but he'd said the theatre was just around the corner. That was where he'd be.

And maybe she'd been meant to walk alone to him, because on the corner there was a shop window full of shoes, and if she'd still believed there was a fair God up there watching over his children, she would have thanked him for putting that shoe shop where he had. Jim's frock deserved better than worn walking shoes.

She was eighteen years old, and for the first time in her life she entered a shoe shop and chose a pair of shoes. Not the school clodhoppers Norman had bought for her, or the solid walking shoes Granny bought, not Laurie's tarty red sandals either, but a pair of black court shoes with two-inch heels. They weren't cheap. She received sixpence change from a one-pound note, but they were worth it.

The shop man wrapped her walking shoes, and she continued on around the corner, walking like Princess Elizabeth, walking so proud to where Jim stood waiting beside a poster advertising Henry Fonda — and his smile wider than Henry Fonda could ever smile, those china cup teeth looking beautiful, looking like he'd finally grown into them, or they'd grown into being a part of him.

She shoved her damp brown paper parcel into the string bag with her walking shoes, then looked him in the eye.

'Just in case I don't ever get around to saying it to you again, you're probably the only truly beautiful man in this world,' she said.

'And you're marrying me tomorrow.'

'I need my father's permission.'

'Wear that dress and that smile and they won't care how old you are,' he said.

The movie was good. Jimmy sat wide eyed through the first ten minutes, swapped laps for the next fifteen, then napped in Jim's arms until it ended just after four thirty.

It was five o'clock when they picked up the ring. The jeweller had engraved the inside. *Jen and Jim, 1942*. She hadn't known Jim had asked for it to be engraved. Tiny, perfect copperplate writing, and how could anyone write that perfectly with an engraving tool? Hidden though, once it was on her finger, their secret. *Jen and Jim, 1942*. Jenny Morrison and Jimmy Hooper all grown up.

She took it off and they looked at it again on the train ride home, then he slid it back onto her finger and she felt married to him.

There was a crowd on that train, but the crowd looked more familiar. The streets from station to boarding house, even the traffic on the roads looked more familiar.

They saw no sign of Nobby and Rosemary that night. Jenny fried yesterday's bread in lard and they ate it with Gertrude's apricot jam while Jimmy demolished two Weet-Bix and washed them down with a banana.

'He's half ape,' Jenny said.

'Look at his father,' Jim said.

They tucked him into his cot with a bottle of his condensed milk brew. After his effort today, he'd drink condensed milk until he was back home with Granny's goats. They stood together then, leaning out of their open window, looking at rooftops, over rooftops, pointing to landmarks, the church they'd seen, the road that led down to the local shopping centre, Jenny knowing where she was now, where the station was, the butcher, where she'd bought the lard, the greengrocer where they'd bought bananas.

Jimmy's empty bottle hit the cot rails, and seconds later hit the floor, then Jim reached for her hand, his thumb playing with the gold band. *Jen and Jim, 1942.* They stood close until Jimmy rolled over onto his stomach. Minutes later, his breathing told them he was down for the count.

They kissed then. Words were no longer necessary, there was no more right or wrong. It was, and that's all that was. They were *Jen and Jim, 1942*, and Jen and Jim were always meant to be.

It wasn't like in the cellar. The bed was wide and comfortable, a wash of moonlight stole in through the window, playing over them, a slim slit of passage light peeped beneath the door, noises in the passage, the wireless playing downstairs. He used two of his army-supplied rubbers. The army had the best of everything; they'd supply the best rubbers.

It wasn't like in the cellar at all. It was like drowning in paradise, then a resurrection to life. And whatever mixed-up beings they might have been in their former lives, they metamorphosed that night into one perfect and complete entity.

VERN AND GERTRUDE

'Are you trying to break a poor bloody man?' Vern said.

'Nice to see you too,' Gertrude said.

The car's nose had come to a halt beside the chicken-wire fence. Gertrude stood behind her gate watching him extricate himself from behind the steering wheel. She'd heard his car coming, had steeled herself to deal with his daughters. When the car hadn't stopped where it usually stopped, she'd steeled herself for the impact. No impact and no daughters with him today.

'You knew that boy was getting leave and you let that little trollop chase up there after him?'

'If you're getting out of that car to make war, then stay in it,' she said, but he was on his feet. She stood long enough to see his leg-throwing walk, to notice his walking stick and trodden down bedroom slippers, long enough to feel the wash of sadness, of pity, then she turned away and walked back to her house, leaving him to negotiate the short distance alone.

'Don't you close that door on me!'

It hadn't been in her mind to close her door — until he told her not to close it. She left a gap wide enough for his walking stick. He came inside.

'You're not welcome here if you're in an argumentative mood,' she said.

'How much leave did they give him?'

'A week.'

'How long have you known?'

'If you'd stop trying to dictate how that boy lives his life, he might have told you he was getting leave. He might have come home to spend it with you.'

'Where are they staying?'

'You're hardly in a fit state to go up there and drag him home.'

'I asked you where they are staying.'

'In Sydney.'

'Where in bloody Sydney, you frustrating bloody woman?'

'Go home, Vern. I've got better things to do than put up with your ill humour.'

'I've been welcome in this house all my life, and I'm not allowing that hot-pants little slut to ruin it.'

'You've done a fair to middling job of ruining it yourself.'

'All I asked is where they're staying.'

'I don't know where they're staying. All I know is that Jenny is sharing a room with the wife of one of Jim's army mates. Now go home.'

'Like hell, she is.'

'Call me a liar again and I'll hit you with your own cursed walking stick.'

'You take offence too bloody easily, that's your trouble. A man was half crippled, heartbroken, half out of his mind and he finds out in a letter that his brainless bloody son has got himself involved with her and joined up to get away from her. What the bloody hell was he supposed to think — even if he'd been capable of thinking?'

'He was supposed to know better than to call me a liar — three times.'

'You knew something was going on between them.'

'I told you I didn't — and if you think I didn't feel as bad as you about what happened, then think again. He started coming down here on Sunday nights to play penny poker with Harry and Joey.'

'And with her.'

'She lives here! Did you expect her to dodge him like she had to dodge you?'

'You've known for weeks that they're sending him overseas and you didn't tell me. I had to hear it third or fourth hand through Maisy Macdonald.'

'You expect me to go crawling back to the door of a man who calls me a liar — three times — then gets his solicitor to send me letters, threatening to take me to court? A man who told me he'd have *my* grandson raised *decently*?'

'I had those letters sent to her, not to you — and she's sixteen bloody years old and not capable of raising dogs.'

'She's eighteen years old and doing a better job of raising that little boy than you did with your own — or he would have wanted to come home to spend his leave with you instead of pleading with her to save him from wasting his week in arguing with you, if you want to know the truth of it.'

'You want to see that little trollop married to him.'

Gertrude turned to the stove and moved her whistling kettle — minus its whistle — over the central hotplate. She picked up her teapot. 'You've got two choices, Vern. You can sit down and drink tea with me or stand there ranting at my empty walls. Like your son, I've got better things to do than waste my time arguing with you. Make up your mind while I empty my teapot.'

He was sitting when she returned, his walking stick propped against her table. She gave an inch.

'Maisy told you that they'd gone up to Sydney?'

'She told Margaret. She cuts her hair every week or two.'

'Maisy booked the ticket. She drove Jenny in to the station. I didn't want her going up there.'

'When are they sending him overseas?'

'He's got leave until the twenty-sixth. I know no more than that.'

'You don't know where they're sending him to?'

'I doubt he knows. He wrote that they were sending his unit over to have a go at the Japs.'

'He's told that bloody solicitor to ignore my instructions, that he's engaged to marry her.'

'He could do a lot worse — and damn near did.'

'Born of a dago trollop and your bastard of a husband, raised by your lunatic daughter and your fool of a son-in-law —'

'If you and Margaret had kept your big mouths shut, Jim would never have known she'd had Jimmy. He must have written to her a dozen times or more after he left. She never wrote back to him. She had no intention of marrying him until you started threatening us with court.'

She measured tea into the pot, poured boiling water, lifted his favourite mug from the dresser hook, fetched the milk from the Coolgardie.

'You gave her the money for the trip.'

'Jim sent money. Maisy paid for her ticket.'

'Interfering bitch of a woman.'

'She's got a good heart — unlike a few I know.'

'That boy is worth thousands —'

'So are you. It doesn't make you any easier to take.' She slid the sugar basin down the table, sent a spoon after it. 'If you'd listened to Jim when he'd tried to tell you he was breaking off his engagement instead of roaring yourself into a stroke, we wouldn't have had a grandson. There was nothing between those two before your stroke. While you were in hospital, he started coming down here every night talking his heart out about you to someone who'd listen, which is more than you ever did, you self-ish, pig-headed, money-hungry sod of a man.'

He sugared his tea, stirred it longer than necessary. 'Who's looking after the other two?'

'Who do you think?'

'They're not here.'

'They sleep here. Maisy and Elsie have them during the day.'

Maybe he sneered. Maybe it was his partial paralysis. She ignored the sneer and sat, drank her tea, wondering if all that was left between them after seventy years was blood — and a grandson of their blood. Watched him pick up his mug with his right hand, pleased to see him using it. Watched him support it with the left. She hadn't expected him to regain a lot of use of his right hand, hadn't expected to see him walking as well as he did.

'What are you doing slopping around town in bedroom slippers?'

'You don't live in town.'

'You've never worn bedroom slippers in your life.'

'You never spent enough time in my bedroom to know what I wore.'

'I spent enough —'

'I don't have to do the bloody things up, do I?'

'If you got rid of some of that belly you'd be able to reach your feet to do them up.'

'That's right. Kick a man when he's down.'

'Get a pair of boots on your feet and you might feel like a man.'

'You're rubbing it in that I'm not a bloody man —'

'I'm telling you to get a pair of boots on your feet.'

'Why wouldn't you marry me?'

'I would have left you in a week — and the longer I know you the better I know it.'

'All I ever wanted was you.'

'Only because you couldn't have me.' She drank her tea, watched his mouth at the mug. Maybe she loved him. Maybe you can't kill that sort of love. 'We've got a grandson, Vern; a beautiful, smart little boy who can wed us tighter than any wedding ring ever could — if you'll let him.'

'He hasn't got a drop of your blood in him.'

'Don't let the name I go by fool you into forgetting who I am — and whatever blood is running in that fool of a girl's veins, then a damn good dose of it got itself transfused into me. She's mine — as much as, *more than*, Amber ever was.'

'That wouldn't stand up in court.'

'Her birth certificate would. As far as the world is concerned, she's my granddaughter.'

'They can do tests on blood these days that will prove she isn't.'

'They'll prove some connection to Amber.'

'Knowing what you know, or reckon you know —'

'I know. She's got Archie's voice, his hair, his eye colour. I've never been more sure of anything in my life.'

'He would have been in his late fifties when she was born.'

'He never aged. When he was up here that time when Amber was going on thirteen, he didn't look his age — and I didn't notice you slowing down in your late fifties.'

'How can you stand looking at her, if you reckon she's his?'

'I could ask how Jim turned into the pleasant boy he did with you and Joanne Nicholas as his parents.'

'You'd stick up for anyone against me, wouldn't you?'

'I'll stick up for her against you. That little girl had the world on a string at fourteen and those raping little bastards came along and cut it.'

'So she goes after some redhead in Melbourne, goes after Jim to nark her sister, goes up to Sydney to get another one and nark me by marrying him.'

Gertrude stood and walked down to the lean-to, opening and closing drawers until she found what she was after. She brought an envelope back to the table, set her reading glasses on her nose and read aloud.

You, dirt beneath my feet? Moon dust maybe, sprinkled down from a moon far too high above my head for me to ever reach. Think back for a minute, Jen. While you were winning talent quests, having your photograph in newspapers, I was the town drongo, tagging around behind Margaret and Sissy and pleased to have someone to tag around behind. I wouldn't wish on anyone what happened to you, but it put the moon within my reach.

I've been giving a bit of thought to how I might have felt about that photograph of your other kids, and all I can say with any honesty is that they are half you, they're Jimmy's half-sisters, and they'd probably grow on me — and even if they didn't, I promise I'd always do the right thing by them. There's one sure way to put a stop to Pop's plans, so stop putting up your barbed-wire fences, and say you'll marry me.

You told me that you'd loved me since you were four years old, since the day I'd taught you the right way to eat an ice-cream. Just try for a second to imagine what that must have been like for me, Jimmy Hooper, town drongo, hearing that, and being able to write that on paper today. It makes me a bigger and better man . . .

'There's love there, Vern — or they believe there is.'

Vern reached for the page, but she folded it, placed it back into its envelope and returned it to the lean-to.

'How do I know that's what's in it?'

'Because I'm not that good at making up words on the spot — and because I told you so.'

'Let me read it for myself.'

'It's my evidence for court. I can't have you damaging it,' she said.

She didn't sit with him again. She emptied her mug and rinsed it with a dash of water from her kettle, then turned, waiting for his mug. He had no intention of leaving. He asked her if she had a biscuit.

'You're as fat as a pig already. You need to cut back on cakes and biscuits. Your father probably died of the sugar disease.'

'What else has a man got left?'

'Life,' she said. 'Which a lot we grew up with haven't got. Get out of the house and live it. Get back to your council meetings, out to your farm. You're bored. That's your trouble. That's why you keep hounding me with your solicitors.'

'I keep hounding you because that boy is a Hooper, and I'll see him raised as a Hooper — and for the umpteenth time, I sent those letters to her, not you.'

'You'll find out how much Hooper I've got left in me if you keep sending them. I'll spend Archie's money on my own solicitor and have you and that streak of misery you call a daughter up on charges of verbal abuse, mental anguish, blackmail and anything else I can think of. Now go home. I've got work to do.'

'I'm not going anywhere.'

'Then go home and get a pair of boots on your feet. I can't stand looking at you in bedroom slippers.'

POLICY

The la-di-da landlady had made it clear on day one that she had a 'no children' policy. On Jenny's fourth morning in Sydney, she was at the clothes line, Jimmy playing with pegs at her feet, not quiet, but not making too much noise, when the landlady approached them.

'Good morning, Mrs Hooper.'

'Good morning,' Jenny said. They'd been keeping Jimmy out of her way — wearing him out by day in parks, on the streets, bringing him home late so he'd be eager to hit that cot and sleep. Jim usually kept him quiet while she did the washing, but this morning he'd gone off alone to the post office to place a call to his father.

'What age is he?' the la-di-da dame said.

'Not ten months yet.' Certain the woman was about to complain of Jimmy's squealing, or his scattering of boarding house pegs, Jenny's reply was defensive. She picked up a handful of the scattered pegs, used them on three more napkins, two pairs of his rompers.

'He keeps you busy,' the woman said.

'He certainly does.' Jenny shook a few creases from her navy print, hung it.

'You've been lucky with the weather.'

'Thankfully.' She collected more scattered pegs. Jimmy had lost interest in them. He was kneeling, studying the landlady. Then he took off across the lawn to get a closer look and Jenny left her pegging to retrieve him. But before she could, the landlady with

254

the 'no children' policy offered him her hands. Jimmy wasn't shy; he accepted her hand and pulled himself up to his feet.

'What a fine strong boy you are,' the landlady said. 'Would you come up to Myrtie, darling?'

Myrtie? Darling?

He didn't protest when she lifted him; he allowed her to wipe his hands with her coverall apron.

'We have a few cats wandering across the lawn, Mrs Hooper,' the landlady said. 'You never know what diseases they might carry.'

'Oh,' Jenny said, and she hung three of Jim's handkerchiefs.

'My husband returned to his unit this morning,' the landlady said. And maybe it was her captain husband who had the no-kids policy; she didn't seem over eager to hand Jimmy back when the bucket and peg basket had been returned to the washhouse. She asked how he'd enjoyed the long trip up from Melbourne, asked how Jenny was enjoying her time in Sydney.

Then Jim came back and the la-di-da landlady returned to the house.

'What's wrong?' he said.

'Nothing — I don't think. Stray cats that walk across her back lawn mainly, and the diseases cats carry. What did your father say?'

'The lines south were busy. I gave up.'

'Everyone is on the phone saying goodbye. Mrs Norris said her husband, Robert, has gone back to his unit — that thousands of servicemen are on the move this week.'

This week, their week. They'd been squeezing every minute from every day, leaving the house early, staying out until nightfall. And when Jimmy was down for the night, they squeezed that night. Drank tea in the kitchen, listened to the wireless in the lodgers' sitting room, sat like kids on the front fence, watching the cars go by, talking, forever talking about nothing and everything, and knowing that when they were finally ready to bid that day goodbye, there was their room and their closed door.

They saw little of Nobby and Rosemary, who were only just thinking about getting out of bed while Jenny and Jim were deciding where they'd eat lunch. They saw little of the other lodgers, except at breakfast time.

Their own labelled milk was in the refrigerator now, their own labelled butter, their block of lard. Jenny borrowed the landlady's iron one evening and it was such a pleasure ironing again with electricity, she ironed every frock she'd brought with her.

She shouldn't have bothered ironing the red dress. She'd never wear it again. But it was such a waste. The fabric was classy, heavy, with a sheen to it that might have told Granny it was a heavy silk.

Jenny could recognise wool, cotton. The lime green frock Laurie had bought for her in Melbourne was cotton. She loathed the shade but liked its style and the way it fit. She wore it on their fifth day in Sydney. There was always a crowd in the city's centre, in the park, too, where they ate lunch, where Jimmy was free to crawl and crow as much as he liked, and where they could laugh at his antics. There was the telephone box on the far side of the park. Sooner or later, Jim would have to call his father.

A busy telephone box. A dozen Yank soldiers were queuing to use it.

'Charlie White reckons that the Japs did Australia a favour when they bombed Pearl Harbor and got the Yanks into the war,' she said.

'We would have been in trouble without them,' Jim said. 'So would England.'

'Go over and queue with them, Jim.'

'It doesn't seem like good sense — paying out money to be yelled at.'

'You'll be sorry if you don't.'

'I'll be sorrier if I give him another stroke.'

They sat watching one group of Yanks replaced by another in the phone box. They were like kids, like fourteen-year-old boys when their mothers weren't watching, Jenny thought. A lot looked like baby-faced boys. The group who had been in the phone box had a tennis ball. They were using it as a hand grenade, pitching it hard at each other, with sound effects. She watched their play for a time then turned to Jim, now lying on his back, Jimmy sitting on him, wearing the army hat.

He was still the same Jim Hooper she'd always known; his ears were still big, his teeth at times looked like china cups, but he wasn't the same. She loved looking at him, watching his big hands holding Jimmy, loved sitting in the park at his side and knowing that they were joined forever in Jimmy.

How did such things happen? How can someone know a mouth forever then suddenly start wanting to kiss it? How can you suddenly love a pair of hands, crave the touch of those hands?

She'd always had a thing about hands. Loved Granny's big work-worn hands, feared Amber's ladylike hands, envied Sissy's fingernails, loved watching the way Norman's hands had turned the pages of a book, the way they'd held a pen. If not for Georgie's hands, the little girl might have become a Cecelia Smith, a Martha Jones . . .

She still couldn't stand to look at Margot's hands. She'd known them as a four-year-old, had seen them pulling the wings off a beautiful butterfly. It wasn't Margot's fault. For the past year she'd been telling herself that six times a week and twice on Sundays. And it wasn't her fault — which didn't change how she felt every time she washed Margot's fathers' stubby hands.

'Margaret told me your sister had a breakdown after I left,' Jim said.

'Amber had the breakdown. Sissy probably drove her to it.'

'Pops said once that your grandmother spent a fortune on doctors when they found your mother that first time.'

'She never mentions it, but she probably did. She still loves her — or loves who she used to be — I don't, and I don't waste one second of my day in thinking about her either.'

'There used to be talk around years ago that you weren't born a Morrison.'

'The twins started it at school. *Old J.C., she went off to have a pee, squatted down behind a tree, dropped her pants and found Jenny. Old J.C. now stinks up the cemetery, since many long years ago,*' she sang.

'How do you remember that?'

'*Ray King is lousy, his mother is a frowsy. He smells like a dog, 'cause his father likes the grog.*'

'Do you remember the one they used to sing about me?'

'I remember all of them.'

'Sing it.'

'I will not.'

'I often wonder what happened to Ray King.'

'Granny says he was probably murdered like Nelly Abbot and Barbie Dobson except they never found his body,' Jenny said. 'Remember the night he saved me from Sissy?'

'The lonely little petunia in the onion patch,' he said.

Jimmy was on his feet, looking as if he was thinking about taking off alone. He changed his mind and took off on all fours. She retrieved him.

'The day I drove you and the kids home from the bridge, Sissy told me you weren't her sister.'

'She's been calling me a stray since I was four years old. Did you ever read *Silas Marner*?' she asked.

He'd read too many books; he didn't remember titles.

'It's about an old weaver who finds little Eppie sitting in his cottage one night and he ends up raising her. When I was ten or eleven, I copied it, and called myself Cara Jeanette. I was left on the doorstep of the post office, wrapped up in brown paper, and Mr Brown, a crippled postmaster decided to raise me.

'I spent half of my life pretending Amber wasn't my real mother — but the twins killed that, too. When Dad was trying to marry me off to one of those mongrels, he brought my birth certificate down. His name and Amber's are on it. And I look a bit like Amber. I've got her build, or the build she used to have before she turned into a rake handle — and I'm the image of my grandfather.'

'How did they . . . the twins . . . that night? You were up on the stage, singing with the band, then you disappeared.'

'Amber bailed me up in the lav and ripped that blue dress half off me. I said a few things Dad didn't like and he locked me in my room. I climbed out the window and was sitting on the oval fence, listening to the band, when they crept up and dragged me over to the cemetery. Anything else you'd like to know? How they held me down on my grandmother's tombstone and took turns?'

'Sorry. It's none of my business.'

'You'd think it was if I married you.'

'Don't get spiky, Jen.'

'Go and make your phone call then. I want to walk over the bridge.'

He took Jimmy with him, perhaps as a buffer between himself and his father, and she sat staring at the phone box and wondering how she might explain how she'd got entangled with Laurie. He hadn't dragged her off and raped her. She didn't hate him either. He wouldn't have touched her if she hadn't lied about being nineteen.

She shook her head, shook Laurie away, and stared at the phone box, knowing Jim's call must have gone through; he'd been in the phone box for several minutes.

Left sitting alone with the stroller, perhaps she looked like fair game. The tennis ball came flying towards her. She caught it, and pitched it back. The Yanks applauded her catch, or her throw, a few called out to her. They didn't speak English, or not Australian English, and she didn't want them talking to her. She stood, tossed her string bag and Jimmy's rubber elephant into the stroller and pushed it across the grass to the phone box, where Jimmy, bored with phone calls, saw her and wanted to get out. She took him from Jim's arms and a minute later Jim ended his call.

'Righto, Pops. Righto. Take care of yourself,' he said, and he hung up. 'He's made up with your grandmother, or that's what it sounded like to me.'

That might have been good news to Jim; it wasn't to Jenny.

They had an appointment at a photographic studio at two. Jim wanted a family photograph and made certain Jenny's ring was well displayed. She signed papers at a bank later, signed them Jennifer Morrison Hooper, because Jim was determined that she was marrying him first thing in the morning, and because she was seriously considering doing it.

And why shouldn't she? Jimmy deserved it, even if she didn't.

They took a ferry to the zoo. She stood a long time watching an elderly tiger pacing backwards and forwards behind the bars of his cage, the tiger's eyes telling her that if he ever got out of that cage, he'd eat her and his keeper before he'd climb back in.

She was out of her cage. She could stay out if she was married. All she'd have to do was lie about her age.

He had the papers. He knew where they had to go.

They walked home across the bridge, Jimmy propped in the stroller, sound asleep. Halfway across, Jenny got down on her knees to kiss the pavement, and when Jim asked what she was doing, she told him she'd sworn to one day kiss the ground that had given Sissy giant blisters. And he got down on his knees and they kissed the pavement together, and for a time they couldn't get up for laughing.

'I was green-eyed jealous when you brought her up here to see this bridge's opening.'

'You wouldn't have wanted to be here the day she got those blisters,' Jim said.

Loved him for kissing that bridge, wanted to tell him she'd marry him tomorrow. Wished she was twenty-one and in control of her own life, wished they could bring a minister out here right now and get married in the middle of that bridge.

They couldn't. His father would get his solicitor to undo it.

'We'll get married on my twenty-first birthday.'

'That's years away. What if you change your mind before then?'

'You might, but I won't.'

They walked again, walked that mile across the bridge and not a blister to show for it, while Jimmy slept on.

He woke up to share their meals at a restaurant. They introduced him to Sydney's moon on the walk home from the station. It was late when they got there — and there was nothing hanging on the clothes line.

'No!' Ten napkins, plus half of the clothes she'd brought for Jimmy, her spare bra — and most of those missing napkins were the new ones Jim had bought. And not a thing they could do about the missing washing but lament its loss.

Jenny was still lamenting, but quietly, as she carried Jimmy upstairs while Jim carried the stroller and their shopping.

'Oh, Mrs Hooper.' The landlady's private door, the one that never opened, was open. She'd brought the washing in.

'Thank G . . . you!' Bundling Jimmy into Jim's arm, Jenny ran down to take the laundry basket, the napkins already folded. 'Thank you so much for your thoughtfulness, Mrs Norris. I thought . . . thought they'd been stolen. Thank you.'

'In these times we never know who might be about at night, dear.' Her private door half closed then suddenly opened again. Maybe she wanted her basket back. Jenny scooped the washing into her arms and offered the basket.

The woman took it, picked up a fallen napkin and placed it on the pile. 'I have been wondering,' she said, 'if perhaps you two young things might like a night out . . . alone? If you would feel secure in entrusting your little boy to my care.'

Would they like a night out alone? Jenny looked up at Jim. He looked down at her, then like the Macdonald twins, they replied as one.

'We'd really appreciate that, Mrs Norris.'

THE CLUB

Friday night was their last night together. Nobby and Rosemary were going to a city club to meet up with a few blokes from their unit. They'd go with them. Mrs Collins in the room next door assured them that if Jimmy woke, she'd hear him. The landlady's private door would remain open.

'I'll hear him if he makes so much as a murmur, dear,' she said when Jenny gave her a bottle of milk, just in case, and three napkins, just in case.

'He shouldn't move, Mrs Norris. Thank you so much.'

They got away just before eight, Jenny wearing her green linen, her black high heels and the pearl-in-a-cage earrings. Her eyebrows required no darkening, her lashes no lengthening. She'd been a beautiful child; she'd grown into a beautiful woman. And tonight, walking away from the house holding Jim's hand, she felt beautiful. She didn't care where she was going, just that she was all dressed up, and was going out to dance with the best man in the entire world.

Rosemary and Nobby had walked ahead to the corner, hoping to hail a taxi. By the time Jim and Jenny caught up they'd decided to give up hoping and take the train.

It was nice walking out with another couple, feeling like part of the world again. Nice waiting with the crowd, catching the train, riding in a taxi when they got to the city.

It dropped them at the entrance to the club on the outskirts of the city. It didn't look fancy, but it was popular. There was a crowd inside — and four blokes from the boys' unit waiting there to insult them — and flirt with their girls.

Rosemary drank lemon squash. Jenny did likewise. Two country girls, they sat side by side, their backs to the wall, both out of their element. Everyone was smoking. Rosemary lit a cigarette so Jenny lit one.

There was a small dance floor down the far end, and beside it a little grey-headed chap playing a piano. A few couples were dancing. Paddy wanted to dance and he didn't have a girl. Jenny danced with him, then she had to have a dance with Davo. His own girl refused to dance with him. Jenny found out why; he thought he could jitterbug.

Artie and Mavis could. Mavis, who drank gin squash, was wearing a full skirt and showed the tops of her stockings when she twirled.

Noisy, smoky, loud, and that's about all Jenny had to say for her night out in Sydney. By eleven she was yawning for fresh air and her bed, and maybe the old chap on the piano wanted his own bed. He started playing the old tunes.

'You sang that at someone's funeral,' Jim said.

'She sings too?' Paddy said. He'd been asking all night what a good-looking sheila like her saw in a lop-eared coot like Hoop. That's what they called him. They all had nicknames, Bull and Nobby, Paddy, Davo and Hoop. It was so good to see Jim as one of the pack. He'd never been part of any pack.

'She came third in a radio talent quest,' Jim said.

'Years ago,' Jenny yawned.

'How old are you, Jen?' Rosemary asked.

'Old enough to have a ten-month-old baby who will be awake at six.'

'She's still got the prize money,' Jim said, ignoring her hint, taking her bag and helping himself to her envelope. *Willama Radio Talent Quest. Third prize awarded to Miss Jennifer Morrison.*

'On your feet,' Paddy said. She protested and clung to Jim's arm but he wouldn't save her. He wanted her to sing. Paddy and Nobby marched her to the piano player and told the old chap to play 'Danny Boy'.

'I'm sorry,' she said. 'Take no notice of them.'

'She won a talent quest,' Paddy said. 'We want to hear her.'

'Do you want to sing, dear?' the elfin man asked.

'I haven't in years.'

'Years and years,' Paddy said. 'Look at her. She's so damn old.'

The little pianist struck a note. 'How's the key for you?' he said.

She didn't know much about keys, and she didn't want to make a fool of herself. This wasn't Woody Creek or Willama. This was a Sydney club and she wasn't good enough to sing at a Sydney club.

But Jim thought she was, and his mates thought she was Jim's missus, and tonight in that dress and high heels she felt almost good enough. And tomorrow she'd have to start the long crawl back into her cage, so why not sing tonight?

She moved nearer to the pianist and gave him a note. 'I sing it down there somewhere,' she said.

He hit the right note, played the introduction, she cleared her throat. Not a yawn left in her now. Not a note either. She placed her handbag on the piano. He repeated the introduction and she sang, but quietly.

'Shut up,' Paddy yelled. 'We can't hear her.'

She upped the volume, as she had on the night of the ball. And the laughter quietened as eyes turned to see who was up there singing.

She sang it through, but the old chap kept playing, so she repeated the second verse.

Clapping then, whistling too — and, 'Can you do Vera Lynn's "We'll Meet Again"?' And, 'Do you know "The White Cliffs of Dover"?'

The old chap started playing, so she sang 'The White Cliffs of Dover', confusing a few of the words but no one complained. She sang 'We'll Meet Again'. And after that, she couldn't get away. For half an hour she couldn't get away, not until a swarm of Yanks came in, and while one took over the piano two attempted to take over Jenny.

Bull hadn't been named Bull for no good reason. He was almost as tall as Jim and twice as broad in the chest and shoulders. A Yank kid landed on his bum and slid across the dance floor.

Jim got Jenny out to the street, Nobby and Rosemary behind them. Paddy, Bull and Artie remained behind to handle the Yanks; they may have been fighting side by side in the war, but that didn't mean they had to like them.

Nobby walked around the corner, looking for a taxi. Jenny, Rosemary and Jim were waiting at the kerb when the pianist came out to the street.

'I hoped I'd catch you, dear.'

She'd left her snakeskin handbag on top of the piano. 'Bless you,' she said. 'And thanks for letting me sing.'

'You have a beautiful voice,' he said. 'Do you sing professionally?'

'No!'

'You should. I and two companions play at a few functions around the city. Your voice would be a more than welcome addition to our little band.'

'I'm going home tomorrow,' she said.

'Sydney's loss,' he said, and he offered an envelope. She took it, thinking it was her talent quest envelope, thinking he'd looked in her bag to find her name. She returned it to her bag, thanked him again, and as Mavis and Artie joined their group, the little man walked around the corner and disappeared into a side lane.

'What did he want?' leg-flashing, gin-squash-drinking Mavis asked.

'I forgot my handbag. It's got my return ticket in it.'

'He's an old queen if ever I saw one,' she said.

'Is he?' Jenny replied. She'd never heard the expression, didn't have a clue why he was a queen, except his accent sounded English. 'He's a brilliant pianist.'

'They're all arty-farty and they give me the creeps,' Mavis said.

Nobby had whistled in a taxi, and how that driver knew where to go, Jenny didn't know. There was so much city, roads leading off roads, and onto more roads, but the driver found his way to the boarding house, and the boys tipped him well.

It was late, well after midnight, when they crept in, Nobby and Rosemary heading down the ground floor passage, Jenny and

Jim heading for the stairs, when Mrs Norris, dressing gown clad, popped her head out from behind her private door.

'The dear mite didn't stir,' she said.

'Bless you,' Jenny said, wanting to bless the world tonight. She could still sing. She could still do it. And she had been good enough to sing in Sydney, too. She was so happy tonight, so honest-to-God happy. How long since she'd been honest-to-God happy?

'We have to pick up those photos in the morning,' Jim said.

'I'll have to buy more condensed milk for the trip home.' Home? Number five was home. Jim was home. Woody Creek wasn't.

'You'll have to hang around at the station all day.'

'It will be easier hanging around with the stroller than it was hanging around without it.'

It was a saying of goodbye that night. Sad. The kissing was sad, the remembering of things they had to do was sad. Their lovemaking was sad and afterwards the holding of hands, holding on tight to their last night.

His grip eased before her own. She released his hand and rolled over. It wasn't over until tomorrow.

Nowhere to wear her classy green linen and high heels in Woody Creek. No more hot water pouring from the taps — no more taps. No more bathroom and electric iron. No light at the flick of a switch. No more Mrs Hooper.

But she had Jim's ring. *Jen and Jim, 1942.* Like Dora Palmer, she was engaged to be married. And she would marry him, too — when she was twenty-one.

She couldn't sleep — or didn't want to sleep and wake up in tomorrow. Wanted to squeeze the last grains from this night, even if it was already tomorrow.

Crazy Yanks, she thought. Just kids, just drunk kids too far away from home. They had money to burn and tossed it around like it was paper. They'd tossed a bit into the pianist's tip jar.

Brilliant little man, his fingers could draw every song ever written from that piano, and without need of sheet music. Miss Rose had needed her sheet music. Brilliant. And he'd sort of offered her a job, singing with his band. Jenny Morrison — Jennifer Hooper, a singer with a Sydney band.

Wow!

That had been one of her dreams before her dreams had been stolen. Up here in this sprawling world of roads and houses, anything, everything was possible. Back there — back there . . .

She sighed, saw herself dodging Vern again, dodging people when she went into town, always keeping her head low. Nothing was possible in Woody Creek.

And she'd have to see Norman again. And he'd look at the hem of her skirt again. Couldn't look her in the eye.

Guilt? Shame? Something.

Maisy had spoken to him when she'd driven Jenny and Jimmy in to catch the train. He hadn't even looked at his own grandson. At least Vern wanted his grandson; at least he recognised Jimmy's value.

She had no value. Her ring, to Vern, would be as a red rag waved at a bull. And she couldn't stand it. Couldn't stand his snarling daughter. Couldn't stand Margaret wanting to hold Jimmy. Couldn't stand being Jenny Morrison, town slut — not after being Jenny Hooper, club singer, mother of one beautiful boy.

She didn't want anything to do with tomorrow. It was coming though. She could hear the sounds of morning coming to get her.

Weariness swallowed her, carried her away to ride a confusion of crazy dreams. Running down a Geelong street in her lime green dress. Driving a taxi down winding roads, lost. Trying to find someone. Didn't know who. Mary Jolly maybe — or Cara Jeanette, that girl with the magical life.

She woke late to Jimmy, singlet clad, bare bummed and crowing; to Jim, sitting on the floor three feet away, urging him to walk. And he did, or he took one step then flopped to his fat little backside. She watched Jim set him back on his feet.

'Be quiet or you'll wake Mummy.'

Mummy? She'd never been Mummy. Elsie was Mummy to the girls. Through slitted eyes she watched Jim's game, wishing the war had ended while she'd been asleep, wishing they could stay in this room forever, playing Mummies and Daddies forever.

There is no forever in wartime. Jim had to be at Central Station at noon.

Jimmy took another step and this time remained on his feet to crow at his own brilliance. She had to get up to praise him.

'Clever boy.'

'At least I saw him walk,' Jim said.

'I'll write to you about every step he takes, every word he says, every tooth he gets.'

Sad, the packing up of their room, sad laughter when Jimmy tried to take off and landed in her half packed case, a weeping sort of laughter, and when there was nothing left to pack, when they'd checked under the bed, checked the drawers, the wardrobe for the umpteenth time, when they'd kissed while Jimmy tried to climb their legs. Then there was nothing left to do but to pick up that case, that string bag, that stroller, pick up Jimmy, and close the door on their one-roomed home, say goodbye to the landlady and tell her how Jimmy had taken two steps.

'Thank you for everything,' Jenny said.

'You're very welcome, dear,' Mrs Norris said.

A swarm of khaki at the station. The couples stood together, comparing photographs, sharing photographs. Almost time. Jim wore a watch. He knew the time.

'What will you do until your train leaves?'

'Wait for it,' Jenny said.

'Book your case through. It will be easier.'

'I will.'

'Promise you won't take that ring off.'

'I promise.'

He had to go. It was no use telling him to be careful. She told him anyway. No use in saying any of the final foolish words people say at train stations when the train is itching to get on about its business.

'Write as soon as you get home.'

'I will.'

'Show Jimmy my photo every day so he doesn't forget me.'

'I will.'

Nothing left then but that brief train station kiss, holding hands until they had to let go. He backed away, putting distance between their hands, then he smiled his china toothed smile, saluted her, and turned back into a soldier amid the blur of soldiers.

She lifted Jimmy high, wanting him to see his *dada* when she could no longer see him. Caught a glimpse of him at the window, flicked a tear from her eye, and waved Jimmy's arm until he got the idea to wave his own. They waved until the train moved away.

It was over then. She was empty then.

Her string bag wasn't. It bulged with clean napkins, condensed milk, baby bottle and travelling food. Case propped in the stroller. It wasn't easy manhandling the load alone. She settled Jimmy on her hip and, dragging the stroller behind her, made her way to the counter to get rid of that case she could live without until they got to Melbourne.

'All civilian travel south has been cancelled,' a pasty-faced youth said.

'What?'

'All civilian travel south has been cancelled,' he repeated, bored.

'I've got a return ticket for today. It was booked weeks ago,' she said.

'The services get priority,' he said.

'I've got a baby. I've got nowhere to stay.'

He didn't care if she had triplets. 'The services get priority. All civilian travel south has been cancelled,' he said, but louder, perhaps hoping to save repetition. There were two or three behind her.

She gave up. Stepped back. She'd have to camp in the waiting room until . . . until when? She had to find out when. She had to rebook her seat.

'This is ridiculous,' a woman was saying to the man behind the counter. 'My husband is in the services. I've left my children with a neighbour —'

Jimmy wanted to get down. Jenny's arms wanted to put him down. She heaved him higher on her hip and towed the stroller back the way she'd come to join a queue of people trying to rebook their seats.

'Tuesday? What am I supposed to do until Tuesday?' an

elderly woman wailed. 'You can't get a hotel in this hellhole for love nor money.'

Jim had said the same when she'd complained about the la-di-da boarding house. It looked like paradise now. Number five could still be vacant, or Rosemary and Nobby's room. She wondered if Rosemary would be able to get home. She was only going halfway to Melbourne then catching a country train. Maybe she'd be going back to the boarding house. Jenny looked for her in the queue, searching strange faces for one which was now familiar.

Today was Saturday. If she couldn't get a seat before Tuesday she'd have to stay somewhere. She knew how to get back to the boarding house and she had plenty of money to pay for that room. That's what she'd have to do. She stood Jimmy at her side, and opened her handbag to see how much money she had left. A strange envelope caught her eye, the envelope addressed to Mr W.J. Whiteford.

She had the wrong handbag! But she didn't have the wrong handbag. Her talent quest envelope was in it. She stared at the alien envelope, then turned it over. *During business hours* was written there, and what was maybe a Sydney telephone number. And beneath it: *Your beautiful voice was appreciated. Wilfred Whiteford*. And inside the envelope she found three ten-shilling notes! That little man had paid her to sing.

And Jimmy was going to be trodden on. She heaved him up and he wanted the envelope. Jenny, surrounded by Sydney, stared at those three notes. Norman paid Granny ten shillings a week to keep her out of the town — which just went to prove how worthless she was in Woody Creek. Jenny Hooper had value. She'd made thirty shillings just singing half a dozen songs!

Maybe that money wasn't for her singing. Maybe Wilfred Whiteford was an agent for some white slavery mob and he gave out his phone number in the hope that some desperate idiot would ring up.

She found the train going to the station near the boarding house. A middle-aged woman helped lift the stroller on board, a man helped lift it off. Where there is a will there is a way. She sat the case in the stroller and Jimmy on the case, looped the string bag over the handle, and pushed the whole lot the few blocks to the boarding house.

She'd barely knocked on the rent hatch before it slid open. 'My ticket home was cancelled, Mrs Norris. Tuesday is the earliest I can get south. I was hoping . . .'

'You poor dears. Come around to my private door,' Myrtle Norris said.

PRIORITIES

Gertrude would be expecting them on Monday. Maisy had offered to meet the train and drive them home. They had to be told. Mrs Norris, who had a telephone in her parlour, offered to call Jenny's family. Jenny gave her Maisy's number and a pound note to pay for the call and lodgings for three more nights.

So strange to enter number five alone, to sit on that bed to imagine the telephone conversation below, Maisy's strident telephone voice infiltrating that la-di-da parlour. A strange weekend, lonely, Jimmy looking for his father, sad too, knowing he'd forget his daddy before Jim came home.

On Monday, she went early to the local station to rebook her seat south. And of course she'd left it too late. Everyone with cancelled seats on Saturday had rebooked for Tuesday. She could get a seat on Friday's train south, which would mean getting into Melbourne on Saturday then having to wait there all day Sunday.

'What about Saturday?'

'Nope.'

Everyone wanted to travel at the weekend. She booked for the following Monday, then went shopping for bread, milk, apples, two bananas, a bag of oatmeal and half a dozen eggs — which were probably stale. She bought a wedge of cheese. There was lard in the fridge, a scrape of butter. She kept herself busy that morning, sorting through the things she had to do. Maisy would have to be contacted again. How long did it take for a letter to travel interstate? She bought a writing pad, a cheap pen, a bottle of ink, bought a Sydney newspaper, then called into the post office to buy a couple of stamps.

There were four telephone cubby holes in a small room near the post office entrance; two were in use. She knew Maisy's number but didn't know how to make a phone call. The stroller parked in front of a vacant telephone she read the instructions, found the slots for coins, counted her coins.

'We're not dumb, are we?' she said. 'Daddy did it, didn't he?'

'N-dudda,' Jimmy agreed.

So they did it; and it was so easy — except Maisy didn't answer the phone, Jessie did. But that was fine too; distance and Jimmy made it easier to fill the three minutes allocated by the telephone company, and on the telephone, Jessie sounded just like Maisy.

She'd have to pay Mrs Norris a week's rent. She had plenty of money; Jim had given her money to get home, and she still had some of what he'd sent her to buy her ticket to Sydney in the first place — and Wilfred Whiteford's three ten-shilling notes. She took them from the envelope, added them to her total and slid them into the money pocket of her handbag. She looked at the envelope then, at what had to be a telephone number.

During business hours. Your beautiful voice was appreciated. Wilfred Whiteford.

She'd dreamt she was singing with a band last night, singing on the Woody Creek stage in Sissy's rainbow taffeta evening gown. All day that dream had been like an itch in her mind. She wanted so badly to scratch it. There was no harm in calling that number. He probably wouldn't even be there.

She'd need pennies to make a local call. She had plenty of pennies.

So she did it.

30 September 1942
Dear Jim,
All my life, trains and me have been joined. My ticket south was cancelled on Saturday. I was buying a ticket back to the boarding house when I found the envelope that old pianist

from the club gave me when he brought my handbag out. In the dark, I thought it was my talent quest envelope, but it wasn't. It had his name on it and his business phone number.

I know this probably will sound crazy to you — it still does to me — but it seemed like fate, because when I went down to rebook my seat, I couldn't get one until next Monday, so I rang the number on the envelope.

His name is Wilfred Whiteford and he works in some government department in the city, and he must have an important job because he's got a telephone on his desk. Anyway, he told me that he donates his time at that club every Friday night, to do his bit for the war effort, but he also plays with a drummer and a sax player at parties and dances, and they get paid to play. His friend, Andy, used to sing with his band until he broke his hip and Mr Whiteford said they need a singer.

I love singing, and I've hardly opened my mouth in years. When I go home I'll never open it again. I'm stuck here because of the trains until Monday, so I told him I'd go to the club this Friday.

He's got a car, and if this isn't fate, then nothing in the entire world is, because he lives with his friend on that hill we could see from the boarding house window, which is only a mile or two away, and he said he'd pick me up and see me home and to tell my husband that he'll take good care of me.

I spoke to Mrs Collins, and she said she'd be happy to keep an eye on Jimmy. Then I told Mrs Norris, and the end result of that is they are going to share the keeping of an eye on him. He won't move anyway.

The landlady has been very thoughtful to us and is not half as stuck up since we came running back to her in a panic. I was scared she'd give me the 'no kids' policy again, but she asked us into her private rooms and made me a cup of tea, and even offered to call Maisy.

Also, I found that bankbook you hid in my case. I didn't know you'd put money in it, you drongo. You'd already spent far too much on me, but thanks very much anyway. I won't use it, but knowing that it's in there makes me feel safe.

Jimmy did a little run of three steps yesterday. Georgie walked at nine months. Margot didn't until she was eighteen months old.

Love,

Jenny and Jimmy xxx X That one is from Jimmy.

She was midway through writing to Gertrude when the landlady delivered two envelopes to her door, one addressed to *Mrs Jim Hooper*, the second to *Miss Jennifer Morrison or Hooper*.

When she'd phoned, Mrs Norris had given Maisy the boarding house address.

29 September

Dear Jennifer,

Did you go and marry that boy . . .

Dear Jenny,

Your landlady sounds like a Lorna Hooper attempting to talk around a mouthful of marbles, but seems nicer. She said she was making the call for Mrs Jennifer Hooper and Jessie and the girls are all busting to know if you got married to Jim, or if your landlady just thinks you did . . .

Dear Granny,

No, I didn't marry him, but I wish I had. I'll probably be home before you get this, unless they cancel my ticket again, but I was going to write it before I got your letter, so I'm writing it, because you won't believe what's happened up here.

Jim took me to a club on the Friday before he left and the landlady and a schoolteacher kept an eye on Jimmy, who was sound asleep. Anyway, I ended up singing and the pianist at the club offered me a job singing with his band. As I'm stuck up here until next Monday, I told him I'd sing again this Friday. He is very respectable, his name is Wilfred Whiteford, he's almost as old as you, he works in some government department and he's picking me up at the door and driving me home.

You missed out on seeing Jimmy take his first steps. He took off the morning Jim left, and he thinks he's so smart — and he's saying dada. Jim taught him, just said it over and over and over until Jimmy started saying it back.

I won't start another page. I could fill it with what we've been doing, but I'll tell you all about it next week.
Love,
Jenny and Jimmy

Dear Jen,
I don't know where this will find you, or when it will find you, but I gave Pops' address when we booked in, so if you've gone home, the landlady will send it on to you.

It's hard to know where to start or CENSORED the chaps say. I don't know how much is fact and how much is myth. We're supposed to CENSORED. CENSORED or so they said. It sort of CENSORED . . .

Dear Jim,
Your letter looked as if it had been under attack by Japs, or maybe the Yanks got at it. They pretty much left the last line intact . . .

Dear Granny,
I hope you're sitting down. If you're not, then sit down, because I just cancelled my seat on Monday and paid Mrs Norris a month's rent in advance, most of it from money I earned from singing.

I could say that I'm sorry, but that would be a lie, because I'm not the slightest bit sorry. I'm floating on cloud nine this morning and from up where I am, the whole world looks technicolour.

You should see where we are living. It's got leadlight windows in the front and hot water pouring out of taps, two indoor lavs, one upstairs for the lodgers and one for Mrs Norris, plus an outside lav for the men. It's got three bathrooms, including the landlady's, and a gas stove in the kitchen, which I've had

*a few heart attacks lighting. I can't light the gas oven, but one
of the Miss Wilsons did it for me tonight and I made a batch of
your oatmeal biscuits with bought walnuts.*

*Speaking of gas, which leads to the boiling of kettles . . .
would you or Elsie please, please have a spare tea coupon? I'm
reduced to stealing Mrs Collins's used tea-leaves . . .*

All letters to the boarding house were delivered to the one letter-
box, sorted by the landlady then delivered, if the lodger was in. If
not, she placed the letters in her letter rack on the rent hatch shelf
in the lodgers' kitchen. Jim and Maisy's letters were addressed to
Mrs J. Hooper, while Granny made a point of addressing hers to
Jennifer Morrison — and Jenny wished they'd go astray.

26 October 1942
Dear Jenny,
*You get yourself home here where you belong. The girls are
missing you and so am I. I might not admit this to anyone
else, but I'm not as young as I used to be and those two are a
handful. What little I've seen of Sydney was enough to tell me
that it was no place for a single girl. You get yourself home
this week . . .*

5 November 1942
Dear Granny,
*You know and I know that Margot is more Elsie's kid than
mine, and I'll bet she's happier without me. I doubt Georgie
is pining for me and I'll bet you ten pounds that you only miss
me on wash days — and I've got the dirty napkins up here
with me . . .*

It must have been the landlady's husband who hadn't liked kids.
Jenny had barely set eyes on him, and when she had, she'd been
more interested in watching Jim slap his head and click his heels.
He'd looked twenty years younger than his wife, though maybe it
was Mrs Norris's weight and old-lady clothes that made her look
sixty. Up close, her face looked younger, or maybe being with

277

Jimmy made her younger. She was dotty about him — not that anyone could be blamed for that. Mrs Collins was dotty about him. Mr Fitzpatrick called him his young gentleman friend.

And they liked her, too. Mrs Collins popped in to ask her if she felt like a cup of tea some weekends, and if Jenny was in the kitchen when the teacher was making her evening meal, she always put enough tea in the pot for two. She wasn't like a schoolteacher, more like a chatty little grandmother. She had an adult son and three grandchildren who she only saw during the school holidays. They lived in Melbourne.

The landlady wasn't exactly normal, or chatty. She said a lot, but gave little away — like Norman. She never went out, other than to shop and go to church on Sundays. She had no visitors, had a pile of newspapers delivered and read them cover to cover, and every day, at any time of the day, the wireless was playing.

November 1942
Dear Granny,
For your information, I am not pregnant and trying to hide it from you. And no one has ever pined for me, so please stop trying to blackmail me home.

All I've done since I was fourteen is watch my belly blow up like a toad and wash napkins. I know most of it is my fault. I know I'm responsible for Georgie's care, but aren't I responsible for my own care too? You're the only person in the world who has cared what happened to me. Can't you be just a little bit happy for me? This is the first time in my life that I'm doing what I want to do, what I've always wanted to do. And I love what I'm doing. It's like I've finally found out who I am up here.

And as for Jimmy being neglected, you can tell Vern Hooper from me that his grandson is living better up here than he'd ever live back there. Jimmy thinks home is a double storey brick house in a posh suburb. He thinks toast comes out of a toasting machine and hot water comes out of taps. You can tell Vern too that Jim was the one who got me singing again and he's happy that I'm doing it, and while you are about it, tell him that we're officially engaged, and as soon as I turn twenty-one

I'm going to marry Jim. And on that note, I'll close.
Love,
Jenny, waist measurement 24 inches.
PS I'm putting in ten bob for the girls which I made with my
voice. Buy them something nice with it and tell them it's from
me and Jimmy.

November 1942
My dearest Jen and Jimmy,
I like picturing you in our room, seeing Jimmy bum up in his
cot. It was our safe little island away from world wars and
family wars, and knowing that you're still up there lets me
hold onto a bit of that time.

I suppose Jimmy is walking everywhere by now. I'll never
forget the last morning when he took that step then plopped
down on his bare backside. I still laugh about it. The look on
his face was just like Pops looks when something doesn't turn
out the way he expects it to.

He's not happy about you being up there but at least he's
writing to me. I sent him one of the photos we had taken . . .

He wrote pages and pages. At times there were weeks between
his letters, then two or three would come within a couple of days.
She loved his letters, which, as long as he mentioned nothing
about the war, the censor's pen left unmarked. She wrote pages to
him, wore her writing pad away with her letters to Jim.

. . . I feel as if I made some sort of a hop, step and jump from
fourteen to almost nineteen, and I found you and Jimmy
somewhere along the way. Wilfred Whiteford is like my new
Mr Foster, more talkative, more modern, but just as kind. He
drives a modern car that looks a bit like your father's new car
but doesn't always go like a modern car. He mixed his petrol
ration half and half with kerosene, but it gets us to where we
have to go and gets us home again.

I'm learning so much from him, about B flats and C minors,
about Sydney's roads, and maps and all sorts of things . . .

There were gaps in Jenny's education, which she put down to jumping from fourteen to almost nineteen, or living in limbo between those ages. She was back in the real world now and learning something new every day.

With Jim's ring as her shield, she was even learning not to see every male under fifty as a potential rapist. She danced with a few at the club, even sang with a few. There were those who wanted to do more than dance but all she had to do was show them her ring and tell them her husband was fighting the Japs and seven out of ten ended up talking about their own girlfriends, their own wives and kids. Little Wilfred was her shield against the three out of ten who didn't care if she, or they, were married or not.

She loved Friday nights at the clubs, loved her Saturday nights even more, when she sang with Wilfred and his band of merry men and was paid to be a professional singer, and was treated like a paid singer by the men who hired the band. She loved her life, loved every single day of it, and loved Jim for giving her back her life.

Most of what she earned went on food and rent, but she and Jimmy window-shopped and they didn't need money at the public library, which was a king's banquet of books. Like a starving child, she feasted there.

Clothing was a problem. Her only frock, fit to sing in, was her green linen, and at a pinch her navy print. She wore her black skirt and sweater when the nights were cold, but Sydney in November was too hot for woollen skirts and sweaters.

The red dress taunted her every time she opened the wardrobe. On a Friday night in November she decided to wear it, with her red high-heeled sandals. One glance in the mirror told her it would get her more tips — and more trouble from the Yanks.

The lack of clothes would drive her home — and cheeky-faced little Georgie. She planned to be home for Christmas. The war could end soon. According to the wireless the Germans were retreating, or retreating in places.

The Japs weren't.

The news was full of Japanese convoys, and the Solomon Islands and Guadalcanal.

'Guadalcanal was attacked early yesterday morning by flying fortresses under General Kennedy's command. One tail-gunner reported seeing Japanese soldiers crowded like sardines on the ship.'

'How far away are the Solomon Islands, Mrs Collins?'

Mrs Collins usually knew the answers; she'd been teaching school and living at the boarding house since her husband died. And if she didn't know, Miss Robertson, another teacher, who was from England, did. She'd gone on walking holidays through France and Germany as a girl. Sitting with them at night was like a geography lesson. Whether they knew it or not, they were educating Jenny.

'Hitler is hurrying troops and planes from south Russia to Bulgaria and Greece. The Germans are commandeering all shipping lying in Greek harbours. Cairo reports that the Germans are being pounded by medium and heavy bombers. The Germans' rearguard actions are pitifully small affairs as General Montgomery's men pursue the remnants of Rommel's ragged army . . .'

So many cities, in countries Jenny had barely heard of. She heard about them now and found them in the library's huge world atlas.

'My neighbour's twin sons were fighting in Africa,' she told Miss Robertson one night. It was the first time she'd managed to say 'twin' without following it with an internal stream of *Bastard, bastard, bastard*. They were still bastards, but distant bastards. She still dreamed of them, but they were no longer pursuing her. In one dream they were throwing grenades at the Germans which weren't grenades but lemons. Mad dreams, but better — maybe because she loved their mother, who addressed her letters to Jennifer Hooper, and who never once attempted to blackmail her into coming home.

The girls are doing well, and your gran is thrilled that you're using that God-given voice, as is Amy McPherson. We always have a good talk when I cut her hair.

Amy McPherson now, no more Miss Rose, but always Miss Rose to Jenny. She was still teaching at the school. Maisy said she'd wed too late to have her own children — or maybe she'd had enough of other people's children when she locked the door of her schoolroom each afternoon.

Still putting on her Christmas concerts, still wearing that same sharp-cut bob, trimmed by Maisy every month or two.

. . . that's what happens I suppose when you've spent your life practising your hair-cutting skills on ten kids. I seem to have become the local hairdresser. I don't know how old she is but she was teaching there when Maureen started school. Her hair still looks auburn from a distance but up close you can see that she's going grey.

I was telling Amy that Margot has inherited your voice, how she sings with the radio when she's in here. Amy said she'd be a welcome addition to her concerts when she gets to school. She's not much of a talker, Margot, but she can definitely hold a tune . . .

Jenny dreamed of Woody Creek that night, a near pleasant dream until it moved her to Norman's parlour. Too real then. She was sitting across from Amber, working with her on a huge piece of embroidery, acres of it, and scared stiff because she was working her corner with blue thread when she should have been working it with maroon. Still scared of Amber in her dreams. Still woke up with her heart thumping from Amber dreams. Scared too of Amber's blood running in her veins. She'd left her kids in Woody Creek, as Amber had left her and Sissy . . . It wasn't the same though. Every week, when she could afford it, she enclosed a ten-shilling note in her letters to Gertrude. Amber had never written, not in the six years she'd gone missing. Anyway, knowing what Amber was, was being forearmed against ever being like her — like standing with your gun aimed and your pockets full of hand grenades, ready to fight off the enemy as soon as you sighted her peeping over the horizon.

20 November 1942
Dear Jennifer,
Running away from a life that's been less than you might have wanted it to be isn't going to change what went before.

I knew a man once who thought he could keep starting over,
but each time he got started he ended up making the same
mess he'd left behind in the last place. You can't keep re-
creating yourself and leaving the threads of who you are
behind. You'll turn around one day and find yourself tangled
up in them.

Whoever you are calling yourself, whatever tales you
might be telling to your new friends, you are who you are,
and trying to pretend that you're someone else will only lead
to trouble. And I don't care how well the landlady and your
teacher friend look after Jimmy — you can't raise a little boy
in a boarding house room. He's at an age where he's forming
his attachments to people, and he should be forming them with
his sisters and family . . .

25 November 1942
Dear Granny,
Myrtle isn't just a landlady. She's my fairy godmother and
she's a damn sight better mother to me than the one I had. I
had dinner with her the other night and we sat in her parlour
knitting, and not once did she suddenly turn around and stab
me with her knitting needle.

And as for Jimmy forming attachments to his family, that's
a lot of hoo-ha. I spent fourteen years attempting to form an
attachment to my sister and it didn't work. I spent years sleep-
ing in her bed and the best we ever managed was not to kill
each other.

Some people are born outcasts, and I've been an outcast
of that family all of my life, and an outcast of the town, too,
for the last few years. Apart from you and Elsie's mob, and
Maisy, all that's waiting for me back there are sneers and Vern
Hooper . . .

November 1942
Dearest Jen and Jimmy,
By the time this gets to you, Jimmy could have had his birth-
day. Give him a birthday kiss from me.

I wish I was there to hear you singing. I'll never forget the first time I heard you. You were knee-high to a grasshopper and wearing a hat almost as big as you were . . .

She had the dream of her life that night. She was out at the clothes line, maybe Amber's clothes line, and the sky was full of miniature soldiers, swarming like a plague of grasshoppers wearing parachutes. She was pegging out talent quest envelopes, piles of them, Granny's laundry basket was overflowing with them, and those tiny soldiers were landing in it and putting their dirty feet on her white washing. And she was not going to stand for that. She started stepping on the soldiers, crushing their parachutes that weren't parachutes at all, but those tiny umbrella mushrooms that grew in clumps in the bush. Saw the face of one miniature soldier as she was about to crush it beneath her shoe, and it wasn't a Jap's face. It was the twins' face. They all wore the twins' face and there she was, stomping on them, grinding them into the lawn, she squashed an entire battalion of those twins.

3 December 1942
Dear Jenny,
Give Jimmy a kiss from me and his sisters for his birthday. Vern took another bad turn on Tuesday and I ended up taking my life into my hands and driving with him to Willama. Lorna drove, and that girl couldn't drive a goat to a field of clover. The doctors think he might have a touch of sugar diabetes. They are keeping him in for a few days, to starve him back to health, as his doctor said. He won't listen to a thing I tell him.

Margaret showed me a photograph of the three of you taken in Sydney. It's a lovely photograph of you, of all three of you. I hope you've got some feeling for that boy and that you're not just leading him a dance . . .

10 December 1942
Dear Granny,
I've booked my seat for the week before Christmas. I'll be travelling as far as Melbourne with Mrs Collins. I'm glad for

your sake that you're on good terms with Vern, but if I were
you I'd make a lot of hay while the sun is shining because it
won't be shining when I get home. As soon as I step down from
that train, he'll get over his diabetes and start sending his
solicitor's letters . . .

She didn't want to go home, but Mrs Collins was travelling down
to Melbourne to spend the Christmas holidays with her son and
his family, and the opportunity to travel those miles with a companion convinced Jenny to book her seat. She'd told Wilfred she
was going home, she'd told Myrtle.

Then, on her last Friday night at the club, Wilfred told her the
band had two big paying jobs over Christmas and New Year.

It was excuse enough. She cashed in her ticket.

Dear Granny,
I'll say sorry first, sorry repeated twenty times, but Mr White-
ford has got two big jobs over Christmas so I won't be coming
home.
     Please try to imagine what it must be like for me up here,
to be respectable Mrs Jennifer Hooper, the singer, instead
of Jenny Morrison, with TOWN SLUT tattooed on my
forehead . . .

She sang with her elderly gentlemen friends on Christmas Eve.
Wilfred had to be in his late sixties and the other two band mem-
bers looked no younger. It was like going out to a party with
three Normans — but happy Normans. Basil, tall, grey and
courtly, who worked for a solicitor; Peter, round, bald and shy,
who owned a music shop; and Wilfred, a leprechaun with magic
fingers. They knew who she was, and it wasn't Jenny Morrison,
town slut. She'd gone, and she was staying gone, and Jenny
Hooper was staying in Sydney — and if she was staying in Sydney, she needed clothes.

She spent her Christmas Eve earnings on a bottle of black
fabric dye and one of leather dye. She bought a secondhand preserving pan, a long-handled metal spoon and a pound of salt, and

when Jimmy was down for the night, and the lodgers' kitchen was empty, she half filled the preserving pan with hot water and set it on the largest gas ring to boil.

Amberley was deserted, apart from Miss Robertson, one of the men, and the two middle-aged sisters who shared a room. They came down to the kitchen to make a cup of tea at nine, and stayed on to watch Jenny change the personality of her red sandals with black leather dye. The red dress and the gruesome lime green hung over the back of a chair, waiting for their own dose of respectability. She knew the red might not take the dye, but it was useless to her as it was. The lime green would dye; it was a heavy cotton. By nine thirty the water in the pan was boiling. Jenny added the contents of the dye bottle, added salt, gave her brew a good stir then eased in the red frock. It turned black in an instant, so she dropped in the lime green and stirred. The instructions on the bottle said to keep the fabric moving for half an hour. She stirred her brew for an extra ten minutes, desperate for those dresses.

Her fingernails were black, her hands grey when she crawled late into bed. They'd wear clean. The frocks had looked black when she'd hung them dripping on the line — by night they'd looked black. If they dried streaked and useless, she'd know she was meant to go home. She slept, her stained fingers crossed.

The once-lime green was as black as coal and not a streak on it. The once-red was black, but with a slight reddish sheen — and neither one had fallen apart in the dye bath.

She pressed them that morning and tried them on — and the once-lime green looked so smart, so Sydney. She loved it. Dye hadn't altered the neckline of the once-red, but she'd soon fix that. Maybe a white trim, white cuffs on the sleeves.

She wore the ex-lime green on New Year's Eve, with her ultra high-heeled ex-red sandals, and because it was her birthday she took her pearl-in-a-cage earrings and pendant from their box.

Every time she wore them they brought back memories of the old swagman who had found that pendant in the park. He'd said he'd found it — had probably stolen it, because two years later he'd posted the matching earrings to her.

He hadn't looked like a thief. A few of the swaggies were. He hadn't looked like a swaggie either. In his black overcoat, with his foot-long clean white beard, he'd looked like Noah from the Bible — hadn't been as godly — Constable Denham had locked him up for molesting Maryanne Duffy. He'd been found guilty too, but he'd been the first person in the world to give Jenny something beautiful, and for that she'd never forget him.

She'd never forget her nineteenth birthday, either, and driving out to a party with her three elderly gentlemen friends. God only knew how they found some of the halls of the dances, the houses of the revellers, but they did. Maybe New Year's Eve parties in Sydney had always been frantic, or maybe it was the war, but Jenny was paid good money to be there and she sang her heart out.

A hot sweaty night, that one, black dye from her sandals rubbed off on her stockings, dye from her dress turned her bra grey beneath the armpits, but she bought a black bra with her earnings, changed her mind about a white trim for the once-red dress and bought a quarter of a yard of black guipure lace instead. And when it was stitched in across the neckline, that frock screamed expensive, screamed respectability.

She bought Jimmy a tiny sailor-boy suit, with navy shorts that buttoned to a white and navy shirt, and he looked so smart in his new outfit, Mr Fitzpatrick offered to take a photograph.

Dear Jim,
It seems strange writing 1943 but it's going to be the best year. I know you'll look at the photograph before you read this. Mr Fitzpatrick took it for me with three others. Jimmy was being at his most charming. He's not always so charming. He's saying a lot more now and he knows what he's saying. He can say 'car' and 'puppy' and 'bickie' and a heap of things, and he thinks the photograph we had taken at the studio is called Daddy. Everyone talks to him, a few spoil him. He's like a favourite boarding house pet . . .

With Mrs Collins away through much of January, the land-lady claimed babysitting rights. Jenny arrived home one Friday evening to find Jimmy asleep on the landlady's bed. He'd woken so she'd taken him downstairs. Near January's end, Mrs Collins returned, and brought a bundle of her grandson's outgrown clothing back with her, and suddenly Jimmy had a ton of little boy clothes and a few to grow into — and Mrs Norris started inviting him and Jenny to Sunday dinners.

She made an incredible macaroni cheese casserole, a delicious minced steak stew that didn't even taste like meat. She made puddings and rich custards — no wonder she was overweight — but Jimmy loved her dinners. He loved Myrtie, too. If he saw her in the yard, he called her name, ran to her, and reached towards her with willing arms. He loved exploring her private quarters when they ate there on Sunday nights; he had an entire passage to play in, a parlour couch he could climb on, a kitchen table to crawl beneath. Perhaps he was beginning to resent the restriction of number five's closed door.

In February, Jenny wrote in a letter to Maisy that Mrs Norris wasn't la-di-da at all, not in the true sense of the expression. She'd just been born with a plum in her mouth she couldn't swallow when her posh family home had become a lodging house.

Jim knew the Norris family history from Nobby, whose older sister was married to Robert Norris's younger brother. He'd told Jim that Myrtle's father was a paper millionaire who had played the share market and been burnt badly in the depression. He'd taken the long jump off the bridge, Nobby said.

Myrtle Norris never mentioned her parents, never mentioned anything personal. She reminded Jenny of Norman — she said far too much without really saying anything. Jenny knew her husband was an army captain, stationed somewhere in England, but why he was way over there when the Japs were over here, she didn't know.

Their wedding photograph hung in the landlady's parlour. Myrtle had been a plump but pretty bride. She had the shape to have borne more kids than Maisy, had breasts that might have fed a dozen babies, though if she'd had that dozen, they kept their distance — and she never mentioned them. She never mentioned

Robert, apart from once mentioning that he'd taught English at a high school before the war.

Like Norman, she never missed church. She and Miss Robertson walked off together on Sunday mornings at ten thirty on the dot; you could set the clock by them. They looked much of an age too. Jenny had put Miss Robertson's age at mid-fifties, though the more she saw of Myrtle, the younger her face became. She had Norman's big brown puppy dog eyes, expressive when she allowed them to have expression, which they had when she played with Jimmy. She had dark wavy hair and barely a streak of grey in it. Miss Robertson was all grey. Fat was aging. Maybe Myrtle Norris wasn't as old as she dressed.

The lodgers were all middle aged or older. Four were teachers. Miss Robertson taught arithmetic and Latin at a girls' college. Mrs Collins taught English and art at the local high school where Mr Fitzpatrick taught history and geography. Miss Howell, a woman of forty-odd, taught at a local primary school. The two middle-aged Wilson sisters who shared number two worked as sales assistants in one of the big department stores in the city. They looked like sisters and acted like friends. The woman who lived in number six, the room opposite Jenny's, worked in the office at a parachute factory, which may have been why Jenny had dreamt about parachutes.

There were two single middle-aged men downstairs with Mr Fitzpatrick, segregated from the women. One was a salesman, the other worked in a bank. Jenny ran into them occasionally on her way to and from the lodgers' sitting room. Their rooms were at the same end of the house, the back end.

Jenny was out of time, out of place in this house, a child amongst adults. But on weekdays the other lodgers vacated Amberley between eight thirty and five, then the entire house belonged to her, the wireless in the sitting room belonged to her. She sat beside it, copying down the words of new songs, Jimmy climbing on chairs, crawling beneath them, yelling if he wanted to yell. The kitchen was their own between eighty thirty and five. They ate there, fried sausages there, fried cheese sandwiches.

27 February 1943

Dearest Jen and Jimmy,

The weather up here is hard on photographs or maybe I wear them out with looking. He's a real little man now, isn't he? I'd love you to send one of those photos to Pops. Margaret says he's not well. If you could bring yourself to do it, I'd appreciate it.

It's been a brutal week. We kill them but they keep on coming. They're a mad race. They'll kill themselves rather than be taken prisoner.

It's hot up here, humid sticky heat. We're driven mad by insects. We're wet all the time, wet with sweat or rain or both and dropping like flies with malaria, and if we haven't got that, we've got the runs or jungle rot. I oughtn't to be writing this to you. They'll probably black it out, but it gets into your head sometimes and you have to let it out or you'd start swinging from the trees . . .

29 March 1943

Dear Jim,

I know what you mean about things getting into your head and having to let them out. I let this out last Saturday night. Wilfred and his friends have run out of jobs on Saturdays now that the party season is over. I wasn't going to send it, but I read it again a minute ago and I thought why not, because it's true.

When fairy tales were written and dragons flew the skies,
A gentle prince out riding heard strange and mournful
*   cries,*
For a beggar she had fallen, and lay flat out in the dirt.
The prince sprang from his gallant steed: 'Dear lady, are
*   you hurt?'*
'Kind sir,' she said, 'I am unclean, continue on your way
For I'll despoil your garments, if you long with me stay.'
But he reached into the sticky mire and drew her to her feet.
'Full many a year I've searched for you, and now finally
*   we meet.'*

His tears were warm upon her face like raindrops falling
*   down;*
They cleansed her face, her hands, her hair, they cleansed
*   her linen gown.*
He took her to his castle where there were no more tears
And happily ever after reigned a thousand years ...

TOWN GOSSIP

Maisy and her big-mouthed daughters had started it. All over town, Macdonald voices grated. In Charlie's, in the butcher's shop.

'You can't put a lid on that sort of talent.'

'She's in the right place up there.'

'We'll be hearing her on the wireless again one day. You mark my words.'

They'd bruised Sissy with their singing of the stray bitch's praises. Everywhere she went they cut her to ribbons with their praise.

Ribbons fly away.

Sissy had flown away again to that hangdog cur's relatives. One day she wouldn't fly home and Amber knew it.

'Amber, Amber! Open this door.'

Maisy had been hammering at the door for days. The interfering bitch wouldn't get in. The doors were locked, the blinds and curtains closed.

'Amber! If you don't open this door, I'm going to get Denham. Amber!'

Voice like fingernails on slate, like grit on glass, like razor blades slicing bone.

She could hear him too this morning. Every time Sissy flew away, his smell came back. Smelled him when she turned on the tap, tasted him in the water.

Dry. Dry as a wooden god. Had to keep him out of her.

Couldn't keep him out of the house. She'd packed blankets against the slits beneath the doors but he seeped in. You can't block every gap. Could hear him hissing now. Down the chimney. She'd blacked them with newspapers. Paper is only paper.

'Open the door, Amber, or I'm going to get Denham.'

Pretty bud, near ripe for the plucking.

'Shut up.'

What is trapped within your core, pretty Amber?

'Shut up you bastard.'

She'd smelled him in Charlie White's shop that day. As if she hadn't known him. She'd spent years waiting for him to come back.

Pretty bud, near ripe for the plucking.

He'd told her he'd take her away. The only place he'd taken her was in the dirt beneath the bridge.

A father's right, my pretty Amber.

'Bastard.'

He'd liked them young, liked standing down at the creek watching their screaming play.

'I know you,' she'd said that night.

'You are mistaken,' he'd said.

Almost got him. That second time she'd thought she'd got him. He was punishing her for it tonight. He wouldn't shut up.

Pretty bud near ripe for the plucking.

Shall we see what is trapped within your core, my pretty Amber?

Hard to hear him above the ocean roar in her head, the howl of wind in her ears, through a skull vibrating with noise, expanding with the pressure of contained noise.

For months, for years he'd go. He always came back.

She stepped close to the mirror, peering into it, searching for him. Only a wraith of woman behind the glass. Only the erosion of pretty Amber, deep fissures in parched earth. Fingers rose to trace the arid landscape, the ditch mouth, the rutted clay surrounding twin lost lakes.

Ravaged by him. Ruined by him. Burned black by the fire he'd ignited in her belly.

The elements bruise, pretty Amber. The bud unfurls its petals and too soon they fall. A bud should be plucked when in its fullest beauty, my pretty Amber.

Cringed from the memory of what he'd done to her that day — and wanted him to come back and do it again. Wanted . . . to feel . . .

Watched for him by the schoolyard fence, waited for him until she'd grown tired of waiting for him, and she'd wed that hangdog cur for his Queen Victoria vase, his mother's gold-rimmed tea set, his railway house in the centre of town.

Such a pretty bride.

A rose doesn't bloom forever, my pretty bud.

'Shut up!'

'Something has to be done about her, Mrs Foote. She's got Norman locked out, she's had him locked out for days. She won't even open the door to me now,' Maisy said.

'He's the one to talk to, love,' Gertrude said.

'You may as well talk to the man in the moon as Norman. He's staying over at the hotel again. I think he's enjoying his holiday.'

Gertrude's kitchen table was awash with tomatoes but Maisy pulled out a chair and sat. She came most days to pick up her granddaughter.

'The girls are with Elsie this morning,' Gertrude said, hoping she'd take the hint and go.

She didn't take the hint. 'Sissy knew she wasn't right when she left, but she went anyway. She wasn't even home for six weeks this time.'

'Could you take six weeks of living with them?' Gertrude said.

'That's not the point. Amber has crawled around that girl her whole life. Sissy could give something back to her.'

'We each seem to end up with what we deserve, and as far as I'm seeing it lately, Norman and Amber deserve each other. Give it up, love. I realised a few years ago that there are things in this old world I can't fix.'

She couldn't fix Vern's thinking and she'd had about enough of him. Maybe he'd ended up with who he deserved, one overbearing witch of a daughter, and poor simple Margaret who had her hair cut more often than necessary in order to spend an hour or two gossiping with Maisy — who was the worst in the world to gossip with. She'd never learned when to keep her mouth shut.

And Gertrude didn't have an hour or two to waste on gossiping with her, not this morning. She'd picked eight pounds of tomatoes she planned to turn into tomato sauce this morning. Hadn't lit her copper yet. She hadn't filled it.

'Neither one of your granddaughters had what you could call a normal life,' Maisy said.

'We did our best for them and that's all any of us can do. To tell you the truth, I'm pleased Sissy has got a place to go.'

'Have you heard from Jenny lately?'

Gertrude heard from her most weeks, heard more than she wanted to hear at times, though never what she wanted to hear: that Jenny was coming home. She glanced at her visitor, at the thick stack of letters behind her clock.

'I wish she'd write and say she's coming home.'

Maisy balanced a tomato on her palm but made no reply. Jenny's singing was the talk of the town, as was her engagement to Jim Hooper. Margaret Hooper carried a photograph around in her handbag of the three of them, the ring on Jenny's wedding finger showing clearly.

'Jim and my nephew,' she said, flashing it proudly. She made no mention of Jenny, but at least she hadn't cut her out of the photograph.

Maisy always took longer than necessary with Margaret's hair, usually offered her a cup of tea when she was done with her snipping. She got on well enough with Margaret Hooper.

'I suppose that when you come to think of it, Mrs Foote, the same applies to Jenny as it does to Sissy — only more so. I mean, what you said about Sissy being lucky to have some place to go. I know Jenny has got you, which is different to Sissy having them — but not having to face everyone here, it must be like heaven to her. And to tell you the truth, it eases my own guilt a bit — I mean knowing that she's finally getting a chance to do what she was born to do.'

There was no accusation in Maisy's tone. Maybe there should have been. Her words hit one of Gertrude's nerve endings, made her look at her reasons for wanting Jenny home. She needed her at home. Elsie had enough kids of her own without taking on two extra, and two- and three-year-old girls needed constant watching.

She took up her knife and started cutting tomatoes, sawing them in half, dropping the halves into her preserving pan.

She needed Jenny home where she could keep an eye on her, too. Vern swore that she was pregnant. Gertrude had her own thoughts on that, had spent some nights worried sick in imagining her attempting to expel a Hooper among strangers who didn't know the family history.

September to March. She'd been in Sydney for six months. She wouldn't be singing at clubs and parties if she was six months forward, not with a Hooper inside her.

But was she singing in a club? Or was that boy sending home money so she could stay up there? Vern said so.

She cut two more tomatoes. They were overripe, but overripe was good for sauce making.

'You can't raise a baby in a rooming house full of strangers,' Gertrude said.

'When I was nineteen I was managing two babies and had another one on the way,' Maisy said. 'How old were you when you had Amber?'

'Twenty —' Gertrude started, but give a detail like that to Maisy and in twenty-four hours everyone in town would know Gertrude's age. 'I was wed at nineteen.'

'We managed, Mrs Foote. I had money enough, no time, no energy, but somehow I got through it. You did too. We do what we have to do, even if at times we don't know how we're doing it. Jenny is doing the same. Give me a knife and I'll help you with those or you'll be at it all day.'

Gertrude found a second serrated knife and they sat on opposite sides of the table, cutting, tossing overripe tomatoes into the pan. Maisy had been at home in this house since Amber had started at school. She'd done much of her growing up in this kitchen.

'Has Jenny ever been told about her real mother, Mrs Foote?'

Gertrude shook her head and cut two more tomatoes. 'I've thought about it, but there's no right way to tell her, and not much to tell anyway. And given her life these past years, I doubt she needs anything more to deal with.'

'You could be right,' Maisy said. 'It's just . . . no one ever told me about my mother, other than to tell me that she was a slut who didn't care if I was alive or dead. She was sixteen when I was born. They sent her down to some cousin in Melbourne and she ended up getting married. She sent me money and a card for my birthday every year and Aunty Lily kept them from me. I only found out when I married George and was six months pregnant. Then she went and died of consumption before I got to meet her. I never forgave Aunty Lily for that. People need to know where they come from.'

'You're probably right, love, but the longer it goes on, the less I think about telling her — and the less likely it is that she'll hear it from anyone else.'

'There are a few who still mention it, particularly now. She got that voice from someone. Italians are known for their singing.'

Gertrude knew where she'd got her voice. He was no Italian. She wondered if he was in jail or out, alive or dead. She'd spent the greater part of her life in wondering if Archie Foote was alive or dead. She cut a tomato, tossed it, and wished she'd cut that sod's throat with a serrated knife one night when he'd been passed out from the drugs.

'I'm going to telephone the hospital about Amber. That city place they sent her to fixed her up last time.'

There was nothing Gertrude could say. Nothing she wanted to say. She cut tomatoes.

'She could be lying dead inside that house for all I know. I was over there this morning knocking for half an hour. I couldn't hear a sound from inside.'

'Her father could hole up in his room for days. He came out when he got hungry.'

'How did you stand it?'

'I left him, love. I wiped him out of my mind — and I'm trying to do the same with Amber.'

'Something happened between him and Amber, you know.'

'What?' Gertrude's knife stilled.

'I've got my own ideas. I could be wrong.' Two tomato halves splashed into the pan and Maisy reached for another. 'When I look back on how she was in the days after he cleared out — when I look back through an adult's eyes, that is — she was just like one of my girls used to be when they'd broken up with a boyfriend. Bawling, rotten to me. We'd always been best friends, probably because we were the only two kids in town who didn't have fathers. Then suddenly Amber had one who looked like Jesus Christ. He used to come to the school gate done up like a toff, and she'd run to him and leave me standing.'

'He took her out of school?'

'Six or so times, though she was always back before school came out. I was jubilant when he stopped coming. I told her so, and she damn near scratched my eyes out.'

They sliced tomatoes in silence, sliced them until they were done.

'Did you ever get to see that Forester bloke Denham locked up for taking advantage of the Duffy girl?'

Gertrude was opening a new bag of salt. 'What about him?'

'Amber was convinced he was her father. I knew he'd been dead for years, but I couldn't convince her. She told me she was going to confront him. I don't know if she did or not but she stopped talking about him. Remember how she came good after they arrested him?'

Gertrude's memory of the timing of Amber's improvement differed. No one had seen her around until the day of Barbie Dobson's funeral. That was the day Amber had rejoined the human race, long before Forester's arrest.

'When they let him off the murder charge, she was livid, Mrs Foote.'

Gertrude glanced at her visitor, then took her time sprinkling salt over the tomatoes, measuring sugar — not as much as she may have measured before rationing. Two cups of vinegar, plus a dash.

'She swore she saw him back here two weeks ago, staying at the pub. I got George to ask Horrie Bull the chap's name. It wasn't him. Alfred Conti, Horrie said. Amber wouldn't believe me. She's been going downhill since. She's obsessed by her father, Mrs Foote. I reckon he molested her.'

Gertrude spilled too many cloves into her tomatoes. That same thought had been dogging her for years. She should have kept that girl by her side while he'd been around, should have kept her out of school. Should never have lied to her about her father being a good man, a clever doctor.

She stood picking out the excess cloves, unsure if she was picking out too many. Took more care in adding the allspice. Her sauce was tasteless without spices but too many could ruin it. Added mustard seeds, cayenne pepper — and a little bit of that stuff went a very long way.

'Is he still in town?' she said.

'He was only here for two or three days. She stopped eating. She went cleaning mad, complaining about the smell in her house. The last time I saw her, which was three days ago, the broom she held in her hands had more fat on it.'

Gertrude lifted the preserving pan onto the stove. There was a good fire burning beneath but it would take a while to boil.

'You've been a good friend to her.'

'Someone has to care about her.'

'I care, love. I've cared and I've cared and there's nothing I can do. If you get that doctor up here, I'll pay for him.'

'I'll get going then and do it, Mrs Foote.'

TOO MUCH TO CRY ABOUT

Still two days to get through until Friday and Jenny had two shillings in her purse. Living on tips from the club was all very well when there were tips to live on; it was hopeless when there were none. Wilfred and his merry men had one Saturday night booking in March, and nothing so far in April. Summer was the party season. Now it was autumn.

Sydney's autumn was prettier than Woody Creek's. The gardens and parks were more colourful. Jenny spent hours walking, showing Jimmy the pretty gardens, picking up pretty autumn leaves — and wondering what Sydney would look like in winter, wondering what her room would be like in winter. Probably freezing cold. She missed Gertrude's little black stove, missed the black coat she'd lived in through a Melbourne winter.

I'll have to buy a coat, she thought, and they cost a fortune. And she'd need clothing coupons. She could afford to buy one if she withdrew some of Jim's money. She hadn't touched it yet, though she'd have to soon. Jimmy needed a coat too, and new shoes.

He was sitting on the floor, playing with her black sandals, attempting to put one on over his shoe. She sat at her dressing table rereading two letters delivered this morning.

Maisy's letters always sounded like a good chat over a cup of tea.

> . . . we got the top parlour window open and boosted Jessie up
> to get in and open the front door. One look at the state of the

house was enough for the doctor. He told me to get Denham and call the ambulance.

They took her away to Melbourne and, according to Norman, she's back in the same place they took her the last time. Your father paid Nelly Dobson to clean up the house. Me and Jessie gave her a hand and you never saw it in such a state in your life. She'd stuffed newspapers up the chimneys, and the mess she made of the walls. Someone will have to paint her bedroom.

Your sister is staying in Hamilton with one of your cousins. I wrote to her to let her know what's going on with your mother. I haven't heard back. That girl needs her backside kicked from here to kingdom come. She knew her mother wasn't well when she left and after all Amber's done for her, you'd think she'd have a bit of compassion . . .

Jim's letters were still censored, though a few missed out entirely on that black pen.

My dear, precious Jenny and Jimmy,

I love your poem. It's wrapped around my photographs, in my pocket next to my heart. I've read it so many times I can recite it, though when I do, I change 'beggar' to 'goddess'. If I was a poet, I'd write ten thousand pages about the goddess who turned a lop-eared drongo into a king.

I needed your letter and Jimmy's kiss today. We lost Paddy, and Nobby took a bullet in the leg. We've lost a lot of good chaps. I probably shouldn't be writing this. I doubt they'll let you read it.

I wrote to Pops recently about you and Jimmy and asked him to promise me he'd look after both of you if anything happened to me — which it won't, so don't go worrying. He hasn't written back, or maybe he wrote back through Lorna. I can do without her letters. I've always tried to tell myself that she deserves my pity not my anger, though that doesn't seem to work as well over here.

Margaret writes a good letter. She said that your singing at the club is the talk of the town, and so it ought to be. You

handled it the night I was there as if you'd been singing all
your life, which I suppose you have been.

Pops used to tell me that everything, the good, the bad and
the indifferent, all happened for a reason. I do a lot of thinking
about the past lately, and for once, he could be right.

If you hadn't had Margot forced on you, you wouldn't have
had Georgie, Bobby Vevers wouldn't have been trying to pick
you up the night you went to see Gone with the Wind, *I wouldn't*
have decided to see you home, and if all of that had never hap-
pened, Jimmy would never have been born. Apart from you,
he's the best thing that ever happened to me — which I told
Pops when I wrote to him, which might be another reason why
he hasn't written back.

I'm running out of light. It gets dark early. I've got our
photos out and your poem, and just now I crossed out 'beggar'
and wrote in 'goddess' because that's what you are, my sing-
ing goddess. I only wish I was there to hear you.
Love you both.
Yours,
Jim XXXXX

She folded the letter, slid it into its envelope and walked to the
window to look north to where he was — somewhere north, up
where the weather was always hot. No sun on her window yet,
not much sun anywhere today. She'd have to go to the bank and
find out how to make a withdrawal, or go home — unless the
Yanks came back to town and the tips picked up.

It must have been close to noon. She had bread and a little
milk left, some cheese, plenty of lard. Fried cheese sandwiches
for lunch, she thought. They always reminded her of Norman.
He'd loved fried cheese sandwiches. He wouldn't be missing
Amber. He'd be making a mess in her kitchen.

Jimmy had one of her sandals on and was attempting to stand.
He'd grown tall. He'd probably end up as tall as Jim.

She heard footsteps whispering up the passage. Jimmy heard
them too. He tossed the sandal and headed for the door. Myrtie at
his door could mean macaroni cheese, or tomato soup.

There was no invitation to lunch today. Myrtle Norris, who lived in mortal fear of telegrams, had one in her hand — and fear in her big brown eyes. To Jenny, telegrams were a swift means to an end. Maybe Jim had got leave. Maybe he was already back in Australia.

'Thanks,' she said, and she opened it.

She should have feared this one. Shouldn't have opened this one. She threw the thing from her and backed away from it.

Myrtle picked it up. She read it.

SAD NEWS STOP JIM HOOPER MISSING IN ACTION STOP LETTER FOLLOWING STOP COME HOME GRAN

'My dear, dear girl.'

Jimmy sitting on the floor, using a sandal as a hammer. Bang. Bang. Bang. He knew it wasn't true. Bang. Bang. Bang.

Granny just wanted her to go home, that's all. Every time she wrote she nagged her about going home. It was a trick. Vern had probably told her to do it.

Bang. Bang. Bang. The sandal or her heart hammering. But Myrtle had the sandal, had Jimmy in her arms.

Bang. Bang. Bang.

And Jimmy chuckling, wanting to rip up that lying telegram, knowing full well it was a lie. Two hours ago, Daddy had sent him a proxy kiss.

She clasped Jim's letter to her breast, using it to hold her lurching heart inside. He was alive and well in that letter and Granny's bloody telegram wasn't going to kill him.

Couldn't breathe, because Granny would never do such a thing.

And her fool's paradise came crashing down on her, crushing the breath from her lungs.

She was a jinx. Everything she touched, she ruined. If not for her, Jim would have been married now to Sissy and living in Monk's house. She was a disease, a contagious disease. If she hadn't climbed out the window the night of the ball, she wouldn't have been raped. If she hadn't got on the train . . .

Jimmy's arms reaching out to her.

Had to stay away from him. She'd jinx him, too.

Myrtle's eyes leaking, her mouth full up with la-di-da words, opening, closing, making empty talk bubbles.

Blood rushing in Jenny's ears, thumping in her head. Shook her head. Missing. Missing.

'Can I call someone for you, pet?'

No one. Only Jim.

And Jimmy.

And she hadn't wanted Jimmy anyway, not when he'd first got started. She'd willed him out of her. Climbed up on the roof of the shed and jumped, trying to shake him out of her.

Hadn't asked to start loving him.

Hadn't asked to start loving goblin-eared Jimmy Hooper who had taught her how to keep pushing that ice-cream down with her tongue while crunching on the cone so that you had ice-cream left right down to that last bite.

Missing. Not dead. Had to get away, find space to think. Missing meant missing. Lots of soldiers went missing.

That's what they wrote when there was not enough left of the soldier to find.

And she pushed past Myrtle and Jimmy and she ran. Ran back the way she'd walked the first day with Jim, ran fast, attempting to turn back time, ran with his letter in her hand until her lungs started whooping in great breaths, until she knew that no one could turn back time. Walked then, walked anywhere, up hills and down hills, walked while the day grew cooler. Walked north, south, anywhere, the wheels of her mind grinding in circles that all came back to blown to bits — like she'd been willing Maisy's twins to be blown to bits.

The knowledge that Jim had already been blown to bits when she'd read his letter came to her in a street she didn't know. Walked on, searching her mind for a day when he wasn't dead.

She had to leave time for Vern to get the news from the army, time for Granny to hear the news, time for Granny to saddle her horse, ride into town, send off that telegram, time for those words to fly from Woody Creek to Melbourne, from Melbourne to Sydney, time for the telegram to be written on paper, for the boy to ride up the hill and knock on Myrtle's front door.

On Friday night when she'd sung, when she'd danced with two boys in her once-red dress and high-heeled sandals, he'd been . . . missing. On Thursday when she'd sat in the library looking up places in the atlas. Last Wednesday maybe. What had she done last Wednesday? Couldn't remember last Wednesday.

Time wasn't real. It began to lean, to wobble. And the pavement beneath her feet wobbled. And the street ahead grew misty.

Give it up. Just give up. You can't control what you can't control. Just let go and give in. It's no use.

She'd let go the night Margot had come out. She'd let go the night she'd found out what Laurie wanted. Just let go and let whatever happened happen.

Amber let go and ended up in a madhouse.

Jolt in her heart and in her mind. She wasn't Amber. Grasped hold of a picket fence. She wasn't Amber. Never would be Amber. Grasped the point of one splintery picket too hard, drove a splinter into the pad of her palm. And crushed Jim's envelope. Blood on her palm. If she'd got blood on that envelope it would mean he was dead. No blood on it. Slid it in safe beneath her bra strap and stood looking at the hole in her hand. Hurting. But the pain was good. It was something she could take hold of, concentrate on.

A woman at her gate watching her howl. Jenny wiped her eyes and walked on, got around the corner where no one was watching. Walked and howled until the long creeping tendrils of an overgrown rosebush caught her frock with its thorns.

Like Granny's climbing rosebush, always ready to grab. She eased her frock free, wiped her eyes and looked at the bush. It had covered a side fence. Now it wanted the front fence.

One rose, a red rose, still blooming, too high to reach.

'Tis the last rose of summer, left blooming alone.

He'd brought her here. That rose was his final goodbye.

All her lovely companions are faded and gone.

And she wanted that rose. He'd meant her to have it.

Lone one, I'll not leave thee to pine on the stem. All the lovely are sleeping, so sleep thee now with them . . .

If she walked away from that rose, he was dead. She had to reach it, keep it alive in water, then he'd be alive. Just . . . just missing . . . just lying in some jungle somewhere, just shot in the leg like Nobby. If she could get that rose home, they'd find him and take him to a hospital.

She wiped her eyes on her petticoat, wiped her nose on it, and reached into the mass of thorny growth until she found the branch the rose was growing on. Didn't care whose rose it was or who may have been watching her. And she got it, snapped it from its stem.

It smelled of Woody Creek, at sundown, in spring. It steadied her world. They'd find him now. They'd find him and send him home.

And she had to find her own way home.

She turned right at the corner and walked on, smelling the rose. She stood a while beside a larger road, seeking a landmark, a direction. She'd walked one too many roads today and not taken a scrap of notice where she was going. She was lost, didn't know if she should walk right or left. She looked for the sun. It had been lost beneath low clouds all day and the day was almost done. No east, no west, like the day she'd arrived in Sydney.

She had to ask someone, that was all.

She turned into a lane. Only rear gates and back fences there, but it led her to a street of factories. Signs hung beside doors, on doors, over doors, all screaming VACANCY. APPLY WITHIN.

The sound of hammer on metal. Making more guns to kill more boys.

She walked by fast and stood a moment before a boot factory. Everyone busy in there making boots for soldiers to march in — die in.

He wasn't dead. He wasn't dead.

Walked by an old green door in need of paint, a cardboard sign pinned to it with drawing pins. VACANCY MACHINISTS. APPLY WITHIN.

What were they making in there for that bloody war? Uniforms so the boys might die well dressed?

He wasn't dead. Another telegram would come tomorrow saying that they'd found him.

It had been near noon when she'd left the boarding house, was four, four thirty now and the day darkening. She had to find her way back to Jimmy.

She was crossing the road when a crowd of laughing girls came pouring out through a factory door. She watched them light cigarettes, watched them walk in bunches in the opposite direction. They'd lead her to somewhere. She followed them.

They led her to a station, not to her station but it was on her line. She had no money to buy a ticket but she could follow the railway lines back to Myrtle's station, or follow the road that followed the lines.

Night had settled over Sydney before she reached the boarding house. Exhausted, legs more weary than they'd ever been, head still heavy with tears, and Myrtle Norris standing on the porch watching for her.

'Come through, pet.' Jenny walked into warmth. 'Did you speak to your family?'

Myrtle Norris lived in a magical world where telephones rang, where milk was delivered to her door in bottles, where onions were bought by the bunch from the greengrocer. She had no concept of a hut two miles from town, of goats in the front paddock, chooks in the yard, row upon row of vegetables growing between shed and house. Jenny didn't attempt to explain. She just wanted Jimmy. She needed to hold him, have his little hands holding her. She needed to put that rose in water, keep it alive so Jim would live too.

WINDOWS AND DOORS

Bobby Vevers had been missing for weeks before his family learned he'd been taken prisoner by the Japs — and just when they'd got their hopes up about that, the Red Cross got word through that he'd died in the Jap prison camp. One of the Murphy boys had died in Africa, died a hero's death so they said. One of the Dobsons' older boys had been on a boat torpedoed by those killing bastards. Vern Hooper wasn't the first in Woody Creek to lose a son. A boy turned eighteen now and unless he was cross-eyed and had a gammy leg, the army took him. Woody Creek had bred a lot of boys. Vern had bred only one, and one who never would have been called up to fight, being an only son with a sick father and a farm to run.

A man doesn't cry. Vern spent his days walking, cursing the girl responsible.

'Hot-blooded little half-dago bitch. She never would have looked at my boy if he hadn't been engaged to her sister. Bloody little goldie-headed prostitute bitch.'

For two days Gertrude stayed with him in town and ignored his cursing. If blaming Jenny gave him a focus right now, she'd allow it. He wasn't well enough to take the stress of this waiting to hear if Jim was alive or dead. Strip control away from a man accustomed to control and what was left to him? Not much.

He watched her addressing an envelope to Jenny, watched her enclose a money order to cover her fare home.

'Bloody Amberley,' he said. 'She's got that boy up there living in a brothel.'

'It's a respectable boarding house and he's being well cared for,' Gertrude said.

'How do you know he's well cared for? How do you know what the hell she's getting up to? You didn't know what she was getting up to in Melbourne. Selling herself for two bob a time, and that's what she's doing up there now — like her bloody mother . . .'

'She's singing in a club, Vern, and you know it.'

'I don't know it and neither do you.'

'I know it.'

His railing continued too long. Gertrude found herself biting back replies — and not biting back replies to Lorna.

That girl had been carved from granite. If the telegram from the war department had shaken her, she'd absorbed the blow. More male than female, Lorna, born with Vern's desire for control. Some man had been saved a mess of pain by her spinsterhood.

Gertrude remained in town until Saturday morning, when she told Vern it was time she went home, that she had two little girls to see to.

'You've always had someone else to put before me, haven't you?' he said.

'I've put no man before you, and there's nothing to stop you from spending a few days out there with me.'

Nothing to stop him but two illegitimate kids and a lack of comfort, a lack of conveniences.

She went home, and on Tuesday learned from Maisy that Vern had been admitted to hospital. Maybe he needed to be there. Maybe his daughters needed him to be there.

Gertrude's letter and the ten-pound money order arrived in Myrtle's mailbox on Tuesday morning and Jenny wasn't there to receive it.

She'd waited at the boarding house all day Thursday, at the gate through Friday, certain another telegram would come. By Sunday, when Myrtle and Miss Robertson walked off to church, the rose petals had started drooping, and she couldn't, wouldn't allow them to fall. She'd taken the flower from the glass of water and pressed it flat between the pages of *Rebecca*, had weighted those pages down with a brick she found behind the washhouse.

A busy day Sunday. The landlady had knocked on her door around midday to invite her down for lunch. She'd brought her minister home from church, a Reverend Nightingale, and he looked more underfed blue crane than nightingale.

'God has a master plan for all of us,' he'd said, shaking her hand with fingers that collapsed under her small pressure. And maybe that was the first real thing Jenny had noticed since Wednesday. She'd shaken a few hands, but never one that collapsed into spiders' legs.

He'd prayed before they'd eaten. She felt embarrassed for him praying in Myrtle's parlour. Hadn't listened to his words, just wondered why all ministers used that same high-pitched sing-song voice. Maybe God had a hearing loss. Maybe that's why he didn't hear most people's prayers. Maybe she should have done her own praying in singsong tones.

She'd prayed for Jim every single night since he'd left. Please God, keep him away from the Japs. Please God, let him come home soon. Please God, make the war end. She'd believed in God when she was a kid, like she'd believed in Father Christmas. At five she'd woken up to the fat man with the fake beard. It had taken a few more years to work out that God was Father Christmas for grown-ups.

Myrtle had never worked it out. She stood with her head bowed while the minister prayed for Jim's safety and for the safety of the other fighting boys — while at that same moment, thousands of boys were being shot, bombed, drowned, blown to pieces. Jenny stared at the parlour wall, praying that his praying would end soon. Jimmy wanted to eat.

He saw it first. He jabbered, pointed to the wall. The minister had called down a scrap of heaven; there was a rainbow behind him. Jenny turned to find its source. Only the sun, shining in through Myrtle's leadlight window, reflecting its colours.

But the praying was done. 'Has your son been baptised, Mrs Hooper?' the minister said.

Jenny shook her head as she carried Jimmy closer to that pretty wall.

'Pretty,' she said. 'Pretty rainbow.'

'Pity,' he mimicked.

'Daddy painted a pretty rainbow for Jimmy,' she said.

'Dad-dada,' he said.

Had the girls mimicked so many words at his age? She couldn't remember. She could remember every detail of Jimmy's growth. In some future year, she'd tell him that he'd said 'dada' before he was ten months old, that he'd said 'pretty' at seventeen months old, that he'd crawled at six months, walked at ten, cut his first tooth at eight months.

'What a clever boy you are,' Myrtle said.

'Perhaps we could take care of that next Sunday, Mrs Hooper.'

She brushed the hair from Jimmy's eyes. Too much hair, like his father. He needed a haircut. 'I'm going home,' she said. 'But thank you very much for your thoughtfulness.'

She had to go home. Jim had created Mrs Jennifer Hooper. He'd created the club singer. She'd already gone. Myrtle had telephoned Wilfred at work on Friday morning.

That afternoon she started packing up number five, and every move she made reminded her of the first time she'd packed it up, and every move too sad. Wanted to howl when she tossed Jimmy's outgrown clothes in a pile on that double bed, clothes he'd worn when Jim had been in this room.

Myrtle's shoes whispering again in the passage at four. Jimmy headed for the door, eager to greet her.

'Mr Whiteford is on the phone, pet. Will you speak with him?'

'Tell him I'm going home on Thursday, Mrs Norris.'

'Of course, pet. Will you have dinner with me tonight?'

'You're doing too much for us, Mrs Norris.'

'I don't enjoy eating alone, pet. We'll be eating leftovers.' She'd put on a spread for her minister — perhaps attempting to fatten him up.

They were washing the few dishes when Wilfred called again. This time Jenny took the telephone.

'We have a function on Saturday night, my dear,' he said. 'At that Hornsby Hall we had such difficulty finding. They have asked specifically for our pretty singer.'

'I can't, Mr Whiteford.'

'Would Jim have wanted you to give up your singing?' he asked.

He shouldn't have said that. It made it sound as if Jim was dead. And he wasn't. It made her realise too that the last thing in the world Jim would ever want was for her to stop singing.

'I can't manage on Friday night tips, Mr Whiteford. If I had someone to look after Jimmy, I'd get a proper job and I'd stay and sing for free.'

'Of course,' he said. 'Forgive my lack of consideration.'

'Is money a problem, Jenny?' Myrtle asked when the phone was back on the hook.

'I've got some in the bank.'

'I'll miss you and this dear boy so much.'

'We'll miss you and Amberley, but it will be better if I'm at home. If any news comes about Jim it will go to his father. Up here I won't hear it for days.'

'You and Jimmy are his next of kin, pet. You have every right to contact the —'

Jenny looked at her landlady, wishing she could tell her the truth. She didn't dare. Didn't want to lose that woman's respect.

'When do you hope to leave?'

'I'll see if I can get a seat south on Thursday. My rent is paid until Thursday.'

'That's of no account —'

'It is to me.'

'I . . . I could not fail to hear your conversation with Mr Whiteford. You must know that I'd be more than happy to care for Jimmy — if you decided to seek employment.'

'I hadn't really thought about it until I said it.'

'Perhaps you should give yourself time to think about it.'

'You mean you'd look after him every day? All day?'

'You must know what a joy he is to me.'

*

On Monday morning, Jenny left Jimmy with Mrs Norris and went to the bank. She withdrew ten pounds then walked to the station to buy her ticket home.

A train was waiting there, and on impulse she bought a ticket and took the train to the station near that street of factories. She found her way back to that heavy green door with the sign still pinned to it and before she could change her mind she rang the rusty old door bell.

A woman with cottons in her hair answered the bell's clamour.

'You're advertising for machinists. I can use a treadle machine.'

'That won't do you much good here.' The green door began to close.

'My husband is missing in action. I've got a little boy to feed.'

'I've seen your type come and go, girl. They last five minutes in this place,' the woman said.

'I promise I'll last more than five minutes.'

'We start at eight,' the woman said. She was closing the door.

'Does that mean . . .'

'You've talked yourself into a five-minute trial, girl. Be on time.' And the door slammed shut.

She had a job! Or a five-minute trial for a job . . .

On Tuesday morning she arrived well before eight, clad in her once-lime green frock, and Maisy's thigh-length black cardigan, and she waited for half an hour in the chill of morning while girls wandered up to that door, smoking girls, talking in bunches. Jenny stood alone, knowing she didn't belong here, scared stiff, or frozen stiff, but the door opened and she followed the crowd into a barn of a room, a cold, high-ceilinged room, with many lights hanging low on lint-covered chains, and beneath those lights, wall to wall machines. The girls separated, chose their machines.

She stood until the forewoman saw her and led her down worn steps to a smaller barn, led her around a tall table that might seat forty to where three girls had taken their positions to snip threads, led her between giant machines to a long workbench with a field of machine heads growing out of it — and nothing, nothing in that cold barn which bore any resemblance to Granny's little treadle sewing machine. She'd talked herself into this. She had to go through with it.

The woman pointed her to a vacant chair set before a dustsheet-covered machine head. 'Sit.'

Four or five girls on either side, a matching number opposite, and at the far end of the workbench a huge belt, like at the sawmills, slapping, driving whatever it was that drove those twenty bench machines.

Her ears were assaulted by the noise. Eyes assaulted by too much. The size of the place. The metal-lined gutter running down the centre of the bench like a water channel — a shirt channel. Bits and pieces of shirt running like small tributaries into the main channel, streams of collars, streams of pockets. Jenny sat in stunned silence while the forewoman instructed. A loud woman; voice on her like a bullocky, Granny might have said. She needed to be loud.

Someone else was louder. 'Mrs Crump!'

And the woman with cottons in her hair, who must have been Mrs Crump, was gone and Jenny left holding a misshapen piece of fabric. And what the hell was she supposed to do with that?

Girl on her left zipping around collars, dozens of them. Cotton running from giant reels, never cut, never tied off like Granny always tied off her threads. Girl opposite, already creating a blockage in her section of the metal channel.

Five minutes the forewoman had given her. Had she been here for five minutes? Jenny was ready to run.

But some of the girls looked like schoolkids. She watched the girl on her left feeding in collar after collar. She turned to the girl on her right and watched her break a needle, heard her swear. Turned quickly back to the girl on her left, who looked fourteen, with a face full of pimples and bottle-top glasses, but had her machine eating the fabric out of her hand and howling for more. She saw how the girl placed the fabric beneath the foot. The machine foot was the same as Granny's. Jenny placed her fabric, then pressed down on the pedal. The machine attacked. She snatched her hand away in time.

Heard the cry of 'Mrs Crump!' from Jenny's right.

'They don't grow on trees, girl,' the forewoman said. She fitted a new needle, and to prove she'd last more than five minutes, Jenny got her machine hopping at a pace she could control. That was the trick, just the barest pressure on that foot pedal, then slam down your heel when you wanted the thing to stop.

Mrs Crump stood behind her, watching her turn that misshapen fabric around as Granny had shown her how to turn the fabric around, with the needle down; watching her following that stitching line back, then with not a word she was gone.

Backwards and forwards Jenny went, up and down that fabric, showing the machine who was boss — until the noise died.

It was like being in Woody Creek when the mills stopped. Like a world-ending silence. She glanced around, wondering why the machines had stopped. There was no blackout; the lights were still on.

'Morning tea,' the girl on her right said. 'And thank Christ for that much.'

Jenny followed the herd through a rear door. Tea was supplied, but she had to bring her own cup.

'Use Barbara's,' a girl said. 'She's off sick today.'

'Sick of work,' another said.

Jenny used Barbara's cup and never in her life had a cup of tea tasted so good. She sat at a rough wooden table. A woman with peroxide blonde hair offered her a biscuit, and her name. Norma — or was she Roma, and the girl beside her with the glasses was Norma? Too many girls. A hive of girls all talking at once.

'Jenny. Jenny Hooper,' she said.

They washed their cups at a grubby sink, queued to use two toilets, clustered before a small mirror to comb their hair, then back they went to the machines.

The forewoman dumped a bundle onto Jenny's section of the workbench. 'Pocket hems,' she said.

It wasn't pockets. It was a bundle of bits tied together with a strip of the same material, a cardboard tag on it.

'Untie it,' the girl with the pimples and bottle-tops said, pushing through more collars — and how could there be so many shirts in the world needing collars?

'Fag it,' the girl on her right said. 'She'll tell me not to come back tomorrow.' Pretty little dark headed girl, she looked sixteen. Her mouth didn't sound sixteen.

Jenny opened her bundle and found what looked like pockets.

'Oh, bugger me dead if I haven't done it again! Mrs Crump!' the dark girl yelled.

'Fools are thick on the ground, girl,' the forewoman said. 'I can pick them up for a penny a dozen.'

'It's the cotton's fault. It keeps bogging up underneath,' the girl argued.

'Keep convincing me that you're a fool and you'll be out that door.'

Jenny stitched the hems of pockets until the machines stopped for lunch. She hadn't brought lunch but she followed two girls to a street of shops five minutes down the road. There she bought a hot pastie with tomato sauce, which she ate on the way back.

'I'm Selma,' one of the girls she'd followed said.

'Jenny. Jenny Hooper.'

All afternoon, she stitched pocket hems, keeping her head down and her fingers safe. And she learned that she'd only thought she'd been living in Sydney these past months. She hadn't. Jim had set her down on some school-teaching, hot water on tap, la-di-da island. This place was the reverse side of that Sydney.

'Have you got the time?' The dark girl on her right wanted the day over.

'No watch.'

'You're married, too?'

'He's fighting the Japs.'

'Mine's up north somewhere. He got me up the duff to get out of going, then had to go anyway, and I got stuck with his mother and a pair of bawling twins. How's that for luck? Twins first pop.'

Jenny nodded, stitched pocket hems, never-ending pocket hems.

'He was getting leave, so I cleared out. I'm staying with my cousin — the blonde on the buttonholer. She got me a week's trial. Do they have to keep you for the full week?'

Jenny had been given a five-minute trial. She stitched faster, her mind centred on shirt pockets until someone turned off the power and her machine freewheeled to a halt.

'And thank Christ for that much,' the girl on her right said.

Dustsheets being spread. Jenny spread her own, tucked it around the bundle of pockets she hoped she'd be allowed to complete in the morning.

'She's coming. She's going to tell me not to bother coming back. I'm Lila, by the way. It's been nice knowing you.'

The forewoman didn't tell them not to come back. Lila was shorter than Jenny, with the figure of a bathing beauty — and a fag in her mouth before they stepped into the gloom of late afternoon. She offered her packet and Jenny needed one. She was a factory girl now, lighting up with a dozen more. Norma, the older woman with the peroxide blonde hair, joined them.

'So, how did it go today then?'

'Fagging awful,' Lila said, and they walked on, Jenny part of a threesome of lint-covered girls, each one flicking cottons from their skirts as they walked, Jenny flicking harder at her black skirt and cardigan.

'Are you in mourning or something?' Lila said.

'Mourning and the joint we work in don't go hand in hand, kiddo. Wear something light coloured tomorrow,' Norma advised.

FINDING JENNY

Money is the grease that oils the cogs of choice. A little of it encourages more. Gertrude's letter was waiting for her, with a ten-pound money order folded inside a sheet of paper urging her to use it to buy a ticket home.

Not much else in the letter, no word of Jim. She wrote of Vern, of his daughters.

Jenny wrote back, about her job, her landlady who had offered to look after Jimmy.

And the weeks passed, and at times three seemed to roll into one, and Jimmy started to think he lived downstairs, seemed to look on Myrtle Norris as a second mother. If he fell, he ran to Myrtle as often as he ran to Jenny. And on dark mornings, when he was lifted from the warmth of his cot and carried grizzling down the freezing passage to the warmth of Myrtle's rooms, he reached out his arms to Myrtle, pleased to go to her.

'We should bring his cot downstairs for the winter, pet. It would be easier for both of you.'

'You're doing too much for us already, Myrt.' No more la-di-da landlady now, no more Mrs Norris, just Myrt and Jenny, just friends now, and Myrtle not wanting to accept Jenny's rent money, and refusing to take a penny for looking after Jimmy.

Jenny caught a cold in late June and she gave it to Jimmy. Number five was a freezing tomb of a room and a small single-bar radiator in the sitting room did little to warm more than a patch of skin at a time.

Then Myrtle found a folding bed in the storeroom and what

is the use of arguing against logic? Jenny helped set it up beside Myrtle's bed.

'Dat my big bed,' Jimmy said.

He didn't miss Jenny in the night. She missed him, missed waking up to him in the mornings, but it was easier, and she had more room to move in number five without his cot.

The world kept on turning. People had to learn to turn with it, or fall off the edge into nowhere. She stood on her own two feet now, a factory girl during the week, a singer at weekends, and managing to keep the two sides of her life separated — until late June, until Norma, Barbara and Lila came into the club one night with a mob of Yanks.

Those girls were her weekday friends. She knew their life stories. They spilled them over the lunch room table. She knew that Lila was two years her junior, that she'd left twin sons in Newcastle with her in-laws. She knew that Norma said she was twenty-four, but Jenny guessed that she was probably closer to thirty. She had a nine-year-old son and two school-aged daughters living in a children's home. Barbara, an only child of elderly parents, was going on twenty-one, and wild. Her favourite pastime was picking up Yanks — and doing more than just picking them up, Lila whispered.

They didn't know Jenny's life story. They thought she was Jenny Hooper, that her husband was fighting the Japs. He was, the last time she'd heard from him, so in her mind that's where he remained. She was living a lie in Sydney, so why shouldn't she lie to herself?

By lunchtime on Monday, everyone at the factory knew Jenny sang at a club.

'Dark horse,' they said. 'What else don't we know about you?'

They didn't know she lived in a mansion, that her la-di-da landlady had fallen in love with her son.

July 1943
My darling Robert,

Myrtle wrote pages each Sunday night, emptying out her week of days to her Robert. Her days now spent with Jimmy, her letters were filled with him.

*. . . watching him evolve is such a joy to me. He calls me
Myrtie now and is beginning to speak in sentences. 'Want
bickie, Myrtie,' he says and so clearly. 'Jenny gone-a work,'
he says. I would gladly give all I own if he could be my mine.*

*She's only nineteen years old, far too young, and such a
pretty girl. She'll marry again when the war is over and have
more children.*

*I know little of her family situation, other than that she was
raised by her grandmother. She never mentions her parents,
whom she apparently hasn't seen in years. There is such a
wide-eyed country girl innocence about her, but a deepness,
too. I offered to contact the war department for her regarding
Jim, and she told me she didn't want to make it real.*

*I doubt she was legally married to him. She told me once
that the family had not approved the match . . .*

On the weekends Wilfred Whiteford and his merry men had no
function to attend, Myrtle lost her boy from early Saturday morning until seven o'clock on Monday morning. Those weekends
were long. She spent them watching the stroller leave, waiting
for it to return, and when it did, she was constantly listening for
Jimmy, her eyes turned to the ceiling, wondering if he was running around up there barefoot.

*He has had one severe cold this winter. I don't want him get-
ting another. She's a capable girl, and very frugal. She brought
home a bundle of material scraps from the factory last week,
dyed them the prettiest shade of blue then turned them into
tiny frocks for children her grandmother cares for. She ran up
the larger seams at the factory but hand-stitched the rest then
sat for hours, making such neat buttonholes . . .*

As one long and lonely Sunday loomed before her, Myrtle heard
them in the lodgers' kitchen. Seeking an excuse to go there, she
armed herself with clean tea towels.

Jimmy ran to her. She kissed him, collected the lodgers' soiled
tea towels and stood for a while, watching Jenny squat before the

gas oven, attempting to light it with a burning twist of newspaper. Myrtle got the oven burning for her, then held Jimmy back from the heat while two trays of biscuits slid in. With no good reason to remain longer but no desire to leave, she picked up one oddly shaped section of fabric Jenny had spread on the larger of the two kitchen tables.

'What are you making, pet?'

'Overalls — with long hems this time. He's got his daddy's long legs.'

'Have you been in contact with Jim's people at all?'

Jenny shook her head and went to the sink to wash the mixing bowl, to leave the kitchen as she'd found it. A lot of Amber had rubbed off on her. She liked a tidy kitchen, and liked sewing, too; kept her threads in a shoe box like Amber had. Reels of thread, pins, needles — she'd even made a pincushion.

'Are both of Jim's parents still living?'

'Only his father,' Jenny said. She snipped a length of thread and aimed it at the eye of the needle. 'He's got two older sisters — both old maids.'

'The little girls you sew for, are they nieces?'

'They're little mistakes, Myrt. Granny has — Granny and her adopted daughter have more or less raised them.'

'You said once that she'd raised you?'

'Since I was fourteen.'

'Is your sister still living with her?'

'She's in Melbourne with Dad's relatives — most of the time.'

'You must miss her.' Jenny shook her head and reached for one of the pieces of fabric. 'My brother moved to New Zealand five years ago. I still miss him,' Myrtle said.

'I don't miss her. She's one of the sisters in the tale of Cinderella.' She placed two matching pieces of fabric together and began to join them, her needle flying. Jimmy wanted to climb up, to see what she was doing, so Myrtle lifted him, her heart content with that boy in her arms.

'You're the fairy godmother in the story,' Jenny continued. 'Mine and Jimmy's.'

'What a lovely thing to say.'

'It's true.'

'Does your aunt have her own children?'

'Elsie? She's not my aunt. And she's got six — her four, plus two of her sister's. Have you got children, Myrt?'

The smell of hot biscuits saved Myrtle from replying. They were done, and Jimmy wanted one. Jenny slid two onto a plate and broke them into small pieces, waving a piece to cool it, then popping it too soon into his open mouth. Myrtle flinched, knowing it was too hot. But it wasn't. Not for Jimmy. He wanted more.

'I imagine sometimes what it must have been like for your kids growing up in this house with a fairy godmother,' Jenny said popping a second portion of biscuit into Jimmy's waiting mouth.

'I can't have children, Jenny,' Myrtle said.

'I'm sorry,' Jenny said.

For twenty years, Myrtle had felt sorry for herself. Her brother had two sons. Her sister-in-law had five children. Friends and neighbours had children. Twenty years ago, she'd called many in this street her friends. Not now. She'd cut her ties with those who had been blessed.

Amberley had always been her home. When she'd wed, she'd moved from her virginal room into a larger room, with a double bed, so certain that children would be born of her love for Robert.

Such a protected life she'd led until her father had taken his life. Gone for a walk one night and hadn't returned.

That terrible funeral. That terrible awakening to reality.

He'd borrowed a fortune to play the stock market, and while shares had continued to rise, he'd done well. But what goes up must come down. He'd lost his business; he'd mortgaged the house to pay his broker.

They thought they'd lose Amberley. If not for Robert, they would have lost it. Myrtle had not been raised to work, but she'd been educated, and had applied to the education department for a teaching position. But one wage earner in the family was considered to be enough back in those bad times — and under normal circumstances Robert's wage would have been enough.

Their circumstances had not been normal. Richard, Myrtle's brother, was in his second year at the university and was not prepared to give up his studies. His car had to go. The maids, the yard man had to go. Jewellery was sold for a mere fraction of its true value, as were paintings and furniture. A terrible year, 1930, and all of their economies and Robert's wage, his meagre savings, barely keeping the bank from the door.

It was Robert who had suggested taking in a paying guest. Miss Robertson, one of his teaching colleagues, recently arrived from England, had been seeking more genteel accommodation than that found for her by the education department. She'd moved into an upstairs room and been no trouble at all, so they'd taken in a second teacher, Mr Fitzpatrick, then a third and fourth, Mrs Collins, a widow, and her fourteen-year-old son.

By 1934, all six of the upstairs bedrooms had been let. They'd provided full board, their paying guests eating each night with the family. Not an ideal situation, but one did what one had to do.

In '35, Richard followed a New Zealand girl home; they'd had a hurried little wedding and a son born too soon. Myrtle's mother hadn't lived to meet that tiny boy. Amberley, left jointly to the siblings, was valued, and mortgaged again to pay out Richard's share.

They'd borrowed again in '37, and used that money to turn the small sunroom into a private kitchen, the study into a bathroom, while the large dining room became their private parlour, the parlour their bedroom. They had a door installed in the passage so they might close their rooms off from the rest of the house. Gave the old kitchen over to the lodgers. Two or three had not appreciated fending for themselves; they'd found alternative accommodation; their rooms had soon been let.

With her private door locked, Myrtle saw little of her lodgers. She opened the old serving hatch between the lodgers' kitchen and her parlour each Friday, made change there, signed rent books, then closed it. She employed a woman and her daughter to clean on Monday mornings and to make up the lodgers' beds with clean linen. A laundry van collected the soiled linen on Tuesday mornings and returned it on Fridays. She sorted the mail, took the occasional telephone message, packed the clean linen away.

They'd applied to adopt late in '37, through the church and been told it would be only a matter of time before an infant was placed into her arms. Happy, hopeful years.

Then came the war.

Robert had seen action during the first war, and when it was over he'd spent twelve months in France and Germany. The army needed experienced men. His name had come up on some file and he hadn't argued. She'd wanted him to argue, had begged him to argue; she'd told him that at forty he was too old to go.

He'd considered it his duty.

Hang duty, she'd said.

Lonely weeks, lonely, fearful years — before Jenny and Jimmy came to fill her days. She should have encouraged that girl to return home to her family. Instead, she'd encouraged her to stay.

A godmother, she'd said, a fairy godmother. What a lovely thing to say.

'. . . involved in the fighting, Myrt?'

Myrtle gathered her thoughts. 'Robert? I don't know, pet. He writes that he has seen little action.'

'I would have thought he'd be too old to be called up — not that he's old . . .'

'I attempted to convince him that he was very, very old, but to no avail. Men have this . . . this feeling that it is their duty to fight in wartime.'

'They change duty to suit the situation,' Jenny said. 'A while ago it was a woman's duty to stay home and look after the kids. Now it's their duty to man the factories and equip our valiant fighting men. *Keep the home fires burning, while two hearts are yearning, turn the dark clouds inside out till the boys come home . . .*' Jenny sang, then snipped a thread, and slipped it through the eye of her needle. 'But you wait, Myrt, just wait until it's over and we'll be back to having a baby every year so they'll have an army ready to die in the next war.' She tied a knot in the thread, began to stitch. 'I'm never, not as long as I live, ever having another baby.'

She was a child, and a jaded old woman. There were too many facets to Jenny; they blinded the eye to the flaws that lay beneath the surface. They were there. At times Myrtle glimpsed them, but fleetingly.

My darling Robert,

Mr Howard has informed me that he will be moving out in July. He's marrying a widow with three children! I would never have thought it of him. To me he has always epitomised the confirmed bachelor. He has been with us for over three years and I believed we'd have him for many more.

Given the current housing situation, I dare say it would be selfish not to re-let his room, but I have this awful fear of allowing an unknown male the freedom of my house. How I wish you were here to advise me. I have considered moving Jenny downstairs and offering her full board. She has become to me a favourite niece. This would allow me to put a female lodger into number five. With Jimmy now spending most of his nights with me, she'd manage well enough in one of the smaller rooms . . .

When would it end? Where would it end? The Allies were making headway, so it seemed. Mussolini, Italy's leader, had been overthrown and imprisoned. Myrtle followed the war news, in the newspaper and on the radio, but there were so few details. Perhaps the government, like Robert, believed in protecting those at home from the horror of war.

My darling Robert,

The world is certainly changing. Two women have been elected to the federal parliament, an Enid Lyons and a Dorothy Tangney. I dare say it was only a matter of time. With so many women, the married and unmarried, holding down important positions, I cannot help but wonder what will happen when the men come home. Shall Enid and Dorothy each be given an apron and sent back to their kitchens?

In September, the Italian government, which had been fighting with Germany, signed a truce with the Allies. Then, on the third of October, they declared war on their old allies. There was no understanding the minds of men.

MOSCOW TALKS MARK BIG STEP TO VICTORY the newspaper headlines howled. THE FOREIGN SECRETARIES FROM ENGLAND, AMERICA AND RUSSIA MEET.

And while they spent twelve days sitting around talking in southern Russia, German troops abandoned their equipment in their haste to retreat.

GERMANS CUT TO PIECES WHEN RUSSIANS SWOOP.

How did anyone visualise that? How could anyone begin to imagine what it was like for those boys?

Better not to think about it.

My dear boy has been with me until tonight. Jenny had an engagement with Mr Whiteford and his band on Saturday night. We allowed her to sleep in this morning . . .

THE YANKS

For a month Jenny carried Gertrude's ten-pound money order around in her handbag, and like the seeds Granny planted in the garden, it had taken root and grown. As with many raised during the depression, Jenny had rarely found two pennies to rub together. It was coming in from everywhere now.

On three Saturday nights in a row, Wilfred and his band had parties, then two Fridays in a row the Yanks' boats were in.

And she was making good money at the factory. The forewoman had moved her from the bench machine to one of the big seamers. Everyone had wanted that seamer. Trina, the girl who had been on it, had made a fortune on piecework, and the seamers were always the first asked to do overtime.

She'd paid back the ten pounds of Jim's she'd withdrawn from the bank; now every week or two the total of her own money in there grew. At night, when she sat alone, she worked out on paper how many weeks' rent she had in the bank, how many weeks' food. She'd bought an account book like Norman's, in which every purchase was listed, just as Norman had listed his purchases.

July: New walking shoes. Repairs to old walking shoes.

August: Grey checked double bed blanket. Buttons for the blanket overcoat.

Everyone was wearing blanket coats. Clothing coupons were required for ready-made clothing but not for household goods. She'd borrowed the pattern for a blue blanket shortie jacket from Selma, the girl on the other seamer, and later made her own pattern for a matching coat for Jimmy. He looked so smart and grown up in it, she wasted money on a professional photographer, who took a few shots of him standing alone and one shot of mother and son together. It was the best one, or maybe she thought it was the best one because he looked the image of her around the eyes and nose and brow. Even Lila said so.

Lila had fixed on Jenny as her bosom friend — during working hours. Jenny enjoyed her companionship — during working hours. She knew the names of most of the girls, knew some better than others. Norma was Lila's cousin, Barbara was Norma's best friend. Selma and Betty stuck together, as did Joan and Lois. So many girls, so many cliques, so many stories.

Norma and Barbara liked the Yanks. They came to work on Mondays with packets of Yank chewing gum.

'They'll get more than chewing gum from them if they're not careful,' Lila said. 'They'll end up with VD.'

A school of learning, that factory. 'What's VD?'

'A sex disease. They go to hotels with them.'

'They don't!'

'They do so. And you know Trina from the seamer? Barbara reckons she's had a half-black baby.'

'She didn't!'

'Barbara says so.'

'Has she seen it?'

'She didn't keep it, you ratbag. She had it at some Salvo home and left it there.'

The factory was full of Yank tales. A dead girl was found in a culvert out at Parramatta, and it was blamed on the Yanks.

'Never let them buy you a drink. I heard about a woman who they drugged and had their way with.'

'I saw two white girls getting into a taxi with half a dozen of them nigger Yanks.'

August 1943
Dear Granny,
The Yanks were in on Friday. I'm enclosing ten bob for you to buy something for the girls from me and Jimmy . . .

328

Dear Jenny,

Mr Foster asked after you today and he said to tell you that he had a letter from Mary Jolly and that she asked him to pass on her regards.

You'd remember Mrs Bryant — Nancy, I used to call her. She died suddenly last weekend. It was unexpected though maybe it shouldn't have been. She lost her husband three months ago and those two lived for each other.

Georgina is growing very leggy. She's a good inch taller than Margot. I don't need to write that they've forgotten who you are and I doubt it's much use telling you to come home, or telling you that we don't need your money. Put it in the bank . . .

Dear Granny,

I'm putting plenty in the bank, and it's the best feeling I've had in my life. The weeks go so fast. It's no sooner Monday than its payday again and I get no time to spend it. I made a pile last week and I haven't had time to get near a bank. I worked from eight to eight, Monday to Thursday, and could have worked late on Friday if not for the club, which was bedlam.

You know how a plague of grasshoppers will go for any-thing green? Well the Yanks swarm off their boats and go after anything wearing a skirt, and they don't care if she's already with a bloke. Most of them can dance so a lot of the girls like dancing with them. The Aussie blokes who can't, or won't, dance take offence, then it's on for young and old. The MPs dragged a dozen blokes out of the club last Friday but we made a fortune in tips. We always do when the Yanks are in.

It's sad about Mrs Bryant. I liked her. She always spoke to me in town. She used to bring in cream and things when I was a kid. Say hello to Mr Foster for me and ask . . .

Ask him for Mary's address?

She chewed at the end of her pen, imagined writing again to Mary Jolly, receiving letters from her addressed to Cara Jean-ette Paris. She'd loved the pretence of her childhood pseudonym, had loved weaving Cara's fictional life for Mary. It had been like reading a never-ending book. She could do it again. She could tell her she'd married and was living with her in-laws in a Sydney harbourside mansion. She could tell Mary to address her letters to Mrs Jim Hooper.

No. She wasn't a kid, living in a pretend world — and she wasn't going to use Jim's name in some childish game either. One day, one fine day when the war was over, when Jim . . . when the world got back on track, then she'd get Mary's address and knock on her door.

. . . ask Mr Foster to pass on my regards to Mary. Tell him to tell her that I think about her often.

I'm sending you a photograph of me and Jimmy and one of Jimmy you can give to Maisy to give to Margaret Hooper, and ask Maisy to ask her if they've heard anything at all about Jim because I don't trust Vern . . .

In November, Jenny bought three yards of the prettiest shot taffeta. It was blue, but with a green and purple sheen to it. It reminded her of the colour of the old ball gown. She made it up to wear to Barbara's twenty-first birthday party. Everyone was dressing up for it.

Dear Jenny,
I ran into Sissy in town today. She told me she was home for Christmas. I don't suppose we can expect you home . . .

Dear Granny,
Coming home would mean two days of travelling to get there and two days to get back, and I'm singing over Christmas and New Year anyway. I'm posting a few things for the girls. Tell them they are from Santa Claus . . .

She shouted herself a haircut for her twentieth birthday and watched every snip of the scissors, directing the hairdresser to cut her hair the way Granny had cut it, short, like a boy's, at the sides and back, but full on top.

Twenty had seemed much older when she was fifteen. Now that she was there, it still seemed too young. Maybe next year, when she was twenty-one, she'd feel older.

Jimmy, grown from baby to little boy in Sydney, had never had a boy's haircut. She sat him in the chair when her hair was done, and Jimmy had his first professional trim. It made him look older, less like her, but more like Jim.

Her birthday fell on a Friday, on club night. Needing to mark it in some way, she wore her shot taffeta with her pearl-in-a-cage earrings and new black high-heeled shoes. She powdered her nose, painted her mouth, lengthened her eyebrows just a little. Wilfred told her she looked as pretty as a picture.

It was the wrong night to dress up. The Yanks were in, packs of them in naval uniforms. They were from a different planet; they spoke a different breed of English, had names no self-respecting Australian would tolerate: Hank, Joe Junior, Billy-Bob, Whitworth, Chuck, Link. Most of them looked like kids, many younger than she. She sang their requests, jitterbugged twice with Billy-Bob, a baby-faced kid who looked sixteen. His mates said he could sing. So she sang a song with him — which was a mistake. She couldn't get rid him.

'That's my little boy,' she said, flashing her photographs when her wedding ring didn't work. He wasn't interested in photographs of two-year-old boys. He told her his boat was leaving in the morning, that he had to get back to it tonight.

'I'm sorry,' she said. And just to get rid of Billy-Bob, she danced with Hank, who was more dangerous. The short hairs on the back of her neck told her so — and told her not to drink the lemon squash he bought for her. It was still sitting on the piano at midnight when Billy-Bob wanted a kiss for the New Year.

'I'm married,' she said. 'I've got a two-year-old son. Go away.'

'I'm in love,' he said, drunk enough not to care if she had six kids.

He was an eighteen-year-old kid, heading back to fight a war tomorrow, and she hated that bloody war, hated the thought of any one of those laughing, drinking, rowdy boys being dead next week. She let him kiss her, which was like being kissed by a wet fish with an elastic mouth.

'Happy New Year,' she said. 'Now goodnight.'

'You let me waste my night on you,' he said.

'Then don't waste any more of it. Go away.'

She sang again, sang until one, when Wilfred shared their bounty of tips, and they left the club.

He always parked his car in a lane around the corner, a narrow lane and pitch dark, but they'd walked that way often enough to know each rut, and he held her arm. A courtly gentleman, Wilfred, he opened the car door for her, saw her seated.

The night Jenny had met him, Mavis called him a queen. Back in those days Jenny hadn't known what she meant. Norma, from the factory, called him an old queer, then explained in common language what a queer was. Many gaps in Jenny's education had been filled by the factory girls — who were probably right about Wilfred. He lived with his friend, Andrew, who had broken his hip and could no longer get around. She'd met him once when Wilfred forgot his house key and drove back to get it. Andy had trouble walking, and would not appreciate being roused from his bed to open the door after midnight, Wilfred had said.

He hadn't appreciated opening it at eight. He walked with two sticks and looked old and cantankerous. Maybe he was in pain, but he didn't look the type of friend Wilfred might have chosen to live with — more like a jealous wife who had caught her husband driving around town with another woman . . . or with another singer. Andrew had sung with the group before his accident.

Wilfred had to back the car out of that dark lane. A careful driver, he braked and checked over his shoulder before making the sweep onto the road. Jenny's own head was turned, checking over her shoulder for traffic, when the driver's side door flew open. Little Wilfred grunted, then disappeared.

The mind doesn't always spring to the right conclusion, not in that first split second of time. The car was rolling and without a driver. She grabbed for the steering wheel, her foot stabbing at the brake — thought of Laurie —

'Happy New Year, babe.'

A Yank voice in the dark. Wilfred?

Then hitting out at a large shape with her handbag, handbag

heavy with coins, notes — with everything important she owned. And the bag was dragged from her hand and too late she tried to get out the passenger side door.

Another one pushing in. Pushing her back in.

That's when she screamed, when she kept on screaming. That's when she punched, clawed, clawed at an arm across her throat. It killed her scream.

More of them getting into the back seat. She was dead. She was dead and stuffed up a culvert. She was dead, and the car motor howling for her. Car moving. Gears grinding. Hands dragging, pushing, pulling her over the back of the seat. Screaming again. Screaming until a fist hit her in the jaw. She howled for the pain of that punch. Howled and begged those bastards then, pleading for her life, her arms pinned, legs pinned.

Hands all over her. Fighting those hands until they pinned her arms.

'Please. Please, God. Please.'

Bottle clashing against her teeth. Choking, spitting fire.

'Suck it down, babe. It's party time.'

Knowing she was dead. Murdered in Sydney on her twentieth birthday. And lucky to get to twenty, Vern would say.

That's where dreams get you. That's where singing, where money in the bank gets you.

'Party time. Relax and enjoy it, babe.'

Choking, swallowing so she didn't choke. Fighting to breathe and that bottle clashing into her teeth when the car hit a bump. Liquid burning her mouth, her throat, her face.

You can't fight two. You can't fight two times two. You can't.

Lightning never strikes twice in the same place, Granny used to say.

Lightning strikes when it feels like striking. Lightning strikes where it wants to strike.

'It's expensive stuff, babe. Get it into you.'

'It's your lucky night, babe.'

Lungs whooping for air enough to live, and why bother living anyway. Jim was dead. So stop fighting and die.

Jimmy.

Swallow it. Swallow or choke on it.

They dragged her out. Somewhere. A dark place. Carried her, then tossed her down like a sack of wheat on the sand. Nothing to grip. To hold onto. No reason to hold on.

Spread her legs. Kneeled on her arms. Laughing, passing the bottle and using her like a pack of male dogs. Pack of filthy laughing hyenas.

The shutting down then. The stopping of it. Or the stopping of the world.

I won't see Jimmy grow. I wanted to watch him grow.

SINKING IN SAND

Someone was washing her face with a warm face cloth. Jenny opened her eyes and was face to face with a black labrador.

Sand in her mouth. She spat. Dark, though not quite dark. Ocean somewhere. Close. Wash-wash of water on sand.

The dog, pleased that he'd raised the dead, stood back, laughing at her.

She spat sand, lifted her head, tried to raise herself on her elbow. It sunk in sand and she fell back. She couldn't remember what she was doing there. How she'd got there. Something was choking her. Her bra. Twisted around her neck.

She remembered then, and a howl rasping up through her raw throat she rolled to her knees, cowering, pulling her bra down to where it belonged, her eyes searching for the dog's owner.

The dog, afraid of her howl, backed off, found something else to sniff at, something darker than sand.

Crouching to hide her nakedness, one hand feeling her throat, feeling the hopeless moan in her throat. Head, shoulder, back hurting, throat, jaw hurting. And one earring was gone. Howling then for her missing earring, for her nakedness. Helpless, hurting, hurting everywhere. As the dog moved off to explore further, she saw what he'd been sniffing at: her pretty taffeta dress. She fought her way into the frock, her shoulder screaming, sand showering her face. Her arm went through a ripped sleeve seam, and she moaned for her pretty dress and the hours she'd spent in stitching it, howled for her hurting and her earring, but she got her arm free, got it into the sleeve, got that dress pulled down. Covered, she looked again for morning walkers. Only the dog.

There was an ache in her lower back when she pushed herself to her feet. Pain when she turned her neck. Ache in her jaw, head pounding.

Limped towards the ocean. Miles of water. And one shoe lying in the sand.

Waves wash, wash, washing against the shore. Like at Frankston. But it wasn't Frankston and she wasn't fifteen. Where was she? She rubbed her shoulder, stretched it, stretched her neck, then walked down to the water.

And found her second shoe playing in the waves, washing in, creeping back out to swim again. She reached for it. Saw a stocking stretched like seaweed on the sand. Threw the shoe back in the direction of its mate. And the action hurt. There was something wrong with her shoulder. She stood rubbing it while a wave picked up the stocking, stretched it. Like a snake it swam back to the sand.

She brushed at the skirt of her pretty shot taffeta frock. A crumpled rag now. Ruined, like Amber's old ball gown had been ruined. She should have known better. Should have known better than to buy the fabric. Should have known how it would end. Like her *Alice Blue Gown* — in the lavatory pan when she was ten.

'Bastards,' she howled, to Amber, to the rapists, to the twins, to God and every other bastard who had stolen her life. 'Bastards.'

But she had her life. She wasn't stuffed up a culvert with her throat cut, wasn't stabbed to death like little Barbie Dobson who had never had a life, like Nelly Abbot, who had not been allowed to grow past ten — like Jim Hooper. She had her life. Jimmy was at home with Myrtle. She had her life and she had Jimmy.

She hitched her frock high, then higher, as she waded into the waves, waded in deep enough for salty water to wash her clean. Granny had great belief in salty water. It would cure anything that a cup of tea wouldn't. She felt the sting of its curing where they'd used her, of its cleansing, felt the heat of urine as her bladder released, burning those bastards out of her.

Time stilled as she stood in the waves while the sand cleansed her, her eyes scanning the coastline, seeking landmarks. She didn't know where she was. She didn't know Sydney, she'd had no time to learn Sydney, other than Myrtle's area. She'd worked. She'd worked so hard to put money in the bank. She'd done everything right in Sydney. Everything.

'Wilfred?' She'd forgotten little Wilfred. They hadn't wanted him. They'd wanted her.

'Bastards.'

Wilfred would have gone to the police. They could be out looking for her. How did anyone look for anyone in Sydney?

'Bastards!' she screamed across the water, and the dog, busy chewing on some titbit, looked up and smiled. 'Scavenger hyena bastards.'

The frock's full skirt stuck to wet buttocks, to wet legs as she walked back to where she'd tossed the second shoe. It was wet, sandy. She shook it, found the other one and emptied it of sand. With a shoe in each hand, she watched the dog mouthing something inedible. And he brought her his inedible bone, dropped it at her feet then sat, his tail spraying sand while he waited for praise.

He'd found a watch. She picked it up. The wrist band had been chewed. Its hands told her it was ten past five. She turned it over, wiped away sand and dog saliva with her thumb, and saw the engraving. Neat letters, like the jeweller had engraved inside her ring.

Billy-Bob from Mom and Dad, 7/18/43

'Bastard,' she howled and threw it at the ocean.

It landed short. The dog thought it was a game. He fetched it, returned it to her feet and sat waiting, tail wagging, for more.

'Bastard,' she said. There was no other word left in her.

But that watch was evidence. She took it down to the water, washed it clean, then walked those lapping waves, hoping they might wash in her pink pants. Gone. Washed out to sea. Or in one of the bastard's pockets. With her earring. With her suspender belt.

Aware the game was over, the dog wandered off towards a road. He was friendly. He looked well cared for. His owner could have a telephone. She followed the dog, feeling naked beneath the full skirt of the frock, holding it down, holding it close to her knees.

She searched both sides of that road for Wilfred's car. It wasn't there. There were no cars about. In the distance a milkman's horse clip-clopped about his business. She shook sand from her shoes and slipped them on, one dry, one wet and gritty. Shoes made for dancing, not for walking, but she walked in them, in the direction of the milkman.

He turned a corner and the dog disappeared down the same side street. No use leaving a main road. She had to find a police station. She had to report the rape before the rapists' boat sailed. She had to do everything right this time.

Name?

Jenny Hooper. But I'm not really Jenny Hooper. I'm Jenny Morrison, the town slut with three kids. I've got a sign hanging around my neck saying *Please rape me*.

She couldn't go to the police.

She knew who they were. She had that watch. And one of them had been Hank. Knew his rank Yank smell, his accent.

Party time, babe.

She had to report them.

She'd heard so many horror stories about the Yanks. Hadn't believed half of them. They were just boys sent a long way from home.

Now she believed. Now she had her own story.

She visualised the factory lunch room. 'There were five of them. They chipped my front tooth with their bottle.' She could feel the chip with her tongue. Hoped it wasn't as bad as it felt. Felt it with her fingernail. Just the corner. She felt again for her lost earring. She'd loved those earrings. Knew that one of those bastards was probably fingering it now, and laughing about his night out in good old Sydney.

She had to report them.

The light was better now. People would be about soon. She had to get to somewhere. Had no money to get anywhere even if she found a train. Her snakeskin handbag was gone. Bankbook gone. Jimmy's photograph gone, money, cigarettes, talent quest five-pound note. Everything was gone.

Jimmy wasn't.

Sand between her toes, cutting. She walked on, holding her skirt down.

Jenny was still in sight of the beach when a taxi drove by. She waved to it. The driver didn't see her, or chose not to. He continued on to the corner. But he turned around, drove back.

'Must have been some party, love,' he said.

She opened the rear door, slid into the back seat, and gave him her address. Taxi drivers knew Sydney. He'd take her home. She had money in her room. She hadn't locked her door. She never locked her door. There was a typewritten sign behind it, probably behind all of the doors, warning guests that no responsibility was taken for the loss of personal possessions. Miss Robertson locked her door. Maybe she had something to lose.

'Can you pay me, love?'

'When I get there I can.'

'I've heard that one before. Out you get.'

'Please,' she said. 'Here.' And she handed him the watch.

He squinted at it, shrugged. 'Not much use to me.'

'I'll change it for money when I get there.'

He put the car into gear. She sat staring out the window. They were somewhere south of the city. She knew that much. He knew his city and, with no traffic about, it didn't seem long before he turned into Myrtle's street. Maybe her mind had been wandering.

She asked him to stop on the far side of the road. She said she'd be a couple of minutes. He got out of the car and followed her across the road.

'Please,' she said. 'Just wait. Please.'

'I'll be in after you if you don't come back, love.'

Crept barefoot inside, crept up the stairs — and met Mrs Collins on her way to the WC, Mrs Collins not wearing her glasses, not wanting to be seen without her false teeth. She hurried on her way.

Jenny's emergency money was in a cigarette packet in her bottom drawer. Like Granny she always kept emergency money in her bottom drawer. Her underwear was in the top drawer. She stepped into a pair of pants, then, money in hand, she returned barefoot to the taxi driver. He took her money and handed her the watch.

Back upstairs, she dropped the thing into her bottom drawer and picked up her towel, her once-lime green frock, underwear, soap, the last of Jim's lavender water and a bottle of coconut oil shampoo. She'd get herself clean, then she'd think. Then she'd be able to think.

Washed her hair three times, got the stink of them out of her hair but not out of her head.

She was alive. That's what she had to keep telling herself. She wasn't dead and stuffed up some culvert to rot. She was alive and Jimmy was safe and that's all that mattered. It was over. They'd be on their boat now, maybe gone already.

Leave them to the Japs —

Or talk to Myrtle. Ask her what to do.

She'd be the last person in the world to talk to.

Speak to Wilfred — if he wasn't dead. Such a little man, little leprechaun with magic fingers. Speak to Wilfred. He'd lost his car. He would have gone to the police.

THE DOCTOR

She took two aspros, and for an hour tried to close down her mind in sleep. She couldn't sleep, couldn't lie still. She started cleaning, tidying her drawers, dusting the window frame with one of Jimmy's napkins, polishing the glass with old newspapers. She was wiping dust from the top of the wardrobe when Myrtle knocked at the door.

Jenny wasn't ready to face her.

'Mr Whiteford is on the telephone, pet. Will I ask him to call back?'

'I'm coming,' Jenny said, and she followed Myrtle downstairs.

'Thank God you got home safely,' he said.

'Thank God.' Why do we say thank God when we no longer believe there is a God?

What else was there to say?

'I have your handbag, dear.'

'Thank God.' Or thank the laws of gravity. He'd been snatched from a moving car and flung. He'd landed. The bag had been snatched from the same moving car and flung. It had landed. He'd picked himself up. He'd picked up the bag.

The first night she'd met him he'd chased her out to the street with that snakeskin handbag. More in it now than then.

'I'll come up and get it,' she said.

'Did they . . . harm you?'

'I'll come up now,' she said. The telephone was in the parlour. Myrtle and Jimmy were in the kitchen.

'I have to get my handbag,' she told Myrtle. 'Can Jimmy . . .' But Jimmy wanted to go for a ride, and maybe the normalcy of pushing his stroller up that hill, of being forced to respond to him, would be good for her head.

Walking in comfortable shoes was good, the placing of one foot after the other helped unwind her brain.

Wilfred was out on the street, looking for her, his cheek and brow gravel-scraped, his nose swollen, but he was standing. He told his story while she opened her bag, found her cigarettes and a peppermint to silence Jimmy.

Three cigarettes in the packet. She lit one, and then there were two. Everything else was there. That bag, unlike its owner, led a charmed life. She slid its worn strap over her shoulder.

'Have you been to the police, Mr Whiteford?' He shook his head and she sucked smoke. 'I know who they were.' He looked at the boy sucking the hot peppermint, maybe not enjoying it, but not prepared to discard it. 'One of them was that baby-faced kid who sang with me. I found his watch.'

'Who have you got out there?' a voice grizzled from the doorway.

'I won't be a moment, Andy.'

Jenny eyed the man in the doorway, then turned again to Wilfred. 'You'll have to report that your car was stolen, won't you?'

'Given my personal situation, the police will have little sympathy.' A year ago she may not have understood. This morning she understood. Men who lived with other men were jailed for it. 'My concern is for you. They . . . they took advantage . . .'

They'd taken every advantage. They'd used her like she was a dog on heat. Her hand shook as she drew again on that cigarette, needing that smoke this morning.

'They took my earring too,' she said, then turned to Jimmy, who was still sucking the peppermint. 'Spit it out if it's too hot, darlin',' she said. He wouldn't spit it out. She turned the stroller around. 'I'm relieved that you found my bag.'

'Forgive me for putting you in danger,' he said.

That had been Norman's trick, always wanting someone to give him absolution. She'd given it too, time and time again. No pain in giving it one last time.

'It wasn't your fault. It wasn't mine either. I hope you get your car back.'

Wilfred's car was found parked down near the docks. The front fender was dented, one of the headlights had been broken, but it was otherwise intact. While he was cleaning it, he found Jenny's missing earring jammed down behind the rear seat, and that evening he drove to the boarding house to return it.

It was gold, he said, and quite old, no doubt of monetary value. She didn't care about its monetary value; to Jenny it was beyond price. She put it back in its box in her drawer. She'd tossed the taffeta dress into Myrtle's incinerator and later regretted the impulse. It was gone now, turned to ash like Sissy's daffodil dress. She bought a new suspender belt, new stockings, new pants, needing to replace what they'd taken, to get back to where she'd been. She couldn't get all the way back. Jim was dead. She knew it now. Those bastards had killed the flight of butterflies. Couldn't let them kill all of it. Wouldn't. That night she removed the backing cardboard from the photograph of her, Jim and Jimmy, and she inserted her talent quest envelope and money into the frame. It belonged with him. That part of her would always belong to him.

She went to work. Her shoulder was painful but its pain became her focus. She could massage it, even complain about it. She didn't tell her Yank story in the lunch room. She listened to Norma and Barbara's stories, and massaged the ache. It was getting better. She told herself that when that ache went away, she'd be fine.

On 17 January 1944, the rationing of meat began, which was of no concern to Jenny. She never bought meat, rarely fried sausages. On that same day, Brenda, a pretty kid of sixteen who worked as a presser at the factory, said she was dead meat, said her parents would throw her out, said she was going to throw herself off the bridge, said she'd sat for an hour in a scalding bath then taken a whole packet of laxettes and it hadn't shifted it.

Jenny massaged her shoulder, listening while a few offered advice.

'My aunty swears by a dose of quinine,' Selma said.

'Where the hell do you get quinine unless you've got malaria, and who is going up to New Guinea to get it now?' Barbara said.

'Remember Lois Matthews? She had to get married then lost it a week later.'

'You could lose it, Bren.'

'Where's your boyfriend?'

'He's only seventeen, and Dad hates the sight of him.'

'How far along are you?'

'I've missed twice. Mum is going to murder me.'

'That should get rid of it,' Barbara said.

'Shut up, Barbara!'

'There's an old doctor I know who'll do it for enough money,' Norma said.

'How much is enough?' Brenda said.

'Ten quid.'

'Ten quid!'

'He's a real doctor. He does all of the society dames — and their daughters . . .'

'Where am I going to get ten quid from?'

'Tell your boyfriend he has to pay.'

'He's only an apprentice, and he has to give most of his pay to his mother.'

It was like a radio serial, the ongoing drama of Brenda, who on payday managed, with her boyfriend's help, to raise five pounds. Barbara, the only child of elderly parents who didn't pay a penny in board, gave her two pound. Norma put in ten bob. Jenny put in a pound note and seven and six in change. All Lila could manage was five bob. The rest was raised in sixpences, in two-bob coins.

Norma made the appointment for Mrs Molly Mullins, on a Tuesday. She delivered Brenda to the doctor's surgery and took her home when it was done. Norma, the hay-band blonde, her roots as dark as Lila's at times, may have been as tough as old boots, but she had a good heart.

By Thursday, Brenda was back at work, the weight of the world gone from her shoulders and Norma giving her advice on how not to get caught again.

In February, Jenny returned to the club. She stayed away from that dark lane. Wilfred drove his car to the corner to pick her up, and as they drove through the night streets she gripped a four-inch hat pin in her hand. She'd go for their eyes with it, gouge out their eyes, push the four inches of that pin into their brains. Fear of Sydney was in her now, and something more than fear. Hatred of every Yank was in her, of every baby-faced boy with an accent, every thick-necked, battle-wearied mongrel.

But she took their tips. Once money was in the bank it became a clean number. She sang through February and March, and when April began she told Wilfred she was going home.

'Forgive me,' he said.

Jenny sighed, fed up to the back teeth with forgiveness. Sighed again and sought a reply.

'You let me think I was a famous singer for a while, Mr Whiteford, and I loved every minute of it.'

Out of the car, she looked down the street, dark and unknown tonight. Everything had changed. Even Myrtle's safe street had changed. She closed the car door and walked up the drive. She didn't even wave her hand to him, didn't want to see him or that car again. Every time she sat in it, she smelled them, smelled them on her for hours afterwards. Her shoulder was better but she was far from fine.

After next week she'd be fine, after their countrymen had paid for Norma's doctor friend. That would be her revenge, knowing that every pound note she placed into the abortionist's hand would come from the Yanks. They'd murdered her life so let them pay the cost of murdering what they had left inside her.

Norma made the appointment for Mrs Molly Mullins, on a Tuesday, and it was like a huge signpost stuck in the middle of a road. TUESDAY. She had to get around it, get to the other side of it, that's all. Had to get to Wednesday, then it would be over.

Jenny had tried to keep it a secret, had asked Lila to get the doctor's address from Norma, had said she had a friend who was in trouble. But Norma wouldn't give it up. She'd said she had to make the appointment herself. Barbara, factory clown, Norma's bosom buddy, knew about the Tuesday appointment. She'd had one herself. All three girls would deliver Jenny there and, when it was done, they'd take her home to Lila's boarding house.

Party time, babe.

They rode a train, then took a tram, walked half a block north from the tram stop — not too far to walk back when it was done, if Jenny was still walking. She could barely walk up there. Shaking, scared of bleeding to death, and she couldn't get Granny out of her mind.

But Brenda was at work this morning. She'd lived through it. And Barbara had been here a week before her twenty-first birthday party.

'It's no different to going to the dentist. You just open your legs instead of your mouth,' she said.

'Are you two his agents?' Lila said.

Norma and Barbara laughed. Just four girls walking in the sunshine, walking to a neat little house joined to other neat little houses set a few feet back from the street, an inner city street, to a gate with a brass plaque fixed to it. *Dr Gerald Archibald*.

Jenny hung back reading that plaque while Norma and Barbara went to the door to rattle the knocker.

He opened it.

And Jenny stepped back, stepped back again. She knew him. His hair was shorter, but not short. His white beard had been trimmed to a neat point. He was wearing a striped suit and dark-rimmed glasses. But it was him. Long black overcoat and beard or not, she knew she was looking at old Noah. She'd studied him too often, had spoken to him. He'd given her the earrings and pendant.

She ran.

Lila, who had been holding the gate open, let it slam and took off after her. Didn't catch her until Jenny was around the corner, leaning against a paling fence and lighting a cigarette.

Norma and Barbara found them there. 'What do you think you're doing, you raving idiot?' Norma said.

'She knows him,' Lila said.

'What's that matter?'

'He knows me!'

'What are you going to do then?' Norma said, helping herself to one of Jenny's cigarettes.

'Find another one,' Lila said.

'I don't know another one, you pair of raving idiots.'

'They don't grow on trees, girl,' Barbara quipped, in a fair imitation of Mrs Crump.

'I'll go to the Salvos,' Jenny said.

'They won't do it,' Barbara said.

'Shut up, Barbara,' Norma said. 'What have you got against him?'

'He knows where I come from. He knows the people I know.'

'No one's ever heard of Woody Creek, and he's been up here for almost two years that I know about. Come back and get it over and done with,' Norma said.

But Jenny was walking.

'Where are you going?'

'Work.'

'Old Crumpet won't keep you on. She gave Trina the boot as soon as she found out she'd got caught.'

'Then don't tell her.'

'She'll boot you out when you start showing.'

'Then I won't show.'

They went to work and told a collective lie. They'd spent the night in Newcastle, had gone up there because Lila's twin sons were in hospital, and they'd missed the early train back. Norma worked the big buttonholing machine, Jenny worked one of the big seamers, Barbara and Lila were on the inspection table.

'You're not indispensable,' the forewoman said.

In May Jenny bought a corset, and material to make two straight skirts with elastic waistbands. Sydney was winding down to winter. The black cardigan Maisy had given her was long and bulky. It covered her. She knitted a long bulky sweater.

In June, the Allies went in for the kill.

'Four thousand ships, several thousand smaller craft and eleven thousand first-line aircraft launched an attack on Hitler's Europe today . . .'

It was on Myrtle's wireless, on the factory wireless.

By mid-July a few of Hitler's own officers knew he was a madman and attempted to assassinate him. In late July the forewoman approached Jenny's machine and assassinated her — or murdered her plan.

'Do you intend dropping it on the factory floor, girl?'

'Dropping what?' Jenny said.

'Finish up on Friday.'

'I've got a little boy to feed.' Having a little boy to feed had got her a five-minute trial. Maybe it would buy her another month. All she needed was another month or two. The Salvos had a place where she could go for the last weeks, and a place where she could leave Jimmy. Mrs Molly Mullins had called them last Friday.

'It's factory policy. Your job will be here when it's over.'

'What am I supposed to live on until it's over?'

'You got yourself into that state, girl. Friday. Maureen will be taking over your machine. You can give her a run-through on it today.'

And that was that. Maureen was sitting at the big seamer and Jenny was back on the bench, back where she'd started, filling in time until Friday.

She should have got rid of it. Should have told Myrtle the morning after it had happened. Should have told that taxi driver to take her to the Harbour Bridge and jumped off. What was the use of trying when God had it in for you?

She finished work that Friday. On Saturday she claimed Jimmy early and took him shopping, took him to a movie, needing to dodge Myrtle, whom she'd been dodging for the past month — and when she couldn't dodge, lacing her corset tighter and covering her bloat with a bulky sweater or an overcoat.

She shouldn't have taken Jimmy out all day. He had a cold, and on the run home from the station they got wet. Myrtle was waiting at the door, her eyes disapproving, as if she was the mother and Jenny one of her recalcitrant kids.

'You could have left him with me if you were going to be out so long, Jenny,' she said, lifting Jimmy from the stroller. Jenny tried to reclaim him, tried to get away. 'It's too cold upstairs today,' Myrtle said. 'Stay for dinner.'

It had to happen sooner or later. Myrtle would know on Monday that she had no job to go to. Their coats were wet. Myrtle had taken Jimmy's off and hung it on her coat rack in the passage. Jenny removed her own and hung it. Pulled her sweater down, sucked in her stomach, which had gone beyond hiding.

But Myrtle had her back turned. Jenny sat, allowing the kitchen table to conceal the bulge. They spoke of the rain until the meal was being served. She had to move then, had to spread a cloth, set the table.

Big brown puppy dog eyes confused. Disgust taking the place of confusion but not a word spoken, other than by Myrtle's shoes whispering their disgust as they hurried towards her bedroom. She closed the door and didn't come back.

Jimmy emptied his plate. Jenny emptied her own.

'Where Myrtie gone?' Jimmy said.

'Myrtie's busy.' Jenny washed the plates and cutlery, left Jimmy playing with his cars, and knocked on the bedroom door.

'It's not what you think, Myrt. I was raped on New Year's Eve.' To her own ears it sounded like a lie.

She tried the door. It was locked. No use knocking. Jenny picked up Jimmy and went upstairs to a room as cold as a tomb. Jimmy immediately started coughing. She put him into bed and crawled in with him, held him until they shivered themselves warm.

He was coughing the next morning when Myrtle came to their door. 'You are paid up until Thursday, Mrs Hooper. I'll expect you to be out by ten on Friday morning.'

'I'm still Jenny.' Shoes hissing down the passage. 'I've got nowhere to go, Myrt.'

They ate Weet-Bix for breakfast then went back to bed to keep warm. They shared a tin of tomato soup for lunch and all afternoon snuggled in bed, Jimmy like a little koala clinging to her, a coughing snuffling koala, but he slept for much of the day, and by nightfall he seemed better.

At five, Jenny knocked on Myrtle's private door. It didn't open. They ate fried bread and plum jam, and Jimmy wanted Myrtie.

'We'll see her tomorrow,' Jenny said.

They found her in the laundry and bailed her up there.

'I was raped, Myrt, on New Year's Eve, by five Yanks. I should have told you then but I wanted to pretend it hadn't happened.'

Disgusted, defiled by the close contact, Myrtle pushed by her, left her washing soaking in the trough, under the sign stating that washing must not be left soaking in the troughs.

'Myrtie, where you going?' Jimmy called, but Myrtle, who yesterday had jumped to his every command, was today inured to his charms.

Jenny knocked at the rent hatch on Monday, once the workers had left the house. Myrtle knew who was knocking. The hatch remained closed. On Tuesday she took Jimmy to the phone box on the corner and placed a telephone call to the boarding house. Myrtle hung up when she recognised the voice. On Wednesday Jenny started packing up number five.

Every garment she'd accrued had been hard fought for. She threw nothing away. A skirt too country bumpkin for Sydney would look fine in Woody Creek. Worn out shoes could be repaired in Woody Creek. Her case wouldn't hold half of what was in this room, but, like Gertrude, she'd saved her brown paper bags, saved her string.

She wrapped her three dozen napkins in another, tied the white parcel with string — and she shouldn't have had three dozen napkins. Had they bred in the dark of her wardrobe? Myrtle must have bought them, probably had another dozen downstairs. Jimmy's clothes stuffed into a large brown paper bag, her makeup and shoes tossed into another. Jim's letters she placed in the corner of her case with her bankbook. She glanced at the final numbers. Like a squirrel hoarding nuts for a hard winter, since New Year she'd been stowing away every spare penny. She'd manage. It was just a case of finding someplace to manage in, that was all, just for two months, two and a half months. She wasn't desperate for Myrtle's charity — desperate for her friendship, for her support but the Salvos would support her. Good old Salvos. They'd find a childless couple to take the baby Yank. That's what Granny would want her to do. Maybe that old bloke hadn't been Noah. Maybe Gertrude had got into her head and made her see what wasn't there.

The Salvos wouldn't allow her to keep Jimmy with her at the unmarried mothers' home, but they had places where he'd be well looked after. He mightn't like it, but for a week or two it wouldn't kill him. It wouldn't do him any good either. He'd grown accustomed to two mothers pandering to his every need. How would he survive with no mother?

What she needed was a room where she could stay until it was time. There was no need to be away from him for more than a day or two then. She'd got over having Margot and Georgie fast, and the Yank had been squashed small by her corset, worn small by worry, starved small through lack of appetite.

She picked up the handbag that would forever remind her of Laurie. The shoulder strap, worn through, had been knotted, the clip would barely hold, the coin pocket was worn out. Last week's wages were in a little red purse with a ten-bob note and coins. She had sixty-three pounds in the bank. She'd get a room somewhere.

She looked at the watch she'd never wound. The hands had stopped at twenty to four. Sad-faced watch now. Guilty watch. Probably worth a bob or two. She tossed it into her case with her alarm clock.

On Friday morning she walked down to the telephone box and ordered a taxi, and while waiting for it to arrive she carried her belongings downstairs and piled them beside the stroller outside the lodgers' side door.

Lila lived at a boarding house not far from the factory. They had no vacant rooms but Jenny could leave her belongings in Lila's room while she looked for a place of her own. The taxi driver carried her case to the door, maybe thinking she'd come down in the world. He held his hand out for the money anyway. She paid him. Jimmy didn't like the atmosphere. He clung to her skirt while she dragged her case inside and down the back to number eleven, where she left her load in the corner behind Lila's door. Keys weren't necessary in Myrtle's house. In this place they probably were.

She spent the day searching for a room. She could get one at a hotel, but couldn't afford to stay there for two months. She and

Jimmy spent the night in Lila's bed, and three in one bed didn't make for a good night's sleep. On Saturday the girls went room hunting together. There were no empty rooms in Sydney, or not to be had by pregnant widows with two-year-old sons. There were signs in a few windows advertising private board, but one look at Jimmy and the rooms were no longer available. It was hopeless.

On Monday, when Lila left for work, Jenny left to find a Salvation Army uniform. Maybe they could find her a room. She wasn't asking for charity.

Then the sky started leaking, and it seemed every Salvo in Sydney must have been inside keeping dry, or doing whatever they did when they weren't rattling tins. She had a phone number, but not with her; she hadn't been thinking straight when she'd left Lila's, had just wanted to leave.

And as if they weren't wet enough, Jimmy had to go and wet his pants. And she should have thought of that, too.

He was a big boy. He didn't like wetting his pants. He howled. 'I wan' Myrtie's house. I wan' Myrtie.'

'She's gone, darlin'. We're going to find another house.'

'I wan' Myrtie's house.'

'It's no use wanting, so stop your wanting.'

'I wan' marta soup,' he bawled.

'We'll get some tomato soup at Lila's house.'

'I not wan' dat soup. I wan' Myrtie's marta soup.'

On some future day, when someone says Sydney, I'll think of tomato soup, the smell of urine and pushing this stroller, Jenny thought as she pushed on through heavier rain. In some future year, this is all I'll remember of Sydney.

It came to her, out of the rain, out of the cramp in her belly, and it was so obvious she didn't know why she hadn't thought of it before, or maybe her brain had frozen solid and that's why she'd thought of it.

They caught a train to Myrtle's station. Jimmy recognised it and stopped whingeing. Jenny was finally taking him home where he belonged.

She pushed him up to the front door he was more familiar with than she. She lifted him from the stroller, so he might plead her case, then she lit a cigarette. Sometimes there is no place else to go but into a cigarette packet.

Little hands slapping that fancy door. 'Myrtie, I wan you. Myrtie,' he called. 'Myrtie. I wan' marta soup.'

He got that door open. A little. Enough.

'You love him, Myrt. If I can stay here until this one is born, you can have your own baby to love.'

THE LANDLADY

'How dare you?' Raised in a mansion, educated at an exclusive school for girls, given all that her young heart desired until her marriage failed to produce a child, the wound of her failure was raw. 'How dare you bring that little boy back here?'

Never, never had she let her rooms to couples with children. The sound of her nephew's tears had been an abrasion on her barren womb. She'd locked the door of number five the day Richard and his wife had returned to New Zealand. It had remained locked — until the Hoopers, and had Robert not been home on leave, it wouldn't have been unlocked.

'It's only for a week,' he'd said.

The room was directly over her parlour. She heard too much of what went on in it. And that dear smiling little boy crawling to her across the lawn. And the feel of him in her arms.

She'd made a mistake and would not make another.

Myrtle had watched Jimmy leave in the taxi on Friday, a blur of a day. She'd wept when she'd stripped the bed in number five, when she'd locked that door; had howled into a small sweater she'd been knitting for him.

She'd tried to write to Robert, attempting to justify to him, and to herself, what she'd done.

That girl is not who I had believed her to be. She has got herself with child and Lord knows who is the father. She has no idea of a child's needs. Jimmy has been more my child . . . my heart is breaking.

354

Page after page she'd written, a tirade of accusations and self-pity, which she'd later shredded.

A terrible weekend.

This morning, she'd found some justification for her actions. That girl needed to be with her family at a time like this. She should have gone home months ago. In forcing the issue, Myrtle had done the right thing. She'd felt better this morning.

And now they were back, and that little boy's arms were reaching out to her, eager to cuddle away that desperately lonely weekend. She stepped away from him, steeling herself against him.

But she left the door ajar, and Jimmy didn't need much of a gap to squeeze through. Jenny looked the other way and drew on her cigarette, aware he would need to win this battle for her. And he was winning. He was in, his arms wrapped around one of Myrtle's solid legs, melting her. She lifted him, and he knocked her reading glasses askew with his kisses.

'You've let him wet his pants.'

'I'm going to do the same in a minute. Could I . . .'

Myrtle cleared the doorway and Jenny entered, making haste to Myrtle's private bathroom. She was slow to vacate it, and when she did, they were standing where she'd left them, Jimmy demolishing a banana. Jenny watched it grow shorter, wanting a bite before it was all gone, but Myrtle clung to Jimmy and he clung to his banana.

'You were born to be someone's mother,' Jenny said as she stepped around them and outside to the porch's small shelter. 'It seems so logical. I need somewhere to stay until a baby I don't want is born; you've got an empty room and want a baby you can't have. Between us, we've got the perfect solution to each other's problems.'

Myrtle attempted to put Jimmy down but he didn't want to go down. Something he couldn't understand was going on. Myrtie's house was warm and she had bananas and tomato soup. Outside was wet and cold. He clung to warmth — and to Myrtle.

'I love this little boy,' she wailed. 'I'd take him as my own today.'

'I know you would, but he's mine.'

Myrtle disentangled Jimmy's arms from her neck. 'You have to go, my darling boy.'

'Two months, that's all I'm asking for, Myrt. In two months' time you can have your own baby.'

'Please leave, Mrs Hooper.'

'I'm still Jenny, just pregnant. And it's raining.' Though not raining enough. She needed a downpour.

'I wan' marta soup,' Jimmy said to Myrtle's back. She was getting away.

'She hasn't got any soup, darling. She's used it all up in her veins — and she didn't even bother heating it up.'

The sky came to her rescue. It released its water. Even Jimmy knew she wasn't taking him out in that. He scrambled from the stroller and was back up the steps.

'He knows what he wants and he's not too proud to beg for it,' Jenny said, watching him throw himself at Myrtle's leg.

'Lord help me . . .'

'He won't, but the Salvos will. They've got places for unmarried mothers. The phone number for them will be in your phone book.' Jenny leaned against the brick wall, taking a smidgen of weight from her feet while removing another cigarette. 'They find homes for the babies.'

'What sort of girl are you?'

Jenny shrugged, struck a match and, guarding the flame with cupped hands, she got her cigarette burning and drew in a gasp of smoke. 'Pregnant, desperate,' she said. 'At the end of my tether. Tired, wet —'

'To give your own flesh and blood to a stranger?'

'Until you found out I was pregnant, you weren't a stranger. So far I've only offered it to you.'

'Children are not currency to be exchanged.'

'Trading came before shops and lawyers. Trading something you've got too much of for something the other one hasn't got is as old as time.'

'You give me this little boy today and I'd defy God to take him from me,' Myrtle howled, crushing him to her breasts.

Jenny drew in more smoke. 'I considered jumping off the bridge and leaving him to you in my will, but his grandfather would take him away from you.'

'Then take him home to his grandfather.'

'He's mine.' She sucked on that cigarette, looked at the length of it, annoyed that it was burning away so fast. 'And I can't go home, not like this.'

'If you were, as you say, taken advantage of, your family will understand.'

'Sure.' She sucked more of the cigarette's length away. 'Jimmy's grandfather will have me in court in a week and Granny will probably give evidence for him.'

Myrtle didn't believe her. It was written all over her face. Jenny sighed, too tired for this, feet too cold, backbone becoming unhinged from her hip bones. She had to sit down and there was no place to sit down, so she leaned against cold bricks, sighed and inhaled more smoke.

'It's all about lightning not striking twice in the same place. I was raped when I was fourteen. The girls my grandmother looks after are mine.'

'You disgust me.'

'That's not news,' she said, pitching her butt into the rain. Sheets of rain falling now, water rushing from the roof down a pipe and into the earth. Where did it all go to? So much she didn't know. But she knew she wasn't staying here to see Myrtle's disgust. She stepped out into the rain.

'If you can bring yourself to look after him for half an hour, I'll get the Salvos' number from the exchange.'

'Get out of that rain.'

Hair flattened, rain running down her neck, shoes leaking, Jenny walked through the downpour to the gate, refusing to look back.

'Get out of the rain, you fool of a girl! You can make your phone call inside.'

Myrtle gave her a towel, then disappeared with Jimmy into her bedroom. Jenny left her shoes to drip on the doorstep, took her coat off and shook it, hung it up and walked barefoot into the parlour.

The telephone was on the wall. She glanced at it as she walked to the fire, where, supporting herself with a hand on the mantelpiece, she warmed each foot. Across the passage, Myrtle was attempting to talk Jimmy into a nice warm bath. Jenny wouldn't have refused the offer but Jimmy wanted soup first.

'We'll make you nice and warm, my pet. Then we'll make some tomato soup.'

'Dat's my bed,' he said, reclaiming his world.

'Yes, darling.'

'Dat's my car.'

'You can play with your cars while I make soup. Come now.'

'I wan' soup now!'

'Do as you're told, Jimmy, or we'll go back to Lila's house,' Jenny said.

He didn't want Lila's house. He stopped arguing.

There was a telephone book on a shelf beneath the phone. She was flipping through it when they entered the parlour, Jimmy bathed and clad in an unfamiliar sweater and serge overalls, red bunny-ear slippers. Myrtle went to the kitchen. Jimmy ran to Jenny. He wanted Myrtle's soup, but he wanted Jenny to have soup with him. Little diplomat, James Hooper Morrison, he'd manoeuvre his women back together.

Jenny allowed him to lead her by the hand as far as the kitchen door. Myrtle had cut the crusts from a slice of bread and was pouring soup over it, turning it to a pink sop. Jenny would have offered the soup in a cup, offered the bread uncut, crusts left on for dipping. Myrtle lifted him up to his high chair, tied on his pinny — like her own coverall pinny.

'Have you made your call?'

'I can pay you two months' rent in advance.'

'It's out of the question.'

'Why?'

'It's out of the question.'

'You've got a barbed-wire fence built around you, Myrt. You can't climb over it and won't crawl under it, not even when there's a baby waiting for you on the other side.'

Little bird mouth open, waiting for soup. Myrtle's hand

shaking, she spooned soup in, treating him like a baby when he was Jenny's little man.

'You're locked into some safe little world by lack of imagination.' Myrtle spooned soup and Jimmy swallowed. 'If the church offered you a baby, you'd take it fast enough,' Jenny said.

'There are laws to life. There are procedures that must be followed,' Myrtle said. 'Jimmy can stay with me. He'll be better off in familiar surroundings.'

'And when I come back for him he'll be yours. If I go, he goes. That's the law to my life, my procedure that must be followed,' she said, and she left them to it and walked to the telephone.

Myrtle's eyes followed that swollen stomach, greedy for what lay curled within it. Her feeding spoon wavered. Jimmy's bird mouth was forced to chase.

If her feeding style was erratic, her thoughts were chaotic. Was it out of the question, the room for two more months? Was a baby out of the question?

Adoption was. She'd known that the day Robert had put on his uniform. They'd be considered too old when he came home — if he came home. Trade. That fool of a girl! As if you could barter babies. Just an ignorant factory girl, that's all she was.

A factory girl, yes, ignorant, no, but a fool of a girl anyway. As if Myrtle would be a party to . . . to . . . to . . .

It had been done, and done many times without benefit of judge or lawyer. A girl she'd gone to school with had been raised by a well-off aunt while her tribe of brothers and sisters had fought daily for basic survival.

If Jenny was prepared to disappear . . .

Ridiculous. She'd come back and claim the child. That had happened here in Sydney not long ago. It was in the newspaper. A grandmother had raised her granddaughter as her own for seven long years, then the mother, having wed, was given the child by the courts. Far better never to have a child than to have one only to lose it. The heartbreak would kill.

'All gone, pet. All gone,' she said.

Jenny was back at the door, watching her wipe Jimmy's face, remove his pinny. 'You were born to be a mother.'

'God has a plan for us all. Motherhood was not in his plan for me.'

'How do you know that I'm not part of his plan for you, that this isn't exactly what he had planned for you all along?' Myrtle turned away to the sink and Jenny leaned against the doorjamb, too tired for this but persevering. 'What has changed so much about me in a week? You seemed to like me. Apart from my shape, how have I changed, Myrt?'

Myrtle swung to face her. She was weeping. 'You weren't honest with me.'

'I've always been honest with you.'

'I asked about those girls you sewed for. You could have told me then.'

'I told you they were mistakes Granny was raising — which is the truth. And if you knew my life, you wouldn't expect me to go around telling everyone every single detail about it.'

'Look at the state you've got yourself into!'

'Get me your Bible and I'll swear on it that I was raped on New Year's Eve. Call Mr Whiteford at work tomorrow. He'll tell you.'

'Tell me what you no doubt told him —'

'He'll tell you he was there, that they stole his car!' Jenny said, turning back to the telephone. But she changed her mind. 'I thought you were different, Myrt, but you're just like every la-di-da Mother Grundy I've ever met. You see a lump of something on the footpath and because it's the right colour and shape you think, oops, dog's dung. Nine times out of ten it isn't dung at all, but you're not going to put your foot in it to find out, are you? Hold your nose and walk around it, Myrt.'

'You have no right to attack me!' Myrtle howled.

'And you've got no right not to believe me either. I went to the club on New Year's Eve with Wilfred and I sang my heart out all night. We were in the car, on our way home, when five Yank sailors opened the door, threw Wilfred out on his head and drove me down to a beach and raped me. Five of them. They were taking turns on me when I passed out.'

A green and white striped tea towel mopping her tears, Myrtle attempted to flee the room but Jenny blocked the doorway.

'I woke up naked, my bra twisted around my neck, my dress half the beach away and my underwear gone. How would you like to catch a taxi home with no pants on? How would you like to know that a pair of pink pants you repaired with white cotton are some Yankee boy's souvenir from Sydney?'

Myrtle tried to push her way free, but Jenny stood firm.

'You'd feel violated, Myrt. That's how you'd feel. You'd feel so violated that you'd burn a brand-new dress you loved. And every time you put on a similar pair of pants, you'd want to vomit, so you'd throw them in the incinerator too, and every time you thought about it, you'd want to jump off the bridge so it would finally be over and you wouldn't have to see yourself being treated like the town slut. You're so bloody pure, so full up with your holier than thou sensibilities, there's no room left inside you for anything new to grow. That's why you've never had your own baby. It's got nothing to do with God's plan.'

Jimmy was worried; he didn't know what was going on. Jenny let Myrtle out of the kitchen. She heard the bedroom door slam, heard the fancy passage light fitting rattle its glass, then she lifted Jimmy from his high chair and carried him to a chair close to the parlour fire, held him close and rocked him. In minutes he was asleep, as was she.

She dreamed. Dreamed she was a girl of twelve or thirteen, and she was digging a hole behind Myrtle's washhouse, but the dirt kept falling back in. And she had to be careful where she put that shovel. There was a crop of babies down there, growing like potatoes in the dirt. She didn't want any more but she couldn't leave them down there. Kept pulling them out, miniature babies, dozens of them, covered in dirt.

She woke gasping for breath, relieved to wake, or relieved for a time. She moved Jimmy's head, shook pins and needles from her arm, then carried him sleeping to the couch where she lay down with him, Myrtle's velvet cushion for a pillow, her crocheted knee rug for a blanket.

When next she woke from a dream of dark lanes, the parlour was in darkness and Jimmy was gone. There was a slit of light creeping from beneath the kitchen door, but no sound from the kitchen. Jenny rose and crossed the passage to use the toilet, to peep into Myrtle's room. Jimmy was in his little bed. Myrtle's bed was empty.

Myrtle was in the kitchen, writing to Robert. She told him how she'd put Jenny and her little boy out on the street, told him how they'd come back, how they were now sleeping.

If only you were here to speak your good sense to me. How can a girl of twenty have two children older than Jimmy? He'll turn three in December. I was a child at fifteen, a pampered school child, sharing these rooms with my parents and Richard, with maids to care for the house and a man to take care of the yard.

She has no family support and says she must give up the child. She has suggested we raise it, and of course it is impossible, but as the night hours pass, I find myself asking myself if it really is impossible, my darling, or was she sent to us by God . . .

My mind is a whirlwind, one moment spinning one way, then spinning back. I know you love Amberley, as I do, but we could sell it. We could. We could move to New Zealand with our baby, stay with Richard until we found a home of our own.

She blotted the page, dipped her pen and began filling a third page.

No use at all in pouring her heart out on paper. That letter could take weeks to reach him. His reply could take weeks to return.

Two months. Two months, or perhaps a little longer — if there was any truth in that girl's tale of New Year's Eve.

'And I must not allow myself to think of this foolishness,' she whispered.

She could think of nothing else. A beautiful girl, she would have a beautiful child. Perhaps a little boy like Jimmy —

Ridiculous. They'd leave in the morning. Almost morning now. A strangely silent predawn.

And her pen dipped.

JENNY EXPECTING STOP FAMILY SUPPORT NIL MUST
RELINQUISH BABE FOR ADOPTION STOP WISHES TO
RETAIN NUMBER FIVE UNTIL CONFINEMENT WHEN
ACCOUNT WILL BE SETTLED IN FULL STOP PLEASE
ADVISE RE MY AGREEMENT TO TERMS OF OCCU-
PANCY LOVE MYRTLE

She glanced towards the parlour, then as guilty as a child at the
biscuit tin, she tore the page from the pad and stood, reading her
words. By need the message was cryptic. What she was propos-
ing was illegal. Her words would be transmitted by a stranger's
hand, read by strangers. She read it again, this time in a whisper.

Robert would understand.

GOD'S MASTER PLAN

Myrtle made porridge for breakfast; she served her guests but not herself. She had no appetite this morning but stood watching Jenny clean her plate, watching Jimmy plaster his face, her table and floor. She poured him a glass of milk, poured two cups of tea, and not a word spoken until Jenny rose to wipe Jimmy's face, to wipe the table and lift Jimmy down to play with his cars.

'You feel nothing for it?' Myrtle stated.

'I was pack raped, Myrt. What am I expected to feel for it?'

'The miracle of life.' Myrtle turned to her sink, her eyes filling. 'I'd sell my soul if I could exchange places with you.'

'I'm not asking for your soul, just number five, just until the end of September.'

'They'll place the baby in your arms and you won't part with it.'

'I would have parted with it months ago if I hadn't recognised the doctor.' Myrtle's expression said she didn't understand, or didn't want to. 'If there was a pill I could swallow this morning, I'd swallow ten,' Jenny said. 'I promise you I'll walk away from it more easily than I'll walk away from you and Amberley.' She reached for a cigarette. 'Two months. That's all I'm asking for. At the most, ten more weeks.'

'You smoke too much,' Myrtle said.

'Tell me I can have my room back and I'll stop. We'll stay out of your way, I promise you that, too.'

'I have to go out for half an hour. Shall I take Jimmy with me?'

Jenny nodded. She followed them to the door and lit her cigarette, watched Jimmy climb into the stroller, eager to go.

'I trust you with my most precious possession, but you don't trust me enough to believe I was raped.'

'I should be no more than half an hour,' Myrtle said, and they left.

Jimmy's voice faded in the distance. The cigarette grown too short to hold, Jenny buried it in the garden, then took her damp shoes inside to warm by the fire. Her coat was damp around the shoulders. She draped it over a chair, close to the heat. The world outside was bitterly cold. Myrtle's business this morning must have been urgent to send her out in it.

But brief. They were back in twenty minutes.

'If you don't mind keeping your eye on him for an hour or so, I'll get my things from Lila's. The Salvos' phone number is on the shelf beside the phone.' She took the stroller to transport her load. Taxis cost money and money was her only security now.

Myrtle didn't make the phone call. She prepared lunch for three, her mind not on her task, but with her telegram, perhaps already crossing the ocean. It would find him, as her letters found him.

Jimmy played at her feet, running his wooden car around the table's legs, up chair legs. For him, life was back to normal.

'There was a case recently,' Myrtle greeted Jenny at the door. 'It was in the papers — no more than a year ago — a child raised by her grandmother and claimed by the mother after seven years.'

They lifted the stroller into the passage, the napkins still in it, with the brown paper bags. They placed the red case beside it.

'I won't want to know about it,' Jenny said. Her coat was shrugged off, hung, shoes off, then she walked ahead of Myrtle to the fire and stood with her back to it. 'I'm going home when it's over. That's all I know.' Silence then, the small fire crackling, feeding on new wood. Where did Sydney get its wood? 'Are you thinking about taking it?'

'I'm attempting to explain that what you are suggesting is impossible.'

'Nothing is impossible.'

'How would you suggest we . . . we manage the subterfuge?'

'It sounds like a German submarine,' Jenny said. 'Sub-ter-fusen.'

'It means —'

'I knew what it meant when I was ten years old. And I don't know anything right now.' She shrugged. 'I could give my name at the hospital as Myrtle Norris. No one up here knows who I am.'

'Your condition is obvious. It may appear a little coincidental that you disappear, and I appear with a baby.' She didn't sound like Myrtle. Her eyes didn't look like Myrtle's. They were guarded today, not quite able to hold Jenny's.

'Then I'll disappear now. I'll sleep on your couch and you keep your private door locked,' Jenny said. Hope growing in her heart, just a little hope.

'And Jimmy?'

'You've been looking after him anyway. Tell the lodgers I'm working out of town.'

'The cleaning woman? Her daughter?'

'I'll clean in here. And you start wandering around with a pillow stuffed down your pinny.'

'Let us not stoop to the ridiculous —'

'The publican's wife at home stuffed a pillow down her pinny so she could pass her daughter's son off as her own,' Jenny said.

'You may recall that Robert has been overseas since September of '42.'

'Who counts?'

'Many people.'

'Tell them Robert was flown home on some secret mission. If you told me he'd popped in on New Year's Eve, I wouldn't know if he had or not. People are only interested in their own lives. You were looking after Jimmy, that's all I know about your New Year's Eve.'

It was a parlour game, to Myrtle, a time filler. She played it alone that afternoon while scraping batter into a cake tin, and while the cake baked. She found herself continuing the game in bed that night, raising questions and finding, or not finding, her own answers. She played it in the laundry, at the kitchen sink.

Who was to know Jenny was here, if she were to remain within these rooms? How many came to these rooms? The minister, but only when invited. Robert's sister-in-law visited once or twice a year, but she always phoned before she came. The lodgers were not invited into her private rooms — however, certain among them would remember when Robert left.

Give them all a month's notice. Tell them the house was being sold to a private family. And put it on the market? Her house, though full, had been empty to her — before that girl and Jimmy.

Robert's family would need to be told the truth — a partial truth. They'd known for years that she and Robert had applied to adopt. Her brother knew they'd planned to adopt.

Sell up, go with her adopted child to New Zealand, stay with Richard until Robert came home . . .

The timing was the problem. Were children placed with couples when one parent was overseas fighting?

Doubtful.

But there were more fatherless babes around now than there had ever been, and if she didn't know the legalities of adoption placements, then others would not know.

How long would it take to sell the house? It was hers to sell, the deeds transferred from her father's name to her own when they'd borrowed to pay out her brother's share.

'When exactly is the baby due?'

'Nine months from New Year's Eve — if it comes out clutching a calendar. It could be weeks before. Jimmy and my first came early.'

'Have you seen a doctor?'

'Only from a distance.'

'Your other children's births would have been registered while you were in hospital?'

'Jimmy's was. The others were born at home. Granny registered them. She's the town midwife.'

Jenny's belongings remained in the passage through Wednesday, through Thursday. The Salvation Army's phone number remained on the telephone stand. Myrtle didn't make the call.

She was waiting for something, and Jenny knew it. Her actions, her manner, her obsession with the postman spoke volumes. On the Friday morning she walked to the parlour's large window ten times in one hour to stand and stare out at the street.

She was there when the telegram boy leaned his bike against the front fence. Myrtle had her front door open before he blew his whistle.

No fear of his envelope that day. She ripped it open.

GOD WORKS IN MYSTERIOUS WAYS STOP ALL SUPPORT MUST BE GIVEN STOP TRUST YOUR GOOD INSTINCTS STOP LOVE YOU ROBERT

'We will find a way, Jenny. I will do whatever I must. We want your baby.'

BILLY-BOB

In August Paris was liberated, and Myrtle spoke of the beautiful city she'd seen as a twelve-year-old. Jenny told her that she knew what it must have been like for the French, living under German occupation, having Hitler dictate whether they were allowed to smoke, whether they were allowed to set foot outside the door.

'*Heil* Hitler,' she said each time Myrtle issued a decree.

'I don't find that humorous, Jenny.'

'I don't find living under occupation humorous either.'

You can't live day in, day out with another and keep up a well-mannered pretence. You can't share every meal and not put your elbows on the table.

They got to know each other during those months. Sat together by the fire in the evening, knitting tiny white garments or leafing through the infant section of Myrtle's *Home Doctor* book while Myrtle spoke of travelling to Melbourne so the child could be born there, in a private hospital, under Myrtle's name. They would then go their separate ways, Myrtle and her newborn on a boat bound for New Zealand, Jenny and Jimmy to board the train for Woody Creek.

'Melbourne is too close to home, Myrt. I know girls who work as nurses in Melbourne. We'd be letting the outside world in.'

They argued about Melbourne, about how and where the baby should be born, how and where they'd make the swap, about cigarettes.

'I gave you money to buy me two large packets and you couldn't even buy me a little packet.'

369

'Read that article on the effect of nicotine on the unborn.'

'I read too much and so do you.'

Accustomed to her freedom, accustomed to walking for miles, Jenny was forced to fill her days with reading, with stitching. She unpicked a skirt Myrtle had placed in the Red Cross bag. She was losing weight. Jenny made it into two small skirts for her girls. She unravelled Miss Robertson's navy blue cardigan, found in the same bag, and with the reclaimed wool knitted two small sweaters. She altered a maroon frock Myrtle deemed too old, and offered it to the landlady as a maternity smock.

'You are being ridiculous.'

'You'll look ridiculous when you try to pass off a baby as your own if you don't give the lodgers something to believe.'

'They know when Robert left —'

'Yes, but he was flown home on a secret mission, wasn't he?'

She stitched shoulder and waist tapes to a small round cushion and modelled it with the smock. Such laughter. Myrtle couldn't recall such laughter in these rooms. She conceded a little by discarding her corset. She attempted to walk more slowly up the stairs, more carefully down.

'Hold your stomach when you walk down, as if you're trying to stop the baby shaking around.'

In late August, Robert wrote, expressing his concern at the proposed sale of Amberley. Myrtle had spoken to an agent. She didn't want to sell her childhood home, nor to be a guest in her brother's house. It was a way out, that's all.

'It may be better if the baby is born at the Salvation Army home, Jenny, and we make the transfer in the city. I will let the family know that I am expecting to adopt.'

'His birth certificate will have my name on it, Myrt.'

Myrtle needed her name to be on her baby's papers. That would be her only security — should Jenny change her mind . . .

'We'll take the train up to Brisbane.'

'Start wearing your smock and cushion and I'll have it here and you can pretend you've had it.'

'Alone?'

'I had my first alone.'

'I won't consider it. I'm booking seats on the train. I'll book you into a hospital as my daughter, Myrtle.'

'And I'll probably have it on the train and we'll end up on the front page of the newspaper. You start wearing your cushion and I'll have it here.'

'Wilful girl.'

'You're supposed to be eight months forward, Hitler.'

Myrtle wore her maroon smock in August. It appeared to go unnoticed until Miss Robertson walked off to church alone, until Mrs Collins asked her if there was to be a blessed event.

Myrtle, her face a match for her maroon smock, came to the bedroom where Jenny hid when the hatch was open.

'I lied,' Myrtle said. 'To Mrs Collins. Lord help me. I told that woman a bare-faced lie.'

That was the night she agreed that the baby would be born at home.

Through August, Myrtle gathered necessary items under Jenny's instruction: tins of condensed milk, baby's bottles, old towels, sharp scissors, sterile tape to tie the cord. She bought cigarettes from time to time, but rationed them like a prison warder. She played the wireless day and night, in case of laughter. There was laughter. In case of raised voices. In September Jenny raised her voice.

Myrtle was stressed, Jenny stressed by her, and Jimmy stressed by both of his women; he wouldn't stay in bed.

The argument began over him. Every time he got out of bed, Myrtle gave him what he wanted.

'Will you butt out, Myrt? I told him to get back into his bed. Stop going against me.'

It was after nine before he went down and stayed down, and Jenny needed a cigarette.

'You've had five already today.'

'Then I'll have six.'

'I'll make a cup of tea.'

They were sitting in the kitchen, drinking tea and eating oatmeal biscuits, when Myrtle started the war.

'What do you know about the father?' she said.

371

'I didn't ask their mothers' maiden names. One of them said, *Party time, babe*. He didn't sound well educated —'

'I meant only —'

'You asked me who I'd been playing around with, and that's what you meant.'

'That wasn't what I meant to imply.'

'It's what you think. Admit it — you think I was playing around and I got caught.'

'Please keep your voice down.'

'Admit it, Myrt.'

'You're a pretty girl. I —'

The parlour couch was Jenny's bed; her case lived beneath the parlour table. She dragged it out, opened it and rummaged through clothing which no longer fitted, among the letters, Jim's bunch tied together with navy blue wool, Granny's and Maisy's scattered. She found Billy-Bob's watch beneath the letters and took it to the kitchen where she slid it down the length of the table.

'That's all I know about the father. It's got a name on it, and a date that's probably his birthday. You might be able to track him down through the navy, ask him how far he went in school — though I can't guarantee the baby is his. It could be Hank's. He was a big, ugly, sweat-stinking mongrel and he sounded as if he'd been raised by hogs in the bogs.'

'Please keep your voice down.'

'Then keep your doubts to yourself.'

'Why didn't you come to me when it happened? If you had the boy's name, why didn't you report him to the police?'

'Because if I'd come to you, you would have said to go to the police. And because they would have found out I had three kids and told you, and you would have thought I was lying like you think I'm lying now — and because Wilfred didn't want to report it. He's one of those poofter blokes, and the police probably would have locked him up for sodomy — if there is such a thing in your pristine little world.'

Myrtle ran for the wireless to turn the volume higher. Jenny pursued her, turned her own knob, and lost the station.

'I was lucky I didn't catch VD. That's what I was worried about. They reckon that half the Yanks have got it.'

Myrtle fought for control of the wireless. She found a screeching soprano and Jenny sang 'Ave Maria' with her, but an octave lower.

'You have a beautiful voice. A beautiful voice!'

'So they tell me. I had a beautiful life with you and Jimmy, too, until they spat on it. As if I'd ever want any man touching me after Jim. As if I could ever stand another man touching me. I hate every one of them.' She picked up the watch and pitched it into Myrtle's rubbish bin.

'That's an expensive watch, Jenny!'

'Which must make it a bit better. I mean, a rapist who wears an expensive watch can't be all bad, can he?'

'I can't deal with your sarcasm. I asked the wrong question and I'm sorry. You hear stories about the American Negroes going with our girls. I —'

'Don't want a half-black baby, Myrt?'

'Everything I say is wrong.'

'It will be white. The black Yanks don't get around with the white Yanks. Billy-Bob was a baby-faced blond. Now give me my cigarettes and leave me alone.'

She took her cigarettes and sat before the fire, watching the smoke being drawn up the chimney. Myrtle came to fiddle with the photographs spread along her mantelpiece. Robert was there, clad in shirt and cravat, a younger Myrtle beside him. Jimmy was there. The Yank baby would be up there one day, waving his stars and stripes — and probably the image of Hank the Yank.

'This . . . this deception, this waiting is so very stressful for me, Jenny. You must understand.'

'I understand that your stress is driving me mad. I could at least walk at night.'

'It's too dangerous on the streets at night.'

'What worse can happen to me, Myrt?'

'Women are murdered.' She took the photograph of Robert from its place and stood a while looking it in the eye. 'I have such terrible fear, for you, for the child and for Robert. God chose for me to be barren. Am I going against his will? Will he punish me for my lies?'

'Any God who sits up there flipping through the pages of his account book working out who to punish next isn't worth worrying about.'

'I was raised in the church.'

'Me too. My father has been a church fanatic all his life. I sat in church every Sunday from when I was three years old and absolutely believed that God was sitting up on a cloud, watching over me and my missing mummy. I woke up to him when they found my missing mummy in a madhouse and sent her home to us cured — except she wasn't. I was ten years old and she loathed the sight of me and I never knew why.'

Her cigarette was gone. She tossed it into the coals and watched it spurt green flame — wondered for a moment if Myrtle's theory on smokes being poisonous might be fact, then shrugged and lit another.

'I was fourteen, still at school, when our neighbours' twins raped me. They were drunk. That was their excuse. My mother wasn't. She lied about me going after the twins, lied to my father, the church fanatic, who was too ashamed to come near me, and who ended up trying to marry me off to one of the bastards — for my good name's sake — or his.

'I let them plan their wedding. I let them fix up my mother's wedding dress for me and make a wedding cake, then the night before I was supposed to get married, I threw her wedding dress down Granny's lavatory pit and took off to Melbourne. I ended up pregnant again. It was my fault that time, but if they hadn't been trying to marry me off, I wouldn't have gone to Melbourne. Not that anyone cared about that. After the second one, I wasn't fit to walk the streets according to most in town, including my own sister.

'Then along came Jim. I'd known him nearly all my life. He knew everything about me, but he reached down into the dunghill everyone had made of my life and he pulled out some lost part of me. He got me singing again. And I loved him. I loved everything about him. I loved making love with him. Do you know why he died, Myrt?'

Myrtle didn't know why. She shook her head.

'Because God has got my name written down on a dog-eared page in his account book and it keeps on falling open at that same page, so he has to punish me again for my most grievous sin of living. I was supposed to die like my three brothers and sister died at birth.'

'Don't —'

'It's true. But don't worry, your page is clean. He won't kill Robert. And he's not trying to kill me either. He'd miss his favourite punching bag. Now I'm going for a walk.'

Tonight Myrtle didn't attempt to stop her. She followed her out to the gate, pleaded with her to take care, then watched at her window, at her gate for an hour, until Jenny returned with four large packets of cigarettes.

'Are you trying to kill that child?'

'I'm trying to survive it. Go to bed and leave me alone tonight — please, Myrt.'

It was their worst night. Come morning, Myrtle was afraid to enter her own parlour. She attempted to open the squeaking door silently, and was hit by the maroon velvet cushion, white tape dangling from it like spiders' legs.

'You said you'd do anything and this morning you're doing it.'

'Don't start, Jenny.'

'You're almost nine months pregnant. It could come any time and no one will believe you.'

'We should have gone down to Melbourne.'

'God wants you to have a baby, Myrt. He'll work it out for you. Now put it on.'

Myrtle placed the cushion on a chair and turned on the wireless.

Again it flew, and Jenny sang, to the tune of 'Greensleeves'.

There was a landlady named Myrtle,
who lived in a shell like a turtle.
Until one fine day, she decided to play,
and Myrtle, the turtle proved fertile.

'They'll hear you upstairs.'

'I'll get louder, unless you put your cushion on.'

'Please, Jenny —'

'*Myrtle the turtle was glowing, her stomach was definitely showing* . . . Just try it on for me.'

'Shush!'

Brussels had been liberated. It was on the news! The Allies had the Germans on the run. 'There'll be an end to it soon,' Myrtle said.

'I was having my hair cut when it started. I was fifteen.'

'Shush.'

German retreats, pitched battles in the Pacific, then Myrtle surrendered. She slid her arms through the shoulder straps and allowed Jenny to tie the dangling tapes, tie on a coverall pinny.

'You look ten years younger,' Jenny said. 'You look thinner, too — well, everywhere else you do.'

Was it any wonder? Myrtle's nerves were at breaking point.

A long, long month September and the Yank baby was making no attempt to leave security for the unknown. Jenny wanted it out. Wanted it done.

'Jimmy came early. Margot came early.'

Every day Myrtle rose in hope that this would be the day. Every night she went to bed, hoping to be awakened before dawn.

Then, in the late afternoon of the third day in October, the pains began. They'd been coming on and off for a couple of days but this time they were stronger and they kept on coming.

Myrtle got Jimmy to bed at seven then returned to the kitchen to sit watching the clock.

'Is it . . .?'

Jenny nodded. 'You might spread a few old towels around the bathroom floor.' That's what Granny had done with Georgie, spread towels on the lean-to floor.

Myrtle did as she was bid then returned to stare at that swollen belly, almost ripe for the picking. And suddenly she knew that, like Adam, she had been tempted by forbidden fruit.

'I can't . . . I can't do it, Jenny.'

'Don't take too much notice of that cushion. I'm the one doing it.'

'It's against God's will.'

'Man created God, not the other way around, and I'm having a baby, which is not the time for a religious discussion.'

Myrtle went to the bedroom. Jenny pleased to be rid her, rode down another pain and watched the clock hand tick around the face. Long, aching, grinding pains and not enough space between them to walk to the bedroom. Held onto the doorframe and rode down a big one. Myrtle was on her knees beside her bed, head bowed.

'Don't get too comfortable there. I'm going to need you very soon.'

The bedroom floor was carpeted. She returned to the kitchen to ride down a bone-cruncher. Hank the Yank, slow to make a start, now seemed eager to vacate the premises.

'I'll come in there and have it on your carpet,' Jenny yelled, and another pain hit, right on the tail of the last. She grasped the table, wondering if something had gone wrong, or if rapists' babies knew what their fathers had done and just wanted it over. She could feel its head coming down as she'd felt Margot's head coming down.

Bathroom. 'Myrtle!' No time for the bathroom. Snatched the newspaper, tried to spread a few pages but it was coming out.

She squatted. Granny had made her squat to deliver Georgie. No cast-iron bed to grip so she gripped the handles of the sink cupboard, and as another pain hit, she pushed. Gripped those handles too hard. The doors flew open and she fell to her backside, slamming her head against the refrigerator's door.

Like a turtle on its back; like a beetle with its legs in the air. But beetles and turtles don't turn the air blue with their cursing of la-di-da landladies.

'Save your breath, darlin',' Granny would say. 'Save your breath and push it out. Stay calm, and use your head. The women in Africa have their babies in the fields then go straight back to work.'

Thinking of Granny helped. Granny hadn't allowed her to lie on her back when Georgie was born.

'Giving birth is labour and I don't know of any respectable labour you can do on your back,' she'd said.

Margot had come while she was standing up. God only knew what she'd been doing when they'd dragged Jimmy out.

She rolled to her side, got her knees beneath her, then using the table leg for support, planted her feet in a squat. And she could see into that open sink cupboard. She could see a packet of cornflour, a packet of tea — and two large packets of cigarettes.

'You la-di-da bugger of a woman!' she yelled. 'You said you hadn't bought any.'

Myrtle was at the wireless, turning the volume higher. Joseph Schmidt was belting out 'A Star Fell From Heaven' when the birth waters gushed to the kitchen floor. Myrtle stood frozen, fearing God's retribution, fearing Robert was at that moment lying dead somewhere, punished for her deception; she was blind to what was going on in her kitchen between table and refrigerator. And without Granny's hands to catch it, Hank the Yank nosedived to the floor, landing on the saturated headlines of the morning's *Herald*.

PACIFIC BATTLE. JAPANESE LOSSES HEAVY. US CASUALTIES LIGHT.

That was as close as the infant was likely to get to its fathers — on a US boat somewhere in the Pacific.

Flat on her backside, legs spread, Jenny eyed the bloody, white-coated thing, a cord still connecting it to her. She didn't want to touch it. Wanted to yell, *Get it away from me!* but Granny wasn't here to get it away. She had to touch it.

Myrtle had boiled a pair of scissors, had boiled narrow white tape, wrapped scissors and tape in a sterile towel — and put them in the bathroom. But Jenny and the baby weren't in the bathroom. She couldn't remember what had happened with the others after the lump of them was out. Had something got stuck inside her? Would they have to call the ambulance and ruin everything?

Joseph Schmidt hit a high note when she pushed again. The afterbirth slopped to the floor and it looked like a calf's liver. Hoping it wasn't her own liver. Jenny grabbed a tea towel, a green and white striped thing used a few hours earlier to dry the dinner dishes, and with it lifted the lump of life that should have been squawking and wasn't. She peeled newspaper from it, wiped its face with the tea towel. Poor featureless little Yank, tiny face, flat nose. She wiped its nose. Maybe it had been in there too long, it was overdone or something.

She gave it a shake. It didn't like that. It wailed.

Joseph Schmidt stopped singing to listen. Myrtle stopped trembling and ran to the kitchen.

Her entry into the battlefield was too fast; soft-soled shoes on wet newspaper slide. She skated half a yard across the floor, arms flailing, then her feet went from beneath her and she landed hard, heavy, on her backside, skirt up, knee-length bloomers exposed.

Two women sitting side by side, one of them holding the baby.

'You're a useless bugger of a woman, Myrt,' Jenny sighed as she reached up to open a kitchen drawer. The scissors were kept in there, and a roll of kitchen twine. She used a length of twine to tie two granny knots, to tie a bow, to tie a knot in the bow while some famous tenor sang 'The Lord's Prayer' loud enough to make a glass on the sink vibrate.

Flesh is tough. Myrtle's kitchen scissors weren't sharp, but they chewed Hank the Yank free from that calf's liver, each bite of those chewing scissors sending tremors through Jenny's bowel. She was wrapping him in the striped tea towel when she noticed he had no rapist's tools.

'It's a girl,' she said, transferring the bundle into Myrtle's arms.

Almost done. She lit a cigarette and leaned back against the refrigerator door. It was almost done. She'd do the rest in a minute, or maybe in five minutes. It was almost over.

IT'S A GIRL

Wet and bloody newspapers strewn around her, the green and white wrapped gift in her arms, Myrtle was sobbing her heart out when Jenny turned the volume down on Richard Crooks.

One night while in my bed I lay, there came to me a dream . . .

She crossed the passage to the bathroom, taking her time. She washed, dressed, put on a touch of makeup, knowing now exactly how they were going to make the swap.

An angel walked before me to guide my weary way . . .

She took one last look at Myrtle and the striped tea towel. 'Don't you move a muscle.'

Myrtle wasn't sure she could move and had no intention of trying.

The sun rose in the heavens, the street was paved with gold . . .

African women had their babies and went straight back to work in the fields. They didn't have to climb a staircase. Jenny climbed and counted those steps, walked down the passage to Miss Robertson's door, the unquestionably respectable, maidenly Miss Robertson, teacher of Latin and arithmetic at a posh girl's school.

'Sorry to disturb you so late, Miss Robbo. I just popped in to give Myrt some money for Jimmy's keep and found her with a baby on the kitchen floor. I didn't even know she was pregnant.'

Miss Robertson knew, and disapproved strongly of such goings-on in a woman of Myrtle's age. She was, however, a Christian woman and thus prepared to do what must be done. She woke Mrs Collins.

Myrtle looked sufficiently shaken, as did her kitchen, to have given birth. Miss Robertson wanted to call an ambulance. Myrtle told her she'd call her own doctor in the morning, that she required only a little help to the bathroom.

Mrs Collins cleaned up the worst of the mess, Miss Robertson fetched the kitchen mop and bucket, while Jenny, more familiar with infants than they, sat holding the little Yank.

By the time the big hall clock struck midnight, Myrtle and her infant were tucked up in bed, the two teachers had returned to their rooms and Jenny was allowed to collapse on Myrtle's bed.

They slept that night with the little Yank between them.

Milk leaked from Jenny's breasts while the infant sucked on a weak solution of boiled water and condensed milk, Jimmy watching from a distance, wondering what his women were doing with that white-clad bawling thing.

'Roberta Anne,' Jenny said.

'Marion Louise?' Myrtle said.

'Deborah?'

'Julia?'

'Rebecca.'

'Gladys.'

'Cara Jeanette.'

'Robert's mother's name is Jean. She'd like that.'

So it was done. The baby was registered as *Cara Jeanette Norris. Mother: Myrtle Joyce. Father: Robert John. Witnesses: Miss Matilda D. Robertson and Mrs Margaret J. Collins.*

The little Yank was three weeks old the day Jenny left Sydney. Myrtle booked and paid for Jenny's ticket; packed Jimmy's clothes into one of her own small cases while Jenny crushed what she could into the red case. The napkins wouldn't be travelling south; they were in use again. The stroller wouldn't be travelling; Jimmy was a big boy now.

Myrtle ordered a taxi. She rode with them to the station. Jimmy didn't like the white thing that had become stuck to his Myrtie but he liked riding in the taxi and he loved trains. He didn't understand when Myrtie kissed him goodbye, when she kissed Jenny goodbye and attempted to press two ten-pound notes into her hand.

'Don't dirty it with money,' Jenny said.

'It's for the hotel in Melbourne, for the napkins and your stroller.'

'You've fed us for three months. We'll call it even.'

Myrtle placed the folded notes into Jimmy's pants pocket. He liked things in his pockets, but Jenny took them. She had a great respect for money.

'I wish I hadn't promised to go home.'

'Until I'm caring for her alone, I won't believe she is mine. Each time you hold her I'm terrified you'll change your mind.'

'Your name is on her papers.' Jenny put the money in her handbag and looked at the baby one last time. 'She won't ever know I exist.'

'Robert and I will know, and every day of our lives we'll bless the angel who came into our lives. Now go, pet.'

Jenny touched the tiny hand. By comparison with Jimmy at birth, this one was a midget, weighing in at five pounds five ounces on Myrtle's kitchen scales. She didn't want it, couldn't have kept it even if she had wanted to. She'd just had too much to do with it, that was all. She'd sewn the baby's gown, and made the sleeves too long. Silly little hand lost in that sleeve. She turned back a cuff and offered a finger. Tiny hand gripping her finger, maybe a baby handshake, thanking her for hot water on tap, carpet underfoot, a fairy godmother. A fragile mite, who, like Georgie, had to go and get herself born with Jenny's hands. She wished that hand different. She wished she hadn't given away her pretend name. Didn't know why she had. Should have let her be Marion or Julia.

'I promise you she'll have the best life we can give her, the best schools —'

'You'll spoil her rotten,' Jenny said, easing her finger free and taking Jimmy's hand.

'I want Myrtie to come, too.'

Myrtle was weeping. She must have been the weepiest woman in the world. Jenny backed away.

'I don't suppose you'd write, get Mr Fitzpatrick to take a photo or two? Just so I know you haven't killed her with kindness. Just write care of Mrs Foote, Woody Creek.'

Myrtle didn't reply. Jenny took another step back. 'Please.' Myrtle shook her head and Jenny turned and boarded the train.

'I wan Myrtie to come wiff us.' Jimmy had begun to understand that this was to be a final leaving. 'I wan Myrtie to come, Jenny.'

'She can't come.' Jenny led Jimmy to their compartment, where he climbed onto the seat to look out the window, searching the platform for Myrtle.

Still standing there, still weeping. Jenny pressed her fingers to her lips and blew her a kiss, blew another for Cara Jeanette.

Then the stroller and Myrtle disappeared into the crowd.

NORMAN'S STATION

The trip to Melbourne was interminable, but they got there. Jenny bought a ticket to Woody Creek, then walked Jimmy across the road. Myrtle had booked them a single room at a hotel. They had no luggage, other than their coats and a string bag. Myrtle had booked the cases through. It was a long wait until morning. Afraid she wouldn't wake in time to catch the train, Jenny couldn't sleep.

Jimmy started at daybreak. 'Where's Myrtie's house?'

'A long, long way away.'

'I want Myrtie.'

He kept it up until they got back to the station. Maybe he thought she was taking him back where he belonged. She collected the luggage, ushered him before her into the ladies' room, and dug deep in her case for her corset, bought in May, discarded in July. She hadn't fallen as flat as she should have, and she wanted to wear her green linen frock home, determined that when she stepped off the train at Norman's station, he'd see the singer, not the slut. She found clean underwear, then opened the smaller case packed with Jimmy's clothes. Blue cable-stitch sweater, navy pants, white shirt, he looked like a little toff. She sat him on her case while she dressed for home, painted her lips, rubbed a smear of lipstick into her cheeks for colour. She looked pale, felt pale today.

They ate toasted cheese sandwiches for breakfast, or Jimmy ate them. She took a bite or two but her stomach, laced tight, wasn't interested in food.

'I want Myrtie's porridge,' he said.

'We'll have some of Granny's tomorrow. She makes the best porridge.'

'Where?'

'After we have another ride on a train.'

'On Myrtie's twain?'

'Another one.'

'Not anover one,' he said. 'I want Myrtie's.'

God help her. God help him, too. She found a bench seat beside an ashtray, set her cases at her feet, set Jimmy at her side, fed him a toffee and sat smoking while one of the whalebones in her corset took its revenge. Not much she could do about it other than sit straight. She wanted to slump, wanted Jimmy to stop whingeing.

They called her train. She picked up the cases, the string bag. 'Walk close to me, Jimmy.'

'I want Myrtie,' he said, and he flopped down to his backside.

Cases down again. 'Stand up and walk. I can't carry you and the cases.'

'I don' like more twains.'

'Me either, but we have to get on one more.'

'Why did we hab to?' Jimmy cried.

A soldier, wearing Jim's uniform, his hat, asked if he could give her a hand with the cases.

'Please.'

She heaved Jimmy up to her hip and followed the soldier down the corridor to an empty compartment. He lifted her cases up to the wire racks and tossed his army bag after them. She'd hoped he'd help her out then go. He sat. She hated men looking at her. Wished she'd taken after Norman instead of Amber. Wished she'd worn her black dress and no makeup.

Then another soldier came in to stare, and to laugh when Jimmy told her he didn't like more trains.

'We came down from Sydney yesterday,' she explained.

She had apples in her string bag. She bribed Jimmy silent. He'd grown accustomed to getting what he wanted when he wanted it. He wouldn't survive in Woody Creek. *She* wouldn't survive in Woody Creek. He crunched and she sat, her face turned to the window, as an elderly woman and her decrepit husband joined their group, then two more women and a girl, and thank God, the train moved before any more came.

Then the city was sliding by, backyards like junk heaps, one after the other, a paddock or two, a house or three, then the paddocks grew larger and the houses fewer while the train sang her closer to the last place on earth she wanted to be.

She didn't want to be Jenny Morrison. Didn't want to live in a two and a half roomed shack, fetching water from the creek. She wanted to be Jenny Hooper, factory machinist by day, singer by night.

All gone, Jenny Hooper. Dead and buried, Jenny Hooper. And Jimmy Hooper, too. How would he like being Jimmy Morrison?

And how was she going to lie to Granny? She'd written fairytales to her these past months, written of the factory and the club. She hadn't been at the factory for three months, hadn't been at the club for more. She had to wipe those last months from her mind. Wipe that baby from her mind. Get her mind back to June.

Granny would notice her stomach. Or maybe not. She'd notice the dress, the stockings, notice how tall Jimmy had grown. Then she'd put her arms around her to give her a Granny cuddle, and feel that corset. She'd forgotten Granny's hugs. Could hear her voice in the song of the train wheels. *What are you trying to hide with that corset? Have you come home pregnant?*

She'd have to take it off.

Heard Granny again in the wheels. *You've never had a stomach in your life.*

Too much sitting slumped over a sewing machine, Granny. Too little time walking, Granny. Too many of Myrtle's rich meals, Granny.

She'd fallen flat after the other ones and she'd been so huge with Jimmy. Not enough walking was true. Eating too well was true.

And how did she expect to walk Jimmy home from the station? She'd been crazy to give that stroller away. But she'd wanted to give something, leave something of herself, of Jimmy, to that baby.

It should have been a boy. It should have looked like Hank. Maybe it looked like Billy-Bob. It shouldn't have had her hands.

'Look at all the baa lambs,' she said.

'I don' like baa lambs.'

'Granny might have some baby goats.'

'I don' like baby goats.'

'You used to. You used to drink lots and lots of goat's milk, too.'

'I like Myrtie's milk.'

'We'll stop at a big station soon and we'll buy an ice-cream.'

Jenny sighed for a cup of tea, or for Myrtle. Sighed for that bald-headed baby's hands.

Everything was . . . was not what she'd expected it to be. She'd expected a boy, expected it to come out waving the stars and stripes. She'd expected to look at it and see a rapist in waiting; instead it had been a poor little corset-crushed girl. And it had come so fast, so easy. Like an apology. Like it knew what its fathers had done.

What was it like to grow inside someone who for nine months resented the space you used up, resented the blood supply feeding you, resented every twinge?

Maybe I know, Jenny thought. I know what it's like to live in a house where every breath you take is resented.

The train stopped for twenty minutes at a station midway between Melbourne and Woody Creek. Jimmy demanded cake and lollies. Jenny bought ice-cream and a bottle of lemonade.

One soldier returned to the compartment. Jimmy, full of ice-cream and lemonade, stretched out on the seat for a nap.

'How old is he?' The soldier asked.

'Almost three.'

'I've got a four-year-old and a little tyke I haven't seen yet,' he said.

'They'll be pleased to see you.' She wished he'd go to sleep.

'Is your husband in the services?'

'He died in '43.' That stopped the conversation. He returned to reading his paper and Jenny stood and looked down at her skirt, crushed by sitting. 'Could you keep an eye on him for five minutes for me? I don't think he'll move.'

'Go for your life,' he said.

That was the idea. That whalebone was killing her.

She stripped down to pants and bra in the ladies', in an area too small for stripping and too unstable, with nowhere to hang her frock when it was off. She slung it over her shoulder and her petticoat with it, then unlaced the corset, ripped it off and pitched the pinching thing. Bumped her funny bone on the wall while fighting her way back into her frock, and while she was moaning about that, someone knocked on the door.

She picked up the corset. Couldn't very well walk back to the compartment with it under her arm. Couldn't fold whalebone and stuff it into her handbag either. Should she stuff it behind the lav and get it later? She didn't want it later. Never, for as long as she lived, would she lace on another corset. She'd rather shove it down the lav where it deserved to be shoved. She peered down the hole that went through to the lines, the same hole she'd used to get rid of three of Jimmy's messy nappies two years ago. They'd gone straight through.

'Ashes to ashes,' she said. 'Dust to dust.' And she released it.

With a little encouragement, the corset fell through to spend its life rotting between the railway lines, or caught up on barbwire fence flapping its whalebones at train drivers.

Whoever was knocking on the door had become desperate. Jenny washed her hands, washed her arm up past the elbow, buckled her belt, ran wet fingers through her curls and stepped out. An unhappy old lady pushed past her to get in.

Jimmy was sleeping when she got back to the compartment. The soldier, having babysat, now wanted to talk.

'The Russians are hammering Germany,' he said. 'They won't hold out much longer.'

'Have you been overseas?'

'I've been up north,' he said.

They talked the last miles away, and they were faster miles. Too fast. Each time she glanced out the window, the landscape looked more familiar. Woody Creek coming to get you, Jenny Morrison.

She recognised the stand of blue gums out front of the Tyler place. Recognised the white clay walls of Lewis's dam, the crumbling sheds beside the house.

Then the train was hooting, warning the town, warning Norman. Her heartbeat was warning her to put on her armour against this town.

Past the falling-down back fences, the barking brown dogs, the fig tree leaning over the convent's back fence. Blunt's crossing. Norman's railway yard, with stacks of red and bleeding timber waiting to be loaded.

The train slowed, wheels creeping, stopping, the train hissing its ire.

And there he was, thinner from the rear, shoulders more rounded, and looking so old and she, afraid to face him.

She'd have to, she'd have to leave the cases with him.

The soldier carried her luggage out to the platform. She carried Jimmy and her string bag, her snakeskin handbag, its worn strap replaced by Myrtle's shoe repairer.

Norman didn't recognise her, or not right away, not while she was with the soldier, thanking him for his help.

'A pleasure, love.'

'Enjoy your leave with your family.'

'There's not much doubt about that,' he said, and with a wink directed towards Jimmy, he swung back onto the train.

From the rear he looked a little like Jim — Jim too close in this town.

'Where did we come to, Jenny?' Jimmy asked sleepily.

To hell, she wanted to reply. 'Woody Creek,' she said.

Norman was staring at her. She met his eyes, expecting a word, something.

Two more passengers were ending their journey in Woody Creek — Molly Martin, who lived ten or so miles out, one of her sons at her side. He eyed Jenny as she dragged her cases into the ticket office.

Norman took the Martins' tickets, then he was behind Jenny.

'I'll have to pick my cases up later,' she said.

He was staring at a luggage label on which Myrtle had printed HOOPER in big black letters. Jenny ripped it off.

'Or you might ask Mick Boyle to deliver them if you see him about,' she said.

Norman nodded and reached out a hand. For an instant she thought he was reaching out to her. Then she remembered her ticket. That's all he wanted from her. She gave it up, and with a last glance at his hangdog eyes, took Jimmy's hand and walked west down the platform, away from him.

'Who is dat man, Jenny?'

'Your grandfather,' she said. 'One of them.'

'Why?'

It was difficult to explain family ties to kids, not worth the effort when those ties were broken.

They couldn't get across the lines until the train moved away, she had to stand on Norman's platform and wait.

'Why did we come for to . . . to here?'

'We're going to visit Granny.'

'I don' want Gwanny. I want Myrtie.'

'We can't have Myrtie any more. Now we'll live with Granny.'

'Why?'

The train was moving at last. She took Jimmy's hand and walked him over the lines.

'Cawwy me.'

'You're too big to carry. I'll give you a piggyback later but you have to walk a little way first.'

He walked. The track to the hotel was wider than when she'd left, well used and gravelled now. North Street was unchanged. It smelled the same, of stale beer and peppercorn trees.

'What's dat fing?' Perhaps he meant the grotesque peppercorn tree, or the empty street, or the eddy of dust and grit, dancing it down the centre of the unmade road.

'It's Woody Creek,' she said.

'I don' like woodycweep.'

'Me either, darlin'.'

The road down to the forest looked long; an ice-cream might put off the inevitable. She led him past the butcher's, which stank of dead cows, towards the café, wondering if Mrs Crone was still standing behind the counter, if her bananas were still brown, her apples still withered.

The same old checked lino was on the floor. The same

390

slamming wire door. The same expression on Mrs Crone's face when she recognised her customer.

'Two milk iceblocks, please.' Jimmy would suck on an iceblock longer, and make less of a mess than with an ice-cream.

Pink and brown milk iceblocks, a penny each. She paid for two with a ten-bob note, wanting that sneering, prune-faced old bugger to see she had money in her purse, and she allowed the wire door to slam shut on the way out, too.

Back to the hotel corner then, across the road, praying that the Hoopers weren't looking through their windows. The road was wide. They mightn't recognise her. Nothing but space in this town, space and dust and flies, and trees, and the smell of cut timber. Nothing had changed. Nothing would ever change here.

Jimmy's iceblock lasted him to Macdonald's mill. He bawled when it fell to the dirt, wanting her to pick it up and wash it.

'No taps,' she said. 'Want a piggyback?' He climbed on and she told him about Granny's horse, how Granny sat on his back and said, 'Gee up, Nugget.'

'Why?'

'So he'll go fast.'

'Gee up, Nugget,' he said.

She didn't have the energy of a winded cart horse, but she carried him past John McPherson's land, crossed the road with him on her back and placed him down amid tall trees.

'I don' like here,' he said.

'We already agreed. Woody Creek stinks.'

'Woodycweep stinks,' he repeated.

They chanted together as they headed down the forest road, not a wide road, only a bush track that had found a purpose. Jimmy had no use for it. His head turning from side to side, he sought the road out of this place. There was no way out. Boxed in by tree trunks, bare glimpses of the sky between the overhanging branches, black crows watching from those branches, waiting for prey. The smell of dust, of eucalyptus and honey, the smell of the creek, just a stone's throw away.

A dusty, rutty road. Country kids learned to look down when they walked. A little city slicker, Jimmy looked up, tripped on a rut, fell. Her grip on his hand saved his knees, but he'd walked too far, and he wanted Myrtle's house, so he sat in the Woody Creek dust and bawled for Myrtle, and Jenny squatted beside him, wanting to bawl for her too, but bawling did not a scrap of good in Woody Creek.

If I pretend I'm gay, I do not feel that way,

He looked up at her, his eyes big blue-grey puddles. He liked singing that song. Knew all of the words to it. He let her draw him to his feet, brush the seat of his pants. He brushed dust from the hem of her skirt and they walked on, hand in hand, singing their special song.

As I hold back the tears, to make a smile appear . . .

They sang it loud enough to scare those old crows from the trees, sang it loud enough for Gertrude to hear. She came at a near run, met them at her boundary gate.

A noisy greeting that one; a hugging, kissing greeting, a laughing greeting, Jimmy clinging to Jenny's skirt, not remembering the tall stranger clad in trousers and wearing knitting needles in her hair.

'You've grown into such a big boy,' Gertrude said.

'Woodycweep stinks,' he said.

'What have you been teaching that little boy?'

'That Woody Creek stinks,' Jenny laughed.

A SORRY BUSINESS

The lavatory pit stunk more than she remembered — Amber's wedding dress still rotting down there somewhere. The kitchen had grown narrower, grown darker. Same old washstand and basin, same enamel bucket beneath the washstand. Same bar of Velvet soap in the same old dish. No more soft towels, just a worn and washed-out rag of towel hung where it had hung two years ago, on a bent nail hammered into the side of the washstand.

Two little girls stood staring at the visitors, the redhead looking like a long-handled rag mop, the other one looking like a Macdonald after the vampires had sucked their fill.

'G'day,' Jenny said, and Jimmy hid his face against her skirt, afraid of the dark house, threatened by the two small girls.

He didn't want a drink of milk. He didn't want a biscuit. He wanted to go to a proper house, but Jenny's shoes were off which meant that she was staying for a while. She sat at the table. He climbed up to her lap and buried his face against her when Elsie came with more kids to stare.

'I want Myrtie's house, Jenny,' he wept.

'This is Granny's house. This is where we used to live before we went to Myrtie's house.'

Tea was made and poured, the biscuit tin open on the table, half a dozen kids were sitting in a row on the cane couch eating biscuits when they heard the car. Jenny lifted her head to listen. She'd forgotten the way cars announced their arrival long before they reached Gertrude's gate, forgotten how the trees, the creek funnelled the noise down to this land.

Gertrude went to the door to listen. 'It sounds like Vern.'

'Damn him,' Jenny said.

'Th'ee th'wored,' Margot said.

'What?'

'You swored,' Georgie translated. 'Why did you bring that boy for?'

'That's Jimmy,' Gertrude said. 'You've seen photos of Jimmy.' She stepped outside to get a better view of her boundary gate. 'It's Vern,' she confirmed. 'Did he know you were coming home?'

'How could he?'

'Maisy gave your address to Margaret back when Jim first went missing.'

'Why? So they could kidnap Jimmy?'

'Vern's half-brother is dying from the legs up. Vern and his daughters have been spending a lot of time with him in the city. I dare say Margaret might have got in touch with you had there been news of Jim.'

'You're pipedreaming, Granny.'

Elsie herded her kids out the door. She'd seen too much of Vern Hooper in her youth and had no desire to continue the association. 'We'll pop over again when he's gone, lovey,' she said. 'Good to see you home.' Margot went with her. Georgie thought about staying, but not for long.

'One of them must have seen you walking by,' Gertrude said. 'I didn't know they'd come home.'

'I thought you'd made up with him.'

'He's been in and out of hospital, down and back to a city doctor, I haven't seen a lot of him.'

'I can't face him, Granny, and Jimmy doesn't need it today.'

'He's got his daughters with him.' Gertrude's expression suggested she was less than pleased to see them at his side. She cleared away the biscuit tin and Elsie's mug, and gave the table a quick wipe down.

'Tell them I've got smallpox. Tell him I came home pregnant,' Jenny said.

'You'll go straight back to where you came from if you are.' Gertrude made no comment on smallpox.

Her shoes back on, Jenny carried Jimmy to the door to do her own staring. Vern had his legs out of the car but not the rest of him. One hand on the car door, one on the doorframe, he rocked himself to his feet.

'He was never that bad.'

'He's gone downhill this past year.'

Lorna, a totem pole in black, looked as if she'd stand forever. Margaret wore floral. She looked like one of Beatrix Potter's mother rats, complete with her bustle, or bustle buttocks, on show as she bent to remove something from the car boot.

'They've got Norman spying for them, Granny! They've brought my cases down.'

Gertrude walked out to greet them, and to carry one of the cases inside. Vern, on his feet now, appeared to have his work cut out in carrying himself. Lorna carried nothing but her sneer.

Jimmy had had enough of strangers. He howled.

'It's all right,' Jenny lied. It wasn't. It was all wrong.

'I don' want dis house,' he wailed.

She carried him to the lean-to, wanting to drop him through the window hatch and climb out after him, to run. 'Look at the pretty flowers,' she said. Faded, worn wallpaper, stained by small hands, split where the wood behind it had moved. 'Be a big boy for Jenny.'

She heard footsteps in the kitchen, chair legs scraping, creaking as one of the chairs took Vern's weight. She couldn't hide from them. Gertrude wouldn't let her hide. She brought the cases through to the lean-to, signalling with a nod for Jenny to go out and face her visitors.

Better to face them today while she and Jimmy were clad in their Sunday best. She followed Gertrude back to the kitchen, pulled up a chair and sat.

'A big boy,' Vern said.

'He'll be three in December,' Jenny replied.

Margaret's protruding eyes stared at Jimmy, Lorna sneered down her eagle beak nose, Vern looked from the boy to Gertrude, who was rattling around in her cupboard looking for matching cups and saucers.

'Have you heard anything definite from the war department?' Jenny said.

They'd heard nothing. Lorna's scowl said very clearly that Jenny had no right to ask.

She'd always had a beaked nose. It had grown longer, or the spectacles she now wore accentuated its size. Her eyes were close set, small, black, near hidden beneath heavy dry lids. Her ears were huge, her jaw long, her cheeks sunken. She was a caricature of a woman.

Margaret hadn't changed in the face, hadn't changed in the years Jenny had known her. A little heavier, breasts a little larger, maybe more a rotund Mother Chihuahua now rather than Mother Rat. She had a chihuahua's eyes.

Tension was growing in Jenny's back, in her neck, in the arms holding Jimmy. She'd been travelling for two days. She needed to sit back and relax.

Gertrude carried the conversation. Good manners and tea got them through the first fifteen minutes. Jenny hoped they'd go when their teacups were empty and when they didn't, she stood.

'We'll go over and get the girls home, Granny.'

There was a point to Vern's visit. He got to the point.

'We've been staying down in the city,' he said. 'We've had some legal advice from a chap down there.'

'I've had my own legal advice, Mr Hooper.'

She'd spoken to Basil, from Wilfred's band; he worked for a solicitor and knew a lot about the law. He'd told her to hang onto Jim's letters, in particular the letter stating that he'd asked his family to take care of her should anything happen to him.

'No doubt you have,' he said with meaning. She didn't understand his meaning, or maybe she did. Jim's mother had left him a fortune. She walked to the open door and stood looking out.

'He made a will when he joined up, before his boy was born.'

'As if I care about his money!'

'How do you think you're going to raise that boy without his money?'

'I've been working to raise him.'

'There's no singing clubs up here, girl.'

'We won't be staying here.' They'd be getting out of here tomorrow, that's what they'd be doing.

'As far as I see it, we can do this decently between ourselves, or we can do it the other way. There's no court in the land that would refuse my claim.'

'My legal adviser told me that any grandfather who had lost one wife to childbirth and nearly killed another one, and who wouldn't even take me down to the hospital when his grandson was being born, hasn't got Buckley's hope in any court of taking a three-year-old boy away from his mother — not when the mother was engaged to his son.' Basil had thought she'd been married to Jim, but engaged was almost married.

That hit Vern where it hurt. He stood, determined to intimidate her with his size, and Jenny stepped back to the table, no taller than when she'd left, as slim, a little older, but much, much stronger, strong enough now.

'My boy would never have gone near that war if not for you. His blood is on your hands, girlie.'

'That's enough, Vern,' Gertrude said.

'Don't you take her part in this —'

'I'm taking our grandson's part. He doesn't know where he is, and he doesn't need this — not after travelling two days to get here. Sit down and calm down, Vern, or leave.'

'If she had one skerrick of feeling for my boy, she'd do the right thing by him.'

'I did the right thing by him when he was alive — which is more than you ever did for him.'

Jimmy was afraid of the giants in that house that wasn't a house. He rarely cried. He was screaming now.

'Take him over to Elsie's,' Gertrude said.

He didn't need more strangers and Jenny was past doing what she was told to do. She carried him into the lean-to and got the old green curtain between him and the strangers, but Jimmy liked the lean-to no more than that kitchen full of giants. He clung to Jenny's neck and screamed for Myrtie.

She sat on the bed, rocking him and staring at the weather-stained wallpaper beside the window, which wasn't a window, just a flywired hole in the wall with two warped shutters to keep the weather out. She shouldn't have brought Jimmy here. She should have known this would happen as soon as she hit town. She should have booked in to that Melbourne hotel for a week, looked around for a live-in job.

Vern and his daughters didn't leave. She couldn't hear what was said above Jimmy's wail. Rocked and soothed him, kissing his hot little face until he buried it at her breast and sobbed out the last of his tears. Then she heard them, or heard Gertrude.

'They're home, Vern. Be content with that.'

'You haven't got a bed for him. You haven't got room to swing a bloody cat in this place.'

'I'll find room. And you and your girls can find room in that little boy's life if you don't make him the meat in your tasteless sandwich.'

'We won't have Jim's boy raised by a little trollop who can't keep her pants on,' Lorna said.

Jenny couldn't let that pass. Couldn't and wouldn't. 'You're just jealous that no one ever wanted to get your pants off,' she said, quietly, but loud enough.

'Jennifer!'

'Jim was a decent, God-fearing boy until you seduced him with your wiles.' Lorna liked the last word.

'God-fearing and Lorna-fearing,' Jenny replied. 'I've got a letter in that case from Jim telling me how you told him he'd be better off blowing out his own brains rather than marry me.'

'Stop it, Jenny!' Gertrude said, and her rafters rattled with the stamp of her boot. Jimmy clung tighter, but lifted his head to see if the roof was falling in. 'Take your girl home, Vern. She's not welcome in my house.'

'House?' Lorna scoffed.

'My house, and you'll leave it now,' Gertrude said. 'Out with you, you evil-minded, evil-mouthed . . .'

They left the kitchen. Jenny got Jimmy's head onto a pillow and lay with him, holding him close, stroking his skinny little-boy neck, kissing his hair. She heard the car start, heard it leave, heard Gertrude walk down to lift the curtain, and like Norman, Jenny lifted a hand for silence. Jimmy's eyes were closing.

Once he was asleep, she eased herself away and rolled carefully from the bed.

Gertrude was peeling potatoes. 'You'll need to step lightly around them, darlin'.'

'I'm through with stepping lightly. You just get stepped on. What right has he got? Jimmy is strong, he's healthy, he's well dressed. Anyone can see he's been well looked after.'

'He's a man, darlin', and he thinks he's got the right. What decided you to come home?'

Jenny couldn't tell her the truth, couldn't even tell her that Myrtle had her own baby to care for. She'd written too much in her letters about her la-di-da landlady. Lie number one coming up. 'I've got a week off.'

'Those little girls don't know who you are.' Little girls peeping at Jenny from either side of Gertrude.

'They're better off not knowing me.'

'You're the only mother they'll ever have.'

'As far as the Hoopers and most in this town are concerned, I'm the town slut. They can do without knowing that.'

'They can do without hearing that sort of language coming from their mother.'

'They'll only hear it for a day or two. If I stay here, the Hoopers will keep hounding me.'

'He's got no more right to that little boy than I have, than your own father has. As long as he's well fed and has a warm bed to sleep in, Vern hasn't got a leg to stand on in court. He knows it, too. And if he didn't before today, then he does now. What's that on your dress?'

Jenny looked down. Her left breast still leaked at times. Here came lie number two. 'Jimmy must have dribbled on me. It needs a wash,' she said.

'It's a lovely frock. Take it off and rinse it out before it stains.'

'What's one stain more or less? This is Woody Creek and I'm Jenny Morrison.'

ADAPTABILITY

The following afternoon, Vern came with Jim's Willama solicitor. Gertrude was out with her chooks; Georgie was halfway out the door to stare at the visitors when Jenny grabbed her skirt, drew her indoors, closed the door then slid the old slide bolt, stiff with lack of use.

Myrtle had packed Jimmy's fleet of wooden cars. He'd spent half of his life *vroom*ing them around in Sydney and was pleased to have them back in his hands. As was Jenny. With his hands full of cars, he couldn't hold onto her skirt. He wasn't yet *vroom-vroom*ing, but he'd found a garage for his fleet beneath the bottom shelf of Gertrude's washstand.

Vern and the solicitor were hammering on the locked door.

'Little pig, little pig, let me in,' Jenny whispered. 'Oh, no, not by the hair on my chinny-chin-chin —'

Jimmy wanted more, so she told him the story of 'The Three Little Pigs' while those outside demanded to be let in.

'Why did you shut that door for?' the redhead asked.

'I don't like visitors,' Jenny whispered, finger to her lips.

'Why?' Georgie whispered conspiratorially.

'Because I have to make them cups of tea.'

'Why?'

They were squatting between table and door, Jenny urging Jimmy to give his car a push. It wasn't leaving his hands.

Margot stood back from the trio. She didn't like that closed door, or Granny not being let in.

'Show me if it still goes,' Jenny said to Jimmy. 'Push it. Georgie will push it back.' Having no kids to share with at Myrtle's house, he hadn't learned the art.

'Has he got uver things?' the redhead said.

'What other things?'

'From Syndey.'

'Sydney,' Jenny corrected. 'He's got some books.'

The books had accounted for much of the weight in his small case. Myrtle had bought him three picture books. Jenny had purchased one, secondhand, though whether for him or herself she was uncertain. She'd found it a year ago, at a street stall run by a bunch of kids doing their bit for the war effort, and the instant she'd seen its cover, she'd recognised it. She'd turned the pages of an identical book at Norman's station when she was four or five years old. Jim may have grown out of fairies, but he'd known she'd believed in them. He'd brought it with him to the station and she'd sat for an hour turning the pages. A magical book back then and it still retained a little of its magic. Glossy fairies, perched amid apple blossoms and in roses, cheeky pixies hiding behind a bunch of cherries, using a bluebell's stem as a slippery slide, peeping out through windows cut into their mushroom houses.

She fetched it now and stood at the table turning the pages for the girls, who stared at it wide-eyed and silent. They recognised its magic. Jimmy had seen it too often, but he came to get his share, or his share of Jenny. They were still turning pages when the car motor faded in the distance.

'Open this door, you ratbag of a girl,' Gertrude demanded.

'Give me the password,' Jenny yelled back.

'Open this door now!'

'Incorrect. Try again.'

'I'll have a piece of your hide when you do.'

'Incorrect. Last try.'

'They've gone! Open this door!'

'Lucky. We were just about to shoot you as another Hooper spy.'

They let her in, Jenny and Georgie wearing identical smiles. The locked door hadn't pleased Granny or Vern, but it had won

Georgie over, got Jimmy shooting his car across the floor to Georgie and she shooting it back.

She was a talking machine. 'Why did you and him live in Syndey for and not here wiff us for?'

'Sydney,' Jenny corrected. 'I had to make some money.'

'How did you make some?'

'On a sewing machine.'

'Money can't get sewed on machines!' Georgie scoffed.

'I made shirts to sell and got some money for the shirts.'

That was logical. Georgie nodded. She was uncombed, dusty, barefoot and leggy, but beautiful anyway. Not a freckle on her face, dark lashes, well-defined brows — Laurie in female form.

'Get your brush and I'll do your hair.'

'Why?'

'Because you look like a rag mop.'

'Why?'

'Because I said so. Where's your brush?'

'I don't like hair brushed.'

Gertrude got the brush and Jenny brushed, and because she brushed Georgie's hair, she brushed Margot's, who stood before her, jaw clenched, fists clenched.

Did I once stand with my fists clenched, wanting to get away when Amber brushed my hair? Jenny wondered. She couldn't remember Amber ever taking a brush to her hair — only Norman. She could remember his timid hands wielding the brush.

'How old are you, Margot?'

'Five,' Georgie said. 'When I get five, I can go to school.'

'I asked Margot. Do you go to school, Margot?' Jenny asked, brushing white hair, as white, as sparse as her father's. And not a murmur out of her. Georgie did the talking.

'She can't walk that far.'

Maybe she couldn't. She had her father's short legs along with their hair, she had their thickness of body, their hands.

'I bet you can walk that far,' Jenny said.

'I can walk a long, long, long way, and I can swim, and I can run more faster even than you.'

'You could run faster than me when you were ten months old, kiddo.'

'Go over to Elsie's, love. I want to talk to your mother,' Gertrude said.

'Our muvver?'

'Of course she's your mother,' Gertrude said.

'Why does she call you Granny for like everyone calls you Granny for then?'

'I'm her grandmother.'

'Her grandmuvver!'

'Go over to Elsie, you chatterbox.'

'And him too,' she said, looking at Jimmy.

'He can go later.'

'I want to go later, too.'

Gertrude gave up trying to get rid of her. 'That was a stupid thing to do.'

'It worked.'

'I told him I'd take Jimmy up there for lunch on Friday —'

'And me,' Georgie said.

'You can have lunch with Jenny,' Gertrude said.

'He won't go, and even if he was willing, I wouldn't let him — and I won't be here anyway.'

'You can stay until Friday. He said he'd pick us up at twelve.'

'As if Jimmy will let me out of his sight.'

'Kids are adaptable,' Gertrude said, and turned to the watching girls. 'Go out and see if the chooks have laid some more eggs.' They didn't move. She clapped her hands. 'Skedaddle, I said, both of you. Take your brother with you and show him how we get eggs.'

They skedaddled. From the doorway Jimmy watched them go.

'He's got a right to know his grandfather and Vern has got a right to know him,' Gertrude said.

'You take him in there on Friday and they'll kidnap him.'

'If I don't take him in, we'll spend the next week in court. Locking a grandfather away from a grandson he hasn't seen in two years won't go down well with a judge. It was a stupid thing to do.'

Jimmy had ventured out to the yard, a car in each hand. They watched him.

'I told Vern out there that he'd catch more flies with honey than he would with vinegar. I'm telling you the same.'

'I swat flies, Granny.'

'People need to know where they came from, who they came from. Like it or not, that little boy is a Hooper.'

'I'd rather not know where I came from.'

'Stop talking back and listen to me. That little boy could end up owning everything Vern's got, everything Jim had. Vern's not going to live forever — I don't know how he's lived this long.'

'Everything he owns will go to his daughters.'

'A man like Vern puts no store in women.'

'Then why has he been coming down here for the past twenty years?'

'I'm his cousin,' Gertrude said.

'Pull the other one, Granny. It's made out of rubber.'

'Sydney didn't change you for the better, my girl.'

'A lot of things didn't change me for the better, Granny.'

But people do need their own people, even when their people live in a two and a half roomed shack. There were moments when being home was close to bliss. She'd missed that old wood stove with its oven always waiting hot to bake potatoes, to bake puddings — and how she'd missed its warmth on cold nights.

She'd missed Granny's garden, being able to walk outside to pick a bunch of silverbeet, to pull up a carrot, an onion. And be it from goat or cow, having gallons of free milk placed fresh each day into the Coolgardie safe was riches, as was the glut of eggs filling the safe's lower shelves. She made egg custards, made bread pudding, made egg and vegetable pies with pastry almost as light as Amber's, made macaroni cheese casseroles as tasty as Myrtle's.

'You learned something worthwhile in that place,' Gertrude said.

The knots in her neck and shoulders unravelled in Granny's house. Myrtle, Sydney, Amberley, began their slow slide into the mists of once upon a time. She told Gertrude of her struggle to light the gas oven, told her how Mrs Collins had nearly blown herself up one night, or singed her hair and eyebrows. She displayed her once-red frock, now a respectable near black, and she modelled her blanket overcoat. Gertrude looked impressed.

'You've come a long way with your sewing,' she said.

'Necessity is the mother of all learning,' Jenny said. She flashed the total in her bankbook. Gertrude was impressed with that too, if not by the name on the book's cover.

Jenny didn't unpack her case, not fully. She slid it beneath her bed, Jim's letters still inside with Maisy's bulky cardigan, the elastic-waisted skirts. She'd fix those waists when she had time. The fabric was good. Billy-Bob's watch remained hidden in one corner. She should have thrown it away . . . or sold it before she'd left Sydney . . . or taken it to a jeweller and asked him to grind that engraving off so she could wear it. It was a nice watch, small enough for a woman to wear. She'd never owned a watch. Given time she might be able to look at that name. Given a year or two that New Year's Eve might fade, the Yanks might become the villains in a book she'd read about Wilfred the Leprechaun and Myrtle the fairy godmother — and the factory pixies. Maybe — in time.

She missed Amberley's bathroom, taps, sinks, but that missing was balanced by Granny's shelves of apricot jam, chutney and tomato sauce, she could gaze on when she sat in the old tin tub in the shed's partitioned corner. She loved Granny's glut of butter coupons; Gertrude had never wasted money on butter. Jimmy liked butter on his bread. Gertrude barely spent a penny on clothing. She had a book full of clothing coupons.

'If I'd had them in Sydney, I could have sold them on the black market, Granny. There are classy shops up there that will buy them from you — so the toffs' wives don't have to wear the same ball gown twice.'

'That goes on down here,' Gertrude said.

She missed the crisp sheets and fresh towels supplied on Mondays. Granny's sheets were patched and old, their crispness long boiled away. Her wash trough was still slimy; her clothes line prop, two years older, hadn't grown out of its bad habit of falling down in a strong wind.

At least things had changed for the better in town. A few sneered at her when she rode in on a borrowed bike, but many nodded now, and Jessie Macdonald-Palmer grabbed her in Charlie's shop and danced her in a circle.

Hilda sneered, but clipped her coupon and sold her a pound of butter. She sneered again when Jenny asked for two packets of cigarettes.

Granny didn't approve of Jenny's smoking. She smoked one in the orchard before Vern drove down on Friday, drove down alone to collect his lunch guests. Jimmy was pleased to be getting dressed up to go for a ride in a car. He liked cars. But when the moment came to leave and he realised Jenny wasn't going with him, he cried and clung to her. She lifted him into the car to sit on Gertrude's lap, and for the next two hours imagined that car continuing down the road to Melbourne.

She smoked two cigarettes in the two hours he was away, but at two thirty they returned, Jimmy clutching a large and brightly painted tin truck.

'Dat's a tip twuck,' he said, offering it to Jenny for inspection.

'Grandpa gave it to you, didn't he?' Gertrude said.

'Buying him with toys?' Jenny said.

'Don't look for the bad in everything he does.'

Jimmy wanted his truck back. She gave it to him and he ran inside to load the rest of his fleet onto his truck's tray.

'*Vrooom, vrooom, vrooom.*'

'He's a decent man when he gets what he wants. Thwart him and you've made a bad enemy.'

'Most of us are decent when we get what we want. That's no character reference.'

'Try to put yourself in his place. He owns three mansions and he's sitting up there in one of them, dependent on his daughters and loathing that dependency. Be he right or wrong, he swears that Jim wouldn't have gone near that war if not for you. And now you've come home with Jim's son and you expect him to live in a hovel with a family of darkies living next door.'

406

'How can you call them that?'

'I'm calling them what his daughters call them, what he said to me today, what most in town say when my back is turned — and what a judge in a courtroom would say.'

'I thought he liked Joey.'

'He's got nothing against Joey, not personally. It's his race he's got a problem with. Our grandfather lost a lot of stock to the blacks when he first settled that land. He had no respect for them, and the older Vern gets the more like the old coot he becomes.'

'What was his father like?'

'Weak as water. My dad had the gumption to break away. Vern's father stayed and kowtowed to the old man all his life. He died young.'

'What about your grandfather?'

'We thought he was immortal, darlin'. He was the toughest old pommy coot you'd be likely to meet in a month of Sundays. Honest to a fault. Ask him for a potato and he'd give you a sackful, but steal one from his acre paddock and you'd made an enemy for life — as had your kids yet unborn. Vern's the same. As far as he's concerned, you stole his son. If he decides to go after Jimmy, he'll spend his last penny on raking up every bit of mud he can find to throw in your face.'

'Teddy frows mud sometimes,' Georgie chimed in.

'Take your brother outside,' Gertrude said. 'Go out and get a load of dirt in that truck.'

Kids are adaptable. Jimmy liked having other kids to play with; he loved stealing warm eggs from the hens' nests, was wide eyed with wonder when Gertrude let him hold a newly hatched chicken. He liked watching milk squirt from goat to bucket.

Jenny watched him squat with Georgie, loading his tip truck with dirt. He'd never played in Sydney's dust. Did Sydney have dust? He'd never had a dirty face, dirty hands and feet, had never been bathed in a small tin tub.

'You've got a good little boy there.'

'I know it.'

'Vern is picking us up again next Friday.'

'I won't be here.'

'Carting him back to Sydney will be the fastest way to end up in court. Vern was on your side until you came home pregnant with Georgie. He would have got over Georgie if you hadn't gone after Jim.'

'I didn't go after Jim.'

'From the day you heard that Sissy was engaged to him, I saw your intent written all over your face, my girl.'

'I didn't go after him.'

'You wanted to throw a spanner in your sister's wedding plans and don't bother denying it to me. You wouldn't have looked at that boy twice if he hadn't got himself engaged to Sissy.'

'I looked at him twice because he came down here more than twice telling me that he didn't want to marry Sissy. And the reason he kept coming down here telling me was because I was the only person in the world who'd listen to him. If you think I'd have a baby just to nark Sissy, then all I can say to you is that you should have had a few more of them, because the only person having a baby narks is the one who is having it.'

Jenny walked to the door, then turned back. 'And while we're on the subject, Jim Hooper was the only decent man I've ever known in my life, and how he got that way is one of God's miracles because he didn't get it from his bloody father. And if you ever so much as think about saying that to me again, then I'm gone, Granny, and I'm gone for good and so are Jimmy and Georgie. I've got sixty pounds in the bank and twenty in my purse — and I know that I can sing, and that I can hold my own in a factory too, and that some people even like me for who I am. I'm here with you because I want to be here with you, not because I have to be here.'

She went outside to squat with her kids in the dust.

BEDS

Gertrude was beyond the age of sharing her bed. She'd been sharing it with the girls since Jenny stole their lean-to bed. Two weeks of sharing was two weeks too long. She tolerated it until the following Friday, then before lunching with Vern and his daughters, she walked up to Fulton's and ordered a brand-new bed. It could arrive as early as Monday and they needed to find space enough for it.

On Saturday they cleared out the northern end of her long bedroom, dragging dusty old trunks out to the more honest light of the kitchen, where ancient treasures might be relabelled junk and pitched.

The kids enjoyed it, all three draping themselves in scarfs from Germany, a silk shawl bought in Japan, pulling on shoes with turned-up toes worn by Gertrude when she'd dined at the captain's table. A history lesson, a geography lesson, the contents of Gertrude's trunks.

They found a sheet-wrapped, well-flattened surprise down the bottom of her camphor wood trunk.

'My wedding gown,' Gertrude said. 'It's got to be.' She took it to the table to unwrap, expecting it to fall apart. It was as stiff as a board, a fine brocade, a little yellowed but intact.

'It must have been beautiful, Granny.'

'I felt like a princess in it. My grandfather paid for its making.' She opened its folds carefully, held it high by the shoulders, gave it a gentle shake — and her marriage lines, wrapped with the frock, fluttered to the floor.

Jenny pounced on the paper.

'That's where it was!' Gertrude said. 'I spent weeks looking for that when Archie was declared dead. I talked myself into thinking I'd burnt it.'

Archibald Gerald Foote. Physician. Age 23. Gertrude Maria Hooper. Age 19.

'Archibald Gerald?' Jenny said, that name on paper, the profession, ringing alarm bells. Archibald Gerald Foote, physician, who had aborted Gertrude's son. Gerald Archibald, Sydney abortionist — old Noah, who had hung around this town for years during the depression!

Ridiculous. Of course it was ridiculous. As if Gertrude wouldn't have recognised her own husband. As if Amber wouldn't have recognised her own father.

But would they have seen him up close enough to recognise? She had. How much of him could they have recognised anyway, with that beard, that long hair, his glasses and black coat?

It was the answer to everything though. It was the answer to why he'd given her that pearl-in-a-cage pendant, why he'd posted the matching earrings. He'd known she was his granddaughter. Maybe he'd noticed her resemblance to him. That had to be it. Old men didn't go around giving ten-year-old girls antique pendants just for the hell of it.

A shudder travelled down her spine. Maybe some old men did. Maybe he'd offered a trinket to Nelly Abbot, to Barbie Dobson . . . If I'd told Constable Denham old Noah had given me that pendant, would Nelly and Barby have been alive today?

'You look like a stunned plover,' Gertrude said.

'I was . . . thinking. Do you remember that old bloke they locked up for interfering with one of the Duffy kids?' Gertrude remembered him. 'Did you ever get a good look at him, Granny?' Gertrude's head was down, working hard at refolding the wedding gown back into its original creases. 'Did you ever see him close up?'

'Why?'

'Because I saw him in Sydney and he was calling himself Dr Gerald Archibald,' Jenny said. 'A girl from the factory got

410

herself into trouble. He got rid of it.' She didn't mention her own appointment with him.

'What were you doing mixing with girls like that?'

'Do you remember what he was calling himself when he was here?'

Gertrude remembered. She placed the sheet-wrapped gown into the bottom of her camphor wood trunk and picked up a necklace of shells and coral she hadn't laid eyes on in fifty years. As she lifted it, the aged thread broke, scattering shells to every corner.

Chasing them amused the kids, but didn't change the subject.

'It was something longish, I know that much. Could it have been Archibald?'

'Forester,' Gertrude said. 'Albert Forester. And there's probably thousands who look like him.'

'It was him. I used to talk to him. I gave him a sausage wrapped in bread for his dinner one night, and he told me that I had a voice that would charm the angels. He used to wear a ring on his little finger. He was still wearing it.'

'Did he recognise you?'

'I was standing at his gate when he opened the door. He wasn't looking at me. I couldn't believe it. He was dressed up like a toff, with only a little beard, but it was him.'

'How long ago?'

Take care, Jenny Morrison. Take great care. 'A few months before I left the factory.'

Gertrude turned back to the scattered beads. Everyone has secrets they don't wish to share. Gertrude had a secret she'd never share. Now Jenny had one of her own. Neither one pushed the subject further, not that day.

They trod on shells, picked up coral beads, swept them up for days. Ten years from that day, a shell would turn up in the dustpan, but they cleared enough space down the northern end of Gertrude's bedroom, and when the new bed arrived on Tuesday, there was space for it.

The weather warmed. Pleasant days, pleasant evenings of sitting beneath the stars, the night birds calling, the frogs' chorus from the creek carrying.

411

And Vern turning up every Friday, and Jimmy happy to go with him now—which hurt like hell.

Gertrude's happiness hurt, too.

'Why don't you marry him and be done with it, Granny?'

'It would be the sensible thing to do.'

'Then why don't you?'

'He hasn't asked me lately. He's found himself a new focus in Jimmy.'

'You love him, don't you?'

'I was probably born loving him, darlin'.'

'Then why marry Itchy-foot? How could anyone force themselves to do the bed bit if they weren't in love?'

'That's not the sort of question you ask your grandmother and you watch your mouth around those girls. They're growing up.'

'It's better for them to learn about it from us than on a tombstone.'

'That's enough of that talk!'

'It happened, Granny. I can't hide from it, so why should you? And you didn't answer my question.'

'Marrying Vern was out of the question by the time I wed Archie.'

'Why?'

'You're as bad as Georgie with your questions.'

'I told you once your life was like a storybook to me.'

'I've told you before. If Vern had married me back then he would have lost that land to his half-brother, and a boy of nineteen is too young to be thinking of marriage anyway.'

'So getting that farm was more important to him than getting you. Jim would have given up everything for me. I should have given up everything for him. I should have gone to Queensland with him.'

'And I should have waited until the old chap died and married Vern, but I didn't. We could spend our lives kicking ourselves for the things we did or didn't do. All that does is leave bruises.'

'Vern would know if the Japs had taken Jim prisoner, wouldn't he?'

'Tom Vevers's boy was in a prison camp. They knew. I think the Red Cross gets lists of the boys' names and contacts the families.'

'Bastard war.'

'Don't use that language in front of those girls!'

Jenny spied on Vern and his lunch guests when he drove them home the following Friday, spied through the bedroom hatch, and saw more than she wanted to see, saw Jimmy kiss his grandfather, saw Gertrude kiss Vern's cheek.

They came in smiling, Gertrude with a load of shopping, Jimmy with another toy in a box.

Vern never came into the house. He'd sent no solicitor's letters. He'd decided to woo Jimmy to his side with drives in cars, with presents. He was wooing Gertrude to his side, too. He could no longer haul a wheat bag, but he sent one of his farm labourers down with half a dozen bags of wheat for her chooks. He sent down a giant load of mill-ends, too green to burn yet, but they'd dry out over summer. That little black stove ate a lot of wood in winter.

And what am I doing thinking about next winter? Jenny thought. I can't be here next winter.

There were pages of advertisements for work in the back of Saturday's newspapers. *Country girl, for light cleaning. Must be good with children.*

'If she's got kids, she might take a widow with a kid.'

'You're not the type to be doing the bidding of society dames.'

'I've cleaned. I'm a good cleaner.'

'You'd need references.'

'I'll clean up this place for you and you can write me one.'

'You'll leave this place alone, my girl. I'm having trouble finding anything as it is.'

Jenny borrowed Lenny's bike and rode into town to place a call to a woman from Camberwell, who wasn't interested in employing a widow with two kids. She wrote in reply to an advertisement for an experienced housekeeper to live in on a property in Gippsland, *some cooking required.*

A widower replied, asking for a photograph.

'He's got more than cooking and cleaning and childcare on his mind,' Gertrude said.

He made it pretty obvious. He wrote again, suggesting Jenny meet him in Melbourne for an interview.

The Friday lunches continued, the kisses for Grandpa, the toys, the lollies. You could set your clock by Vern on Fridays. Jimmy watching for him now, running to him, Gertrude not far behind him.

'Traitors,' Jenny said.

'What's traitors?' Georgie asked.

'They are.'

'Why?'

'Because I said so,' Jenny said.

Too much time to think on Friday afternoons, to wonder if Myrtle had killed that baby with kindness, to wonder what she'd do if she and Jimmy, plus an extra, turned up again on her doorstep, wondering and watching the clock's hands creep around, past two thirty, close to three thirty.

Then Jimmy running inside with a brown paper bag.

Kids are easily bought. Sitting on Grandpa's lap driving a real car was beyond price. Four chocolate frogs in a brown paper bag is like gold to a three-year-old.

'Share them with your sisters.'

'Poppy sayed dey is for me.'

'And I say share them with your sisters.'

He shared them, one each for the girls and two for him, until Jenny stole his extra frog and made a point of sharing it with Gertrude.

'He wouldn't miss me if I took off and left you with the three of them.'

'Vern and his daughters would have no argument with it,' Gertrude said.

'I'm existing, surviving around the perimeters of everyone's lives like a stray dog. I'm fed, but I don't belong. Sissy used to call me a stray bitch.'

'Those girls will learn bad language soon enough without you teaching it to them.'

Jimmy learned to call Elsie 'Mummy', and hearing that word on his lips ripped a hole in Jenny's bowel. *Go to Mummy*, Jim used to say. *Where's Mummy*?

She'd never been Mummy to those girls — she didn't want to be Mummy to anyone, but there was no way she'd let Jimmy start using that name for Elsie.

414

Georgie fixed it while Jenny was still wondering how.

'Elsie is Teddy and Brian and all of them other kids' Mummy, not yours,' she said.

It was sickening how she loved that kid; it was that aching form of love, that wanting to grab her, hold her, kiss her cheeky face. She couldn't yet. Too scared of frightening her away. Jenny stood listening, tears blurring her eyes.

'You have to say Elsie for her, like I say Elsie,' Georgie instructed.

'Margot sayed Mummy.'

'That's 'cause Elsie gived her milk, is why, 'cause Margot didn't like goat's milk.' Then that so familiar finger pointed in Jenny's direction. 'She's our muvver.'

'Dat's Jenny,' Jimmy argued.

'And our muvver, too.'

'Why?'

''Cause . . .'cause I said so is why, and we live here and not at Elsie's, and 'cause she cooks good puddings and everything for us.'

And there you go, Jenny-muvver Morrison, pudding maker, egg collector, water carrier, washerwoman. Poor Jenny-muvver Morrison, not twenty-one yet. Accept your lot, Jenny-muvver Morrison. You're worn out with running away. Accept your lot in life. Give in to it.

But what about your dreams, Jenny-muvver Morrison? What about Cara Jeanette, that famous singer who married a handsome film star and went to live in Paris?

You left her behind, Jenny-muvver Morrison, left her up in Sydney to live out those dreams in the house of the fairy godmother.

MOTHERHOOD

Jimmy turned three on the third of December. Jenny gave him three kisses and two pairs of homemade shorts. Granny gave him three tiny pullet's eggs and told him he could have all three for breakfast. He didn't want to eat them. He wanted to get tiny chickens out of them. One had leaked into the pocket of his brand-new shorts before Vern and Margaret arrived with a bright red tricycle. And it was no common tricycle either; it had mudguards and a bell on the shiny handlebars. They presented him with a cake, fancy iced, *Jimmy* written on it in blue and underlined by three blue candles. For the first time since October, Gertrude invited them inside for a cup of tea.

The cake looked too fine to cut, but they lit the candles and Jenny lifted Jimmy up so he might blow them out. Margaret, who had baked and iced the artwork, was offered a knife to cut it. She served fat, cream-filled wedges onto an assortment of plates and they ate cake, drank tea. It was a more civil gathering with the third Hooper missing.

Then it was Christmas, and the Hoopers came again, all three of them this time, toting a green pedal car, two shirts and a pair of leather sandals.

Jenny couldn't stand Lorna's ever-present sneer. Couldn't stand seeing Jimmy sitting on Vern's lap, couldn't stand hearing him call Margaret 'Aunty Maggie'. Couldn't and didn't have to.

She left them to it, took the girls down to the creek and tried to teach Margot to swim. Georgie had been swimming since she'd learnt to walk. Margot screamed if a splash of water wet her face. Left Margot sitting on the bank while she and Georgie played.

Not five years old yet, but that little girl was a sponge eager to soak up the world. They stayed at the creek until they heard the Hoopers' car drive away, when they returned to find Jimmy playing log buggies, his pedal car loaded with firewood and roped to the rear of his tricycle.

'*Vroom, vroom, vroom*.' Around and around the yard he drove in wide circles.

'I want a grandpa too that buys fings.'

'*Things*,' Jenny corrected. 'Poke your tongue out and blow.'

Jimmy's new shirts and sandals still on the table, Jenny tossed them onto the cane couch. Jimmy didn't need shop-bought shirts; she made his shirts. He didn't need new sandals either; he had shoes.

Santa's present to Georgie, a large rag doll with hair redder than Georgie's own, was tossed with the shorts but fell to the floor. 'Not fair,' Georgie said.

'No it's not,' Jenny agreed, picking up the thrown doll.

'Stop encouraging her bad behaviour,' Gertrude scolded.

'It's got nothing to do with bad behaviour. It's pure unadulterated envy, and I understand it,' Jenny said.

'Where's my grandpa and aunties to buy fings?' Georgie pushed her advantage.

'Your grandpa spent all of his money on your aunty.'

'Stop that, Jennifer!'

'It's true.'

'You're acting like one of the kids.'

'Why did he spend all his money for?' Georgie asked.

'Because your aunty Sissy is so big she needs six buckets of food every night for her dinner and two miles of material to make one dress, and even two chairs to sit on at the table because her bottom is so wide it falls over the sides of one chair.'

'How big?'

Jenny stretched her arms to their full extent. 'Bigger even.'

'Stop that now,' Gertrude said.

'Can I see . . . how big? Can her and my grandpa come here one day?'

'She's in Melbourne,' Gertrude said. 'Now go outside and play with your brother.'

Full of questions, little Georgie, and like a dog with a bone too big to chew, she worried it for days. Give her one answer, and she found ten more questions, and trying to sidetrack her was like trying to sidetrack ants from a jar of jam. They kept finding their way back to it.

'Where does my grandpa and Aunty Sissy live?'

'Near the trains.'

'Can we go there and see them?'

'No.'

'Why?'

'There's no room in their house for us.'

''Cause Aunty Sissy is too big. And her muvver is too?'

Jenny had no intention of discussing Aunty Sissy's mother. She changed the subject. 'Mo*ther*. If you can't say your *th*s you won't be able to go to school with Teddy next year.'

'I done wan' *th*cool,' Margot said. She had no difficulty saying *th*, just couldn't say an *s* to save her life.

'Fa*ther*,' Jenny said. '*Sss*-chool,' she said.

'Jimmy's farver got dead. Did my farver and Margot's get dead too?'

'Fa*ther*.'

Maybe they practised saying fa*ther* once too often during the days between Christmas and New Year. Maybe words take wing, become caught up on some air current — maybe those air currents infiltrate dreams.

On the night before her birthday, Jenny dreamed of Laurie. He was at Norman's station unloading Granny's trunks, dozens of them. She knew she'd been home for months. Where had those trunks been? She knew she'd packed that Sydney baby into one of those trunks, and she had to find it, feed it. Laurie was standing there, laughing while she threw clothes everywhere, searching for that baby, knowing it was in one of those trunks, knowing she had to feed it.

She woke gasping for air, her arms reaching out to hold Jimmy. He no longer shared her bed. He'd deserted her for the girls' bed in Granny's room.

Little traitor.

418

She sat up and stared at faded rosebuds, sat for long minutes, not wanting to rise and face this day. She'd told Jim she'd marry him when she was twenty-one. She was twenty-one and he was dead and she wanted a cigarette, needed one.

Twenty-one, finally in control of her own life and she had no life to control. She had money in the bank — well, Jenny Hooper had money in the bank that Jenny Morrison couldn't get at, not in Woody Creek. She was twenty-one and sleeping alone in a sagging bed, beneath a corrugated-iron roof where birds congregated to jitterbug over head, she was gasping for a smoke and didn't dare to light one — not inside.

Mad Barbara's parents had given her a huge party to celebrate her coming of age. They'd given her a silver key to the door. No key to the door for Jenny — no keyhole in Granny's front door in which to place a key, and that door left hanging wide open now, day and night, a curtain of hessian hung across it, dampened down so a cooler breeze might blow through, and a few of the million flies and mozzies wouldn't.

Hot as hell already and not eight o'clock yet. God help this room by noon.

She rose and pulled on homemade shorts, cut from Gertrude's trouser pattern. They weren't short shorts, but they offered a freedom she hadn't previously known. She fastened her bra, slid her arms into a light cotton shirt, cut from the pattern Gertrude used for her own shirts, cut smaller. Like Gertrude, she dressed for comfort now, for convenience.

Give me a year or two and I'll be wearing trousers and work boots, she thought. Not yet though. She slid her feet into canvas shoes and went out to the kitchen.

There was a present waiting for her on the kitchen table. Four kisses waiting for her, one given grudgingly. Margot liked El*th*ie be*th*t — and didn't mind saying it, didn't mind showing it. And who could blame her for that? Jenny liked Georgie best. She tried not to show it though.

She opened the parcel before breakfast and found a length of the prettiest deep blue linen, three yards of it. 'It's beautiful, Granny. Thank you.'

'I saw it in Blunt's and thought it would match your eyes,' Gertrude said, serving out five bowls of porridge.

Elsie came over with her kids and a cake at noon and the kids sang 'Happy Birthday'. Jenny ate a slice of cake, then took off to the orchard with her packet of cigarettes.

She'd thought she'd get a card from Myrtle, a card and a photograph of that baby. It would be almost three months old. But there'd been no birthday card, no Christmas card, not even a card for Jimmy's birthday.

Lila from the factory had known Jenny would be turning twenty-one on New Year's Eve. The factory girls took up collections to buy presents. Jenny had put in her coins. They knew where she lived, or Lila and Norma knew. There was probably a heap of letters at the post office — addressed to Jenny Hooper — or they'd been given to Lorna Hooper and she was standing at the stove, burning them.

Mr Foster would know who they were meant for, dear Mr Foster who came from his back room whenever he heard her voice in the post office. Something could come on Monday. Lila's mind was as disorganised as her boarding house room. Myrtle's wasn't. She would have posted that photograph a week early.

There'd be no photograph, not for her twenty-first birthday, not ever. I have to forget about the baby, Jenny thought. She lit a second cigarette from the first, buried the butt deep into the earth, and leaned back against the trunk of the old apple tree, trying to smoke that baby out of her head. Some things become jammed in the deep recesses of the brain. Some things are unmovable.

The chewing of a lemon leaf disguised the smell of smoke on her breath. Stolen mint rubbed between the hands washed them clean of cigarettes.

She spent the afternoon of her twenty-first birthday in a spider-riddled shed and at the clothes line, labouring for three kids, while a paddock away they played with Elsie's kids.

'I've got to do something, Granny. I've got to go somewhere. People don't live like this.'

'A good few live a lot worse,' Gertrude said.

'And a hell of a lot live much better.'

'Your father spent his life chasing after something better.'

'I wish he had —'

'You know who I mean. Amber's father.'

'Have you still got your wedding photograph?'

'It's somewhere.' Washing, wringing, tossing worn-out sheets into a worn-out cane basket.

'It used to hang on the wall when I was a kid.'

'It hung there for your mother's sake.'

'Do you ever see her to talk to?'

'She hasn't spoken to me in years.'

They rinsed and wrung, carried the used rinsing water to the garden in buckets, fetched clean water to the trough.

'We'll have to fill that tank tomorrow.'

'It's 1945 tomorrow and we're still living in 1845.'

'This shed wasn't built in 1845.'

'Damn close to it.'

'Stop your swearing.'

'"Damn" isn't swearing.'

'I've heard worse out of your mouth, my girl.'

Ragged towels were hung, little frocks, checked shirts, cotton working trousers.

'The last time you saw Itchy-foot was when Amber was twelve.'

'Going on thirteen.'

'Where was he between then and when he died?'

'Somewhere between sunrise and sunset.'

'How did he die?'

'He was jailed in Egypt for stealing, or so I heard. His family tracked him to a jail in Egypt after his father died, and could find no record of him ever getting out of it. The family had him declared dead back in '33.'

'Was he a thief when you knew him?'

'He had the conscience of a cobra and the morals of a cockroach.'

'Vern would say it runs in the family.'

He had. 'I worry about Sissy being like him at times,' Gertrude said.

'Sissy? I'm the one who's like him.'

'You got the best of him. She got his selfish ways. She comes home from your father's relatives, and a week or so later she's taken to her bed and Norman sends her back.'

'She's found a new way to get what she wants, that all.'

'I don't know what's going to happen to that girl.'

'I don't care what happens to her. I haven't got a skerrick of feeling for her, just anger . . . anger that I ended up with a sister I can't stand. The Macdonald girls still stick together like glue. Georgie and Margot aren't even full sisters and they don't try to kill each other.'

They filled the line with washing and before hanging the last load brought in the sheets to make room on the line. Together they folded them, put them away on a shelf in Gertrude's wardrobe.

'I used to think I'd be in Paris when I was twenty-one, that I'd be a famous singer. And look at me.'

'Look at you, flashing those beautiful legs.'

'I'm twenty-one and I've got three kids!'

'And strength enough to handle anything. I don't know where you got it, but you've got the resilience of Indian rubber. I've seen it in you all your life. The night you were born, I told Nancy that you were a little survivor. There you were, this wee scrap of a bald-headed mite, but wailing loud enough for her to hear you across two paddocks —' Gertrude closed her mouth fast and turned away, walked to the stove to check the firebox.

'Nancy Bryant? What paddock?'

'I'll tell you one day.'

'Tell me now before the kids come home. What's Nancy got to do with me being born?' But Gertrude was going out to feed her chooks. 'Walking away is Norman's trick, not yours, Granny. I'm allowed to vote. I'm supposed to be an adult. What paddock?'

Gertrude had got herself into something she couldn't get out of. Maybe it was time. She'd considered telling Jenny this morning, had considered giving her the stranger's brooch for her twenty-first birthday. That's what Ernie Ogden had said to do with it. She'd also promised Norman she'd never say a word.

'Your mother lost a little boy after Sissy —'

'I know all that stuff; it's on the tombstone. How come I was born in a paddock?'

Left with nowhere to go but to the truth, Gertrude took the long road to it, hoping to find an escape route on the way. 'Your grandmother died a few days before you were born. The town was full of Norman's relatives up for the funeral. Amber had a house full.'

'And she took off on one of her night walks?' Jenny said.

Her words offered Gertrude the way out she was looking for. 'Nancy and her old dog found you. She heard a baby crying and they followed your cry, darlin', and found you near the railway line, just behind their land.'

'Is that why she hates me? The shock of being on her own in the dark with a screaming baby?'

'Losing Leonora April seemed to be the turning point in Amber's life — and maybe the ruination of Sissy, too. Norman sent them down to your Uncle Charles.'

'Why didn't she take me?'

'You had a wonderful time here with your dad. He took you everywhere with him, brought you down here every Sunday. He and Vern built that lean-to.'

The sun eventually went down on Jenny's twenty-first birthday and there wasn't enough water in the tank to shout herself a bath. At seven, she left Gertrude to put the kids into bed and commandeered Lenny to harness the horse up to the water barrel cart. Nugget wasn't fond of Jenny; maybe he knew she was afraid of him. Lenny led him down to the creek, where the horse snorted his disdain as they backed him up to Gertrude's water-pumping log.

Jenny had never fetched the water without Gertrude at her side, but they got the barrel close enough, got the hose into clear water, slapped at swarming mosquitoes and pumped that drum full. Lenny led the horse back and they pumped their load into the tank.

'That will do until morning,' Gertrude yelled from the doorway.

'I'm twenty-one, Granny,' Jenny yelled, and she turned the horse and the barrel around and went back for another load, singing as she walked.

'I'm twenty-one today, twenty-one today, I've got the key to the door . . .'

It was growing dark when they returned with the second barrel full, Gertrude waiting out at the tank with her lantern.

'That's enough, I said.'

'Never put off until tomorrow what you don't want to do today — you'll feel less like doing it tomorrow,' Jenny said, slapping the horse on the rump, showing him who was the boss tonight.

'Don't turn my own words back on me, my girl. I've just got enough sense to stay away from the creek in the dark. There are snakes by the hundred down there.'

'You said snakes don't like horses, Gran,' Lenny yelled. He was enjoying himself. He liked Jenny, liked having her to himself.

'At least take the lantern with you. You'll be sucking up duckweed.'

'Then we'll drink duckweed,' Jenny yelled. 'I'll wash my hair in duckweed. *My grandmother says I can do as I like, I shout hip-hip hooray, for I'm a jolly good fellow, I'm twenty-one today.*'

It was well after eight when they released Nugget to his paddock. No rub down tonight, no bucket of oats in appreciation, and they'd made him wait on the bank looking down his nose with disapproval while they'd had a swim.

COMING TO TERMS

She should have seen the bike leaning against the fence. She didn't. The door was open, the hessian curtain hanging limp and newly wet down. She drew it back and saw the three kids who should have been in bed an hour ago sitting pyjama-clad at the table, Gertrude sitting opposite.

And him, seated on Vern's chair.

She took a step back, almost turned on her heel and took off for Elsie's house, but he'd seen her lift the curtain.

'You have reached your majority,' he said.

'That must be a relief to you,' she said.

He'd never been good at deciphering sarcasm. He nodded, cleared his throat and held out a small parcel. She remained in the doorway. He cleared his throat again, placed the gift down and glanced at the cluster of her children.

The circle of yellow lamplight was glowing on the three small faces, on three small heads, glowing in three pairs of staring eyes. He had not allowed for the children, had not expected to see her children, to be introduced to them as 'Grandpa'. He was indeed their grandfather, though he had not previously considered himself as such.

He should not have come here.

He glanced at Jenny. She was a woman but not dressed in a womanly way. Unable to look at her bare legs, at the damp clinging shirt, his eyes were forced to look at her face, to see her disdain. He should have foreseen it, should have foreseen the hurt her disdain might cause him. He had not.

'The boy has your eyes,' he said.

'Margot has got the Macdonalds',' she replied accusingly.

'Yes.' He'd never learnt to take his punishment like a man. He cleared his throat and looked to Gertrude for assistance.

'Sit down and stop flashing your legs at your father. You're embarrassing him.'

'You said he was my grandfa*tha*,' Georgie said.

'Jenny's father is your grandfather,' Gertrude explained. 'Let that curtain down before every mozzie in Woody Creek comes in for supper.'

Jenny allowed the curtain to fall, glanced at the gold-wrapped parcel, oblong, book shaped, probably a Bible. No doubt he thought she needed it. She didn't reach for it but walked around the table to the hot end. There was little space between table and stove.

Gertrude slid the gift towards her, the kids' eyes followed it. They'd never seen a present wrapped in gold paper and tied with a blue ribbon.

Jenny didn't need a Bible. She glanced at him, watched him remove his glasses, polish them on a crumpled handkerchief. Too much of his face was exposed when he took his glasses off. It was too easy to see those abused bloodhound eyes — those lost puppy dog eyes — all that remained of her childhood daddy who had taken her riding on the back of his bike. The rest of him was Amber's fool, Sissy's dupe.

Georgie's fingers, itching to touch that gold paper, reached out to finger the blue bow. She'd wished for a grandpa like Jimmy had, and she'd got one, and one who brought presents.

'Fingers off. Jenny will open it,' Gertrude said.

Bible or not, she had to open it — if just to see how much he thought she was worth. Maybe Sissy's hand-me-down Bible? She undid the ribbon, unwrapped the paper. Gertrude took it, folded it to put away, to use again.

Not a Bible. She'd exposed a small flat box with a brass clip. She looked at Norman. He was watching her fingers, so she flipped the clip and opened the lid. And saw a glitter of blue, a deep and gorgeous blue.

426

Something deep down at her core threatened to break open. Her stomach shuddering, the shudder crept up her chest, to her throat. She had to sit down. There was no chair to sit on. She had to think about how he'd tried to marry her off at fifteen. She had to concentrate on that, on all the bad things, or she was going to howl.

'What a beautiful thing.' Gertrude was on her feet, touching the stones with a work-worn finger. The kids, now kneeling on their chairs, leaned across the table so they might see more.

Not a word could Jenny say; if she tried to open her mouth, she'd bawl. She stared at the necklet, hardly daring to touch it for fear that it wasn't really there. But it was, and it had matching earrings, dainty drop earrings for pierced ears. He'd remembered Granny making those holes through her lobes. Or just a lucky accident?

But it wasn't. He hadn't chosen red or yellow stones. He'd bought blue, the blue of her Alice Blue Gown, the one she'd worn when she sang at the school concert when she was ten years old. The blue of her eyes.

She looked at his hangdog eyes then, and her hand went to her mouth to hold the howl in. Had to hold it in. Couldn't hold the words in. They wanted out, and whether she howled or not, they came out.

'It's beautiful, Daddy.' Her voice was low, but she didn't howl.

'Daddy?' Jimmy questioned.

Thank God for kids.

''Cause he's her fa-*tha*, like Harry is everyone's fa-*tha*,' Georgie explained.

The kids made it easier. Georgie told Norman that Aunty Sissy could come with him next time and have her and Jimmy's chairs. Jimmy wasn't so certain about that, but he'd saved the candles from his birthday cake and he wanted to put them on a cake and sing 'Happy Birthday'. A small half of Elsie's fruitcake had been placed into the tin. They poked bent candles into it, lit them and sang. Jenny blew them out.

Norman had little to say. He ate a slice of cake, drank a mug of tea, then they walked him out to the gate, watching his bike light fade out of sight.

'What a surprise,' Gertrude said as Jenny took the necklace from its box and the kids brushed their teeth again, went to bed again. 'It will go well with the linen.'

It would. Jenny fetched the blue linen from her room and placed the necklet on it. It was perfect. Nowhere to wear it, but at least she'd own something beautiful. She still wanted to cry for Norman, or for herself, or for Jim . . . or for that fool of a woman who had gone walking along a bloody railway line when she was nine months pregnant! She wanted to go to bed and howl her heart out for things that might have been.

She didn't though. She draped the fabric over her shoulders, held the necklet to her throat and tried to see enough in the small washstand mirror.

'I might try to copy the style of the green linen, Granny.'

Gertrude knew her limitations, and Jenny's. 'Get Miss Blunt to make it up for you,' she said, and she went to bed.

Jenny returned the necklet to its box, then took the green linen from her wardrobe to study how it had been made. Maybe she'd take it and the blue material in to Miss Blunt. She had money enough to pay for its making and that material deserved better than her homemade efforts.

Her case, never fully unpacked, was drawn from beneath her bed and heaved onto it, opened. The emptying of it would be the final admission that she was going nowhere — which was exactly where she was going. Like Myrtle's minister had said, God had a master plan for all. His plan for Jenny was Woody Creek and she may as well stop fighting it. He'd allowed her those two years in Sydney only because of his master plan for Myrtle. What had happened up there was exactly what he'd meant to happen, right from the start, right from the cancelled seat on the train, right from Wilfred and the club. Just components of dear old God's master plan for Myrtle — as had been the Jap bombs dropped on Pearl Harbor. If America hadn't come into the war, Billy-Bob would have stayed home on the farm.

The lamp was burning in the kitchen, wasting kerosene. Jenny wasn't ready for bed. She carried it to her lean-to, cleared space for it on her dressing table and set it down. The framed photograph taken of her and Jim and Jimmy lived on her dressing table. She picked it up, and considered God's master plan for Vern. Was he meant to lose his son then have a second go at ruining Jimmy?

'You're a womb, Jenny Morrison, God's flesh and blood chalice for the pouring out of his blessings on his favourites.'

And the girls? Who were they meant for? Maisy had plenty of grandchildren and no one would ever come looking for Georgie. Maybe I foiled his plans. I was probably meant to sign both of them away. Or if I hadn't had them, I wouldn't have had Jimmy for Vern. And if I hadn't had Jimmy, I wouldn't have gone to Sydney. No baby for Myrtle.

Jenny kissed her finger and placed the kiss on Jim's photograph. She'd promised to show the photo to Jimmy every day. For a time she had.

How easily we forget.

But it wasn't forgetting; it was putting away the flight of the butterflies, and knowing that what they'd had had been too close to magic to last.

She picked up Billy-Bob's watch. It was still real enough to burn her hand. She dropped it back into the case where it landed on Jim's letters. Snatched them away from it, not wanting them polluted. With the bundle of letters in her hand, Jenny stood looking at the rose she'd picked on the day of that telegram and dried between the pages of *Rebecca*. It was in its own envelope now, tied up with Jim's letters. Dead and brittle, its colour faded, but that dusty old rose scent still clung to the envelope. She had to put it away. Life was for the living, Gertrude said.

And she had to put that baby away too. She'd done the right thing by it. Even if she'd brought it home, even if Granny had come around to accepting it, Jenny knew she would have ended up feeling about Cara as she felt about Margot. You can control what you say, what you do, but you can't control what you feel. She couldn't even control what she felt for Norman. So pleased he'd remembered her birthday. She'd thought he'd forgotten her. And choosing blue, and those earrings. Just so pleased.

She sighed and glanced up at an old shoe box, still there on top of the wardrobe. She lifted it down, wiped dust from its lid with her hand, opened it. There was a sheet of newspaper on top, folded to fit. She took it to the lamp to study the newsprint photograph of the water pistol bandit. He looked even more like Clark Gable in black and white.

The paper placed down, she removed the embroidered purse she'd seen before, probably Amber's. She'd done exquisite embroidery and no doubt had embroidered that purse, the pretty pinks, maroons, greens, beads mixed in with the silks, intricate work.

There was something heavy inside it. She opened it and removed a brooch pinned to a handkerchief, a pretty brooch, but like most of Gertrude's treasures not worth much. She removed an old luggage label. Someone had written on it with red ink. It must have been raining the day they'd travelled; the ink had bled. She wondered where Amber had been. Or maybe it was Gertrude's label, saved from her trip home from India. Maybe she'd worn that brooch home from India.

Just history. Just old history. Gertrude's house was full of it.

Had the brooch not been pinned to cover the handkerchief's embroidered initials, Jenny may have seen the *J.C.*, may have questioned it. She didn't see it. She read the few words written on the sheet of writing paper she found inside the purse. *Albert Forester* — old Noah, the swaggie cum abortionist, who would have recognised her as easily as she'd recognised him had she been the one knocking on his door that morning. Dear old God had held her back from the door. He couldn't allow her to interfere with his master plan for Myrtle.

Why had Gertrude kept that sheet of paper? Why had she kept that old luggage label? Why had she kept all of that junk in her trunks for half a century? She was a collector, that's why. Maybe God's master plan for Gertrude was to collect lost souls and nurse them back to health — and she'd collect Norman if she could. She'd told him tonight he was welcome to come down any time.

Georgie would welcome him. Jimmy had Vern and his Aunty Maggie. Margot had Nanna Maisy and Mummy Elsie.

Jenny looked again at the water pistol bandit's face, then carefully unfolded the page of newsprint she'd folded into that box five years ago. She was reading, remembering, until old floorboards creaked. She folded it fast, and glanced over her shoulder, expecting Gertrude to pop her head around the curtain and tell her to stop wasting kerosene. But Gertrude didn't appear. The house was full of aged creaks.

I shouldn't have kept that newspaper. I ought to burn it, she thought.

You can't change history by burning it.

She placed it in the bottom of the empty shoe box, burying it with Jim's letters and her bankbook, then burying the lot beneath the embroidered purse. The lid on, the box back on top of the wardrobe, she returned to the emptying of her case.

She pulled out the framed photograph of Jimmy in his sailor's suit; just a small frame, cheap. The photograph of her and Jimmy. She placed them beside the family photograph and looked again at Jim.

If he'd lived. If he'd lived . . .

He hadn't.

The alarm clock she'd lived by in Sydney, unwound since Sydney, was pleased to be ticking again. She set it on the dressing table, then reached for Billy-Bob's watch.

Smash it. Bury it.

Gold doesn't rust away.

Chuck it into the stove then. Let it melt away.

And one morning Granny will find a lump of gold, studded with its many jewelled movements, and somewhere within that lump of metal, his name will remain.

You can't melt history, can't rewrite it the way you want it to read. It's there, behind you, unpleasant but intact.

She wound the watch and held it to her ear. It ticked, like the alarm clock, eager to be in service. She set it to the approximate time and looked at the broken band.

I'll buy a new band and wear it, she thought. Mr Cox might sell bands, and if he didn't, he'd be able to order one.

She took the watch and the lamp back to the kitchen, seeking something sharp enough to mutilate the engraving. The point of the tin opener would do it.

431

And Cara Jeanette might not have been his anyway. His was a convenient name to wear the blame, that's all — and the mutilation of his name would only make it more obvious.

She'd found that watch on a beach in Sydney, came upon a dog chewing it, an overweight black labrador. The marks of his teeth were on it. He'd chewed the leather band. No need to lie about where she'd found that watch — unless she scratched off the name.

Could I wear it against my skin? I just decided to forget about Cara Jeanette. If I wear his watch I'll never forget her.

You won't forget her anyway, Jenny Morrison.

THREE OLD MEN

George Macdonald hadn't altered in twenty years. He was short and stocky, his only hair his verandah eyebrows and what grew out of his ears. He was no heavier today than he'd been at forty when he'd bought his wedding suit, which he'd worn to seven of his eight daughters' weddings, and if the eighth ever caught herself a man, he'd be happy enough to wear it again. His legs were short, his head appeared to be attached directly to his shoulders. He had no room for a collar, rarely wore one, didn't look good when he did, but whatever he'd been made of, like his wedding suit, it didn't look like wearing out soon. He was the first man at his mill every morning and the last to leave at night.

Vern Hooper resented him more every year. George was no more than three or four years Vern's junior, he had a young energetic wife, umpteen grandkids and twin sons who had joined up the day war was declared. George was proud to tell anyone, whether they asked or not, that neither twin had a scratch on him. He resented George's *I'm on my way to someplace* strut. There was nothing about George Macdonald that Vern didn't resent.

He also resented Charlie White, who still took it into his head some Saturdays to ride by Vern's house and keep on riding. Vern knew where he was riding — and what did Gertrude find to talk to him about for three hours? He resented Charlie's ability to push those bike pedals, resented his muscular calves, and the riding shorts he wore to show off his calves.

There was too much height in Vern's bones — and every inch of them aching today. His farm was making him money. His mill was making him more. He had money coming out of his ears, and what could it buy him? Nothing that he wanted, not a new set of legs — nor his grandson — though he'd spent enough on solicitors to buy him ten times over.

He resented his big-talking city solicitor too, who kept assuring him that it was only a matter of time. Vern didn't have the time.

If he'd had his health, he would have gone up to Sydney and claimed Jimmy the day the news had come through. If he'd had his health, he might have wed Gertrude and been raising that boy now, out at Monk's house. But he didn't have his health, so he was sitting on the verandah, watching the road and resenting the whole bloody world.

He'd been sitting there at twelve forty when Charlie White had ridden north. His fob watch told him the time was now going on for four and Charlie was still down there. That's when Vern started doing laps of the verandah, walking the circle, forcing his bones to move when every one of the elongated bastards begged him to stop, when Margaret begged him to stop.

'You'll walk yourself into another turn, Father.'

Maybe he would, but he'd go down walking.

He pitched his stick on his second circumnavigation and he forced his mind to recall the morning old Cecelia Morrison died, to recall lifting her out of the dunny and the weight of the coffin he'd helped drop into her grave. That kept him walking. Old Cecelia, weighing in at half a ton, dead in a dunny at sixty.

He had to lose some of his girth. His solicitor had said on the phone this morning that his health would play a large part in the claiming of Jimmy. He'd said that a judge wasn't going to take that boy away from his mother and give him into the care of a grandfather unlikely to see him through his childhood years, not while that girl had good family support, not when she wore a ring on her wedding finger with his son's name on it, which more or less made them engaged to be wed.

'Hot-blooded little half-dago bitch of a girl,' Vern muttered as he walked another circle. If she hadn't gone after Jim, he would have been out at the farm today. If she hadn't gone after Jim, his grandson would have never been born either. He loved that boy.

434

He'd let things get away from him these past years. He'd given in, become a useless, dependent old bastard.

'Put your cardigan on, Father, you'll catch a chill,' Margaret called as he passed the kitchen window.

Bloody cardigans buttoning up over his fat belly. He'd never worn a cardigan in his life until he'd grown his belly. He'd get rid of it, and his old man cardigans. And he'd get that boy. Out of the top drawer, that one, a man's boy. He could kick a football. He could run like the wind, he could chant every nursery rhyme ever written, and sing like that wild little bitch who had mothered him. Something out of the box, that boy.

He pushed off from the verandah post and continued his walk.

'Where is your walking cane, Father?'

Just a matter of time. Just a matter of determination. Just a matter of waiting until the time was right, the solicitor had said this morning.

Time. He had never spent enough of it with Jim. Had never found enough of it to spend with him. All he had now was time, and how much of it he had left would depend on how he used it — or so Gertrude said. Get some of that weight off you and your legs won't have so much to carry around, she said. Eat more greens and less cakes.

He didn't like greens and did like cake. 'Expects a man to chew on cabbage leaves,' he muttered and did another lap of his verandah, his bad ankle killing him. He'd thrown that leg since his stroke. Gertrude had told him years ago that boots would support his ankle. He didn't take a woman's advice easily.

'You've done enough, Father. You mustn't exhaust yourself. Come inside and I'll make you a cup of tea,' Margaret called through the window.

Drink more water, Gertrude said. Stay away from her cakes and sticky puddings.

'Get me a glass of water,' he said.

'I've just now iced a sponge, dear.'

'Are you trying to kill me with your cakes, girl?'

Maybe she was. Maybe they had some conspiracy. Get rid of the old man and we'll get the lot. And they probably would.

435

Lorna was more man than woman. She'd manage. She'd taken over the bookwork. She wrote most of the cheques even if he did still sign them. And it wasn't right that a man had to rely on women. A man needed a son.

He'd get that boy.

Things had changed since women had got the vote, and changed a lot more with the men away fighting. Hundreds of war widows were out there caring for fatherless kids, and in worse living conditions than a two and a half roomed shack. While she was living a decent life, it wasn't a good time to test their position in court, the solicitor said. No use starting a battle unless we're dead certain of winning it. A girl like her will put a foot wrong sometime. That's when we make our move, the solicitor had said.

A girl who looked like her wouldn't live long as a nun; Vern was willing to place a bet on that. She'd pick up with some bloke soon, and the worse she picked up with the better, or the better for Vern's chances in court.

Until then . . .

You have to be seen to be doing the right thing, the solicitor had advised him a week or two after that hot-pants little half-dago bitch had locked him out. He'd been doing the right thing these past months, paying a quid a week for Jimmy's keep, paying it through his city solicitor who kept records of what he sent. He should have started paying sooner, though the courts would take into consideration his ill health at the time Jim went missing — or so the solicitor said. He'd got a letter from Vern's doctor, itemising his hospital admissions, and on paper it sounded as if he'd been at death's door. He had to get himself healthy. Had to get a pair of boots, too, though Christ only knew how he was going to do them up.

And he was going down there to see what Charlie White was getting up to. Half past four. What the bloody hell can she find to talk to him about for four bloody hours?

'Pass my keys out, Lorna.'

'I'll drive you, Father.'

'Your sister not killing me fast enough with her bloody cakes? Give me my keys, I said.'

A TIME OF LEARNING

'Jimmy gets everything,' Georgie said. He had wooden cars, books, trucks, a trike, a pedal car, new sandals, chocolate frogs, an aunty who made fancy birthday cakes with candles, a framed photograph of his father.

'Where did you get his father's picture from?'

'From Sydney.'

'Everything is from Syndey. Why didn't you get mine too, and Margot's, from Syndey.'

'I didn't have any money.'

'You could make more shirts and get more money.'

'I didn't know how to make shirts when you and Margot were born.'

'You could make some jumpers then.'

'I didn't think of that.'

They'd spent the afternoon unravelling Granny's old green cardigan. Twenty years had worn the elbows and wristbands ragged, but the wool in the body and upper sleeves was good enough to reuse.

'I want you to go to Syndey and get one for me.'

'Syd-ney,' Jenny corrected. 'And one what?'

'Photo. And I can go this time and not Jimmy.'

'You have to go to school.'

'When school gets holidays, then we can go.'

'One day maybe.'

All three kids had watched enthralled as the pieces of that well-known cardigan had become a never-ending length of crinkled green yarn, racing backwards and forwards along leaning stitches. The last inch of the cardigan gone, the knitting needles had come out; now one large dark green ball was becoming something new.

Jenny's knitting wasn't growing fast enough for Jimmy. He was outside, riding his tricycle in circles. Margot had gone home with Elsie. Georgie remained to watch.

She'd known she had a mummy who worked in Sydney who could make things. Dresses and new pants had come in parcels, money had come in envelopes and photos, too. She'd always known she had a baby brother. Hadn't known Vern would be his grandpa, that he'd have two aunties and a photo of a father with big teeth.

'You're like a witch,' Georgie said.

'I've been called worse, kiddo. Why am I like a witch?'

'Witches can make different things into different things. Witches make people into different things.'

'Watch out I don't turn you into a green-eyed lizard.'

Most little girls are cute, some are pretty. Georgie was beyond pretty. She had Jenny's hands, was a little like her around the mouth. The rest was Laurie. She may also have inherited his desire to get what she wanted from life.

'You could say some magic and get my father from Syndey.'

'He might be a big green-eyed lizard.'

Always ready to laugh, eager to learn, easy to love.

'What will Margot's be?'

'Purple frogs.'

'And Jimmy's?'

'A . . . a long skinny stick insect, dressed in a fine black suit.'

'And Granny's?'

'Big Billy Goat Gruff. Who's that clip-clopping over my bridge . . .'

'I'll give you billy goat,' Gertrude said.

Elsie's kids had bikes, the older kids rode to school, the younger ones clinging onto seats behind them. Georgie would have ridden a bike if she'd had one to ride. Margot couldn't ride Jimmy's

438

trike. Scared of bikes, scared of water, scared of school. There was something wrong with that kid's head.

Gertrude harnessed her horse each school morning, and until late February she harnessed the horse in the afternoon to fetch them home. Then Jenny started walking in to collect them from school.

Walking the diagonal is always shorter than walking the angles. She brought them home via the diagonal short cut through Joe Flanagan's wood paddock, which led through his forest paddock to Granny's back fence and in through her orchard, which was fine until they had a confrontation with Flanagan's bull. They'd backed off. The bull had put his head down, but they'd made it back to the fence, Jenny damn near dragging Margot through it. That kid had no survival instinct. That was the end of taking the short cut home.

In March Norman came again. He brought a block of chocolate. He wasn't Grandpa material, didn't stay long, but the kids enjoyed his chocolate.

Gertrude stitched a mill worker's finger in March. Paul Jenner drove her out to look at his youngest girl's throat. Polio could start with a sore throat. Gertrude diagnosed inflamed tonsils, prescribed a salt gargle and aspro every four hours, and while she was out prescribing, Jenny baked her first cake.

It sank in the middle. She did her best to disguise the dent with icing, did her best to write Georgie in pink icing. It was a poor replica of Jimmy's birthday cake, but Georgie thought it was pretty.

Sissy would have turned twenty-six that same day. Perhaps a Duckworth baked her a cake. Had Norman posted her a gift?

In April, Elsie made Margot a birthday cake, a better cake than Jenny's second effort, which she hid away. Six candles were placed into Elsie's fruitcake, and they sang 'Happy Birthday' while the rain poured down, turning the yard to mud but filling that tank.

'I liked my cake best,' Georgie said.

'Don't have any of Margot's then,' Joany, Elsie's ten-year-old, said.

'I like Aunty Maggie's cake best,' Jimmy said. 'Wiff cream.'

Then out of that rain storm came Maisy with a doll in a box for Margot, and a photograph of Sissy holidaying in Tasmania with two cousins.

'She looks more like her Duckworth grandmother every day,' Gertrude said.

'Margot looks more like her fathers every time I see her,' Maisy said, sounding more pleased about that likeness than she had a right to sound.

'Fathers?' Nothing got by Georgie. 'She said fathers.' In the plural.

''Cause they're twins,' too-knowledgeable Joany Hall said.

'Why are they twins?'

'Because they look exactly the same,' Joany said. She had Margot's doll. Georgie wanted a turn at holding it. It had big blue eyes that went to sleep when it was laid down. There was too much competition today. She couldn't get a hand on it.

'Let your sister hold the dolly for a while, Margot,' Maisy said.

'Ith's my birthday prethent,' Margot said.

'I bought it for both of you to play with.'

'Are her fathers for both too?' Georgie said.

'You wouldn't want . . .' Jenny started. Wrong thing to say. 'You've got your own father,' she added fast. Also wrong.

'Where?'

'Sydney.'

They were drinking tea when Maisy spoke of Amber. 'She's on her way down again, Mrs Foote. She'd got him locked out.' Gertrude made no comment. 'She was fine while Sissy was home. She was even getting out of the house a bit. I've got the doctor coming up on Wednesday. They fixed her the last time.'

'How did she get broken?' Georgie said.

That doll would get broken in a minute. Teddy Hall had it, checking out how its head was connected to its body.

You can't hold a conversation in a room full of kids, and you can't send them out to play in the rain. Kids can have too much togetherness when the arena of play is limited, and Elsie's mob still thought Margot was one of their own.

Georgie wasn't. Georgie had never lived with them — and she couldn't get a hand on that doll. She gave up and stood beside Jenny and Jenny's arm went around her. That little girl felt like a part of her. Jenny could almost feel the blood flowing between them. She kissed her hair, and Georgie leaned closer.

Maisy left at three, her wheels slipping and sliding through mud and sheets of water. Elsie and her mob went skating home fifteen minutes later, Margot behind them with her doll.

'That doll stays home here, Margot,' Jenny said. May as well have spoken to the door. Georgie left Jenny's side and ran after her sister.

She could run! She caught up to Margot and pushed her.

'Naughty girl,' Gertrude chastised as she ran to retrieve the muddy screamer. Georgie retrieved the doll. 'You're bigger than your sister and you mustn't push her.'

'She's six, and Jenny said.'

'Jenny said the doll was to stay inside, so stop your bawling, Margot. You disobeyed me so you deserved to land in the mud,' Jenny said, taking charge of that kid, stripping off her muddy clothes.

'She's not the one you should be scolding.'

'Georgie was obeying me, and you sympathising with Margot is only encouraging her to disobey me the next time, Granny.'

'You lean towards —'

'Don't say it — and anyway, someone has to. Over there . . .' She signalled with the back of her hand towards Elsie's house. 'They all do their fair share of leaning towards the other one.'

Jenny washed Margot, dressed her in her nightgown and told her to wear it until she learned to do as she was told, and that if she didn't stop her bawling about a bit of mud, she'd wear it to school, too. Margot stood at the door and bellowed louder while Jenny washed the doll's clothes and Georgie sat at the table watching and having her turn with the doll.

'You're rewarding bad behaviour.'

'I'm rewarding respect for something beautiful. She was saving the doll's life the only way she knew how. Its head would have been off by now. Elsie's kids would have had its eyes out just to see how they worked, and you know it. I've been pussy-footing around you-know-who ever since I came home, bending over backwards in trying to do the right thing and getting nowhere fast. All I'm doing by making allowances is creating another spoiled brat like Sissy.'

'Why is Sissy a brat?' Georgie asked.

'She eats too much. Stop your bawling, Margot, or you can go to bed until you learn to obey me.'

'If you'd been here when they were growing —'

'Well, I wasn't here, and Georgie doesn't hold it against me.'

IS HITLER DEAD?

Elsie came skating across the paddock in May, and Gertrude ran to meet her, afraid for Joey, afraid one of the kids was injured.

'I just heard it on the news, Mum. They're saying that Hitler is dead. They said he's been killed in action.'

People all over the word would remember what they were doing the day they heard that piece of news. Jenny was cutting vegies for her chicken soup.

The vegies waited long to be cut while the women sat around Elsie's wireless, listening for confirmation of that madman's death, and speaking of Joey, who was fighting up north.

'If Hitler is dead, it's over, isn't it, Mum?'

'It's over in Europe,' Gertrude said.

But was he dead? No confirmation came that day.

The Melbourne newspapers came in on the train at ten, and by ten the following morning, a crowd was waiting at the newsagent's. Jenny waited with them. She got her hands on a copy of the *Sun*, and stood with others reading the front page. Which posed the same question they'd heard yesterday on the wireless.

IS HITLER DEAD?

If there was one man on earth that half the world wished dead it was Adolf Hitler. Tales of atrocities had been filtering back as the Russians and the Allies made their way through war-torn Germany. The Nazis had lost the war months back but their maniac leader refused to surrender.

Prominent military observers emphasised that the report of Hitler's death was subject to many interpretations. The obituary notice on German radio may have been a screen for his escape. There can be no certainty that Hitler is dead until the body is produced and fingerprints checked.

The emergence of Admiral Doenitz as the new head of state will at the most only briefly delay the collapse of the Reich. It is widely believed that Admiral Doenitz cannot command sufficient army support to continue the struggle.

Confirmation of Hitler's death didn't come, not positively, but on 7 May, the news came through that Germany had surrendered.

'Thank God.'

'Fank God,' Jimmy said.

'*Th*ank, not fank,' Georgie said. 'You have to poke your tongue out and blow.'

Teach one kid a new trick and she'll teach the rest — if they want to learn.

'George Macdonald was saying that the twins are somewhere in Germany,' Harry said that night. 'He reckons they haven't got a scratch on them.'

'Hitler thought he was seeing double and aimed between them,' Jenny said.

'*Old Macdonald had a farm* . . . .' Jimmy sang.

'He's got your voice,' Harry said.

'He gets everything,' Georgie said. 'And Margot, too. Why did she get two fathers and not me?'

'She didn't,' Jenny said.

'Joany said twins,' Georgie said. She knew all about twins now. The kids at school said she and Margot were twins because they wore the same blue overcoats, the same matching pixie bonnets, the same dark green cardigans. They said they were bastards, too.

'What's basards, Jenny?'

'A word you don't ever say.'

'The kids at school say it.'

'Only stupid kids. Are you stupid?'

'I can read.'

She could. She was barely five years old, and wilful, and Jenny loved her wilfulness. In little Georgie, she saw the child she might have been.

She tried to like Margot, tried to seek out things in her to like. Elsie and Maisy said she could sing, but would that kid sing for Jenny, sing with Jenny? Not on your life. And if she could, she'd probably got it from her fathers. They could hold a tune.

She wondered what Cara Jeanette had got from her fathers. Wondered if Captain Robert Norris had survived the war. Wondered if Myrtle had sold Amberley. If Billy-Bob's boat had been among the boats sunk by the Japs' kamikaze pilots. Wondered if she dared to claim his watch. It kept such good time.

She made the decision to claim it one night. They were sitting around the stove, Jenny telling stories about Sydney; the tale of Mrs Collins's singed hair always made the kids laugh. She told them about little Wilfred, the leprechaun with magic fingers who could play any tune ever written. Then she told the tale of the fat black Labrador on the Sydney beach one summer morning, how he'd dropped a watch at her feet, wanting her to play fetch with him.

She brought the watch out later to show the kids the indentations in the gold where the dog had tried to chew his metal bone. Showed them the inscription and told Georgie to read it.

'*Billy-Bob from Mom and Dad*. Who's Billy-Bob, Jenny?'

'A boy who lost his watch on a beach,' Jenny said. That wasn't a lie. 'He must have been a Yankee. Australians don't have such funny names. The Yanks all had funny names: Hank and Chuck, Whitworth and Link, Billy-Bob . . .'

The kids laughed at those names and their laughter was healing.

She told them then of an old schoolteacher with a wooden leg who had used four pegs to hang his shirts on the clothes line, how he'd used two pegs to hang each sock. They laughed at that, too. They knew how precious Granny's pegs were — there were never enough of them.

The newsagent sold Jenny a leather watchband, and with a watch on her wrist, she was never late, never early when picking the kids up from school. Time ticked no faster. The winter of '45 was long.

She had a confrontation with Vern on a freezing Friday when she came in from school with the girls and found his car in the yard, found him sitting at the table, Jimmy on his lap. She nodded, though she didn't want to. She told the girls to say good afternoon to Jimmy's grandfather. And he looked at them the way he might have looked at a nest of flea-infested rats with rabies.

Vern needed to see those kids clothed in rags, needed to see them blue with the cold, not pink cheeked and dressed up like the town toffs in matching overcoats and bonnets. He lived for the day he'd come down here and see that girl with her belly sticking out.

She'd clad herself in grey trousers and blue sweater. Flat bellied, bright eyed, windblown and beautiful — and why couldn't she pick up with some wife-bashing, child-abusing, drunken bastard of a man?

'You must be seen to be doing the right thing, Mr Hooper,' his fool of a solicitor kept saying. 'A girl with her history will make a mistake, Mr Hooper.'

He paid her money each week for Jimmy's keep, and resented her spending it to clothe George Macdonald's granddaughter and that redhead, father unknown. He resented Jimmy wriggling to get down from his lap. Tried to hold onto him. Had to let him go to her.

He'd bided his time in going after that boy, and where had that got him?

Vern watched her take the girls' coats off, hang them behind the door, watched her pouring mugs of milk, handing those kids two biscuits each — and he'd done enough of biding his time.

'Trying to make silk purses out of sows' ears doesn't alter what they are,' he said.

'I dare say you'd be the authority on that, Mr Hooper. I'll bet you've spent a fortune in your time,' she said.

'Jennifer!'

'That boy is my grandson, and I'm telling you now that you won't raise him as a bastard in this town.'

'Some are born bastards. Some just grow old and become bastards,' Jenny said.

'Jennifer!' Gertrude repeated.

'Don't chastise me, Granny. He said it first.'

'I didn't grow to my age to listen to the two I love best in this world arguing in my kitchen. Take the kids over to Elsie.'

'This is where I live. This is where his grandson lives. He can leave any time he likes.'

In June, Germany was partitioned into four occupation zones, British and American, Russian and French. In June, Horrie Bull and his wife sold the hotel.

Everyone knew their son was their grandson. Everyone knew that schoolkids have a pecking order. Like hens in a crowded pen, they'll peck at the weak until they draw blood, then cackle while they bleed.

The Bulls had the good sense to get that boy out of town before he started school — and they had money enough to do it. Money meant options. Those who had too little of the stuff had no options.

By June's end, the Yanks were throwing everything they had at the Japs. It was just a matter of time, the newspapers said. Just a matter of a few thousand more boys dying.

Then, on 5 July, John Curtin, prime minister through most of the war years, died in his sleep. It didn't seem fair that he'd been denied the end of that war.

'He was only sixty! He was only a boy,' Gertrude said.

Only sixty! Sixty is very old when you're twenty-one.

'How old are you, Granny?'

'None of your business.'

'Amber must be going on fifty. You were in your late twenties when she was born.'

'Stop your totalling up of my years and get that washing in before it's blown to China.'

'Have you ever been to China?'

'Not China. I glimpsed Japan.' She patted the ivory pins she

447

still wore in her hair. 'Your father bought them when his boat docked there.'

'I'm not Amber, and when did he have a boat?'

'He did a lot of ship doctoring — and you knew who I meant. You'll have to start making allowances for me soon. I'm so old I'm losing my memory.'

'I didn't say you were old; I just asked how old you were.'

'It's still none of your business, my girl.'

The winds were evil through July. They whipped Granny's house. For hour after hour, July's winds attempted to blow that old house from the face of the earth. It stood up to it better than Elsie's. It whistled beneath Elsie's house, rocked it.

'We ought to build a new room on here — somewhere.'

'Building costs money.'

'If you'd admit your age, you'd be eligible for the old age pension.'

'Keep your insults to yourself.'

'You've got no income?'

'My chooks keep pace with inflation.'

There was time to observe when the winds kept them indoors, when wind-whipped rain thrashed the low roof, rattled the shutters, seeped in through gaps, when drafts seeped in and the curtains swayed and the only warmth came from the stove. There was time to notice the silver showing at Gertrude's scalp when they sat close at night, when the thought of leaving the stove to go to their beds encouraged them to sit too late, when talk turned to the past, to the future, even to Sissy.

'It's weird how Sissy got your hair and I got Itchy-foot's. It's as if we both bypassed Norman and Amber. What was Grandma Cecelia's hair like?'

'Grey. Straight. Fine,' Gertrude said.

'Does Sissy really look like her?'

'The image, though your grandma was a lot broader when she died.'

'How did she die?'

'She took a stroke at sixty.'

'And I was born a few days later.'

'The night of her funeral, as I recall.'

For days the winds howled, hens with ruffled feathers unintentionally took flight across the yard, trees came down. One fell across the forest road and for two days the kids couldn't go to school.

Sending them to school in this weather was asking for trouble. Gertrude harnessed her horse into the old cart and drove them in on the Monday, and drove them home with the flu. Then Jenny caught it. Gertrude and Jimmy looked after them, until they too went down with it.

Gertrude was never unwell. In Jenny's lifetime she couldn't recall her grandmother taking to her bed ill. She was in bed for the best part of a week with the flu, her lungs creating their own wind storm, her cough in the night putting fear into Jenny. Fear of a future without Gertrude. Fear of the future.

She wore trousers now, like Gertrude. Was she to become a second Gertrude, her life spent here, milking goats, feeding chooks, cleaning out chook pens and spreading barrow loads of stinking manure on garden beds?

Jenny worked like a slave during the ten days of Gertrude's illness while Lenny harnessed the horse to deliver the kids to school — which was excuse enough for him to retire from the classroom. He was thirteen, or near enough to it. He'd been repeating grade six, and he'd had enough of grade six.

The new hotel owners came to town to place their stamp on the corner pub. They gave the old building a coat of paint and had a fancy brass plaque made and screwed over the front door. *Erected in 1870.*

Gertrude, not getting about yet, but keeping her hands busy with knitting by the stove, spoke of the old days, of her parents, of when Amber was a girl.

'How long has this house been standing, Granny?'

'I arrived in the bedroom while my dad was hammering down the kitchen floor.'

'How long after the hotel was built?'

'I'm onto you, my girl.' She was still coughing, had lost a little weight, but her mind was as sharp as a tack.

Where there is a will there is a way. Jenny unwrapped Gertrude's wedding dress. Her marriage lines were still wrapped with it, and the date of Gertrude's birth made her heart turn over. Granny was all she had, and in August, she'd turn seventy-six.

She rewrapped the wedding lines, and the gown, hid that knowledge away deep in the camphor wood trunk.

Knowledge, like history can't be buried. Far better to confront it, to deal with it.

She stole one of Gertrude's old tin plates and took it out to the shed, where with ancient hammer and rusty nail she hammered that date into metal, and when it was done, she found a sharper nail and hammered a nail-hole boarder. On Gertrude's birthday, she nailed her plaque over the old front door.

Ejected 2.8.1869.

'You damn fool of a girl, take that thing down.'

'It gives your house character.'

'You've ruined one of my good plates — and you've spelt it wrong.'

'I spelt it right.'

'Who told you?'

'You should have burnt your marriage lines.'

The Yanks finished the war four days after Gertrude's birthday. They dropped an experimental bomb on Hiroshima and turned the city and its people to ash.

IT CAME BY PARACHUTE, the newspapers screamed.

IT EXPLODED IN MIDAIR.

WEAPON HAS EFFECT LIKE EARTHQUAKE.

ATOMIC BOMB HAILED AS REVOLUTION IN SCIENCE AND WARFARE.

The discovery of the atomic bomb is the greatest step forward ever made by man in his efforts to control nature. The bomb seems to have done what we expected. We know now that we can bottle it and release it. The next thing will be to discover how to harness it.

Tens of thousands were disintegrated, burned, maimed by that bomb, but the Japs didn't surrender, not that day. Three days later Russia declared war on Japan and invaded Manchuria while the Yanks dropped another of their experimental bombs on Nagasaki — and let it be known they had a few more to test.

The war ended on 14 August.

For five years, eleven months and eleven days Australia had been at war. The day wirelesses and newspapers screamed PEACE, staid old Melbourne crowds danced in the street.

Papers full of peace. Pages of photographs, tales told by pilots who'd flown over a prison camp and seen groups of Australian internees cheering below, a few waving hurriedly scribbled messages to those back home. Euphoric days, those first days of peace.

Vern's half-brother didn't live to see it. His funeral announcement was at the back of one of those newspapers. His death had been expected. If Gertrude hadn't been keeping an eye on the death columns for the announcement, she wouldn't have known her sister-in-law, Victoria Foote, had died at the age of seventy-one.

Howard Hooper's name was in the same column. Like Vern he'd been her half-cousin, but so much younger. She'd barely known him as a boy and had seen him three times in the years since. Two weeks ago Vern and his daughters had gone down to Melbourne to be with him.

'He was only sixty-three,' she said. 'His father died young.'

'How old was your grandfather when he died?'

'Ninety-two and still ruling the roost. He died with his boots on, and after a good meal,' Gertrude said. 'That's the way I'd like to go.'

'You're not going anywhere — ever.'

Howard Hooper was survived by his wife, one son and two grandsons. Gertrude got out her pen and ink to write them a line of condolence. She wrote no letter to the family of Victoria Foote. She had no husband to write to, no family to mourn her. *Loved cousin of* . . . so the newspaper said.

'Was she the one Itchy-foot was supposed to have raped?' Jenny asked.

'There was no supposed about it,' Gertrude said. 'It says that she passed away peacefully in her Hawthorn home. I doubt she'd known much peace in the past fifty years, the poor soul.'

'Did you see much of her?'

'We left her father's house six weeks after we wed. According to one of your grandfather's cousins, the only time she left that house was when they took her off to a mental hospital.'

PEACE

Bobby Vevers had died in a Japanese prison camp. When photographs of those who had survived similar conditions started finding their way into the newspapers, no one wondered why Bobby Vevers had died. Joss Palmer, an army medic, was one of the first to see the men they carried out of Burma, or to see the skin and bones of what were once men. Joss's letters to Jessie arrived uncensored now. Those at home were finally hearing the truth.

I saw Billy Roberts and didn't recognise him. He was near on six foot, must have weighed around twelve stone when he joined up. He's a walking skeleton now — and barely walking. He recognised me, and his smile looked like a death mask. Most of the chaps we're getting in will need months of rehabilitation before they're repatriated to Australia.

Joss wouldn't be home for a while but a few of the boys stationed around Australia started arriving home.

WHERE WILL THEY LIVE? the headlines shouted. With no war to write about, journalists were already attempting to take the shine off peace.

It was a question which would have to be answered. In the next twelve months tens of thousands of men would be unloaded from the armed forces, many returning to wives, to fiancées, and expecting to set up homes. There was a serious housing shortage in Australia. Even in Woody Creek there was a housing shortage.

'It's one thing to take in your daughter and grandkids, another to take in their husbands. He's not the boy she married, I can tell you that. The kids don't even know him.'

'What they seem to forget is that we've been keeping this country going while they've been away. Now we're supposed to go back to the way it was five years ago.'

'He's forgotten how to live as a family man.'

Joey Hall had been in a hospital in Brisbane. He came home in November. He'd forgotten how to share a sleep-out with a bunch of rambunctious kids. On his second night in Woody Creek, he carried his mattress across to Gertrude's shed and tossed it onto the floor in the partitioned-off back corner he and Harry had once called a bedroom, the corner that housed Gertrude's preserves, Jenny's bathtub.

'You can have it back in a day or two,' he said. 'I won't be staying.'

'That's what I said a year ago,' Jenny said. 'Elsie and Granny won't let you go. They've been counting the days.' As had she.

'There's nothing here for me, Jen,' he said. Jim had always called her Jen; Joey had picked up the habit back when they'd played penny poker.

'George Macdonald said you could have your job back.'

'That's what I mean by nothing,' he said. 'I'm going back up north, up to the sugar country. I met a nurse who came from Bundaberg.'

'Girlfriend?'

'Maybe.'

'Are you going to marry her?'

'Maybe. She thinks I get my colouring from my grandfather, the Spanish pirate.'

'You looked more like a pirate when you had your moustache.'

'I'll grow it again.'

'Would she care who your grandfather was?'

'Her folk would.'

'You can't . . .' Can't hide from who you are? Yes you can. She'd hidden in Sydney and it was a fine thing to do . . . or it was for a time. 'You can't go until we give them a good thrashing at five hundred,' she said.

He stayed five days. They played cards on Saturday night, played until midnight on Sunday, Lenny, Joey and Jenny against Harry, Elsie and Gertrude. Like a party, that night, like a going-away party, and when Gertrude went home, when Elsie and Harry went to bed, Jenny, Joey and Lenny sat on, playing three-handed canasta until dawn.

She walked with Joey to the station the night he left, waited with him, smoking his cigarettes, uncaring who stared. Norman stared. He probably heard Joey tell her to get out of this place any way she could.

'You were going to be a famous singer, Jen,' he said.

'I was going to be a lot of things. I gave up daydreaming when Jim died.'

'You're only twenty-one.'

'Almost twenty-two. I'm working on developing a ten-year plan, Joey. By the time I'm thirty, the kids will be in their teens. I'll still be young enough to . . .'

The train was coming. She kissed his cheek, stood waving his train away, wanting him to go off and be whoever he wanted to be. As Granny had said this morning, he'd never be more than Darkie Hall in Woody Creek.

And the boys kept on coming home. Like Joey, a few didn't stay long. A few wives left with them, a few left without their wives.

Billy Roberts came home, and Jenny, who had sat in a class-room with him for years, barely recognised him.

He recognised her. 'It's a tonic seeing you, Jenny,' he said. He still looked as if he needed a tonic.

'You too, Billy.'

'I hear you've got three nippers now.'

'I hear you were a bit of a hero in that Jap camp,' she said, understanding his meaning, hoping he understood her own.

'I wouldn't mind seeing a bit more of you sometime,' he said.

'You're seeing about as much of me as you're likely to, Billy. The kids keep me busy.'

They kept on coming, and Billy Roberts was not the only one who looked at her with anticipation. Johnny Lewis, brother of Weasel, damn near propositioned her when she was walking the kids home from school one afternoon.

Then, on a Saturday in late November, when summer was flexing her muscles, eager to give spring the old heave-o, one of those Saturdays when Charlie White looked at his bike and wanted to ride, one of those days when Jenny craved ice-cream, she dressed the girls in matching floral, clad Jimmy in shorts and sandals and walked them into town.

Georgie and Jimmy had legs bred to walk. Margot's were short, but she walked now, and with less complaints. They were near King's corner when Jenny saw the two too familiar khaki-clad shapes walking elbow to elbow half a block ahead.

These past years her skin had grown thick enough to handle Billy Roberts and Johnny Lewis, but not them. She couldn't face them. She turned tail and fled.

The kids had walked for ice-cream and they wanted ice-cream. They grizzled for ice-cream. And why should they miss out because of a pair of stumpy-legged, no-necked, raping bastards?

She turned down King Street towards the school end of town, turned right into Blunt's Road, then headed back to the café.

Mrs Crone, busy doing nothing, had always enjoyed the power she wielded over kids. Jenny's bunch were waiting expectantly in a line at the counter when the wire door opened.

'G'day,' they chorused. 'We heard you'd been a busy girl.'

Not a flinch from Jenny; not the slightest turn of her head, until Georgie pulled on her arm, wanting her to see what she could see. All three kids had lost interest in ice-cream. They were staring at identical strangers who looked like George Macdonald in uniform.

'They're Maisy's twins,' Georgie accused.

'Remember that swear word I said you weren't ever allowed to say? That's who they are. Four ice-creams when you're ready, Mrs Crone.'

'Make them double-headers,' one twin said.

'Make them what I ordered — when you're ready Mrs Crone.'

'Make up your minds,' Mrs Crone snarled.

'Double-headers,' one twin said. The other one was offering Margot a two-shilling coin. As she reached for it, Jenny dragged her back by her skirt, held her skirt and turned to watch the ice-cream scoop dig deep into the freezer.

A double-header, and Jimmy's hand reaching to take it. Jenny's arm was longer. She took it from Mrs Crone's hand, and mashed it into the nearest twin's ear, ground it into his ear — and Mrs Crone stopped sneering to stand open mouthed.

Pushed, pulled, dragged three open-mouthed kids out to the street, two looking back to their lost ice-cream, all three wanting to know why.

'Walk, I said!'

'You said we'd get an ice-cream.'

'We'll get it later.'

'Why did they give Margot money for?'

'They didn't give her money, now stop your *why*ing and walk.'

'Maisy's twins means Margot's fathers, that's why,' Georgie accused.

'I want ice-cream,' Jimmy wailed.

'I wan' ithe-cweam,' Margot grizzled.

And those mongrels were out on the street and Jenny wanted to run away and leave those little buggers howling.

'Walk. We'll go and see your grandpa.' Bribery can work with kids at times.

'Why did Margot get two fathers and a nanna and Jimmy get one father and two grandpas and aunties and everything, and I didn't get anything?'

'Stop it, Georgie.'

'I want my father and a double ice-cream.'

'Your father gave you something a damn sight better than ice-cream, you brat of a kid. He gave you his beautiful hair and his eyes —'

That did it. Georgie flopped to her backside and bawled. She didn't do it often but when she did she could make more noise than the other two combined.

The men hanging around the hotel were staring, and Jimmy was clearly planning to join the protest. Jenny dragged him up by his collar. Tried to lift Georgie. Try lifting a well-grown five-year-old kid when that five-year-old kid doesn't want to be lifted. And that pair of khaki-clad mongrels smirking at her, one still digging ice-cream out of his ear.

'He can't see me . . . with no eyes,' Georgie bawled.

'Oh, Jesus! Of course he's got eyes. I meant his eyes are exactly the same as your eyes.'

'And hair.'

'Lots of hair, exactly the colour of your hair. Now get up.'

'I want you to get him.'

'Stop your bawling and I'll find you a picture of him.'

'Where?'

'In the newspaper.'

It was a mistake, but it got that kid on her feet. Jenny walked them across the road, climbed between fence wires and led them through long grass to the station.

Norman was surprised, probably embarrassed, but he offered his biscuits, and like locusts the kids ate until Jenny told them to stop. The twins stood out front of the hotel for a time, then went inside, and finally the kids got their ice-creams, double-headers.

Most kids nag. Georgie could keep it up longer than most. She was still nagging about her father's photograph when she went to bed.

At eight, when Gertrude headed off across the goat paddock with her towel and nightwear, Jenny lifted the old shoe box down from the wardrobe and retrieved the newsprint mugshot of the water pistol bandit.

She'd need a frame. Jimmy's sailor suit photograph donated its frame. She found an empty Weeties packet, cut and trimmed Willy Weeties to fit the frame, then trimmed the newspaper to fit the cardboard. She didn't trim off his name; Georgie would need to see that. She didn't trim off the bit below his name, stating that he'd been charged with numerous offences, but it would be folded over the edge of the cardboard.

She made flour and water glue in a cup, and while it was cooling Gertrude came in and caught her.

'You could have found something better than that,' she said. 'Get her a nice picture out of one of Elsie's magazines.'

'He's her father, Granny.'

'What?'

'He's her father.'

'What's he doing in the newspaper?' Gertrude reached for the newspaper.

She wasn't often speechless. She snatched up her reading glasses and couldn't get them on with her hair wrapped in a towel, so she pitched the towel. Her hair was never left hanging. It hung and dripped that night.

'That's that boy . . .'

'Who held up a jeweller with a leaking water pistol and stole cars to make his getaway in — Laurence George Morgan.'

'I'm burning the thing.'

'You're not, Granny.'

'You don't want that little girl seeing something like that!'

'She wants her father.'

'He's a jailbird!'

'They only gave him three years. He'd be out by now. Give it to me.'

'Where have you been keeping that thing all this time?'

'Put away in case I needed it. I learned that from you.'

'You didn't learn to keep things like this,' Gertrude said, evading Jenny's hand and walking to the stove.

'Don't you dare burn it!' Gertrude had opened the firebox. 'Don't you dare, Granny.' She couldn't make a grab for that paper. It was old, never meant to stand the test of time. 'Please give it to me.'

'There are things kids are better off not knowing, and this is one of them.'

'If a kid doesn't know the truth, she makes up her own.'

'Tell her he died in the war.'

'Lie to her?'

'You'd be doing her a service.'

'Like you and Dad did me a service when I was her age.'

'We never lied to you.'

'You did so. You told me my mummy was very sick so the doctors had sent her away to get better. Maisy told me that my mummy was up in heaven with God, that she was one of his angels. My mother damn near killed me when I was three years old, then she tried to cut Dad's head off and they put her in a madhouse, Granny. And I would have been better off growing up knowing that instead of making a fool of myself by trying to love her when she came home.'

'She was only in that place for a few months. She disappeared from the Willama hospital and for years we didn't know if she was dead or alive. The constable we used to have up here found her six years after she disappeared. How were we supposed to explain that to a little girl?'

'You should have tried — or you should have warned me to run like hell if I ever set eyes on her again.'

'We thought she was well when she came home.'

'She's never been well. I saw her today. I took the kids to the station and she was standing at the fence down behind the lavatory, murdering me with her eyes — or murdering my kids — like she probably murdered Nelly Abbot because she looked like me.'

'Stop that!'

'And so did little Barbie.'

'Stop that now!'

'She hated me enough at the hospital to try — probably tried to burn all of us in our beds. I hate her, Granny, and I'm scared of her.'

'She's on her pills again, according to Maisy.'

'Then they're not doing her much good. Norman has got his ticket office set up like a kitchen — icebox, double burner primus. By the smell of the place, he fried steak and onions for his dinner last night.'

'Did he say anything?'

'He asked after your health, though I doubt he heard my reply. He mentioned the weather, the Nazi trials in Nuremberg — please give me that paper, Granny.'

'You can't show something like this to a little girl.'

'Forewarned is forearmed you used to say, and there's more of me in that kid than my hands. She needs the truth. And so do I. Did having me in a paddock traumatise my mother? Did I look too much like her father? Did he rape her like he raped his sister?'

'I don't know what he did to her — other than pass on his own weakness of the mind. He was incapable of loving anyone. I doubt that your mother is capable of feeling love.'

'Don't give me that garbage! She crawled all over Sissy. All my life she crawled all over her.'

'She left her for those same six years she left you. No mother leaves her kids if she loves them.'

'I left Georgie for two years. I love her.'

'You weren't much more than a child yourself, and she knew where you were.'

Jenny's hand was still out for the paper. Gertrude closed the firebox. 'What were you doing with a boy like that . . . with a common thief?'

'He wasn't common, and I didn't know he was a thief.'

'Parasites,' Gertrude said. 'Anyone who will live off the labour of others is no more than a parasite.'

The old newspaper was back in Jenny's hand. She continued her project. 'Remember me telling you once that Amber was a parasite, living off Sissy, a flea on a fly?'

'You were probably closer to the truth than you knew,' Gertrude said as she drew a part in her hair.

'The flea is feeding: Sissy's washing was on the clothes line,' Jenny said.

Laurie's mug shot looked like newspaper pasted over cardboard when she was done, but a frame will improve any picture. Maybe Gertrude was right. Maybe she'd live to regret it.

And maybe she wouldn't. She gave it to Georgie at the breakfast table the following morning, and that little kid's eyes turned into glistening emeralds.

'He's in the newspaper, like a fil-um star?' she said.

461

'He was very famous when you were born,' Jenny said.

'Is he a fil-um star?'

'A bit like a film star.'

'Margot hasn't got a picture.'

'The camera broke when the man was trying to take one,' Jenny said.

'Jennifer!' Gertrude warned.

'That's the same like my name,' Georgie said. There was enough print exposed above the frame to see *Laurence George Morgan*.

Georgie wanted to take it to school to show all the kids who said she didn't have a father. Jenny told her the glass would get broken, that her father was so special that there was no other picture of him in the whole world. It remained safe on Monday beneath Georgie's pillow.

She showed it to Charlie when he rode down on Saturday with his offerings for the chooks. He showed great interest, so when Vern arrived to see what Charlie was up to, Georgie showed her Daddy to him.

He showed more interest than Charlie. The sticky-nosed old bugger took the picture from its frame.

Jenny, her back to him, her foot busy on the sewing machine treadle, didn't see what he'd done until Georgie pulled at her elbow. She turned as Gertrude reached for it.

Vern didn't give it up. 'No wonder you wouldn't tell me,' he said.

'Put it back in the frame, Vern,' Gertrude said.

'Letting a kid flash something like that around,' Vern said, and Charlie rose to take his leave.

Georgie didn't understand what the fuss was about. 'He was like a fil-um star,' she said.

The fabric left beneath the foot of the machine, the scissors on the bench, Jenny walked to the table. 'Seen enough?' she said.

'You give something like that to a kid to flash around and you expect me to leave that boy down here —'

'Most would have the manners not to take it out of its frame. And don't bother trying to turn this to your own advantage,' she said.

'It will go down well in court,' he said.

'If you want Jim's letters read out in court, go for it, Mr Hooper. You'll come out of it looking like the old bully you are.'

They should have seen it coming. They didn't. Jenny shouldn't have left those scissors where Georgie could reach them. They were small but had vicious little points. Vern got them driven into his backside.

He dropped the water pistol bandit's mug shot. It skidded beneath the table, Georgie dived after it, and was out the door, her daddy safe in her hands.

There was an uproar then. Vern bleeding through his trousers, Jenny on the attack, Gertrude backing her up, Charlie clearing the doorway as Jenny pursued Vern out to the yard.

'I'll get that boy if it's the last thing I do,' he swore.

'You take me to court, you mean-hearted old coot, and I'll go after Jim's money. Jimmy is his rightful heir, not you.'

The car roared up the track and Jenny came in breathing hard and wanting a cigarette. She went to the lean-to to get her hidden packet.

'Get Georgie home,' Gertrude said. 'She has to learn that she can't do things like that.'

'The stickybeaking old bugger deserved it,' Jenny said, removing a cigarette and lighting it. 'She showed him her prize possession and he pulled it apart and sneered.'

'Stickybeak old bugger Vern,' Georgie said at the window.

DESTINY

Everyone in town knew Jimmy was Vern's grandson, that he was the reason Sissy's wedding had been called off, and if a few didn't know, then a passing glance was enough to tell them he was a Hooper. He had the Hooper jaw, the mouth. He had their long limbs, their large feet and hands. He turned four in December and would have passed for a six-year-old.

He and his Aunty Sissy were destined to meet sooner or later. It happened on a Thursday morning, at Blunt's. The girls needed new socks and Sissy needed a new frock to wear to one of the Duckworth cousins' weddings.

'You shouldn't be allowed to bring your bastards into respectable shops,' Sissy snarled.

'If you'd stood in the doorway we wouldn't have been able to get in,' Jenny said, which was true enough. Holidaying with Duckworths was never good for the waistline. Sissy, who holidayed nine or ten months of the year, took up space enough for two at the drapery counter.

Broad browed, heavy jawed, flat in the face — other than her small parrot-beak nose, legacy of her paternal grandmother — she was taller than old Cecelia, almost as tall as Gertrude, and at twenty-six a formidable presence.

If not for a motorbike pulling into the gutter out the front of Blunt's, and Jimmy running out to have a closer look at it, there might have been a slanging match in Blunt's shop that day.

The bike rider was a stranger. Sissy vacated the premises. Jenny retrieved Jimmy and led him by the hand to the northern end of the shop, unchanged in twenty years, where she helped herself to four pairs of white socks from a box marked *Girls' white socks*.

The stranger wanted a shirt with an attached collar, sixteen and a half inch neck. And there was something about him that looked familiar to Jenny. She placed the box back where it belonged and walked to a rack of frocks from where she could get a better look at the stranger's face. Her fingers handled the fabrics, but her mind was not on frocks. She was thinking army, sorting through the names of the boys who had been away, attempting to visualise the Dobson boys older. They were all blonds. Maybe . . .

'I'll t-t-take the white,' he said.

And she knew him — or knew that stutter. The boy at the school concert, the ringmaster on the night Sissy had tripped her onstage, the night she'd ripped the petals from her petunia costume. His name was on the tip of her tongue.

Ray King is lousy, his mother is a frowsy . . .

'Ray King.' It came out. She hadn't meant it to. He turned when he heard his name, seeking the speaker; she had to come out from behind a rack of frocks.

'I went to school with you. I'm Jenny Morrison.'

Big brown innocent lamb's eyes taking in her face as he ran his fingers through thick butter-yellow hair. He'd had no hair at school, always clipped to the scalp. Always big boned — he'd been a giant to her at school.

'The p-petunia,' he said. 'The petunia in the aaa-onion patch.'

'That's me. I thought you'd drowned or been murdered.' He'd disappeared soon after his mother's funeral. She remembered the town searching for him, remembered the twins telling everyone the fish had eaten him.

'B-been in M-melbourne.' He spoke in gusts, but he spoke. He'd made few attempts to speak as a kid.

'What are you doing back here?'

He had a sister on a property out of town — or he'd had a sister. He was up here for her funeral.

Molly Martin was being buried today. His sister? She must have been closer to Amber's age than his. He was Sissy's age,

Jim's age. Not as tall as Jim but well over six foot. An image came to her then of his father, a giant woodcutter with huge arms and shoulders, swinging an axe and making the woodchips fly. Memories rushing her now. Henry King. Big Henry King, crippled by a falling tree.

And she had to stop smiling at him. He'd think she was interested when she wasn't — not in that way. She was just interested to know he was alive, as was Miss Blunt, and her father, who had been nodding off in his invalid chair, his hearing aid turned off.

'Raymond King,' Miss Blunt yelled, fiddling the knobs to tune her father in. 'Ray King. The boy who went missing back during the depression. Henry King's boy. Big Henry King, the woodcutter. He won all of the woodchops at the gymkhanas, Father.' Mr Blunt's memory of today was not always clear, but he could remember his yesterdays.

Jenny counted out coins enough for the socks and left them to talk about Big Henry.

'G-good to s-see you,' Ray said.

'You too,' she said, and with Jimmy's hand in her own, she walked off towards the butcher's shop. There she bought a lump of corned beef. Granny and the kids liked it. She bought a pound of sausages, she bought two loaves of bread at the bakery, then followed her usual route home, down Blunt's Road, over Hooper, left into King Street, which brought her back to her road down near Macdonald's mill — and meant she avoided the Hoopers' house. She hadn't seen Vern since the scissors episode — nor had Gertrude and Jimmy.

It would have been far better if she'd had another slanging match with him that day. King Street hadn't been named for King George or any of his predecessors. It had been named for Big Henry's crumbling shack, still standing on the corner opposite Macdonald's mill. And that motorbike was parked out front of it. There was no sign of its rider.

She increased her pace down the far side of the street, keeping her head to the fore and hoping to hurry Jimmy past the bike. He didn't want to be hurried. He wanted to stand and stare, and with two string bags of shopping and no hand to hold him back, he crossed over to get one last look at that shiny new bike.

At that moment the bike's owner emerged from the far side of the shack. There was nothing Jenny could do but cross over and watch Ray lift Jimmy up to sit on the saddle.

'Your b-b-b-boy reminds me of s-someone.'

'Jim Hooper,' Jenny said.

'L-living with the family?'

She glanced towards Hooper's corner. 'Jim was . . . he died in the war. I live with my grandmother. You'd remember Mrs Foote.'

'L-looked after my d-dad when they l-let him out of h-h —'

'Hospital,' she said. And of course she would have. Jimmy was gripping the handlebars, *vroom-vroom*ing his brains out. She placed her shopping down and watched him ride.

'W-would you t-trust me to give him a ride? I c-could take your bags d-down for you.' He couldn't hold her gaze, afraid of his offer — as was she. But how could she not trust a boy who had left Sissy standing on stage in her baggy white bloomers? She studied his face, and his shy eyes dared a glance back.

'He'd love it. Just a little way though, just down to the bridge and back.' She picked up her shopping and walked on ahead.

They passed her and a minute later were back, Jimmy sitting up front, hanging onto the handlebars. He didn't want to get off.

'G-give us your bags,' Ray offered again, so Jenny gave up the heaviest of them and off they rode, backwards and forwards all the way to Gertrude's gate.

She thanked him at the gate, but when she opened it he rode on through, rode on down to the walnut tree.

Granny was in the yard waiting to see who wanted her, or who wanted her eggs.

'Look who I found in town,' Jenny said. 'Remember Ray King, the ringmaster I hid behind the night Sissy roughed me up at the school concert?'

'Well, I never!' Gertrude said. 'Well, who would ever believe that? Of course. You'd be up for Molly's funeral.' She knew Molly Martin was his sister. She probably knew his mother's maiden name along with his grandmother's.

He was in no hurry to leave, and fifteen minutes later, when Gertrude offered him a cup of tea, he didn't say no. He was Lazarus, risen from dead and sitting eating oatmeal biscuits in their kitchen. They wanted to know where he'd been, how he'd got there. He didn't tell them much other than that he'd found his way to Melbourne, that he had a house there, that he'd been married but his wife had died the week before the war ended. And no, he didn't have children, and no, he hadn't been in the army.

'F-f-flat feet,' he said.

They didn't ask where he worked. He had an office man's hands, or maybe a shopkeeper's — or a bank robber's. Though it would be hard to hold up a bank if you stuttered.

He stayed for an hour. When he was leaving, Jimmy told him his head nearly hit the roof, like Grandpa's head.

'*I'm the king of the castle and you're the dirty rascal*,' Ray chanted, with not a trace of a stutter.

He was no movie star. His nose looked to have been broken at some stage, but he had nice teeth, beautiful dark eyes, nice hair.

Jimmy ran ahead to the bike and again Ray lifted him up to the saddle.

'You and your g-gran w-wouldn't be g-going to the f-f —'

'Funeral?' Jenny said. 'I barely knew her, Ray.'

'M-m-me either,' he said. 'H-hoped I could h-hide behind you, this time.'

That shy smile again. Beautiful white teeth behind it. Maybe he'd always had those teeth, just hadn't smiled often.

'Your cousins will be there,' she said.

'H-haven't seen any of them s-since I left.'

He needed someone to hide behind, and she knew that feeling. She lifted Jimmy down. 'Which church, Ray?'

'Catholic,' Gertrude replied for him. Molly Martin had borne eleven babies and raised eight of them.

'I'll p-pick you up, d-drop you b-back.'

Riding on that bike must feel a bit like flying. Was craving a ride on it any reason to go to the funeral of a woman she'd barely known?

'Would it upset anyone's sensibilities if I went with him, Granny?'

'I ought to go myself. I delivered most of Molly's children.'

Jenny didn't like hats, or they didn't like her hair. She owned one Laurie had bought for her, a ratbag of a hat. Gertrude owned a black wide-brimmed felt hat. It looked just as ridiculous. She also owned a small black hat. Jenny tried it with her once-red dress, and it looked too dressed up for a Woody Creek funeral. They borrowed Elsie's navy beret and Jenny swapped her once-red for her navy print. It was faded but more suitable.

She'd sung at a couple of funerals years ago, the last time at Barbie Dobson's. A different funeral this one. The church had been crowded for Barbie, but only a handful of mourners came to say goodbye to Molly Martin, and most of them were her kids and grandkids. Jenny recognised a few of the boys. A few recognised her. She recognised a middle-aged man as Ray's brother by his build, his hair, though his was greying. Ray didn't speak to him. Ray didn't speak to anyone until his sister was in her grave, until his brother approached him.

'Someone told me you were alive,' he said.

'Someone told me you were too,' Ray said, his voice as cold as a tombstone on a frosty morning, and no stutter. Then he reached for Jenny's hand and walked her fast to his bike.

'Who?' She sounded like Georgie.

'The last of them. I'll go to his f-funeral, too.'

The ride into town had been sedate. Now he went too fast out the Willama road, and that was flying, the wind in her face, tangling her hair. She had to cling to him. Then he turned the bike around and went even faster back to town; maybe he didn't want that clinging to end. She clung to the seat when they put-putted through town, through the bush. This time he rode no further than the boundary gate.

'W-would you c-c-come out w-with me sometime?' he said, his eyes turned towards the bush.

'I don't go out much, Ray.'

'S-signs around for a dance at the hall on New Year's Eve.'

'I haven't danced since I lived in Sydney, but thanks anyway.'

He knew rejection when he met it head on, and his eyes were afraid of rejection.

And why shouldn't she go to a dance with him if he wanted to take her to a dance? She'd be twenty-two on New Year's Eve. She had a beautiful blue dress she'd never worn, and Norman's necklace.

'It's a long way to come just for a country dance.'

'Only a f-few hours on the b-bike,' he said, the hope of the outcast in his lost lamb's eyes.

Ray was always an outcast in the playground, as was Jim when she was small. Why did he keep reminding her of Jim?

Because like Jim, he'd been a part of that better time, the time before Amber had come home.

Why was she drawn to outcasts?

Blame Norman, the original outcast. She'd grown up loving him. She still did in her heart, she'd just learned not to let her heart rule her head.

'If you decide to come up, I'll go with you, Ray, but if you find that you can't make it, then don't worry. I won't expect you until I hear your bike coming down the track.'

'Y-y-you'll hear it,' he said.

Ray King was the talk of Woody Creek that week — as was Jenny Morrison.

'I spoke to him in the café. He said he'd been living in Melbourne.'

'She was in Melbourne for months. She must have known him down there.'

'Can two yellow-haired people have a redheaded kid?'

'One of Henry King's wife's sisters had red hair. The one that died young of the diphtheria.'

'I seen him with that boy on his bike the morning of the funeral.'

'I saw her clinging on to the back of his bike heading out towards Willama and going like the clappers.'

'Wanting to get somewhere fast — I'd be doing the same if she was on the back of my bike.'

THE BEST NIGHT

'His wife probably isn't even dead. Someone probably told him about me and he's decided to try his luck. Every time I go into town, the blokes on the pub corner expect me to start spruiking: "Sixpence a ride and discount for twins."'

'Watch your mouth around those girls!' Gertrude said. Jenny was having a haircut, in the yard, in the sun, the cut curls glinting like gold in the dust.

'He won't come. I hope he doesn't.'

'Don't bother lying to me. You're dying to wear your father's necklace.'

'I'll lose it when he rapes me halfway home.'

'I told you to watch your mouth. You sound like a Sydney tart lately.'

Jenny had a bath at Elsie's that afternoon. She washed her hair, added a little lemon juice to the rinsing water. At seven she put on her stockings, just in case. She hadn't heard from him since he'd dropped her home after the funeral. She knew he wouldn't turn up, and just to prove she wasn't expecting him, she got the cards out and played switch with the kids.

They were in their bed before eight, just in case. No need for him to know she had three kids — if he didn't know already — if he came.

She was trimming ragged fingernails when the kids peeped from the bedroom curtain. They'd heard the bike. Gertrude sent them back, told them to be as quiet as three little mice. Jenny ran for the lean-to to snatch her blue linen from its hanger.

Miss Blunt had made it up in a similar style to the green, and Jenny loved it, though blue frocks had always been her nemesis. Its skirt would probably get caught in his bike chain, or he'd rip it when he dragged her off the bike to rape her.

She slipped Norman's blue earrings into her lobes, had trouble doing up the matching necklet, but she got it done up and loved it anew. She was sliding her feet into her black high heels, unworn since Sydney, when Granny invited Ray into the kitchen.

'She's still making herself beautiful,' Granny said.

'Sh-she's already that, Mrs F-foote' he said — and his stutter made Jenny's heart ache, when she didn't want it to ache for anyone but Jim. She was going to a dance, that's all. She wanted to dance and she couldn't dance alone, that's all. And he probably couldn't dance, and she'd be stuck with him treading all over her feet all night and end up with her skirt caught up in his bike chain, ripped to shreds in the dirt and Norman's earrings lost — when he raped her.

The hall was crowded, as crowded as it had been on the night of the ball; the music had changed little. And he was a brilliant dancer, better than her, and he could jitterbug better than the Yanks. She danced with him all night, refused an offer from Billy Roberts and three more. Why dance with less when you could dance with the best?

She saw Sissy at ten, sitting near the supper room door, saw Amber stuck like a flea to Sissy's side. Saw them murdering her with their eyes when Norman spoke to her, his poor old face near swallowed in a smile at the sight of his necklet at her throat. She saw Sissy's mouth snarling 'slut' near midnight, when she and Ray took over the centre of the dance floor and showed Woody Creek how the jitterbug was done.

It was the best night. It was the absolute best night she'd ever had in Woody Creek bar none. As nights go, she could only think of two in her life which may have been better: the talent quest night and that night at the club with Jim.

She told Ray about the factory in Sydney, about her landlady who'd looked after Jimmy. She kept her mouth shut about the girls. She told him how Jim had been engaged to Sissy, how he'd broken it off and joined the army. She told him that she'd been engaged to Jim for six months before he'd gone missing.

He didn't drag her off the bike and rape her in the dust; he didn't even try to kiss her goodnight. Apart from when they danced, he didn't touch her.

'If I c-come up again, w-would you —'

'There's things you'll find out about me, Ray. Tonight has been perfect and I don't want it spoiled.'

'I w-won't spoil it. W-will you?'

'Petrol is still rationed, isn't it?'

'B-bikes don't use much. W-will you?'

'I'm not who you think I am.'

'Y-you're not saying you won't,' he said.

She went to the pictures with him the following Saturday night. They walked into town and walked home in the moonlight, holding hands.

'N-next S-Saturday,' he said.

'It's too far for you to keep on coming up here every weekend.'

'M-m-marry me and I w-won't have to keep on c-coming up. I've got a h-house.'

'Now you're being crazy. You don't even know me.'

'You r-remembered me. I l-l-love you f-for that.'

She ached for him, wanted to cry for him. She'd had four kids — three; she had to forget about Cara. She'd had a week or two of love but no courting, and here he was, travelling for hours, wasting his petrol, sitting at her side through a lousy picture show, telling her he loved her.

The moon was peeping over the walnut tree when he drew her close and kissed her. She felt shy, felt sixteen, felt embarrassed, but not much else.

'Marry me,' he whispered.

'You don't ask people you don't know to marry you just because you're missing your wife.'

'I know you,' he said.

'You don't. I've got three kids, not one. I can't ever marry anyone.'

'M-me, you can. I've g-got none. N-no one.'

She didn't have the heart to push him away when he kissed her again, just waited until he was done then stepped away, aware she'd let him think there was some chance for them. There wasn't.

'It's not that I don't like you. You're probably the most decent bloke I've met since Jim, but there's no future in it, Ray.' She opened the gate, stepped through and closed it between them.

'I'm n-not giving up,' he said. 'N-next S-Saturday.'

'Stop wasting your petrol on me.'

'I'm n-not w-wasting it. I love you.'

She sighed and turned back. 'I was raped by the Macdonald twins when I was fourteen. I got myself into strife again at fifteen. I had three kids before I was eighteen and I'm never, not as long as I live, having another one.'

'I d-d-don't blame you,' he said. 'Three is enough to f-f-feed these days. S-see you on S-saturday.'

And he rode away.

THE TEMPORARY STATIONMASTER

Sissy had returned to the Duckworths on the Wednesday following New Year's Eve. They were good Christian folk; they'd always taken in the family widows, the maiden aunts and fallen cousins, the Duckworths with drinking problems. They shared the problem, moved the visitor from house to house, never allowing the problematic one to grow too comfortable in any one residence, thus all visitors could be welcomed with open arms in the sure and certain knowledge that those same arms would, in a month or two, be raised to wave them on their way to the next host.

Norman and his mother had been shunted between Duckworths for the first sixteen years of his life, as Sissy was now shunted, six weeks here, four weeks there, a few final weeks with the now elderly Charles, the parson, and his alcoholic son Reginald — which was usually enough to send Sissy scuttling home. She was with Aunt Olive and Olive's daughter, Betty, in Hamilton, when Norman went missing.

He had been at the station on Saturday; several had seen him there. But when the train came in at ten on Monday morning, he wasn't there to meet it. He'd damn near lived at that station these last years and for the past thirty years had met every train. Norman was, if nothing else, a reliable man.

Amber said he'd spent a very quiet Sunday, and that he'd left for the station before she'd risen on Monday morning. She'd presumed he'd gone to the station, though occasionally he had taken a quick constitutional before going to work.

No one had seen him out walking on Monday morning, and on Monday afternoon Denham came to Gertrude's door to ask if Jenny had seen her father.

She hadn't, not since New Year's Eve. Gertrude had. He'd ridden down on Saturday night while Jenny was at the movies with Ray. He'd stayed for a cup of tea, had mentioned speaking to Jenny at the dance, but said little more. He'd left around nine with a dozen eggs and a few tomatoes.

Some in town thought he could have been in church on Sunday. Others stated that he definitely had not been seated in his normal pew. This was unusual for Norman, though not unheard of. In the past six or eight years he'd been missing from that pew two or three times.

His bike was in the washhouse. Gertrude's eggs and tomatoes were in the icebox at the station, with three sausages, butter, milk and half a loaf of bread.

By six that evening, Denham was walking the stretch of bush beside the creek which Norman had been known to frequent. He liked birds, had spent some time down by the creek with his binoculars. He found no sign of Norman.

On Tuesday morning, Denham contacted Charles Duckworth, who said he had not heard from his nephew in ten days. He and Reginald informed the rest of the Duckworth clan that Norman was missing.

Aunt Olive and Betty informed Sissy, who was not overly concerned; she had no intention of going home so soon.

'He'll turn up.'

A railway department chap arrived to look after Norman's station, and his face was enough to frighten kids, though a few came to stare at him while their fathers searched the bush for Norman, poked around in the creek, dodged snakes in the reed beds. A lost child might remain lost for days in that forest, if he wandered in deep enough, but a man who had lived in Woody Creek for thirty years wasn't going to wander off and get himself lost in the bush. A man of Norman's years was more likely to have gone walking and suffered a heart attack. Denham expected to find him lying dead behind a log.

They hadn't found him by nightfall and searching in the dark for a dead man would achieve nothing. The men went home.

'I reckon he's taken off on her,' they said.

'And about time, the poor simple-minded bastard.'

'He's gone out walking on Sunday and kept on going. I'll bet you any money you like.'

'He wasn't the type to take off on her. That poor fool stuck by her through thick and thin.'

'Who's to say what type he was? I know him no better today than I did when he landed in this town back after that first war.'

'Speaking of which, have you seen the bloke they sent up to replace him? He's been shot up bad somewhere.'

'He's got a wife, too. How does a wife look at that for the rest of her life?'

'They say Jim Hooper is a mess.'

'Jim Hooper is dead. He died two years back.'

'Not according to Gloria Bull.'

'Horrie's girl?'

'She's nursing at one of those veterans' hospitals in Melbourne. Her mother writes to Madge. Her last letter said young Gloria was nursing Jim Hooper.'

'She's got him mixed up with one of the other boys.'

'Could be.'

The temporary stationmaster with the shot-up face opened Norman's side gate at ten past eight on Tuesday night. He'd brought Norman's supplies from the station icebox. It was out of ice, had been out of ice since he'd arrived at ten that morning. The eggs felt warm, the butter in a screw-topped jar had melted, the four sausages, wrapped in brown paper, would go off fast without ice.

Amber, on her way back up from the lavatory, didn't see him on her dark verandah until it was too late; she'd already opened the back door.

He asked if there was news on her husband. She stepped inside before she told him how her husband had left for work before she'd risen.

He mentioned the icebox being out of ice and offered a small carton containing Norman's foodstuffs. And those sausages must have been off. He hadn't noticed any smell about them when he'd opened the icebox, but they smelled bad now. Or something did.

He stepped forward to hand her the carton and Amber slammed the door in his face.

You ill-mannered bitch of a woman, he thought, then he stepped back suddenly.

The temporary stationmaster had been through a long war. His nose was telling him where Norman Morrison would be found. He placed the carton on a cane chair and went for reinforcements.

Denham and the temporary stationmaster found Norman Morrison on his bed, buried beneath blankets and a feather quilt, a slim-bladed carving knife buried up to the handle between his ribs, his face mashed to meat, the cast iron frying pan used to cause the damage buried with him beneath the bedding.

There must have been blood. They held their breath and looked for blood. There was no sign of it. Not a splatter on the wall, on the window. Nothing, other than what had leaked into the bedding, to the mattress, sprayed the curtains. Brown, rusty blood. The house smelled like a charnel house but it looked immaculate. They glanced into the parlour, the bedrooms, the bathroom.

Amber was in the bathroom, standing on a chair, cleaning out a small bathroom cabinet, carefully wiping each box, each jar and bottle.

'I'd like you to take a walk over the road with me, Mrs Morrison,' Denham said.

'Wait in the parlour,' she replied. 'I'll be done shortly.'

GOODBYE NORMAN

Someone had to make the decisions. Sissy was too distraught, which left Jenny, who was too shocked to cry. Numb. Walking in circles dry eyed, cursing her mother to hell. She walked until Maisy and Gertrude took her to Willama to see him.

She saw his gentle old hand, all they'd allow her to see, all Gertrude would allow her to see. She held it and howled her heart out.

Someone had to choose a coffin. She howled when she spoke to the undertaker, when she spoke to the minister, when she told him where she wanted Norman to sleep. Twenty-two years ago, Norman had chosen his mother's tombstone with its three chubby angels. One had lost its nose and a wing, one head had been knocked off and cemented back on, but she'd grown up loving those angels. He'd sleep beneath them. The funeral would be on Friday, at eleven, which would give Sissy plenty of time to get home.

Sissy didn't make the trip. Only eight Duckworths arrived on Friday's train: the three Box Hill cousins, Aunt Louise, her husband and unmarried daughter, and Charles and alcoholic Reginald. Aunt Olive and Betty couldn't leave Sissy. She was out of her mind with grief, Aunt Louise said.

The hotel was full of Duckworths and newspaper men. Murder was big news. For two days it made the front page of every Melbourne newspaper. With the war over, newspaper men were scratching for any news they could get.

AMBER MORRISON JAILED IN '32 FOR KNIFE ATTACK ON BOYFRIEND.
OLD INVESTIGATIONS REOPENED.

Police have reopened investigations into the deaths of two Woody Creek schoolgirls. The brother of Nelly Abbot, a ten-year-old girl slashed and battered to death in 1933, told reporters today that there is little doubt in the minds of Woody Creek residents that his sister was the brutal killer's first victim. The parents of a second victim, Barbara Dobson, were not available for comment.

The city police left town before the funeral. There was no mystery to solve here. They had the killer in a city jail.

OLD MYSTERY SOLVED, Friday morning's newspapers screamed, and beneath those black headlines they'd printed archival photographs of Nelly Abbot and little Barbie Dobson.

Vern Hooper read every word. He'd spent half an hour on the telephone with his city solicitor, Lorna and Margaret at his elbows.

They'd bided their time; now their time had arrived. They were going after Jimmy with their pockets full of ammunition and their solicitor was convinced they'd get him. The boy's maternal grandfather had been murdered and his maternal grandmother charged with his murder. That snake-eyed bitch of a woman had as good as handed Vern his boy and if she hadn't, then Jimmy's soldier father would.

Vern didn't want to go to Norman's funeral. He'd been keeping his distance from Gertrude; she could read him too easily. And there had been whispers in town about Jim. She would have heard them.

Maisy drove Jenny and Gertrude into town. She sat with them in the front pew. The coffin, flower bedecked, was too close; Jenny couldn't look up without seeing it. Thank God she'd made her peace with him. She wished she'd made a greater peace with him, wished she'd put her arms around him, held his face between her hands, kissed him.

So many people in that church, Duckworths and newspaper men, farmers in town to do their weekly shopping, just in for a look. Norman would have liked the crowd.

Jenny sat head down, wanting it over. She didn't hear much of the service. She'd told the minister to talk about how Norman had loved playing poker on Friday nights, how he would come home happy and fry cheese sandwiches in the kitchen. She'd told him to talk about how he used to ride his bike out of town to pick mushrooms, to pick bunches of wild daffodils, about how he'd loved watching the birds down at the bridge, how he could name every type of bird in Woody Creek. She'd told him too that she didn't want Uncle Charles standing up there talking about a Norman the people in this town didn't know.

When it was over she didn't know what he'd said about Norman.

She stood while the six pallbearers carried the coffin out, while the organist played something morbid and knew she was going to howl, and Vern Hooper and his daughters were not going to see her howl, and those newspaper men were not going to feature her tears on tomorrow's front page.

Chin down, she gripped Granny's hand.

He was leaving. He was halfway out and they wanted her to move, to follow his coffin out. She couldn't do it. Couldn't let him be carried away like that. She knew what she had to do. Sometimes there's no choice.

She lifted her chin, sucked air in through her teeth, stared at the stained glass window, and opened her mouth.

She sang him from that church, sang him on his way with the Twenty-third Psalm, because he'd loved it, because he'd told her once that her singing had made him proud. Shuddering and shaking, but she sang it loud, sang it strong for Norman, and the organist gave up on her morbid melody and followed Jenny's voice. She sang her heart out for Norman, holding her tears inside, holding them in until the song was done, until Gertrude put her arms around her and stopped her from shuddering apart.

They walked out hand in hand. Mr Foster was outside. She released Gertrude's hand to grip his, then to grip John

McPherson's. Miss Rose kissed her cheek. Miss Blunt kissed her cheek. Charlie patted her shoulder. There was no pat on the shoulder from Vern, no offer of his hand. He couldn't look at her. Margaret glanced her way, her fishbowl eyes blinking. Lorna sneered.

Gertrude and Maisy walked with Jenny behind the coffin. The walk to the cemetery was good, the placing of one foot in front of the other was good. Eight Duckworths walked beside and behind her, Cousin Reginald eyeing her like a good brandy he'd love to taste but knew he couldn't afford.

The bank manager spoke to her at the graveside. Denham chased away two men with cameras then stood behind her, protecting her back. A good man, a good cop. His wife was there. She nodded. A few nodded. A few shook her hand, kissed her cheek. There was no sign of the Hoopers at the graveside. She looked for them. Maisy saw her scanning the faces.

'He's got a good crowd, love,' she said. 'He would have liked that.'

He got a good crowd but it was over by midday. Norman was gone into the earth by midday, Mr Foster gone back to his post office, the bank manager back to his bank, Miss Blunt back behind her counter and the undertaker on his way home to Willama.

It wasn't over for Jenny and Gertrude. Norman's house had to be emptied. The railway department was sending up a permanent replacement for Norman, a married man with three kids who'd require the stationmaster's house. Someone had to empty it and Sissy was in no fit state, so it was said.

'That poor girl. I don't know what is to become of her,' Aunt Louise said.

Poor, poor Sissy. No more money from Norman until the estate was sorted out — if there was anything left of the estate to sort out. Poor, poor Sissy, her hairdresser locked up in a Melbourne jail. Poor Sissy would have to get a job — or just keep moving forever between Duckworths.

Jenny hadn't stepped inside the railway house since the night of the ball when Norman had carried her, kicking, through the back door; the night she'd fought the junk room window open, the night her world had gone mad.

Denham had the keys. He unlocked the doors. Gertrude and Maisy entered first, then the three Box Hill cousins, Reginald behind them. Far better the house be full before Jenny stepped inside.

There was a lingering smell of that crazy bitch's evil in these rooms. And where did you start on emptying her out? You opened the windows, the doors and allowed the wind to blow her evil from this town.

Norman's window had been left open, his room already stripped bare. The smell of hell and brimstone clung there — or the smell of sulfur. The kitchen shovel used as a tray for the burning of it still sat on two bricks in the centre of the room.

The parlour was unchanged. There'd been good times once in that parlour. Jenny turned on the wireless, and to the sound of modern music, she made a start while Gertrude made a start in the kitchen.

Maisy directed the Duckworth men, who couldn't get out of Woody Creek until the train went through that night. She had a big shed in her backyard and rooms to spare. She'd store Norman's furniture until it was needed. Mick Boyle had offered his dray to move the furniture across the road.

The men and Maisy emptied Amber's room, then moved into Sissy's. Jenny wrapped Norman's peacock feathers in an old sheet, wrapped the blue-green vase in newspaper, then piece by piece emptied her grandmother's cabinet of that prized tea set, wrapping each item in newspaper before placing it carefully into a cardboard carton. The Queen Victoria vase was wrapped, the wedding photograph was taken down.

Jenny looked at Norman and his pretty bride, who had never looked at her. For years, that pretty bride had been the only mother Jenny had known. It was Amber, but it wasn't. She wrapped it.

Norman's clothes were folded into a chaff bag. The church ladies would hand them out to the needy. Maisy packed Sissy's clothes into a case which would return with the Duckworths to the city.

'What should I do with that wedding frock, Mrs Foote?' Sissy's wedding frock, which Norman had paid dearly for, was already packed with tissue paper into a long box.

'It's no use sending that down to her. I'll see if Miss Blunt can sell it to someone,' Gertrude said.

'Give it to her,' Jenny said.

'What should I do with Amber's clothes, Mrs Foote?'

'Burn them,' Jenny said.

In the late afternoon they turned off Norman's wireless and carried it out to the dray, rolled up the velvet carpet. Gertrude thought it might cover the uneven boards in the lean-to but Jenny didn't want it there. It was loaded onto the dray to be stored in Maisy's shed. Norman's wireless would move down to Gertrude's house. Harry might be able to connect it up to a truck battery. Mick Boyle said he'd deliver it, if not tonight then tomorrow.

They loaded sheets, pillow slips and towels into the rear of Maisy's car with a few pots and pans and the pantry items. Gertrude could use them. A few books were loaded into Maisy's car too, including Norman's book on birds.

The Duckworth men left with the train at seven. Jenny stood at Norman's back fence, watching until it was out of sight. She waved to it, wanting to believe that Norman's spirit was on it, going home with the Duckworths. She knew she should have wept for him, but not in this place. Too many tears had already been poured into the black hole of that railway house.

They'd forgotten about the washhouse. Norman's bike was out there; the child's bike seat was there, roped to a rafter, his tool box was behind the door.

Jenny wheeled the bike out, ran her hands over the handlebars, and told herself that maybe in time Norman would have taken his grandchildren riding, that maybe, in time, he would have told them he was proud of them.

Probably not.

'Ready, darlin'?' Maisy and Gertrude were waiting for her on the back verandah. The electricity had been turned off.

Jenny carried the tool box to Maisy's car. It was heavy but she was strong. Gertrude said so. She untied the rope holding the child's seat. They loaded it.

'I'll ride his bike home, Granny.'

Gertrude didn't argue. She and Maisy drove away and the house was Jenny's own, just for a while.

She walked the rooms in the dark, checking the windows, her footsteps sounding hollow in the empty rooms. She touched walls, attempting to find the ghost of little Jenny, who had for a time lived happily in this house with Norman.

There was nothing left of her. Just the rattle of Sissy's undraped window. She locked the front door, and for the last time walked that passage. Out to the back verandah then, key in the back door lock. She turned it.

Finished. The end.

Constable Denham had asked her to drop the keys back to him when they were done. As she walked over the road, she looked back. Just an empty railway house, waiting for its new family.

The stars were out. She stood for a moment, staring up at a sky ablaze with tiny candles. Norman had believed emphatically in God and an afterlife. If he'd been right, then he was already up there calling God's meetings to order. If he was wrong . . .

Denham sat on his verandah smoking, waiting for the keys. She crossed the road.

JULIANA CONTI

The lamp was burning when Gertrude and Maisy entered the house, the kettle singing. They'd driven away at ten forty that morning and had told Elsie to expect them when she saw them. Elsie had anticipated their arrival home. She'd lit that lamp and left a casserole in the oven.

There'd been two burials today for Gertrude: Norman's and Amber's. There'd be no more fooling herself. She'd lost her daughter many years ago. Today she'd gone into that hole with Norman. It was over.

It was over, but a terrible sadness lingered in her heart, an awful guilt, an aching emptiness.

She dumped an armful of linen onto her old cane couch, worn ragged by climbing kids. She'd looked at Norman's couch today and considered replacing her own with it, but it would have taken up more space than she had to spare.

Maisy dumped a second load of linen. They went back and forth to the car unloading it.

Jenny had wanted the tool box. Together the women lifted it out and placed it beside Gertrude's cart, just until tomorrow. Pots and pans, superior to Gertrude's, were carried in and piled on her table. The child's bike seat was placed in the cart, just until tomorrow.

'Off you go now, love, and thanks for everything,' Gertrude said. The motor had been left running, the car lights left blazing.

'I know Jenny said to get rid of Amber's clothes. It's just . . . her mother will need something for the trial.'

'There'll be no trial. Denham was saying today that they've got all of her old medical records.'

She'd slashed and smashed that man while he'd slept, and probably on the Saturday night when he'd ridden home with his eggs and tomatoes.

Why had he ridden down? Had he come to speak about Amber, or to get away from her? He'd said little. He should have — should have cursed Gertrude for bringing Amber back into his life. But that had never been Norman's way. He'd never blamed her. Hadn't needed to. She'd been blaming herself for years. It was her fault that those little schoolgirls had been murdered — and maybe those newborn baby boys at the hospital the day before she attacked Jenny. The police were now trying to connect her with their deaths. It was possible — if she'd believed one of them to be Jenny's newborn. That's what Jenny believed.

All my fault, Gertrude thought. I should have listened to Vern when Ogden found her at the asylum. He told me to walk away. Norman wanted me to walk away. So many lives lost because of my interference. Jenny's life ruined because of my interference.

'It's so terrible, Mrs Foote. It's just . . . it's all so . . . unbelievable. I've known her since I was five years old.'

'I've known her longer, love, and it goes beyond finding words to describe it. Go home now and put your feet up. It's been a long day for all of us.'

'I just hope Jenny is —'

'She's strong.' Gertrude hoped she was strong enough. 'She's had no time alone since they found her dad. She needs tonight.' As did Gertrude. She wanted to sit out beneath the stars and let the moon wash her soul clean. Maisy didn't understand that need to be alone. Maybe she'd never been alone.

'Amber had a couple of nice things. They'd fit Jenny.'

Gertrude released a sigh from deep, deep down. 'Jenny would go naked before she'd wear any of them — and I'd see her running around naked before I'd let her. If it wasn't such a waste, I'd tell you to burn the lot.' She kissed Maisy's cheek, thanked her again for her help, and finally, finally the night swallowed up those car lights.

The kettle was boiling. The casserole was hot but Gertrude wasn't hungry.

'A cup of tea,' she sighed. 'A cup of tea and some silence.'

And she heard boards move in the lean-to.

'Jenny, is that you, darlin'?' How had she beaten her home? She couldn't have. 'Is that one of you kids?'

It wasn't Jenny, or one of Elsie's kids.

'Something a little stronger than tea might go down well, Tru.'

He came out from behind the green curtain, his dark-rimmed glasses a contrast against the white hair, the white well-trimmed beard. He was wearing a dark suit and hat, holding a book in his hand, the book Jenny had been reading when Denham rode down to tell them Norman had been found — one of his own books.

Gertrude dropped her teapot. It bounced across the floor, tea and tea-leaves spraying, the lid rolling.

'I thought that woman would never leave,' he said.

Shock, guilt, loss, weariness threatening to overwhelm her, Gertrude grabbed for her mantelpiece and pleaded with her legs not to let her down, not now, not in front of him.

They'd held her up on the day she'd hunted him with her rifle when Amber was thirteen, but she had no rifle tonight. She'd given it to Harry years ago. Her poker was leaning against the stove hob. A good solid poker. She reached for it, gripped it.

'Get out of my house, you viper.'

And the viper laughed at her. 'I had hoped we were past the age of combat, Tru.'

How long had he been here? Long enough to find the money she kept in her bottom drawer, to find Jenny's prized earrings. And the stranger's brooch! He'd come from the lean-to. That brooch was in a shoe box on top of the lean-to wardrobe. He'd found that brooch —

She took a reflex step towards the lean-to. Took that same step back, closer to her boiling kettle. She'd scald him if she had to. She'd smash his head in with that poker and feel no more than if she smashed in the head of a striking snake.

The table was between them, the open door to her right. She wanted him out that door but was afraid the brooch and Jenny's earrings would go with him.

If she yelled, Harry and Lenny would come. The last time a snake had slithered into her house, she'd yelled loud enough to bring them running.

Harry and Elsie thought he was dead. Only Vern knew he wasn't, Vern who hadn't been able to meet her eyes at the funeral. Vern, who she knew too well, who made every post a winner. He was going to use what had happened to go after Jimmy. She knew it in her bones.

Men and their bastardry.

And that bastard had retrieved the teapot, picked up the lid and placed it on the pot. He held it out and, when she didn't take it, he placed it down amid the clutter on her table and drew Vern's chair out — thinking to sit?

'You won't sit down in my house.'

'Have pity,' he said. 'The legs grow old and weary.' He had to be eighty. He didn't look it. 'Where is the girl?'

'Your daughter is on her way to a madhouse for life, where you drove her, like you drove your own sister, you bastard of a man. You've ruined everything you've ever touched.'

'Yes, yes, yes,' he said. 'I was led to believe I would find Jennifer with you.' And he sat and placed his hat on the teapot, and had the audacity to smile. 'You always were one for truth, Tru. There comes a time when the truth must out. I have a vested interest in that girl.'

'You think I don't know about your vested interest? You think I didn't know it every time I cut that little girl's hair, every time I heard her sing? You think I didn't see you in her every time I looked into her face?' She didn't like the sound of her voice; she had to hold herself together. She breathed deeply as she raised the poker. 'You're a greater fool than I gave you credit for being, Archie Foote.'

Her knowledge took him aback. He'd had a very fine tale to tell, and she'd taken the shine off it — but only for an instant. He'd always had the recoil of a striking snake.

'In different circumstances we may have made a formidable team, Tru —'

'Who was her mother?'

'You have brandy.' More statement than question.

Two bottles stood side by side on top of her dresser, an inch of rum in one, three inches of brandy in the other.

'Who was she?'

'A tenacious woman. I attempted to return her to her husband. Alas, she would not go. Just a wee nip for the heart; it's not all it used to be.'

She could have swung that poker at his head there and then, and kept on swinging it. Could have dragged him down to the orchard by his skinny ankles and planted him. Whatever had gone wrong with Amber, he'd been the cause of it. She hated him as she'd hated no other in her life. She feared him, too, or had once. There was not much left of him now to fear. And he had the answers. For twenty-two years she'd wanted answers. Play her cards right and she may yet wring something worthwhile from that bastard of a man — and from this bastard of a week.

She reached for one of her drinking glasses, then for the bottle of brandy. His aging hand wanted it. She placed the glass down but held onto the bottle.

'Still withholding your favours, Tru,' he said. 'Tut-tut.'

'That woman died on my couch. Who was she?'

'What's in a name? You know me — love 'em and leave 'em wanting more.' He had the glass. She had the brandy. Again he smiled. 'Juliana Conti, if I recall correctly — a rich man's wife I borrowed for a time.'

He'd never told the truth if a lie would do as well, but the name matched the initials on the handkerchief. She poured half an inch into his glass.

'You had her out to Monk's place.'

'No.' He sipped, grimaced. 'All water long passed under the bridge, Tru.' He emptied the glass and, grimace or not, held it out for just a little more.

'She was running from you the night she died,' Gertrude said.

'On the contrary, I assure you.' The glass was extended but

Gertrude wasn't pouring. 'Had I the answers, they would all be yours tonight — even for such poor brandy. Alas, the answers are not mine to give, having unsuccessfully attempted to return her to the bosom of her family, I made a hasty retreat to the sanctuary of my cousin. When last I saw Signora Conti, she was cursing me to hell in a hotel room. I can only assume she took it into her head to pursue me.'

Gertrude gave him the bottle. He poured a good splash. 'A little water may cut it. Would you have such a thing in this god-forsaken hole?'

She wasn't fetching him water. 'You knew Jenny was yours when you were up here that time at Duffy's.'

'During my blue period,' he said. 'I heard her voice at an infants' concert. Woody Creek hadn't bred it. I heard her today. She has an incredible range and a unique tone. She wants only for guidance.'

'Down the same path you guided Amber.'

He sipped. 'You are speaking to a dead man newly arisen and cleansed of all sin — or too old to sin more. Yea, though I walk through the valley of the shadow of death, I will fear no evil . . .' He sipped again. 'Were I a believer, no doubt I'd cringe in fear of hell for my most grievous, previous sins. Again, alas.' Another sip. 'My dear sister Victoria having so very conveniently gone to her maker, I now find myself in possession of the old bastard's house and money. He wasted my voice. I'll take great delight in spending his money on putting his illegitimate granddaughter on the world stage.'

He'd always craved the limelight. He'd had the voice. He'd charmed the natives out of the jungles with it — had charmed an eighteen-year-old fool of a girl with his voice.

'If you hadn't spent your life —' She fell silent and turned towards the door. She'd heard something.

'Jennifer?' he said.

It would be Jenny, but she lied. 'It will be Harry come over to check that I'm home.'

Archie Foote had never been a fighting man. Having no desire to be thrown out, he stood and reached for his hat. 'For my own satisfaction only, tell me, Tru — was the brooch found on Juliana that night?'

Relief washed from Gertrude's head to her heels. He didn't have it. 'What brooch?'

'A classic. Quite a spectacular thing. The woman never moved without it. I have walked the path she must have taken many times, combed the area where she was found — during my blue period.'

Gertrude was at the door. It was dark out tonight; she saw no sign of Jenny. She could have heard them talking and gone directly to Elsie's house. The girls and Jimmy were over there. Gertrude hoped she'd gone over there. She didn't want Jenny walking in on this.

'Someone found it,' he said. 'By the look of this place — and the quality of your brandy — it wasn't you.' He'd taken a wallet from his breast pocket and as she walked back to the light she saw him slide a photograph free. 'It was worth a small fortune,' he said. 'The brooch.'

And the wire gate's old hinge complained.

'She's just lost the father she loved.' The poker was placed back on her hearth. 'If you've got a shred of a heart left inside you, you'll go.'

'I'm all heart, Tru — as you know.' He placed the photograph on the table and picked up his hat. 'I'll give you tonight.'

He was standing in the doorway when Jenny walked in. She glanced at him once and saw an elderly man clad in a dark suit, glanced at him twice and saw Gerald Archibald, the Sydney abortionist. Her eyes widened.

'Your voice was an angel's today, my dear. It is a lucky father who has his own angel to sing him home to heaven,' he said.

She heard old Noah in his voice and looked at Gertrude, busy counting eggs into a brown paper bag.

'Half a dozen, you said?'

He played the game. He'd always enjoyed playing games. 'Half a dozen will do very nicely. There is nothing so nice as an egg fresh from the hen, Jennifer.'

'I saw you up in Sydney,' Jenny said.

'Such a pretty city. It puts staid old Melbourne Town to shame.' He took a coin from his pocket, exchanged it for the half dozen eggs. 'No doubt our paths will cross again very soon, my dear.' And he raised his hat and left with his eggs.

Jenny stood looking at the bottle of brandy, at the glass, while Gertrude stood in the yard watching the narrow beam of a torch move briskly up her track.

He'd been twenty-three when she was nineteen, which meant he was now over eighty. He'd played the ageing stroke-affected destitute back in '35 when she'd stitched up the second gash in his head. Tonight he was playing the sprightly old gentleman. A great performer had been lost to the stage.

'Did he walk all the way down here for eggs?' Jenny asked, joining Gertrude.

A car motor answered her question, car lights glowed on the trees. They watched as the car turned around. He hadn't walked from town.

Back in the kitchen Gertrude picked up the photograph he'd left on the table. She held it close to the lamp, wondering why he'd left it — until she made out the brooch pinned to the woman's hat.

It was her. There was no doubting that. She put her reading glasses on and stared at the dark, foreign-looking face. Even without the brooch she would have recognised her. Juliana Conti, he'd said. Finally, after all these years, she had a name to fit the initials on the handkerchief.

'Who is it?' Jenny asked.

'A ghost from the past, darlin'. Can you make me a cup of tea? My old legs feel worn out tonight.'

She didn't sit and rest her weary legs. She went to the lean-to, thinking to hide the photograph away in the shoe box with the rest of that woman's possessions. But the time for hiding was past. He'd be back. He was probably staying at the hotel, signed in as Archie Foote this time. He'd be down here again tomorrow; obsession was that man's middle name. Jenny had to be told tonight.

Gertrude stood weighing the box in her hand, watching the

shadows play on the curtain as the tea was made, as pots and pans were moved from the table to the floor.

'It's poured, Granny. I'll go over and get the kids home.'

'Wait, darlin'.' Right or wrong, it had to be done tonight. 'Leave them there for a while. There's something I need to talk to you about.' She'd promised Norman she'd never say a word about what they'd done that day, but a promise can't outlive the man it was given to.

THE BROOCH

Two large mugs of tea sat on the cleared end of the old table. Gertrude found space between them for the dusty old shoe box. How to start? Where to start? Once she removed that lid, it had to start. She wanted Jenny sitting at her side, wanted a mouthful of tea before she began. She added sugar, stirred, allowing Jenny to remove the lid of the box, to retrieve a bundle of letters, a bankbook.

'He looked so guilty at the funeral, Granny. He's going to start again, isn't he?'

Gertrude looked at her without comprehension, looked at the letters. Vern. Maybe he was. He'd looked guilty — but he hadn't been himself for months, had been keeping his distance. There was something going on with him, though what he was up to wasn't important tonight.

'Sit with me, darlin'. I've got something I have to tell you.'

'He's going to use what she did against me in court, isn't he?'

'If it comes to the crunch, I'll join ranks with the devil to keep him from taking Jimmy. What I need to talk to you about has got nothing to do with Vern.' She didn't know where to start. There was no right way to make a start, so she started the wrong way.

'It's to do with you, darlin'. To do with your birth. You weren't born to Amber. I know it's the wrong time —'

'I've had enough, Granny. Just because the whole bloody world has gone stark raving mad, doesn't mean you can, too.'

'It's true, darlin'.'

'Stop it!'

'I should have told you that day when we were talking about

495

Nancy Bryant following your cry across the paddock. She found you lying in the scrub with your dying mother. She and Lonnie brought you down here. That's the woman who bore you.' Gertrude held out the photograph. 'I learned her name tonight. She was Juliana Conti. She died on my couch a few hours after you were born.'

'You've gone senile and I'm going to get Elsie and Harry.'

'Sit down, darlin', and hear me out.' She took the stranger's purse from the box, opened and upended it, emptying its contents onto the table. 'I've almost told you a hundred times but I never knew how to start and I had so little to tell you that was fact.' She unpinned the brooch from the handkerchief. 'Look. It's the same as the one on her hat.'

She looked at it, because Gertrude wanted her to look, and because she'd seen that brooch before. She compared it with the one in the photograph, because Gertrude wanted her to. So it was the same. It meant nothing to her, as the photograph of the woman meant nothing to her.

'All we found on her the night you were born was that little purse and these few things.' She'd spread the handkerchief, folded too long, but the entwined blue *J.C.* still visible in its corner. 'Norman named you for those initials.'

That J.C. meant something. That J.C. meant the little grey tombstone at the cemetery. J.C. LEFT THIS LIFE 31.12.1923. The date was right, too. That's why the twins had tormented her with J.C.

She stood before Gertrude, holding that handkerchief, her eyes, his eyes, doubting, but waiting for more.

'It was in the newspapers at the time. Remember that old bookmark you found in one of Archie's books?'

'I'm going to get the kids.'

'It's the truth, darlin'. Every word of it.'

'I don't care if it's the truth or not. Can't you see what you're doing with your truth?'

'There's a reason you had to be told tonight.'

'You don't understand, do you? You think you're taking Amber away, but you're taking everything away. You're taking you away and you're all I've got left.'

'As if you could ever get rid of me.' Gertrude was up, grasping her, kissing her. 'Never, my darlin' girl, never until the day you bury me will you get rid of me. And you won't get rid of me then either. I'll be out there somewhere nagging at your elbow all day long. You and Elsie and those little kids are my life. You know that.'

They heard the goat paddock gate open, heard Harry announce himself with his cough. Jenny stepped back to the table.

Perhaps he felt the tension in the room. He didn't come in. 'Just letting you know we've put the kids down for the night,' he said.

'Thanks, Harry,' Gertrude said.

'Everything jake over here, is it?'

'We'll sort it out tomorrow,' Gertrude said.

Jenny was staring at Amber's preserving pan, packed tonight with spices and sauces from Norman's kitchen. She lifted the handle, wondering if a smear of blue dye might remain on it, might remain beneath the rim. She sorted through the spices. Cinnamon and cloves for Amber's apple pies, mixed herbs for her seasonings. Curry powder and ground ginger for her soups and stews. Vanilla for her cakes and custards, nutmeg. Amber's hand had been on every one of those containers. Amber, not her mother.

For one minute or five, Harry leaned in the doorway, speaking of inconsequential things. He gave Jenny time, time to realise she might have been given the answer to why Amber had loathed the sight of her, gave her time to pick up the photograph of Juliana Conti, to look that stranger in the eyes — and have her look back.

Maybe it was true. Stray bitch, Sissy had called her. And Vern's 'hot-pants little half-dago bitch.' Even Jim had suggested she hadn't been born a Morrison.

A foreign face. Juliana Conti. A foreign-sounding name . . .

Norman, too. 'You are a golden songbird, hatched into a nest of grey sparrows. You are a classical portrait, framed in gold and hung in a gallery of fools.'

The shape of that woman's face was familiar, the shape of her eyes. If she could see the hands . . . But there were no hands to see, just the head and shoulders.

Itchy-foot's bookmark. The dead woman in the coffin had her hands folded across her breasts. Which book? What had she been reading?

Itchy-foot's book.

Archibald Gerald Foote . . .

'No.'

This was madness. What she was thinking was madness.

Harry was leaving.

'Thanks, Harry,' she said, placing the photograph down, picking up the brooch.

'Those stones are real,' Gertrude said. 'It's worth a king's ransom.'

'Finish your story, Granny,' Jenny said, and she sat down.

Gertrude told her of Nancy Bryant and her old dog, told of the constable's boy coming to her door and telling her that Amber was in labour.

'Elsie was twelve years old at the time; she had broken her leg. I didn't know how long I'd be in there that night so I loaded both of you into the cart and took you into town with me. We lost little Simon that night. Amber heard you crying and thought you were him come alive. She screamed for you and your Uncle Charles gave you to her.'

The brooch in her closed hand. Jenny pressed its edges into her palm, wanting it to hurt, to imprint her hand, wanting to force some connection to it. Just metal and stones; it meant nothing.

'It must have been pinned onto her coat that night. That old black coat behind the door belonged to her.'

'Your coat?'

'She was wearing it over the gold crepe frock you wore to the talent quest. The shoes you wore that night belonged to her.'

Jenny turned to the coat which hung summer and winter behind the door. Rarely worn. Rarely off her back during the months she'd spent in Melbourne with Laurie. A nun's habit, he'd called it. It had kept her warm. Her mother's coat had kept her warm. Her mother.

'I put the coat and frock into my wash trough with a bundle of blood-stained towels. The brooch must have fallen off. Joey found it under my wash trough when you were three years old. It belongs to you. The constable gave it to me to keep for you when he left town. He said there'd come a day when you wanted to own something that belonged to your mother.'

'She's dark.'

'You've got the Mediterranean complexion.'

'I'm more like . . . him.'

'There's a reason for that, darlin'.' Gertrude unfolded the sheet of writing paper, placed years ago into that purse. She passed it to Jenny. 'You'd remember that name.'

Jenny had seen the sheet of paper. *Albert Forester. No fixed address. Inquired after identifying jewellery.* She'd seen Albert Forester tonight, or Gerald Archibald, or Itchy-foot —

'He's Itchy-foot. He's your husband. Jesus Christ, Granny.'

No chastisement tonight for her blaspheming. 'He's your father, darlin'. He went missing in Egypt a few months after you were born. I thought he was dead until the night Denham charged Albert Forester with murdering those two little girls. They took me up to the jail to put a stitch in his head, and even in the state he was in I recognised him. I've never told another living soul — other than Vern.'

Jenny lifted a hand, knowing now why old Noah had given her that pendant, why he'd posted the matching earrings. She knew why he'd come down here tonight. It hadn't been to buy eggs.

Ice crystals creeping into her brain. Ice water trickling down her spine, and Gertrude speaking about an antique luggage label.

'It was in her purse. *Destination Three Pines Siding, Via Woody Creek* — there was enough of it left to work it out. The only answer I've ever been able to come up with is that your mother followed Archie up there and got off the train at the siding. The Monk family and their visitors had always used the old siding. They had a sawmill and general store out there when I was a girl. By the time you were born there was nothing left but derelict buildings. A stranger offloaded there at night would have found herself out in the middle of nowhere, wheat fields stretching for miles and not a house in sight. She was probably trying to follow the lines back into town when you came.'

'A rabbit wearing white gloves just went running by your door, Granny. I'm late, I'm late, for a very important date.'

'Had I known any real facts, I would have told you sooner. He told me tonight . . . that you were his.'

'My mother is no longer a murderess, but my father is a conscienceless monster.'

'If I told you any different now I'd be lying. He gave you the only good he had in him to give. You've got his voice. He was good enough to be on the stage. His family pushing him into doctoring could have been his undoing. When they work with drugs all day I dare say it's easy to start using the things.'

'Elsie knows?'

'Not that he's your father. She was here the night they carried you in. Maisy knows you weren't born to Amber. Your parson uncle, Ernie and Mary Ogden,' Gertrude said. 'There'd be others. We kept thinking that you'd be claimed by your own people. When no one came forward, Norman said it was God's will that they raise you. Amber agreed at the time. She looked after you well — for months. But we did the wrong thing. Ernie Ogden was the constable up here then, and was the nicest chap you'd meet in a month of Sundays, but no stickler for the law. He thought you'd be better off with Amber and Norman than growing up in an orphanage. He said the easiest way to go about Norman adopting you would be to register you in place of Simon.'

'You fiddled my birth certificate?'

Gertrude nodded. 'You couldn't do it nowadays, but back then Woody Creek was so cut off from everywhere. I was the midwife, he was the law . . .'

'Oh, you could do it,' Jenny said. 'Where there's a will, there's always a way.' She walked to the door. 'You just wrote the perfect story,' she said. 'Born beside a railway line, raised in a railway house by the stationmaster and his mad wife, and so the heroine grew to adulthood with her unwed mother's lack of morals and her father's lack of conscience — and I've already written the ending.'

'You've got strength enough to write any ending that you want to write, darlin'.'

500

'All done,' Jenny said. 'It's out of my hands — gone to the publishers.'

Her heartbeat had gone wild. It was pounding the air from her lungs as fast as she drew it in. She stepped outside into the dark, needing more air than could be had in Gertrude's kitchen.

And so goes the continuing saga, the convoluted circle of life, the ripples within ripples, forever circling out and going nowhere.

She walked fast up the dark track, seeing that toddling little girl growing up in Sydney, growing up with a stranger's hands and wondering forever where she'd got those hands.

Where there was a will, there was a way. She'd had the will. She'd found the way.

Through the boundary gate and across the road to the track leading down to the creek, down to Gertrude's water pumping log. She stood on it, watching the flow of dark water while the reed beds gossiped about what she'd done, and sleepless fish plopped up to stare and to make their own ripples in the slick dark water.

I made another me, she thought. *I made another outcast. Cara Jeanette Norris. Jennifer Carolyn Morrison. We don't exist. We're nothing. We belong nowhere.*

She'll belong. Myrtle's not Amber. She'll make a fairytale life for Cara. She'll grow up in that beautiful old house with two adoring parents. She'll go to the best schools, wear the prettiest dresses. She'll be the me I was supposed to be. No sister to —

Sissy isn't my sister. Sissy isn't my sister.

She laughed then, and her laughter was a howl in the dark and the creek picked it up and carried it. Sissy wasn't her sister, but Amber was. She couldn't shake off that murdering bitch; she was joined to her by his blood.

She laughed and howled while her mind raced in circles, and she could find no way out of those circles. Had to get away from her mind. Walk.

She turned away from the creek and walked back to the road.

Amber had walked in the night and done terrible things.

Jenny spun on her heel and ran back to Gertrude's water dipping log, the broad trunk of a tree long fallen, worn near white by the years. Walked out to where the log disappeared beneath deep water. She could go no further.

She had to go further. She had to get out of this town, get Jimmy and Georgie out of this town. That's what she had to do. Take all of those kids and go . . . somewhere. Start again. Somewhere. She was strong. Granny said so. She was strong enough to do what she had to do . . . strong enough to be . . . to be someone.

Sydney Bauer
Matter of Trust

'It's Marilyn . . . she's missing.'

It's been a long time since criminal defence attorney David Cavanaugh has heard his childhood friend Chris Kincaid speak of Marilyn Maloney; for hers is a name from their past, from a time when David, Chris, and the third in their gang of three, Mike, vowed never to let a girl get in the way of their friendship.

But now Chris is the 'successful, happily married US Senator for New Jersey', and when he pleads with David to return home to Newark to help him locate the girl he 'used' to love, David reluctantly agrees, leaving his wife and baby daughter behind in Boston.

What starts out as a favour to a friend soon turns into a major homicide investigation when a woman's bruised and battered body is hauled from the freezing waters of the Passaic. Marilyn is dead, Chris is charged with her murder and David faces the harrowing responsibility of defending one childhood friend accused of killing another.

Buried family secrets, devastating lies and a seemingly uncatchable killer plague David as he races toward a trial which appears impossible to win. Worse still, he soon discovers that proving Chris's innocence is linked to an unthinkable mistake . . . made by someone very close to him, many years before . . .

'Bauer hurtles readers into a world of intrigue'
DAVID BALDACCI

Christine Stinson
Getting Even With Fran

Cecilia thought nothing could ever induce her to attend her high school reunion. Thirty years after leaving St Agnes Ladies College, she's a successful lawyer with no desire to see her archenemy, Fran, again.

But when Cecilia's husband upends her life, she changes her mind. After all, this reunion could be the perfect opportunity to settle old scores.

Cecilia's not the only one still carrying baggage from her school years.

Sharon has an old bone to pick with goody-two-shoes Anne.

Facing her own mortality, Nellie decides to confront past demons, too.

Kerry's determined to show up on the night looking svelte, or at least not the 'fat girl' of old.

Barb will be there, but only if she can keep her past a secret.

When these seven women come together, each must decide to get along . . . or get even.

Getting Even With Fran is a warm, engaging tale of letting go of the past. It's for anyone who's ever had a friend – or an enemy.